The Children Return

Children of Ennaris
The Children Return
The Blood Rises
Ennarisi Unite
Children of Destiny

The Children Return

Children of Ennaris I

James K. McVey

James K. McVey

ISBNs:

EPUB: 978-1-923211-04-9
Paperback: 978-1-923211-00-1
Kindle: 978-1-923211-08-7

First Printing, 2024

Book Cover Design by M. Yankevich, Novelized, at https://www.novelizedbookcovers.com/

CONTENTS

CONTENTS

CONTENTS

For Stephanie, whose support and encouragement made this and many other things possible.

Drewflin smiled broadly as he watched Marjory play with Marflin, their son. It was a simple game, one taught to all truly gifted children as early as possible, although few mastered it as easily as Marflin had done, Drewflin thought with fatherly pride. A small ball made from graffet was passed back and forth using the power of their minds only. The mother created the path and the child repeated the pattern. Over time the passing became increasingly intricate, and thus difficult, testing and training the child's mind to be open to different paths, to be accepting of potential outcomes that did not follow the norm. That was the educators' idea, anyway. Drewflin just knew that Marflin loved playing the game with his mother, both seated cross-legged, facing each other.

A chime sounded, repeated every two sendons. Drewflin looked around but could see nothing. The sound persisted. It became more insistent. Marjory and Marflin looked at him and both smiled. But the peaceful scene now was further away than it had been a moment before and was receding further and faster all the time. Drewflin panicked and started to stand, arm outreached as his life partner and son sped away from him. Around him the light faded from bright day to late afternoon, then a dim twilight, and finally the darkest of night. The feeling of loss raged through Drewflin as he watched the dark swallow his family into nothingness.

The dark became absolute. But the chime remained. In the distance a colder light came into being, doing nothing to chase the dark away. Drewflin tried and failed to hold onto the image of Marjory and Marflin, as the light drew nearer and the chime grew more insistent...

The depths of the man-made cavern were dimly lit. A single console showed signs of activity. A few small lights on the console glowed green, red and amber, combining to produce a wan twilight. Other consoles were dark. They were ranged around the walls of the cavern like silent sentinels. Each had a hard-backed chair placed in front of it.

A new light, yellow in colour, burst into life on the single active console. It glowed brightly for a few heartbeats, then was joined by a second, and a third, and then a fourth. Soon, a whole array of yellow lights was burning on the console.

Now a chamber off to one side was suffused with a faint white light, stark and cold in tone, that gradually strengthened as panel after panel around the wall illuminated. The light softened and became warmer in tone, the initial harshness being chased away. There was no glare now, even though the light was at full intensity. A stasis chamber was revealed.

Arranged at regular intervals around the walls of the chamber were six low couches. They stretched out from the wall. Each couch comprised a solid base with a light mattress on top and a cushion for the head to rest on close to the wall. Only one couch was occupied. On it lay a tall man, dressed in a simple robe of dusty brown with green markings around the cuffs and hem. Dark brown breeches clothed his long legs and bare feet stuck out from the leg ends. A low dome over his head misted faintly and a series of stud lights began to flash, slowly at first but then faster, in a peculiar sequence. A chime repeated every two sendons, slowly growing in volume.

The man stirred. As he did so the dome raised and folded back into a niche in the wall. It revealed a long face with a pronounced nose and deep set eyes surmounted by a mop of unruly sandy hair. His eyes, when he forced them to open, were a muddy green colour that changed to sea green as his energy reserves kicked in. He groaned, tried to sit and failed, tried a second time and succeeded. He slumped slightly, fighting for balance. He tried to speak, but his throat was too dry, and all he managed was a strangled gurgle. His face set determinedly and he tried again.

"A drink," he uttered brokenly.

A small panel brightened briefly in the wall alongside the couch, and then raised. The shelf behind the panel extended itself along the side of the couch, taking a beaker of amber liquid up to the seated man. He reached out unsteadily and carefully grasped the beaker with both hands, took it to his lips and sipped the contents. After a few moments and some further sips, he swallowed the remaining contents in one long draught. He grimaced at the astringent mouth feel.

The restorative effect was almost immediate. His skin tone, which was pale and wan when he first awoke, developed a golden tan colour with the glow of health within moments. The man returned the beaker to the shelf with sure hands, after which the shelf slid noiselessly into its alcove before the panel dropped back into place. He stretched once and stood in one fluid motion. Or that was the intention. Long out of use, his long legs buckled and he hastily pulled himself onto the edge of the couch once more.

"Idiot," he muttered to himself in a voice with a strong timbre.

A few minutes of muscle flexing and he felt more able to try again. Success this time. He walked slowly around the room a few times to make sure everything was in working order, then exited the chamber and entered the main cavern.

"Light, please," he said conversationally.

The main cavern's darkness was dispelled as illumination panels lit, flooding it with the same sequence of harsh then warm, bright light. The man stood quite still and examined the cavern to see if any changes had occurred since his last awakening. The same walls were as solid as ever. The floor, comprised of an intricate mosaic depicting the surrounding star system, was clean and felt a little warm to the touch when he bent and laid his hands on it, as he did each time even though he knew what the result would be. The consoles – three of them now had lights glowing – were free of dust and seemed intact. The man nodded to himself, his inspection complete.

"What cycle is it?" the man asked.

"It is the 82,791st cycle of sequence Dritera in the Tenth Era," a voice replied from a speaker in the nearest console, only the merest hint of intonation betraying that it was artificially generated.

The man nodded again.

"Why have you awakened me?" he asked the cavern. "I was not due to wake for a further hundred cycles or more."

"There has been an incident," the voice replied diffidently. "It may be that the time prophesied is at hand."

"What sort of incident?"

"A micro-meteorite damaged one of the power nodes that protects the stasis chamber of Mage Goroth. Repairs have been effected to the power node but the stasis has been compromised. I estimate it will fail in fifty-two point nine cycles."

"I see," the man nodded after a few moments. "And do you have an estimate of how long it would be before Goroth recovers?"

"Zero point two cycles," replied the voice promptly.

"So, fifty-three cycles before it begins again." He sighed and his heart sank. "We are too few to battle Goroth alone. Are there any Mages in the planetary population yet?"

"None of power. The available sensor nodes have detected few with true latent power, and the newer religions act to make such people outcasts. Mages are now little more than legend."

"Is that so?"

"My apologies, Mage Drewflin," the voice continued with no hint of apology, "but it is the result of your own policy and that of the last Gathering."

"Yes, I know. Perhaps we should have returned to the world more frequently. But we must husband our strength while we await the prophesied battle. How many other Mages survive?"

The artificial voice seemed to hesitate for a moment, as though reluctant to impart bad news.

"Three. Mages Ragnor, Raglin and Trabor are the only surviving Mages apart from yourself. All are in stasis still. I am sorry to inform you that Battle Mage Marjory died five hundred and twenty five cycles ago."

The news shook him, hard. Drewflin bowed his head in grief for a long moment, shock causing him to stare at the far wall without seeing it. His shoulders hunched. He stayed like that for a long time as he tried and failed to process the news, tried again and succeeded, wishing he could not. His life partner, mother of their only child who was himself lost so long ago, and one of the most powerful Mages ever seen, dead.

"How did she die?"

"The circumstances are uncertain," the artificial intelligence stated apologetically. "The Battle Mage was awakened on the usual schedule. She spent a long time reviewing the defence shield's logs before departing the cavern. After five cycles she returned and made an entry in the secure cybercrypt and then returned to the outside world. I lost her life signs approximately one hundred and thirty-seven cycles later."

Drewflin looked hopefully at the cabinet, as though addressing a person. "Did you check thoroughly?"

"Yes." The voice sounded both sorrowed and contrite. "But I could find no indications of her on any of the scanners or sensors and all in the vicinity were active. None of the defence mechanisms were breached or in any way interfered with. My conclusion is that the Battle Mage perished."

That seemed to be a logical conclusion and Drewflin accepted it, unwillingly, stifling the spark of hope that said that if there was no proof then there was the possibility of Marjory being alive still.

"Ah Marjory, my love, you were to stand by my side during the battle, as we did before," he muttered.

He then brought himself back to almost upright with a huge effort of will. Drewflin sighed heavily. Could he do this? Did he have a choice? Maybe he could, and no, there was no choice.

"So now we have only myself and three Mages of moderate powers, and none of us battle-trained." He drew himself up even straighter, squaring his shoulders, making an extra effort to shrug off the weight of Marjory's death, if only momentarily. "But we have to find a solution. Show me the defences."

The floor's mosaic came alive. The home system and those in the immediate vicinity were shown in vivid detail. Stars, planets, moons, asteroid belts, a small comet passing through the periphery, all were shown by the display. A number of points glowed brightly through the solar system. Overlapping circles centred on each point completely covered the home planet and its moons.

"Defences are still intact," said the voice.

"Contacts?"

"Several vessels from two separate civilisations have surveyed the home systems recently. The home planet may have been detected due to the power break, but our shields have not been detected."

"Two? Have you any information about the civilisations?"

"Little beyond what we could glean from their on-board systems. They both appear to be reasonably advanced in technology. Both appear to be in expansionist phases. Our long range sensors and scans of their systems as they passed allow me to deduce the approximate locations of the home worlds. They originate in different quadrants of the galaxy and both are expanding. They appear to be on a war footing when their vessels meet. Their capabilities are approximately equal militarily. However, their governing philosophies are at odds. One adopts a federationist style, similar to our own in the past, but the other imposes harsh rule and forcibly subjugates the peoples it conquers."

"And the races that make up these civilisations?"

"The federationist civilisation often has a mix of peoples on its vessels. We have noted probabilities ranging from five to sixty percent that each of the races represented were affected by Ennaris' genetic colonists. Except one."

"And what about that one exception?" Drewflin asked, a frown of forced concentration creasing his brow.

"Over ninety-nine percent certainty." The voice was unemotional.

To Drewflin, however, the impact was overwhelming, momentarily pushing away the effect of Marjory's death. "Over ninety-nine percent," he gasped. "Do we have any images of this race?"

"Several images of racial subgroups are available from data extracted from ship systems. They bear clear resemblance to our racial sub-groups of the past. Do you wish to have them displayed?"

"Yes," said Drewflin tightly.

A section of the rock wall appeared to dissolve, revealing a large monitor. A series of images displayed people who looked remarkably like those of his own planet in a variety of strange clothes. All bore racial characteristics reminiscent of the home planet's sub-cultures, or at least how they had been many, many cycles ago. In many, sub-racial inbreeding was evident from the mix of features, as they were universally in his own people after so long. Drewflin found himself enthralled. The sequence of images ended too soon for him, and the rock covering reformed over the monitor.

"Where is the home world of that race?" he asked after a few deep breaths to calm himself from the excitement engendered by the images.

"My best extrapolation put the position in this vicinity," said the voice. "I did not seek to breach that section of the command systems as it shows advanced protective capabilities. As a result, I have had to extrapolate from other factors."

The floor display reconfigured to become a star map of the galaxy, with a section near one end of one spiral arm shaded.

Drewflin nodded. "Were there any genetic colonisations in that sector?" he asked.

"Yes, from the 114,954th cycle of sequence Alperna of the Tenth Era. Several planets were colonised in that sector, but reports expected all but two to yield nothing. One attempt was given moderate prospects and was subject to forty-three missions. The last report indicated that evolution was progressing very slowly. That was a little over ten thousand cycles ago. It was not considered feasible to do more than monitor that planet until the next evolutionary change occurred."

"Where?" asked Drewflin tersely.

The star map narrowed to a single system, showing a yellow star and an array of planets, moons and asteroid fields in orbit around it.

"The seventh planet," said the voice. "On evolutionary extrapolations, the race selected for genetic colonisation on that planet would not yet have attained the characteristics displayed on the images, if it survived the harsh climate.

"However, the other attempt is the most likely to be the source of this race." The bright star dimmed as another flared, toward the bottom of the shaded area. The star chart moved to show a different solar system. "The third planet of this star, designated Xanthor-514, also known as Ordoreth, was expected to yield an advanced civilisation. Two hundred and eighty-one visits by genetic colonists were made. The last one was around seven thousand cycles ago and was an extended mission. Each time, reports indicated rapid evolution. The last expedition was led by Goroth and Zuss." The voice abruptly halted, expectantly.

"Zuss? That may explain it. I thought Ordoreth sounded familiar."

Drewflin was quiet for a long time, lost in thought. Finally he roused himself and walked to the middle of the floor display.

"Change the display to show Xanthor-514, please. Geophysical display. The latest images from the archives will be fine."

He waited until the display was ready. The floor now showed a single planet circled by a sole satellite, then asked, "What is the likelihood that Xanthor-514 has produced Mages?"

"That planet's evolutionary pattern was altered more markedly than most," the voice replied. "It was an experimental process that tried to create an alternative home planet in the event we had to flee our own. Several species of large reptilian and avian creatures were destroyed or altered to ensure the chosen species would come to dominate the planet. And so it seems they did. Mission reports show a steady progression, although faster than expected in the final reports. Many of the expeditions were quite short but at least twenty-five were long term and interventions were extensive as the races developed. But reports also spoke of the powers of our Mages being diminished on that planet, and weaker Mages lost most of their gifts until returning home. So, while the genetic possibility is quite strong, it is unlikely any Mages have developed."

Drewflin was nodding to himself thoughtfully. "But that also means they have not been discouraged actively, does it not?"

"Very likely. However, primitive civilisations tend to distrust anything seen as supernatural, especially as they strive to modernise. It is possible that any budding Mages were discriminated against. If so, there may be very little to work with."

Drewflin's thoughts raced. He took an intuitive leap. Could this be how it was meant to be? It was against most people's expectations but, then again, who could know how prophecies were meant to be met. The stories always had prophesies fulfilled in some strange way.

"The Prophesy says we must look to our children for help," he mused. "We expected that to mean the young of this planet, our home planet. But what if it meant our children of long ago colonisations."

"There is little likelihood of success," said the voice dispassionately.

"Perhaps. But we must hope. It's something Marjory and I contemplated at times although without believing it was possible, and not as a saviour of Ennaris. I'll also seek to reintroduce the magi to our own people, also as we discussed. We must hope one or the other comes to our aid." He walked to the console nearest the chamber where he awoke. "Let's invite them to visit. De-activate the planetary cloak, but keep the defensive shields active."

"The cloak has been deactivated. You realise the second civilisation can also see us now? It also shows signs of being raised by Ennaris."

"How likely?"

"Very likely, greater than eighty percent," the voice paused. "The home planet is Nikera-7 or Andoreth."

"Goroth's last expedition?" Drewflin lifted his head, eyes wide open.

"Yes."

"And this second civilisation is the authoritarian civilisation?"

"Yes. There is a single race on all of their ships that we have scanned to date. They call their leader Likud."

Drewflin started once more. Likud's name was enough to rekindle the anger that had supposedly been long buried.

"Is that likely to be a real person or a title?"

"It appears to be both," the voice replied.

"Could it be him still? The implications of that are ... profound, if so."

"I have no firm information about that," said the voice. "There are no images of their leader, which is unusual from our experience of authoritarian civilisations encountered in the past. But they have as much chance to see us as the federation. Do you wish to remain uncloaked still?"

"Yes. It's a chance we have to take. Please wake the others. Then we need to be brought up to date on events over the last two thousand cycles. There is much to do." He paused and looked to another door on the far side of the cavern as the realisation that he was now without Marjory crashed back down on him. "But first, I must say farewell."

Head bowed, the Mage Drewflin walked slowly to the cybercrypt. The first tear made its way down his cheek.

In the dark nothingness of stasis, Goroth stirred. He could detect nothing, could hear nothing, could feel nothing. And yet... Something had happened. Something had changed. He could *think*! He could link coherent thoughts together.

A few moments, or days, or tendays, maybe even cycles passed as he absorbed that. Time had no meaning when locked in stasis. But once he had considered what the change may presage, the banished Mage started to plan.

He tested the bands that confined him. Repeatedly. The bands remained stubbornly resistant to any pressure. Finally, he located the point where the bands thinned, where the energy strands had worn, or been damaged by something. He considered. Finally, he prepared a mental probe, an infinitesimally narrow filament of thought, and gently pushed it through the weakening spot. He reached out to Grensor, grateful at finding his old comrade alive still. Grensor was startled to have such contact and Goroth sensed some uncertainty as they connected. With the mental connection made, Goroth pushed his plan into Grensor's thought and held it there for a time, unable to sense if Grensor understood or not, until the stasis pulsed and his contact was cut. The weakness that he had identified was gone.

Goroth hoped it was enough. He went back to his planning. Testing, probing, pushing against the confines of the stasis chamber in which he was bound. He *would* return to Ennaris and finish what he started.

In the vastness of interstellar space it is very easy to miss events that occur quite close. This was not one of those times. By a quirk of fate, perhaps, or possibly very good planning, a tiny and very old sensor, floating in a predefined orbit that held it close to the planet's location, noted the moment the planet's cloak was dropped. The sensor recorded the event and then, as per its programming, sent a short burst to a specified location via an ultra-tight beam. The sensor then re-oriented itself, checked and double-checked its position, and flew into one of the twin suns around which the planet orbited. A new sensor activated in its place.

Meanwhile, the receiving station stripped the originating address from the message packet and discarded it, re-wrapped the message in a new packet and re-transmitted it to a defined location, after which the transmitter purged its memory, entered a restart sequence and, once on-line again, recommenced its watch.

The third station repeated the process, as did the fourth. The fifth station, however, the fourth to receive the message after the original ill-fated sensor dispatched it, sent a query and received a response before it, too, repackaged the message and sent it to the address received in that response. It, too, purged its memory and rebooted.

The sixth station, the fifth receiver of the message, identified the message and routed it to its final destination before reinitialising. A small discrete light embedded in a console in a very private cabin, quiescent for the hundreds of cycles that this particular vessel had been in service, started to flash. The cabin's occupant started slightly, stared at the light for a few moments as though not believing what was seen, breathed deeply for a few moments, and then began to implement long-prepared plans.

By another quirk of fate a passing ship also recorded the sudden appearance of a planet where there had never been a planet recorded before, although it was not recognised until the ship had returned to its home base. The recording was sent through the normal channels and was brought to Likud's attention as part of a routine report. It took Likud, the leader of the Empire for which the ship was a scout, a moment to recognise the import of that event. And then he directed the attention of his huge military apparatus to find out more, and started his own preparations.

1. Sunburst

The fabric of space shimmered. Suddenly, it seemed from nothing, there was a ship.

It was a huge ship as deep space vessels were measured. Its skin was scarred and pitted. Sections were blackened by multiple hits or near hits from power weapons, and there was a broad groove down one side, as though it had been hit by a sizable object. On the large bulge atop the vessel that housed the living and command positions was an equally large sunburst. It was scored across where one blast had almost breached the protective shields. But it was intact. And its crew and passengers were intact.

On the control deck of the Union Lightship *Sunburst* Captain Ezara Pantella ordered a defensive configuration as the ship swung into orbit around the planet now beneath its keel. Probes were ejected to test the planet's atmosphere, as the normal testing equipment had been damaged during the recent running battle. Six weapons platforms that had been jury-rigged ingeniously from asteroid mining equipment destined for a different mission were launched as substitutes for the normal screen of smaller defence and attack vessels. The last of those had been destroyed in the last ambush.

On the operations deck final preparations for the upcoming mission were under way. Equipment packs were checked, weapons were tested. There was no harmful haste, but all knew the timetable was tight. The enemy would almost certainly know where they were very soon. No time was to be wasted. But details were important, and the vessel's overall commander, Grand Admiral Mavin Serra, was not one to risk failure because of rushed instructions.

With a brief nod to the mission leader, Serra led the way to the large conference room. She gestured to the chairs ranged around the table in the centre of the room, and the four members of the team sat, at ease but attentive. Tall and imperious looking, with dark hair that fell down her back and a hawkish gaze that had pinned many who had earned her wrath, Serra wore black tunic and trousers without visible rank insignia. Black piping extended down both thighs with what looked like narrow stiletto handles protruding from the top. Her many detractors, and as the youngest ever Grand Admiral she had many detractors, thought them to be an odd affectation. The few who knew Serra well thought that was unlikely, for she did nothing for show. None ever asked about them.

Serra sighed as she took her place at the head of the table.

"March," she said without preamble, looking to the mission leader, "and the rest of you, there's something you should know about this mission." She spoke in Standard, as a common language for all of the participants, each of whom had a different native tongue drawn from human history.

"It was all a joke and we can go home now?" The suggestion came from Capes, the team's communications specialist.

"Not quite," Serra replied, almost smothering a smile. She had always enjoyed the company of these people who made the riskiest missions seem routine, and these were the finest that the forces of the Union had available. "But there are a few unusual aspects. Not the least of it being the members selected for this team."

March glanced around the table. "There does seem to be a pretty high expertise level here," he suggested. "Almost all of us were teamed with other partners already. Why pull us apart like this and throw us together without any time to know the styles of the others?"

Mavin Serra nodded, almost to herself. "Some of this comes from the Council, some from my reading of the situation." She noticed the guarded looks exchanged by the members of the team and smiled, openly now. "As senior Fleet admiral and commander of a Lightship, especially this ship, I have a certain latitude in how I perform team briefings.

"Anyhow, I feel you should know some of the politics behind this mission. Essentially, the Council feels it needs a win, or some of the less ... ah ... dedicated adherents to the principals of the Union may decide to leave. There are efforts to determine whether those members are being influenced by Empire agents, as has happened all too often, but the feeling is that a demonstration of the value of Union membership is needed. This planet, called Ennaris by its inhabitants, was not known until very recently. How that can be is something that you need not be worried about.

"For now, the key factor is that the Council has decided its victory will come here, being seen to protect a world that is not part of the Union, yet, and then helping the people of the planet to evolve under the Union's protection. Why this planet? Because the Enemy's agents are known to have a toe-hold here, but no more. A survey ship a short time ago found that some of the local religions were being corrupted, but the process was in the early stages. One or two local movements have sprung up. Normal things: priests going off the rails and slowly taking their congregations with them, local rulers closing down temples and churches or taking them over. It is very likely that the inhabitants are not aware that they are being misled. More recently, a survey team noted that the northern part of the main continent was, um, sickening."

March looked up and squinted slightly. "Sickening?"

"That's how the survey team described it. Essentially, this is an agrarian culture, slightly higher than Earth medieval but it's uneven. Some basic mining, and some fairly advanced metalwork for the period, but the metal is used for basic things, really. There is a small upper class in some parts who roam around and create mayhem. Some of them seem to be practising forms of genocide lately, which we think may be aimed at reducing the number of people who can resist a takeover. There also appears to have been an increase in the number of wars in the past few years."

The Grand Admiral grimaced. "It is a classic tactic, one practised by many on Earth over the centuries. Subvert or influence the ruling class or other key figures and you have the country, or the planet in this case, especially if you combine that with some sort of crisis."

"And the sick land?"

"It's actually a sort of waste land. The best guess of our experts is rapid, unplanned and indiscriminate industrialisation on a large but local scale. It's only a guess, of course, and probably not a good one. Signs of heavy industry are lacking. It may be the sign of significant damage from past events."

"And that's been enough to put together this team?" March asked sceptically, eyebrows raised.

"We expect the Empire is probably preparing for a complete take-over. But the last indications were that they are still gearing up, so we have a chance to stop it almost before it starts. The enemy's agents have been quite crude in how they have established a presence, far more so than normal, so we speculate that they are not experienced and prob-ably not very senior. This planet is not in a well-travelled part of the galaxy and would appear to have little overall significance. Maybe they were all that was available to Likud at the time. So the thinking is that it should be relatively simple to correct the situation."

There was a short silence, broken by March. "Are you sure it's not a joke?"

"Quite sure."

"Let's go over this a little more completely," said March. He started counting off on his fingers. "An out-of-the-way planet. Low level Empire agents. Early culture in the target population. And a political desire for a good win. Right?"

"That seems to be it. But you forgot to throw in the best individual team members in the Warriors of the Light."

"That," stated March emphatically, "is where it gets screwy. Why not a less experienced team, or even one of our normal teams with the members intact. And why the flagship?"

"Oh, I invited myself to this one," Serra said with a quirk of her lips. "After discussing the mission with the Union Council. And you said it yourself. 'A political desire for a good win.' And yes, you four are considered the best. March, you must be the best team leader and strategist we have. Capes is the foremost communications and negotiations expert. Jonas is our number one combat and weapons expert. And," she faced the final member of the team, "Clay is the first Champion of the Light for many years. You four guarantee good publicity."

"It also makes it resemble using a neutron blaster to kill flies." Capes said in her lower-timbred, almost husky voice. "Better publicity if a lower ranked team did it. But there's more to it. Right?" She looked at Serra with eyebrows raised. "You keep referring to others' views. I'm guessing you have a different one."

"This is my own interpretation from here." Serra stopped and scratched her neck, just where it always seemed to irritate. "There's more to this than we have been told officially and more than I can tell you. Normally, I wouldn't even suggest that let alone say it openly, but all of you are somewhat different to our normal team members. In my opinion this planet is more important to the Empire than it may seem, and the Council found out about it. And that's why you are involved."

"But why the Champion of the Light? A standard Warrior team is three members." March was a shade touchy. Officially, the Champion outranked every Warrior of the Light.

"It also adds weight to my argument." Serra was aware of March's concern, but was also impatient with what she saw as a petty attitude. She reined in her temper before releasing it, as she noticed Clay smile slightly. "You, March, will be team leader. The official explanation for the Champion's presence on a standard mission is that Clay is being disciplined for his recent very public criticism of the Council. Thus, his presence at a low level planetary problem."

Jonas glanced at Clay. "You criticised the Council of the Union in public?"

Clay shrugged. "It seemed the right thing to do at the time."

"What was it about?" Capes was regarding Clay with awe.

No-one criticised the Council, at least in public. The Council kept the Union's influence intact throughout the galaxy, although there had been rumblings in some quarters about imperialist leanings for some time now.

Clay pursed his lips momentarily, considering his reply. "I expressed the opinion that the Council pays too much attention to human planets and not enough attention to other races. They are supposed to be even-handed. Anyway, one of the Council, Aldas, publicly said that I had no business making comments about the Council's policies. I called him a donkey, or words to that effect."

The Admiral was amused. "Words to that effect? I have a different recollection."

Clay looked momentarily embarrassed. Then he grinned broadly. "A braying jackass, to be more precise."

There was moment's pause, as everyone considered the incredible event of a Champion of the Light criticising the Council he was pledged to protect and serve. Capes rocked with silent chuckling, and Jonas smiled grimly.

Jonas regarded Clay speculatively. "So, how did you become the Champion?"

"Well, it chose me," Clay replied.

"Oh?"

"Have you ever been part of a Shakar review?" asked Clay.

"No. I've heard of it but no-one has been able to explain what it is."

"With good reason," said Clay with a brief grin. "Anyone who has ever been part of a review will avoid talking about it like the plague."

"Do you?"

"No. I'm in a pretty unique position because I became Champion. Most don't want to remember anything about it. It's one of the reasons those who have been reviewed are never teamed with a Champion. Not that there have been many of us." Clay surveyed the array of raised eyebrows and paused. He seemed to make a decision. "Okay," he said, "I'll tell you about it, the short form at least. The Shakar sits in a vault in the main centre for the Union and is brought out for the ceremony." He grinned. "It hates that."

"It hates that?" Jonas queried, astonished.

"The Shakar is aware. It tests candidates. Of course, most people are not aware they are candidates for anything. In my case, I was successful at my previous five assignments and was instructed to attend the ceremony. No one told me what it was but I, arrogant as ever, thought it was an award." Clay smiled grimly. "Have you ever been forced to look at yourself? Honestly? Really honestly?" he asked the table. "Because that's what the Shakar does."

Clay paused, his eyes focused somewhere far away, but not misted or sentimental. Rather they were hard, flint hard, as he remembered his Shakar review.

"They call it a review," he said quietly, "but that hides the reality of something that takes bare moments and feels like it lasts a lifetime. Put briefly, you pass or you fail the Shakar review. You know if you pass or not after only a few moments.

"The Shakar reams through your deepest self, and uncovers aspects of yourself that you never knew, or hid from yourself. It exposes you to yourself, and that's the hardest viewing of all. Not only do you see yourself as you truly are, but also as others see you. And you see your potential."

Clay paused and glanced around the group. "Imagine how you would feel to know that your most prized quality meant nothing, or that almost everyone has identified a failing that you have not. Or that you have hidden your true qualities from yourself."

"So it exposes truths about yourself?" asked Capes, eyes shining at the imagined grandness of the test.

"Many have been shattered," said Clay with no emotion. "They were the best of the best, but had no ability to evaluate themselves. At the end, they had to fall back on their own selves. They had to burrow deep inside and accept what was shown, and gather it in, add it to themselves, and then come back."

Another glance around the group.

"Some never did. They stayed withdrawn for many years, some till they died. Others who were stronger returned to service and were haunted. Some shrugged off the failure.

"And it was a failure. They were made to know that they failed, and that is also part of the test. The Shakar includes the candidate in every part of the test and it is absolutely impartial, brutally so if one were to ascribe emotions as well as a form of awareness to the stone."

"Stone?" asked Capes.

"Yes," replied Clay, surprised. "Didn't you know the Shakar is a stone? Of course not, if you've never seen the review and no-one has spoken of it to you. Yes, the Shakar is a stone, a rock. It is of a size to fit perfectly in the palm of your hand. No matter what size your hand may be, it fits perfectly. It feels rough but has no edges or sharp points. In fact, it looks completely smooth.

"When you hold it, you're invited to lose yourself to the stone, to give yourself over to it. And when you fail the test, you feel the failure to your very marrow."

"And when you pass the test?" asked Jonas.

Clay nodded. "Then you are Champion. The stone glows from within and you feel an odd sense of possibilities." He laughed. "Each Champion knows of those who went before, and each knows that if he or she succeeds, there will be no more. He or she will be the last."

"But what do you have to succeed at?"

"Ah," Clay raised one finger, "that is what none of us have ever known. But supposedly he or she will know when the time comes."

March sighed heavily, breaking the silence. "For whatever reasons, we're here. And it's almost time to go." He turned to the Admiral. "Anything else?"

"Nothing but my best wishes. As you know, we survived two ambushes on our way here, but we lost our escort ships. We will try to convince the Empire cruisers following us that this was a feint, like the last two planet-falls over the last two days. So, we will have to leave the system immediately. We will throw a couple more feints after this. We cannot monitor your progress, as we normally would for a few days. You will be alone."

"Any ideas on how we were ambushed?" Clay spoke quietly, but all awaited the reply.

"Nothing I care to share at the moment." She looked at each in turn. "But they knew where we were. Be very careful. Although it seems simple, I don't like the feel of this one."

There was no answer to that. March, Jonas and Capes filed from the conference room, leaving Serra and Clay.

Clay smiled faintly, as though amused. "There's always more to these things, is there not?"

"Always," Serra confirmed grimly. "But you will have to find out what that is for yourself."

"But you know, or think you know." A statement, not a question. "This mission was your idea, wasn't it? You made sure that the Union Council would order that it be undertaken. You made sure you had the best of the best available. Am I right? Why?"

"At the risk of melodrama, it may the most important event in the galaxy for longer than I care to think." Serra replied, avoiding the questions but confirming Clay's suppositions at the same time.

"And I may not see you again, right?" The smile was gone, replaced by a tense wariness that Clay never displayed in public or on a mission. "Are there any private instructions?"

"If all goes as I hope, we will meet again, although perhaps not for a long time." She paused, marshalling her thoughts and emotions, then reached for Clay's arm, gripping it lightly below the elbow with surprising strength. "Take care, Clay Anders, for success or failure of this mission may rest with you more than any of the others. The Union's security forces uncovered an Empire spy a couple of days ago. They think she passed details of this mission to the Empire."

"Including the route, I'm betting."

"Yes. I only found out shortly before this briefing. It is possible even the landing location was compromised."

Clay's eyebrows lifted slightly at the Admiral's words. "So, they may be waiting. What happens if I fail?"

"All will be lost."

"Well, I'm not afraid of death."

"I said nothing about your death being the cost. If you fail, the entire galaxy will be endangered."

"The entire galaxy," Clay said, his tone flat.

"You find it hard to believe, but the stakes are that high."

"And I'm supposed to take care of it? Alone?"

"Not alone. Help will be available if you can find it. But you are the key. Part of the key," she amended. She half turned as though listening. "And now it is time to make your own preparations. Do not expect any assistance from us for a very long time – our paths will be difficult before we will be in a position to provide direct support. But if all comes to pass as we hope, we will provide assistance in the end."

"You sound as though you know what will occur," said Clay as he stood to leave. "And in my memory, you've never said anything the least bit mystical. Why now?"

The Grand Admiral smiled grimly as she, too, rose. "Because," she said, "now is when it is needed. I do not know what will occur but I do have faith."

They each made their private preparations, after which the team reported to the transport chief. Serra was in attendance to see them off. At that moment the proximity klaxon sounded. With a weary shake of her head, Serra gave them a wave and stepped into the chute that would take her to the command centre. The transport officials bustled around the team, making last moment changes, checking kits. The team members were bundled into the projection rooms and stood awaiting the signal.

The transport chief displayed a map of the northern-most of two continents on the planet, and zoomed in to show a small section seemingly comprised of hills and valleys. What seemed to be a small town showed on the north-east of the visible map. He pointed to a mark. Depth markings indicated the hidden store was almost fifty metres beneath the top of a craggy hill.

"Your main kit has been transported to a natural cavern, here," he said as he placed one finger on the mark. "Access is via an entry cave we located here." He pointed to another mark among rocks on a second hill. "The Admiral directed that your additional kit should be included. It will not be included in the mission equipment list returned to the Council."

He hesitated, tempted to ask why the Admiral would do such a thing, but merely said, "That's it. Good luck."

The transport chief led the team to the projection pad and waited whilst each team member took his or her place. Only when each mission member had signalled ready did he move to the transmission console.

The four Warriors were vividly aware of the possibility that they may never see their recent shipmates again. Each projected confidence, outwardly at least. As the power indicator moved up to the critical mark, the alarms sounded a more strident tone. Warning panels began to flash red. With the computer in control, there was nothing to do but pray the ship's defensive shields would hold off the enemy, giving enough time for the team to be away. The mission was not to be aborted. It was, officially, too important. Every mission was too important but this one topped them all.

In the control centre, the Admiral watched as first one vessel, then a second and a third, flashed onto the edge of the battle screens. Although far away, the images registered in amazing detail, enough to see that the ships were a heavy cruiser and two light cruisers. Mavin Serra watched as the enemy vessels arranged themselves for a front-on attack. She smiled. Three to one would seem almost insufficient to them, she thought. The enemy always preferred to work from a position of overwhelming strength. A stray thought protruded: perhaps they needed numbers to make up for their lack of imagination. She pushed the thought aside, as she had many times before. Enough time for that later. For now, she needed to buy some time for the mission team.

The Admiral turned to her second officer and nodded once. Almost immediately, the battle computer's screens winked and the light cruiser closest to *Sunburst* disappeared from the screens, as the makeshift defensive platforms burst to life and bombarded it with everything that had. Immediately afterwards the defensive platforms were showered by the two remaining enemy ships and all but two were destroyed. Those two platforms directed their fire to the second light cruiser, creating a brief distraction while the heavy cruiser directed its considerable fire-power to destroy the two platforms.

On the bridge of the Lightship, Serra called her youngest ensign to her and placed one hand over his shoulder. He was so much like another whose loss she mourned still. There was connection, and Serra believed in such connections.

"Denton," she said calmly, "I need you to hold something for me and keep it safe. Take this and guard it until I ask for it to be returned. Wear it at all times. It will keep you safe."

Her eyes bored into those of the young man as she looped a medallion in the shape of a small bird on a chain over his head to hang around his neck.

"Aye, Admiral," he replied seriously. "And when will that be?"

"Trust in me and yourself. You may have to wait a long time."

The young man nodded once, shortly.

Serra next turned to Captain Pantella. "Abandon ship immediately we jump. Denton will be with you. Dispersal pattern four, I think.

Please order *Fendaristil* to be readied. Denton, when it is ready, activate my private screen. You know the one."

After receiving affirmative nods from each she turned to her console. The shields on the final two defensive platforms were about to fail. Serra touched the communicator's activation pad and spoke quietly.

"Time to go," she said.

The transport chief, unable to see the battle screen, but experienced enough to be aware of what was happening, moved the indicator past the threshold. At the last moment, the chief and his entire crew stood to attention and saluted. The projection panels brightened briefly beyond the capacity of the eye to adjust, and then faded. The team was gone.

The chief leaned on the communicator's pad. "Team away," he muttered.

Immediately the enemy heavy cruiser was subjected to a prolonged bombardment from *Sunburst*. The main blasters fired burst after burst, interspersed by shots from the main railgun, turning the formerly uniform dimness of space into a blazing inferno. But the ship did not maintain the intense volume of fire for long and the bombardment ended as abruptly as it began. Power was transferred to the defensive shields. *Sunburst*, the flagship and the most advanced ship of the Union fleet, began taking hits in turn. The shields flared as each bolt hit. The forward screen began to glow faintly yellow.

Grand Admiral Serra, intently watching her monitors for the first sign of weakness, again nodded to the ship's captain. *Sunburst* began to break away from the oncoming enemy vessels. When far enough away from the planet, and with its shields now glowing almost orange, *Sunburst* shimmered and was gone. After a startled moment, the two remaining enemy vessels turned to the same heading, accelerated to battle speed, and vanished.

2. Team One

As they waited for the dislocated feeling normally experienced during transportation to pass, the four members of the Warrior team moved into defensive positions. They had landed at night, in a large clearing within a grove of trees about five hundred metres from the base of the hill under which their mission equipment had been deposited. The trees, while alien, were at least green-leaved and had brownish bark, as far as the scans had shown. They looked like trees, Clay thought, unlike some of the "trees" found on other planets. Blue sky normally, although it was night now, so that showed more as a dark bowl overhead. The sky was clear, with myriad stars arrayed in unfamiliar configurations but as yet without the planet's two moons. Grass felt quite lush underfoot where they had landed. There was an oxygen-nitrogen atmosphere. It was all pretty normal for a human-class planet. Nearby was a large heap of logs - tree trunks that had been cut and dragged judging by the scuffed ground - with scattered branches and dry vegetation. Probably some farmer clearing space, Clay thought, instinctively moving to the slight shelter offered by the jumble of logs.

The night was quiet, with a very light breeze barely moving the air. Was the lack of noise a good sign or not? One problem with dropping into a new planet was not knowing the local conditions, and that included knowing what was normal for night-life. Of course, having a group of people suddenly appear in their midst probably caused most night creatures to go quiet. The air temperature was pleasant, neither hot nor cold, which was as expected. The planet had an overall temperate climate in large part, aside from a moderately large polar region that was being treated as north and a smaller icy region that was deemed to be south. The top coast of the northern continent was included in the northern polar region, while the southern icy pole appeared to be over ocean only.

With practised discipline, a defensive perimeter was established quickly. Clay was the first to fully recover from the transportation effects, and set up the small tracking unit that would indicate approaching life forms. He then checked his personal defences, smiling grimly as he contemplated the consternation that would ensue if the Admiral knew what he carried. Almost no-one knew the latitude allowed him as Champion of the Light in choice of weaponry and outfitting. If he wanted nothing but a corkscrew, he would have it with no questions asked. His smile broadened as he continued the thought that Serra probably did have a good idea - she had transported Clay relatively often, as the flagship normally did carry the Champion, and she was not the type to miss much. And she had known Clay before he became Champion. In fact, she had arranged for him to be Shakar tested.

Clay shifted his small pack to a more comfortable position and glanced to the other members of the team. March gave a thumbs up signal and then gestured for Jonas and Capes to join him. Clay checked his timepiece, set to the local time periods. It had only gone fully dark a short time before, he knew, and there were about ten standard hours until dawn. Their briefing equated the local day to about twenty-five standard hours, so only a little longer than a standard day. In any event, Clay knew that the advanced technology timepiece would be left with his other modern equipment when they reached the equipment cache.

Clay's attention was drawn to a sudden blaze to the north-east, about where the small town was located. Their scans had indicated a gathering of people in that general vicinity, so it may have been that their landing coincided with a local festival. That could be advantageous, he thought, on the basis that most people in a largely agrarian culture would attend such a festival. If so, fewer people would have a chance of stumbling on them by mistake. The blaze must be a large bonfire, he thought.

Fireworks began to spread streaks of particoloured fire across the night sky, the explosions carrying to the four team members faintly. So, they had some form of gunpowder, which may indicate the types of weapons that may be encountered. Clay decided to wait a moment longer before joining the others.

March, Jonas and Capes had assembled their primary defence armaments. Standard procedure decreed that only local weaponry should be carried by team members, but initial planet-fall normally saw the teams carrying their choice of weapons until they reached the equipment cache, always located away from the landing zone. March held a light-emitting beam weapon - a 'blaster', as it was normally called with a nod to ancient fiction books. Jonas carried an ultra-carbine that fired hardened carbon-ceramic pellets and Capes a smaller alpha-wave handgun. The three crouched in a small group a short distance from the log pile while March checked his bearings. He nodded to himself, satisfied at what the readings said, and signed to Clay to join the group.

"Right," March said and stood.

Jonas and Capes started to rise with him when the tracking unit's display changed abruptly from green to yellow to red, concentric circles flashing to indicate movement on all sides of the team. Before he could react, a blaster beam speared from the surrounding grove and seemed to pin March to empty air before he collapsed. Jonas and Capes dived to the ground and rolled apart immediately, releasing the safety switches on their weapons and looking for the source of the beam. But already blaster bolts, interspersed with kinetic shots, were searching out the team members, creating a blanket of charged particles and slugs throughout the small clearing. Both Jonas and Capes were trapped in the open.

Capes leaped to her feet and sprinted across the clearing, firing into the trees in a constant stream of energy blasts from her hand-gun. She cried out and spun as an energy bolt clipped her left leg. With a final effort she pushed the pain aside and dived into the log pile close to Clay, where she slumped to the ground. The incoming fire was concentrated on the logs now, volley after volley coming from every point of the compass. The clearing had become a killing zone. Jonas was lying prone in a tiny depression behind a small stump. He was aghast at the volume of attacking weaponry, as well as the thought that they had walked into a trap with only their few hand weapons. Nevertheless, he looked for targets and returned fire as quickly as he could. Pausing, he looked to Clay, over ten metres away and lying amid the logs and branches, partly hidden from view, and moaned in frustration as he realised that the Champion did not hold a weapon at all. Even while energy blasts flew past him or hit the inadequate shelter he had taken, a tickle of curiosity tugged at Jonas as he saw Clay, having settled into a small hollow, rummaging through his pack. A burst of energy passed too close and Jonas returned his attention to the extreme danger surrounding him. It appeared he was the only member of the team able to fight. March was dead and Capes injured. March's body was still the target of occasional blaster bolts, and Capes had not moved after making the shelter of the log pile.

The firing lessened, and Jonas decided to hold fire, determined to take a few of the attackers with him. They had been warned that the Empire had established a foot-hold on the planet, and the opposition must be those enemy agents, for energy weapons were far above the local culture's capabilities. But the number indicated by the almost constant fire coming from all around made a mockery of the estimates of numbers. It was odd, though - Empire agents normally used local weaponry, also, because enemy agents usually tried to infiltrate the population, to establish influence by stealth. Using advanced technology would lose them as much influence as it would the Union Warriors.

Jonas looked again to Clay, and wished he had not. Clay was holding a small disk in his right hand, while from one of the jumpsuit pockets he extracted a smaller cylinder with his left hand. The cylinder was inserted into a hole in the disk, a small lever was pushed over to hold the cylinder in place, and Clay pressed a small button located atop the cylinder. A tiny light blinked on the disk's edge.

Jonas' mouth went dry. He ignored the reduced volume of enemy beams and slugs criss-crossing the clearing, which were still deadly despite being of lesser intensity. He slowly looked up from the disk's blinking light to Clay's face, making eye contact for the first time. Clay winked. A bolt hitting Jonas' stump jarred his attention back into focus, but even as he commenced fire at the shadowy figures he could now see behind the screen of trees, his mind saw the disk. Crude technology for the ultimate defence. He had never seen a blitz mine, but recognised it immediately. He prayed it would not be needed. He shook himself out of his reverie and laid down fire against the attackers, swivelling periodically to keep the enemy agents back on the other side of the clearing.

Clay removed another device from his pocket. He touched a tiny pad on its side, activating a small balloon inflater attached to the top of the device, and when the balloon was inflated, released it. The device shot into the air, too fast to be hit by the beams of energy aimed toward it. Clay drew a small beam pistol from the holster attached to his left leg. Jonas watched, enthralled despite his dire straits. Clay closed his eyes, obviously composing himself. Capes could not see the balloon and its hanging device, for by now it was far above the trees. He had recognised it as a backup flare, normally having a small atmospheric-pressure keyed charge attached to kick it into life at a pre-set altitude. Clay pointed his pistol upward, still with closed eyes, and fired.

Immediately, the hill was suffused with a soft light. Jonas stared at Clay. He had heard some stories of the Champion having superhuman powers, but had attributed them to the normal media hype. Clay smiled gently and lifted his pistol into view, bringing Jonas' attention back to the moment.

Shadows could now be seen more clearly, vaguely humanoid although without having a defined shape. Clay drew a second pistol from a holster on his right leg and commenced a withering fire, alternating blasts from the left and right pistols that caused mayhem in the attackers' ranks. It seemed Clay never missed, but a single pistol bolt often was not enough to take out one of the Empire agents. Jonas recommenced firing, concentrating his fire with Clay, so that a target was bracketed by both Warriors. First one, then another and a third shadow flared momentarily into a black deeper than anything Capes had seen, before dissolving. Jonas shook his head in dismay as he realised that they faced the enemy in far greater numbers than had ever been faced before. The Admiral had been right - this planet was not subject to just a simple enemy incursion.

The Empire agents hesitated as several more of their number were killed. But Jonas was seized by a fierce exhilaration as the enemy agents were diminished in number, knowing that with each Empire agent destroyed he and Clay gave the enemy hard blows, for Empire agents were far from plentiful. Normally, the human Warriors fought subverted members of human or other races, rarely seeing even the one Empire agent that normally directed them. He raised himself on one knee, firing at any target possible. He counted a dozen shadows in front of him, and had hit several, when a bolt took him from behind, pitching him forward with his face registering shock. He looked to Clay one more time, with just enough time before dying to see the Champion struck a glancing blow by a beam on his right arm and fall.

All firing gradually stopped. Clay, conscious but lying on the ground, looked in turn at the three other team members. His expression registered sorrow and resignation, but no despair. He drew in his attention, calmed his breathing to a regular cadence, and entered a partial trance, enough to block his pain but still leave him fully functional. Enough time later, if there was a later, for pain.

Reaching down to his belt, Clay pressed two small buttons. A faint shimmer, the sole indicator of a personal defence shield, flared briefly and subsided. He picked up the small disk, returned his pistols to their holsters and stood up, hands hanging at his sides. The attackers had held off firing as their commander exerted control, but a final bolt struck against Clay's shields, staggering him but not breaching the field.

Clay walked the short distance to Capes' position and stood straight and still alongside the logs, watching as a steady stream of Empire agents emerged from the trees, appearing to be insubstantial, like pale shadows. Oddly, they were not wearing their usual full-length black robes, using which they appeared to glide just above the ground. Of course, the robes would have made them easier to see, so that may have been the reason. Clay was appalled at the number of shadows that appeared from the trees. He was surrounded several times over. The agents parted respectfully to allow another one - Clay assumed it was the commander of the attackers - to move into the circle. It stopped a short distance away from Clay.

"It is a pleasure to meet you, Champion of the Light. A rare privilege." There was no hint of gloating, but to Clay the voice had the warmth of water freezing.

"The pleasure is all yours," replied Clay easily, seemingly untroubled despite the scorch on his arm.

"I had heard the Champion was hard to kill. It seems the same cannot be said of the other much vaunted members of your party." The Empire commander paused. "March, Jonas and Capes. A truly excellent result." He - all Empire agents seemed to be male - did not look at the dead team members, his attention centred on Clay. "And now the Champion. Your small field will not stop us for long."

Clay smiled. "It's more powerful than you might think. I'm flattered. You must have brought your whole garrison to greet us." His tone turned ironic. "All these soldiers for four people."

The commander answered smoothly, "All wanted to see the mighty Warriors of the Light fall," confirming Clay's assessment that this would comprise the whole force, or almost all of it. Then as though realising he had revealed too much, the commander snarled. "No matter. We have been successful."

"I think not," said Clay, quickly bending to lift and hold the injured Capes close to his side using the injured right arm, before lifting the blitz mine into view with his undamaged arm.

The agents pulled back in horror as Clay released the cylinder's trigger and so flicked the disk high into the air. His left hand blurred as he dropped the cylinder and drew the pistol from its holster in a single fluid motion. He fired one bolt, striking the disk squarely.

Far away, around a bonfire in a field just outside the town boundary, the dancing throng stood and stared as a huge blast rolled across the land, and a fireball rose into the air. When a party from the village investigated the site of the explosion the next day, much of the grove of trees and all living things within a considerable radius of what was the clearing had been devastated. All that remained was a tiny circle of grass in the centre of the devastation.

The sensors surrounding the planet and its systems were extremely sophisticated, more so than any other sensors developed by warring civilisations much younger than the builders of these older-than-ancient devices. Although both the Union and the Empire had seeded their own sensors around the planet, nothing detected the needle-sharp message bursts that speared into space from the surface of the planet via those ancient devices, each aimed unerringly. And if any had detected the messages, they would not have been able to decipher them without very specific skills. Repeated in each burst was at once a message of hope and fear, of exhilarating joy at the prospect of the long-awaited climax to eons of preparation, of despair at the possibility of those preparations being in vain. It was a message of determination, a message of deepest commitment.

But most of all, it was a call to arms.

And throughout the galaxy, the recipients of the message responded as they had planned so long ago. Beings living with developing races calmly activated their own systems that would remove traces of their existence, that would pass their responsibilities onto others long prepared for the tasks, or that would explain absences that were expected to be permanent. Singly, these beings of infinite patience and implacable resolve set in motion plans of such incredible antiquity that the human mind could not comprehend. But then, they were not human.

The younger civilisations' sensors could not detect the return messages either. And those messages, couched in wildly varying terms, held a single common theme.

"At last," they all said, "the time has arrived. I come."

The Guardians were coming home.

3. Varna

Fifty years after Team 1

Varna Barr woke slowly, dragging herself from the depths of what she recognised had been a deep sleep. It was one to which she had succumbed involuntarily but, nonetheless, she knew she had needed it. In a way, she was surprised to be waking at all. She spent a moment waiting for the pain to come. It didn't. She opened her eyes. After a moment of staring through blurry and wavering patches of light and dark, she was able to make out her surroundings. Carefully, so as not to give any potential enemies a chance to see she had awakened, she shifted her eyes left and right, up and down, seeking visual cues to where she was.

She saw walls of pristine white. Bright but not glaring lighting came from the panel in the ceiling. She was in a bed - that was a surprise! - and covered with some sort of soft blanket. Under the blanket she was naked, she could tell. Carefully, she twisted her head to one side and noted the thin tubes running from her arm to the resuss unit standing near the bed. So, a hospital room, she thought.

And with the thought came confirmation.

"Well, hello!" said a tall, red-haired woman who breezed into the room unannounced. "So, you're awake!"

Varna briefly considered denying that statement of the obvious, just to see what would happen, but damped the impulse.

"Yes," she replied instead. A steady voice, another good sign.

"You certainly gave everyone a scare, coming in all bloodied like you were. I have to say the doctors did a great job," the woman continued to natter away, all the while checking Varna's vital signs and pressing various keys and buttons on a control panel. "You looked more dead than alive, you know?"

"No," Varna replied. "I'm afraid I don't know." She thought for a moment, testing the movement of her arms and legs surreptitiously. Everything seemed to be working, a little stiff perhaps, but working. "Can you tell me where I am, please?"

The woman's eyes opened wide. "Why, you're in the medical bay of *Antilles*. You don't remember being brought in?"

"No," Varna replied wearily. "How long have I been unconscious?"

"You were badly injured, you know," the woman replied, "so you were placed in a medical coma. That was twenty-two Standard days ago."

"Three weeks?" Varna's attention and tone sharpened. "I need to see the *Sirius* security chief, immediately."

"Well, I'm sure there will be time for all of that," the woman said, speaking low and slow as though to a child. "And you *have* only just awakened."

"You are a Fleet nurse assigned to *Antilles*?" Varna asked in a neutral tone.

"Yes, of course I am."

"Then I outrank you by a long way," Varna said in an icy tone. "I order you to contact *Antilles'* security chief and inform him that I have regained consciousness, and ask that he informs Flight-Colonel Andruj of *Sirius'* security section."

The nurse started at the change of tone, and re-evaluated the woman lying on the bed in front of her. Varna made direct - very direct - eye contact with the nurse and it was that even more than the command that made the nurse turn and almost run to the control station. For weeks after she would recall vividly the penetrating stare given her by the badly injured woman.

It was almost an hour before Varna had a response to her order.

"So, you wake up and the first thing you do is chew a nurse's head off?" Flight-Colonel Andruj said drolly as he strolled through the door to Varna's room. "I think the poor woman is going to have nightmares for a week."

Varna nodded, a grimace acknowledging Andruj's words. "I'll apologise later. I needed to make sure you had received my last comm."

"You mean the one where you said that Wensor had been suborned by the Likudians and that you thought he was planning to kill the two junior members of the team? And that you were going to try to stop it but thought you would need help?" At Varna's mute nod he continued, "Yes, I received it. It was not well received by most of the command centre, I must say." His voice was held low, and had a note of suppressed anger. "Luckily, Captain Kruwel is not most and she immediately notified me. I managed to get an extract team together and they could locate you by your homer."

"Dreft and Hiller?" Varna asked?

"Both mostly fine. A little shaken up, and probably reconsidering their career choices, but they're both well. It seems when you showed up the others lost interest in the original plan, thinking you were just the first of an attack team. Dreft and Hiller were given a knock-out when they arrived and left alone. You, on the other hand, were treated somewhat differently."

Varna nodded again but responded urgently. "And Wensor? Did you get him?"

"No," Andruj said, watching Varna's face fall. "We think you did."

"Me?" asked Varna, puzzled. "What do you mean?"

"When the team located you, they also found Wensor. You were still held in chains against one wall of what can only be called a dungeon. You were in a pretty bad state. You don't remember?" Andruj watched Varna intently.

"I can recall some of what he did," Varna said, trying and failing to suppress a shudder. "Wensor was ready for me, I think, and managed to surprise me."

"Yes, we think he was tipped off about your call to *Sirius*. Actually, we're pretty sure of that."

"So, what happened to Wensor? My memories don't include being rescued."

"The extract team found Wensor in your cell. He was dead. He had been run through with his own ceremonial sword and it seems he had then been thrown against the stone wall hard enough to break most of the bones in his body."

"I have no memory of that," Varna said thoughtfully. "And you think I did that?"

"Well, some have thought your high psi quotient could explain that," Andruj said carefully.

Varna snorted. "Psi? You know as well as anyone that it doesn't exist. Those of us that test high in psi merely have advanced skills in reading people and their responses. There's nothing like an extra sense like the vids try to promote."

"Well, someone or something did, and you were the only one nearby to our knowledge."

"I'm not sorry Wensor's dead, but I'm pretty sure I didn't kill him. What state was I in?"

"You had two broken arms, four broken ribs - from kicks we think - some pretty extensive marks on your legs, also broken, that looked like strikes with batons, and what seemed to be whip stripes across your back. Your nose was broken and you'd been pretty thoroughly beaten around the head. Some pretty big lumps at the back of your head indicated that you probably had been knocked against the wall, likely as you were being beaten. There was a raft of internal injuries as well. You were lying in a pool of stale urine - not all your own we think. And there were fresh cuts on your arms and chest. We think Wensor was just trying to inflict pain on you when he was killed. Cutting you with his sword."

Varna lifted her head from where she had been staring at the wall and looked Andruj in the eyes. He recognised the fear in them.

"Wensor had threatened to ... do things to me. He and his friends. They would come in and remind me that they would take turns. They would expose themselves to me, showing me what I could look forward to, they said." She took a deep, shuddering breath. "They also used sticks on me, down there."

Andruj nodded. "The doctors found evidence of you being struck repeatedly."

"Did they do the rest?" Varna's vision wavered slightly.

"It appears not, no," Andruj replied in an even tone. "The intention appears to have been to cause pain and damage, no matter what they may have threatened. What they did caused pretty severe damage, however. The doctors can update you on that. Almost everything has been treated successfully - physically, at least, although there remain some injuries that need more treatment. They will come good also. You can expect pretty intense examination of your state of mind, though."

Varna just nodded and closed her eyes, resting her head against the pillow once again.

"And you will have a guard day and night."

Varna opened her eyes and looked up. "Why?"

"Wensor had influential friends in the Fleet, and on *Sirius* especially. They tried to make a case for you being turned and that you killed Wensor as part of your traitorous behaviour."

"With two broken arms and legs and enough injuries that I was almost dead?"

Andruj nodded. "The Admiral was wavering when we were able to prove that Wensor was part of a cell within the *Sirius* fleet itself."

"And still I need guards?"

"We don't know we managed to get them all. And there remains some resentment that you uncovered the cell yourself, without trusting anyone else." He snorted. "The brains amongst them seem to conveniently forget that anyone you confided in may well have been part of it."

"How many?"

"In the cell? So far, we have thirty-seven, and we're still working through what we have. Several have implicated Warriors in other fleets, and we believe we have cells on other ships of this fleet."

"There would have to be more, I guess," Varna mused, wincing as she shrugged.

"But we also need to be aware that some may be falsely accused to sow further discord," Andruj returned the shrug. "It'll take time."

Varna watched the security chief as he stopped speaking. The tiny - the minute - movements of his head, the effort to control his hands, the slight strain she could sense in his voice, all told here that there was more.

"And?" she asked.

He sighed and nodded.

"And Admiral Predrick has been replaced, demoted and retired."

"And I'm blamed for that, also," Varna stated bluntly.

"Yes. He was popular and you're being blamed for his fall."

"Even though this cell grew quite large under his command? And I'm guessing there were many missions compromised as a result?" Varna kept her voice calm and level, although with an effort.

"Even so," Andruj nodded, carefully not looking at her.

"And the rest?"

"His replacement will join the fleet shortly. Fleet Admiral Mika Sancer."

"So, he's made Fleet Admiral?" Varna said, smiling at last, albeit wanly.

"He's been making a fuss, apparently, after being informed about your injuries. There are a few people on *Sirius* who are somewhat anxious about him taking command. The number of requests for transfer have jumped well above the norm." Andruj smiled a wintry, security-officer type of smile. "They have all been denied."

"And the requesters have found themselves on your list," Varna guessed.

"There may be nothing in it except the usual fear of change and upheaval. But the Admiral has a reputation for getting to the bottom of things quickly. And being very firm when he does."

Varna nodded, smothering a yawn. "Yes, my father is like that."

"You're tired and I've kept you talking well beyond the time allowed to me." He paused and looked at Varna directly. "You may wish to consider whether you stay with the fleet or not, Sub-Major," Andruj said seriously. "Full Major now, by the way, but I didn't tell you that. This fleet is going to be quite disrupted, and I very much doubt your own safety can be assured, much as I hate to admit that. But more, I would guess that you may find yourself wrapped in cotton wool by the Admiral, and my knowledge of Warriors tells me that's not something you would accept easily."

"Thank you, Colonel," Varna replied formally, then sighed. "I'll consider your suggestion. I'm reluctant to be seen to be running, though."

"Understood. My concern is not just for you, though. I have to make sure we can secure whatever situation we have. While having a known target may seem like a good idea as a way to unmask more of the traitors, the resources that would take away from what I need to do is significant." He smiled to indicate he held no grudge against Varna. "Just saying. But it's part of what you should consider."

She nodded, yawning again.

"I'll be back to see how you're getting on," Andruj said, turning to leave. "I'll have two of the security detachment outside at all times and you may not have noticed but this room can't be accessed any other way. Get well!"

Varna merely nodded to his back as he turned and left the room, the door closing behind him with a small pop. The thought that her father would wrap her in cotton wool made her smile - Andruj did not understand his new Admiral - but the idea of not serving under her father's command would be considered seriously.

She tried to make herself comfortable and was only partially successful. Nevertheless, she made a deliberate effort to slow her breathing. She centred her thoughts, seeking the calm core that she had been taught to find. After a couple of false starts she managed something like the meditative state she sought and slipped into a fitful sleep.

4. Serra Returns

The bridge of the Union Lightship *Starfire* was quiet as it traversed the depths of deep space, moving through a poorly charted and rarely travelled sector. Flight-Colonel Kiri, newly promoted to the role of Executive Officer and on her first cruise with *Starfire*, turned as the tone sounded. She raised an eyebrow at the technician manning the nearer console.

"Mr Rork?"

He nodded. "Contact confirmed, Colonel. At the edge of our range. A small vessel, no propulsion systems evident. I'll know more shortly."

As the technician returned to his task, Kiri touched a pad on the command console. Almost immediately, the air above the console shimmered and a holographic image appeared, a man of indeterminate middle age, clean-shaven, short iron-grey hair somewhat tousled. The flight-colonel straightened imperceptibly.

"Admiral Bard," she said, striving to sound competently relaxed. "Sorry to disturb your rest period, but we have a drifter at the edge of our range. Visual in, ah" - she turned to the technician, who held up eight fingers - "eight minutes."

"Very well, Colonel," replied the admiral around a yawn. "Ready a containment field, just in case. I'll be with you in five minutes."

The image disappeared. Kiri relaxed, sinking back in the command chair, only now realising that she had been sitting at attention. She glanced at Rork and scowled as she realised that he had noticed, then smiled ruefully.

"He has that effect every time," she admitted. "Almost like I'm just out of flight school."

"Yeah, I know what you mean," replied Rork. "Something about him, isn't there?" He smiled in turn and turned back to his console.

Kiri thought back to her excitement at being appointed to *Starfire*, the flagship of the First Fleet and commanded by her childhood hero, Admiral Denton Bard. He was a veteran of many battles with the Empire and was rumoured to have taken part in developing many of the more advanced capabilities with which *Starfire* was fitted. The thrill of serving on the ship was yet to fade, but it was also paired to a vague anxiety about letting him down.

"Visual in five minutes," Rork reported, bringing her back to the present.

Kiri touched a stud on her console. "Combat. Prepare a containment field. Co-ordinates in three minutes." Then, to the technician, "Rork, pass the co-ords to Combat as soon as you have them locked in."

"Colonel?"

She turned from her command console. Rork was frowning at his instruments.

"Yes?" she prompted.

"The configuration of the vessel." Rork hesitated. "It's unusual. It's shielded, and I haven't been able to make it out properly."

"How long ... " She paused as the Admiral strode onto the command bridge.

"As you were," he commanded as the bridge staff came to attention. "And you too, Colonel," he continued as she rose from the command chair. "You still have the bridge. I'm an observer."

"Sir," she replied.

"What have we got?"

"Not sure, Sir." Kiri's frown matched Rork's. "We can't identify the vessel. It's shielded."

"Coming on screen now, Admiral," Rork called from his station. "Magnifying. Should be able to see it now, sir."

"Where, Mr Rork?" Kiri was crisp, efficient, again at attention. "There's nothing visible."

"Relax, Kiri," Bard said as he moved up to stand behind Rork's station. He smiled as the flight-colonel started, surprised again to find herself at attention. He then turned to the view-screen and spoke to Rork. "Location, Rork?"

"Should be lower right quadrant of the screen, sir. I don't understand it. The sensors clearly indicate its presence and position, but we can't see it." He scratched behind his ear. "Must be the screens, sir."

"Hmmm. Any idea of the construction of the craft?"

"Can't penetrate the shields, Sir." Rork tapped his console, deep in thought, oblivious to the admiral standing behind him.

Kiri opened her mouth to say something. But she stopped herself as she realised that Bard was unconcerned about waiting on the technician. She watched Rork, almost hearing the thought processes as he considered and discarded possible means of identifying the craft.

"Can't get past the shield," muttered Rork. "Those damned shields." He snapped his fingers. "That's it! The shields."

His fingers flew as he entered instructions at his console.

"Ahem. Care to let us in on it?"

The admiral carefully showed no expression, but his voice betrayed amusement.

"Uh, sorry, sir," Rork stuttered. "I thought I could recalibrate and identify the shield technology. We normally have all the patterns stored and so don't bother, but I thought it would give us a clue. Sir." He eyed the Admiral uncertainly.

"Good idea. Sorry to disturb you. Please, continue." And Bard moved over to Kiri's position. "Any ideas?"

Kiri shook her head. "Not really, sir. This area has been cleared of enemy ships for thirty years or more, as far as we know. But it could be a booby trap. I have a containment field ready to go when we're close enough and the defensive shields are on line. The midships battery is charged and targeted. We're ready to initiate alert conditions." She shook her head again.

"Good thinking. But?"

"Instinct, sir," said Kiri, relaxed now as she discussed a problem of tactics with the admiral who had intimidated her only minutes before. "I just can't see it as a threat. It's drifting, that's evident." She paused, mentally grasping for a better description, and not finding one. "I don't feel threatened," she finished lamely.

Bard merely nodded, his expression betraying nothing.

"Uh, sir?" called Rork.

"Mr Rork."

Rork pointed to the screen, where a smudge glowed lightly in the lower right quadrant. "I've isolated the shields, sir. The shields are similar to ours but different enough to be difficult. Still can't penetrate them, though. I make the shield radius to be about right for a small ship, but I've never seen a small ship able to generate a shield of that power."

Bard moved ahead of the command console, absorbed in the display on the view-screen. "Magnify," he ordered.

The screen flickered and the smudge reappeared, much larger and centred on the screen. Bard stopped a few paces away from the screen.

"Enhance the shield emissions, please, Mr Rork."

Rork again touched his control pad, slower now as he made fine adjustments. The image on-screen sharpened, the energy flows of the vessel's shields became visible as strands interlocked in an oval, with just the barest hint of the craft's outline visible behind them.

The admiral started. "No! It can't be," he breathed.

Kiri and Rork exchanged puzzled glances.

"It doesn't match anything we have, sir," said Rork. "Ship's computer is unable to match it as friend or foe." He frowned slightly as his comment was not acknowledged.

Bard turned slowly. Tightly suppressed excitement cast an intensity over his normally calm expression. He moved to the command console with studied casualness and pressed a stud.

"Combat. Form a defensive shield immediately, centred on the un-identified vessel. Configure *Starfire* for perimeter defence." He turned to Kiri. "Move us so we can defend that vessel, please."

Kiri held up her hand. "Admiral? *Starfire* ... we ... er ... this is a flagship, sir, not a perimeter defence ship."

He regarded her for a moment, then said gently, "Just do it, Kiri. I'll explain in a little while. And call Captain Jord. He should be here for this."

"Sir," replied Kiri, mystified.

As they waited - Bard apparently calm, although with an air of expectation, Kiri and Rork perplexed, and the rest of the bridge crew uncertain of what was happening - *Starfire* was moved close to the shielded craft. The smaller vessels from the flagship's screen reconfig-ured themselves to form a new screen around the two ships. The larger ships of the flagship's escorting battle group entered a pattern where they could both defend from and attack possible threats.

Captain Jord, ship commander of *Starfire*, arrived at the bridge just as Kiri announced that the defensive perimeter was established. He paused by Rork's station and took in the situation displayed on the main screen and Rork's subsidiary displays. He glanced up and asked, "We're defending an unidentified ship?" A raised eyebrow was the only sign of uncertainty.

"Mr Rork cannot identify the vessel. Its screens are similar to ours, but different enough to perplex both him and the ship's computer. Take a closer look." He gestured to the main view-screen.

Jord stepped forward and examined the display. "That looks famil-iar," he said thoughtfully, "but I can't pin it ...." His eyebrows leapt up and his jaw dropped. "No!" he said, turning to face Bard. "It's not possible."

Bard smiled faintly and said, "It's the only answer."

"Oh my!" Jord turned back to the main view-screen. "Are you going to bring her in?"

"Yes. But we have to lower her screen first."

Jord nodded. Without turning he said, "Kiri, medical team to Hangar Deck Twelve, please. Then, signal all ships. I want all ship captains to report to the hanger deck in thirty minutes. You, too. I think the flagship's executive officer should be with us."

Bard nodded his approval as he moved to the command console, straightening unconsciously as he took a deep breath, letting it out slowly.

"Computer," Admiral Bard said sharply. A blue light winked on at the top of the console, signifying the computer's readiness, and a slightly mechanical voice said "Waiting".

"Forward disruptor batteries to ten percent power."

The blue light blinked. "Ten percent," said the computer.

"Disruptor pattern variation." Bard took another deep breath, paused, then continued firmly, "Access shield pattern Sigma-Beta-3-5-2, transfer to disruptor pattern."

Jord's lips thinned as he chewed his lower lip. Kiri watched, fascinated. She had never seen a sign of perturbation on either Jord or Bard. Rork stared at his console, seeking the slightest change in the unidentified vessel. The rest of the bridge crew, aware of the tension that now enveloped the senior staff, moved about their tasks quietly or stood and watched the proceedings intently.

"Are you sure that's the right pattern?" Jord asked Bard. The admiral nodded.

The light changed colour to orange. "Authorisation for security level A1 required," said the computerised voice.

"A1?" whispered Kiri. "That's the highest we have. What could be so important?"

"An experimental ship," said Bard, having overheard the question. "Or rather, a very old ship with experimental technologies."

He placed his right thumb on a small plate, then tapped a code into the console with his left hand.

The orange light blinked twice, then returned to blue, and the computer said, "Confirmed."

Rork looked up.

"Disruptor pattern has been reconfigured, Admiral."

Bard nodded in acknowledgement.

"Target the shields of that ship. Dead centre. Five seconds exactly." He waited while Rork made sure all was in readiness. Then, "Forward disruptors: fire!"

A dazzling beam erupted from a pod at the centre of *Starfire's* nose. It struck the shields of the unidentified ship in the exact centre. Precisely five seconds later the beam stopped. The targeted shields flickered, flared briefly and died, revealing a small ship. As its shields died, the ship's running lights came on, with a spotlight on the bow illuminating an image of a golden sun radiating light in all directions.

"*Fendaristil*," Bard whispered, now standing beside Jord.

The latter merely nodded.

"Admiral. One life form in stasis on board." Rork peered at his screen. "Female. She has commenced resuscitation." He paused, then asked diffidently, "Admiral, Captain? Is that one of ours?"

"Definitely a friend, Mr Rork," Bard said as he turned, smiling. "Yes, that is an admiral's personal boat. An old one." He grinned as he realised both Kiri and Rork were still very confused. "Your fleet education has been lacking, it seems. You should recognise that insignia. That is the personal boat of the last Grand Admiral of the Fleet."

Admiral Denton Bard was laughing lightly as he left the bridge, followed by Jord.

Kiri sat still, staring at Rork, both faces registering shock that faded into awe together.

"Grand Admiral of the Fleet," Kiri whispered. "Serra!"

She stood slowly, shook her head slightly as though to clear cobwebs, then signalled the deputy watch officer forward to the command chair. She hurried from the bridge.

Forty minutes later Bard and Jord were waiting with the medical team in the hangar bay. Behind them, in a perfect line, stood the fleet's ship captains, with Kiri in the centre. The small vessel had been captured by a tractor beam and pulled gently through the hangar door. As it was deposited carefully on the deck the two senior officers moved forward. They stopped just outside the radius of a blue beam that illuminated the craft and waited again. The light winked out and Bard stepped up to the access hatch in the vessel's side.

Slowly, with almost exaggerated care, Bard raised his right hand and pressed firmly against a blue plate to the side of the hatch. The plate appeared to absorb his hand, prompting the medical team leader to start forward. Jord stopped her with an upraised hand.

Bard's hand was released and he stepped back.

A disembodied voice issued from the plate. "Identify yourself."

"Hello, *Fendaristil*," Bard said quietly.

Bard reached beneath his uniform blouse and removed his identity chip from its chain. He raised it to the blue plate, where a beam scanned it briefly.

"Good day, Admiral," the ship replied, now in a much more natural sounding voice. "Congratulations on your advancement. Please stand clear while I extend the ramp."

The beam disappeared, and Bard stepped back and straightened. He unconsciously smoothed the front of his uniform. Jord followed suit and the medical team, although unaware of the true situation, responded to the atmosphere and formed a line behind the captain. Jord nodded approval.

The hatch cracked open and Bard stepped to one side as it swung down and extended to form a ramp. He moved again to stand in front of the ramp, ahead of and to one side of Jord. The hatch was open to its fullest extent and Bard was about to order the medical team to board the vessel and check for casualties when a figure appeared within the vessel. Bard started, then snapped rigidly to attention, eyes straight ahead. Jord was but a moment behind him, followed by the line of ship captains and the medical team.

Across the fleet, in wardrooms and on bridges, the various ship's complements watched view-screens. All were surprised to see Fleet

Admiral Denton Bard, among the Union's most senior Fleet officers, stand to attention like a junior officer. Murmurs rose as they watched the unidentified person appear at the hatch opening and step onto the ramp. The murmurs faded, then rose anew as they took in the nondescript black clothes, devoid of rank insignia.

Kiri and Rork, all those on the hanger deck, stared at the woman wearing the all-black uniform. Appearing to be about forty standard years old, with long dark hair falling loosely down her back, she stood relaxed on the ramp as she took in the scene before her. The murmur among the assembled fleet audience faltered as the sense of presence penetrated even through the view-screens. All conversation died as she walked steadily down the ramp to stand before Bard.

In the hangar, Bard executed a perfect salute and held it until the woman nodded and said, "As you were." Her voice was calm, unhurried, confident. Then, "Denton?" she asked softly, tentatively, eyes searching the admiral's face. Her eyes filled with tears.

Silence was absolute in the hanger. As one, the watchers' attention switched to Bard. Astonishment reached new levels as the admiral's normally impassive mien cracked, his expression momentarily suffused with immense joy before it was brought under control again. One tear ran unheeded from his left eye and down his cheek. Kiri found herself brushing tears away as well, without quite knowing why. The intense emotion all witnessed was made more evident by the immediate return of Bard's impassive expression.

"Fleet Admiral Denton Bard, commanding First Fleet, Force 1, reporting, Admiral," said Bard, his voice rock steady again, but the tear was still on his cheek. Then, waving Jord forward, "Captain Jord, captain of the flagship *Starfire*."

Jord's salute was every bit as formal as Bard's had been, delivered with as much respect. Jord was struggling to maintain his composure, too.

The woman nodded and smiled to Jord, accepting the salute. "Jord, too. The Guardians are smiling on me."

In the hanger and in wardrooms across the fleet, recognition was dawning on some of the older hands, and jaws were dropping and staying dropped.

Hands trembling slightly, Bard unbuttoned his uniform blouse and reached in, grasping hold of a thin chain and lifting over his head a pendant in the shape of a small bird. Mutely, he held it out to Grand Admiral Marvin Serra, who smiled gently and took it from him. She lifted it over her head and settled it carefully in place around her neck.

"Thank you, Denton," she said.

Bard, speaking carefully, said, "Computer!"

"Waiting," announced the computer tersely.

"Command over-ride. Authorisation 1-3-2-9-0."

"Confirmed."

"Register change of command, First Fleet, Force 1. New commander, Grand Admiral Mavin Serra."

"Confirmed," said the computer. "Grand Admiral Mavin Serra voice print restored from archive."

"I was in archive storage?" asked the Grand Admiral, amusement rich in her voice.

Bard smiled broadly. "Admiral, allow me to give you a tour of your new flagship."

Serra held up her right hand and said, "One moment, Denton. I need something first."

"Anything, Admiral," Bard replied, turning to face her.

"You don't happen to have any real coffee on this ship, do you?"

Laughing aloud, Bard gestured Serra forward and the two admirals left the hangar bay together, with Jord in close attendance. All eyes followed the trio.

In the hanger, for a long moment after they had left, a pin dropping would have had a profoundly shattering effect.

5. Grensor Acts

Grensor picked up the reed and dipped it in the watery ink. Carefully, he located the place on the map and made a small mark. He stood back and considered.

The map had been drawn, by him, from a much older map and then adjusted to cater for the changes caused by the rebellion, at least as far as he had been able to determine them. With no real technology working outside certain surprising exceptions, of which he was taking full benefit, he had been forced to fall back on rudimentary methods, which meant spies being sent throughout the twin continents, rumour being recorded and copies of local maps obtained. He snorted to himself. Once he would have waved his hand over a viewscreen and demanded that a map of the planet be displayed and it would have had exquisite detail. Now, he was not even sure he had the continents marked correctly, let alone anything else.

Still, it was as good as he would get. Each of the marks represented a target. Each represented the location where a potential enemy was growing, quite literally. For each represented somewhere where his spies and informants had reported that children were displaying signs of the old gifts. The foment he had been able to create long ago had caused the gifts to be treated with suspicion and almost destroyed. Of course, at that time he had merely built on the fear of Mages of those who survived the fall of Ennaris' civilisation, but it had been a useful tool to reduce potential enemies.

Drewflin and the Council Mages were reduced in number to almost none. The damage was so great that they were unable to effect significant change. Grensor sought to foment strife to keep them occupied. Initially, that was merely to stop them from trying to find him, for he was sure they knew he had survived. But, after a short time he decided to use it as a weapon against those who could oppose him. And so, using the dramatic reduction in learning that followed Ennaris' descent into near barbarity, and the consequent rise in superstition, he created an environment of hatred and fear against those with gifts. That had worked well although, in more recent times, the people were less inclined to act against the gifted.

The damage was done, however. Many who displayed gifts were killed, some by truly horrendous means that caused even Grensor's stomach to clench when he thought of it. In killing the gifted, of course, he also killed future generations of gifted, because it had long been recognised that the gifts came from peculiar mixes of DNA.

There was one group, though, who stubbornly and persistently stood against his attempts to destroy the remaining vestiges of the gifts, at least outside his controlled area. The Blood! These remnants of the old world valued the gifted even as the number born with gifts dwindled away. Grensor had made periodic attempts to reduce their numbers, and he had been partly successful. But the Blood were war-born people and his assassins and the subverted rulers he could influence into attacking them over the centuries had not succeeded in eradicating them. Still, the gifts had dwindled as a result of his efforts, and he had been satisfied. Until now.

It was time to try again. His map held the locations of many who had shown gifts, almost all children. The gifts were resurfacing. Was it coincidence that they were returning just as he had received that astounding contact with Goroth? Just as Likud had reached out to him and provided his own people to help Grensor to rebuild? Unlikely. Grensor did not believe in coincidence. He would have to revisit the Prophecy again, see if it held any clues. But for now, he had his next campaign to rid him of potential problems to consider.

Grensor had another tool available, one that he had been experimenting with for a very long while now. For so long he had been unable to do anything to progress these experiments but he had found a new round of gifted amongst his own people, segregated for so long behind the walls of the tall mountains that separated the twin kingdoms from the expansive grasslands to their south. The result of careful and persistent inbreeding, those gifted included some who were able to generate enough energy to power Grensor's old equipment, once repaired and, in some cases, rebuilt. This was one of the exceptions to the technology interdiction that had plagued him since Goroth was captured. He was able to restart those experiments and this time he had the people of the twin kingdoms to use as resources. And they formed the basis of his new super soldiers.

His first real batch was ready for him to send out to deal with the new gifted children. There had been some false starts over the last few decades, as there always were with these sorts of things. However, Grensor had been among the most gifted of the scientists of his time and he was able to sort out most of the problems. The strength and extreme aggression remained, of course, and there was the troubling problem that most would not stay bound to orders they were given, but Grensor solved that problem using Likud's Andorethi soldiers, who could control them telepathically. That had been a welcome surprise.

Grensor realised that he had distracted himself from the task at hand. He shook himself back to the moment and started to prepare for the dispatch of his super soldiers, his ghazrak, to target the children. Still, he thought wistfully, it would have been nice to see those gifts return to Ennaris.

6. Wardroom

The wardroom was settled again. Normal habits of discipline had been overturned temporarily as the various vessel commanders, each with long records imbued with varying levels of distinction, cheered loudly on the Grand Admiral's entrance. All crowded closer, eager to be near a legend. Mavin Serra was left in no doubt about her welcome, and she warmly returned each salutation, while struggling to remember a new sea of faces.

Now the commanders had dispersed to their ships, each lighter of heart. The disappearance of Serra and her flagship, *Sunburst*, had been shrouded in mystery. Now, over fifty years on, Serra was found, and the mystery was revived. Throughout the fleet, officers and crew discussed the few known details and many rumours that had grown up around the event. Memories were revived of Serra's exploits in halting the expansion of the Likudian Empire into the territory claimed by the confederation of planets that comprised the Union.

In the wardroom, Grand Admiral Mavin Serra reclined in an easy chair. Bard and Jord occupied similar chairs nearby. Serra held a huge mug of coffee, a sunburst representation on its side having been applied to it hastily by the galley staff. Her eyes had misted as the chief steward served it to her upon her repeated request for real coffee, but she had smiled and accepted it with but a brief nod. The chief steward had returned to the galley beaming.

"Well, that was quite a welcome, gentlemen," said Serra dryly as she sipped her coffee.

"It's not every day we have a Grand Admiral turn up unannounced," Bard returned with a smile. "Especially after having drifted through at least two enemy-held sectors, judging by the rate and direction of drift."

"And you were lucky," continued Jord. "We may be the only two left who would have recognised that shield signature. I believe that everyone else from the old experimental crew has died, and a fair number of the next group, too."

"All of them?" asked Serra, eyes wide in distress. "That crew was the cream of the crop. How can all but you be gone? It has only been, what, fifty-five years."

Bard nodded gently. "A large number of them died under strange circumstances. Belton flew his ship into an asteroid belt. All hands lost. Stepf had a drive system malfunction and his destroyer imploded. Markin was ambushed after receiving top secret orders directing him to a remote rendezvous point only to find an Empire cruiser waiting for him. An investigation turned up no leak. And there have been others in a similar line. All odd, all unexplained. The result was the loss, in a very short period of time, of an entire team of brilliant Fleet officers."

"And no-one suspected anything?" Serra asked wryly.

"Sure," said Jord, "especially us. But we couldn't find anything or anyone to tie the events to. Most of the incidents and accidents happened in the first ten years or so after *Sunburst* went missing. There have been none for about fifteen years. But the damage was done. And, of course, there are only us left of the original crew. A small number of the second crew remain but most were not as involved in developing the technology as we were."

The three officers brooded together on the loss of so many erstwhile shipmates. Finally, Bard roused and turned to Serra.

"Enough of that, now. *Sunburst* was not exactly an easy target, but we know you - we - lost the whole screen and all stingers before going missing after we abandoned ship. Tell us what happened."

Serra frowned. "I suppose it should be confidential, but I may need your help so I will tell you. I don't have to ask if this room is secured?

Good. Well, then," and she settled herself in her chair, "start at the start, eh? Denton knows part of it because he was there.

"We received orders to transport a special team to a planet on the rim of the galaxy. The planet had been discovered shortly before, which was a strange event because the systems in that area had been charted and searched for hundreds of years. The scans missed that planet time after time. I pushed the Council to investigate and took the job when they agreed.

"The scans indicated that the planet was essentially a second Earth. Different land mass configurations but otherwise almost identical, down to apparently very similar inhabitants. Very odd indeed. A couple of survey parties found a pre-industrial, more medieval, human-like society with all signs that it had existed for a very long time. That was odd, also, because the society did not seem to have progressed for a long time, but nor did it seem to be stagnant. It was just unchanging. But the final survey also found that the Empire had taken an interest in the planet. Traces of one of their survey parties was found and signs of damage to the planet consistent with the Likudians' usual industrialisation methods were found in an already damaged section of the planet. I'm still not sure that conclusion is right, though.

"So, a team was assembled. By me. Three of the very best Warriors were moved from their own teams for the task, and Clay was included." She stopped immediately, seeing events that had occurred but very recently for her, as she had lost the intervening period during the stasis sleep.

Jord nodded. "The Champion. I remember."

"Supposedly, no-one else knew about the mission except the Council, and I had little chance to report to them. Anyway, we ran into an ambush just after the rendezvous point with Clay's transport. If it was not for the fact that he arrived early we would have been attacked just on the rendezvous time. Pretty coincidental, eh?"

"And Clay was early?" Bard sounded concerned.

"Clay never stuck to rendezvous timetables. He always changed some of the details at the last moment. This time he made it one hour early and a little further inside the planetary system than the plan said. Given that he and I had some history he arranged the change directly with me. We had just picked him up when the ambushing ships arrived. They were surprised, I think, but still managed to take out half of my screen ships and most stingers. There were five heavy cruisers and two light ones. Seven! My people had no chance. We knocked out one and then made the jump to our primary mission launch point, but they followed us.

"This time we were better prepared and managed to damage two Empire cruisers enough to force them to leave the fight. But the other four did enough damage to leave me with only two destroyers as a screen. We decided that a direct run for the target planet was not an option, and planned two intermediate drops as feints, then the real thing, and then another two feints after that. I lost the two destroyers at the first feint, and *Sunburst* was pretty beaten up at the second, but we took another of the cruisers.

"When we made the target planet we had about a quarter of our main batteries on line. Our shields were struggling to come up to full power but we made it. Luckily, final briefing was easy with such an experienced team and I had them down to the drop co-ordinates just as the cruisers arrived. My engineering chief had devised some barrage platforms from mining equipment and shuttles, bless him. Those floating barrage platforms scored a direct hit before the enemy knew they were there, but then all of the platforms were destroyed. We exchanged fire for a few moments and then made our next jump. Everyone got out in the pods during that last jump. I see at least some survived." She smiled as Bard nodded silently. "But our shields failed - actually they were drained of energy - as we came out of the jump.

"I could not jump again straight away. I had to have them find us. So, I entered orbit as though delivering the team. I pulled out of orbit just as the two cruisers arrived, while I was lined up for the jump. Just as *Sunburst* jumped, she was hit. Main engines went out and the jump lasted for a few seconds only. I downloaded the log to *Fendaristil* and entered the final commands, then the sequence to emergency charge the weapons. I had just launched *Fendaristil* when the cruisers found us. They must have jumped further than us and were on a return heading."

Serra's voice had become flatter as she tried to tell her story unemotionally. Now it was devoid of all feeling, toneless and more formal in quality. But her eyes told their own story of distress, frustration and a terrible rage. She was looking beyond the walls of the wardroom, seeing the events that, to her, were so fresh. The two men were silent, their faces carefully expressionless, imagining themselves in the Grand Admiral's place, having to make the many decisions, large and small, that determined the lives and deaths of so many people.

Bard moved to a small bar and poured a measure of a blue liquid into a glass. As he turned to take it to Serra he asked, "Emergency charging weapons would create an overload without adequate release? And *Fendaristil* had the experimental shields?"

"Yes, to both. You may recall that I had you do the shield pattern download to *Fendaristil* sometime before and I had the engineering chief modify the shield pod to boost its output. I'd already tested those designs so I knew they worked. We estimated it would survive even the blast of a dreadnought, although anyone inside would be shaken up a bit. It worked. The *Yaksoo* tried to take us but could not, no matter what it tried. Then the second cruiser moved alongside *Sunburst*, must have been going to board her. They cannot have imagined we left her without taking some defensive measures."

The Grand Admiral shook her head in disbelief.

"Anyway, the proximity alarms must have activated the auto-defence over-ride and she let go with everything. Every missile and gun left to her. The Empire cruisers got caught in it and were destroyed - just blown to bits. The combined shock wave literally blew me out of the system. *Fendaristil* had some engine damage. Light engines were down. I could do little more than try to control stability. When I did get control back completely, I could not locate *Sunburst*, did not know if it survived at all. If it sensed the threat was gone it would have aborted the overload, but I have no idea if it did. I was far down on fuel and a long way from anywhere. So, I set for stasis, set the course to get back into the Union's sector and hoped for the best. Then I went to sleep."

Bard and Jord sat for a moment. Then Jord roused himself to raise his glass in salute and say, "To *Sunburst* and her crew. You made a good fight."

Serra merely raised her glass to join the others, and the three drank their toast to comrades past.

"But you did take out seven cruisers," Jord ventured.

"And lost an entire battle group," said Serra bitterly.

"Having been there for a good part of it, even as young as I was then, I don't think you had much chance, no matter what," said Bard carefully, glancing up from his drink to watch Serra's reaction to his words. "It can't have escaped your notice that we said all of the losses we discussed earlier were on the heels of the loss of *Sunburst*. You - we - were the first of the incidents. The Light only knows what would have happened if those seven cruisers were left intact. They were heavies, from what I recall."

"Five of them were. They must have thought seven would give them a huge advantage," Serra said softly. "And it may have been all for nothing. A day before we dropped them, I received a message that one of the planning team at Fleet had been identified as an enemy agent. The mission was compromised from the start. The team may have dropped into an ambush. I warned Clay about that."

Both Bard and Jord stared and nodded. Bard recalled the Champion, Clay, taking precious time to talk to a young ensign, not very long out of the academy.

"From memory, Clay had proved pretty hard to kill a few times. If he was forewarned then he may have been able to deal with it. But that was over fifty years ago, Admiral."

Serra nodded and stared into the distance. "Only a couple of days for me."

Bard stood and moved to a communications panel on the wall. He pressed a stud on the panel and waited the moment until Colonel Kiri responded from the bridge.

"Colonel, signal all ships. There will be a requiem service for the officers and crew of the *Sunburst* battle group in one hour. And have the chief fire control officer join me in my cabin." He turned back to the others. "Jord will show you to your cabin, Admiral. I'll give you a chance to freshen up before the service. If you will excuse me, I have some preparations to make."

Bard left the wardroom without awaiting Serra's nod.

"...and so, we remember our shipmates from *Sunburst* and her group, valiant men and women who died to protect the peoples of the Union from the forces who would overwhelm it. We will remember them."

One hour later the battle group was arranged in an unusual pattern. The ships were all on a single plane, arrayed in rings centred on *Starfire*. On the bridge, Admiral Denton Bard was completing a tribute to the crews of the *Sunburst* battle group who had died over fifty years earlier, many of whom had been his own ship-mates. Bard stood straight and tall on the bridge.

"All hands," he snapped. "Honour salute! Hold!"

Across the fleet, crews executed copybook salutes, closed fists slapping chests and being held there - the stance was held rigidly by all.

"Fire control!" Bard ordered. "Slave all systems." A pause to allow the command to be enacted. "All view screens as designated." Another pause. "Fire control, execute salute!"

As one, the main energy armaments of all fleet vessels fired, sending an immense amount of energy along converging paths to meet at a point far above the fleet, relative to the plane. On screens through the fleet, men and women stood to attention and watched in awe as the energy streams collided and burst into brilliant coruscations of energy, producing a massive flare radiating from the centre, the ceremonial sunburst salute not seen for over a hundred years.

"Cease fire," said Bard quietly, and the bombardment halted, but the sunburst faded only slowly. When the last flare had died, Bard ordered, "End salute! Dismissed!"

He turned to Grand Admiral Serra, bowed and said formally, "Grand Admiral, *Starfire* is yours."

"Thank you, Admiral. And please thank your crews for me. The *Sunburst* crews would be proud."

Bard nodded shortly.

"And now, Admiral, we have work to do."

Bard raised his eyebrows.

"I want to find out what has been going on. And I have a team to retrieve."

"After fifty years?" Bard gently queried.

Serra nodded. "But they included the Champion of the Light."

"Very well. Do you still have the co-ordinates?"

"Already fed in," said Serra with a smile.

Bard grinned. "This may be interesting. Captain Jord, inform the fleet, please, and get us under way. Standard configuration and velocity."

"Aye, sir," responded the flagship commander.

Defensive ships moved into screening positions, and the fleet slowly picked up speed. They reached the designated co-ordinates and, like the well-drilled team they were, each opened the fabric of space at the precise same moment and vanished.

Far above the fleet's former position, two stray energy beams came together from the salute's residue, flared briefly in a tiny echo of the earlier sunburst, and faded.

7. Varna

Over the next three ship weeks Varna had a small stream of visitors, with Flight-Colonel Andruj visiting every other day and providing a running update on his efforts to discover the extent of the conspiracy in the fleet. The number of those involved had reached over sixty now and morale was dropping rapidly as fleet personnel were unsure of who to trust. Oddly, while some lingering sentiment remained against Varna for her role in and method of uncovering the traitors, she was considered one of the most trustworthy. But Andruj continued to counsel caution.

Among the visitors was the chief counsellor of the fleet, a small woman with fiery red hair who believed the best way to get Varna 'back in the saddle' was to mouth platitudes and cajole her into re-living the experience. Over a handful of sessions Counsellor Major Grinwell succeeded in doing little more than further unsettling the injured woman, whose already damaged self-confidence now dropped even more alarmingly. The Major prescribed sedatives but, if anything, they made Varna's state of mind worse.

Varna found that she was unable to get any rest. Her short periods of sleep invariably ended when she awoke, sweating, with unsettling dreams replaying events that she could not recall clearly. At times her hands shook uncontrollably. At other times she would withdraw into a cocoon that she built around herself.

Her self-belief wavered even further as she replayed the recent events under Major Grinwell's urging. The Counsellor urged her to find ways in which she could have altered the outcome. She felt herself directly responsible for the deaths of three security personnel and upwards of twenty innocents caught in the blast when the Likudians detonated some sort of backup device. Could she have uncovered the truth of Wensor's behaviour without causing the loss of life that she now knew had occurred when the security team confronted Wensor and his planet-based collaborators. She felt little sympathy towards the thirty to forty Likudians - the exact number was hard to judge - but still added their number to her tally. So, her failure to do things better resulted in the deaths of over sixty people, and injury to an unspecified number more. That was a failure of grand proportions, showing extremely poor judgement. She had always been proud of her decision-making. Indeed, she had been commended several times for making the right though difficult call at the right time, usually resulting in lives spared.

Now, she replayed every decision that she had made and found herself having made the wrong call at every step of the way. In reaching this conclusion she was encouraged repeatedly by Major Grinwell, who suggested at each juncture that Varna could have made different decisions that may - not would, but may - have resulted in different outcomes, usually entailing less loss of life. Varna's mood turned away from her normal positive outlook and became dark, unforgiving of herself, approaching self-destructive. Only Varna's inbuilt strength of spirit, despite being so badly battered now, held her back from seeking an abrupt end to the pain and the guilt with which she was wracked.

Then came the day when she was visited by her father. He brought the news that Major Grinwell had been uncovered as one of the main conspirators. She had tried to push Varna in her time of vulnerability into a suicidal frame of mind, all the while reporting that Varna was making progress towards a positive outcome. Mika Sancer then had just held his daughter, saying almost nothing for a long while after breaking the news that the counsellor had done her level best to destroy her. And for the first time, in the arms of the one person in the universe who she trusted above all else, Varna broke down and wept, her copious tears full of bitterness, of fear, of horror, of humiliation. She wept as she had not wept for many years, holding her father in a tight grip as though she would never let go. The little girl who had been now poured out all of her grief, all of her anger. And her father, her rock in what had a become a world of pain and hurt, absorbed it with a stony face that Varna could not see, and murmured words of reassurance and certainty and unconditional love. He stayed until Varna cried herself out and fell asleep, exhausted.

When the Admiral finally left, his stony face caused those who saw him to maintain a distance. His judgement and punishment of the conspirators when he returned to *Sirius* became legend throughout the fleet and beyond. Strangely, though, Varna was never informed of the summary executions of the prime movers, including the erstwhile counsellor, nor the imprisonment of the others for lengths of time that defied what was the norm of the time. She did not find out until much later of the number of fleet officers and Warriors who were left alone in their cells, a single-shot percussion pistol having been provided for their use. All were used.

With the Admiral had come an older man who gave them privacy but slipped into the room and stayed when the Admiral left. He waited patiently until Varna awoke and noticed him sitting in a side chair. She regarded him with suspicion and fear that remained even when the man started speaking. He explained to Varna what had occurred in reality, that every decision she made and every action that she had taken had been reviewed by an independent panel - that did not include her father - and was vindicated. Suspicion stayed even when he informed her that her actions were considered to have been in the best traditions of the Warriors, and not the worst errors as Grinwell had tried to convince her. Two days it took before Varna spoke to him, and then only to ask who he thought he was to try to convince her of anything. And the man smiled at the breakthrough.

"Who I am is of no moment," he said gently. "Know that I have experienced some of what you have experienced, and survived. I believe I grew stronger, in fact. As you will. You're not one to waver and crack as they wanted you to do. They fear such as you, do the Likudians. And those such as you are ever their targets."

"They know of me?" Varna asked, incredulous. "I think not, old man. What have I ever done that was worthy of such attention? This was nothing but the simple revenge of a traitor uncovered."

"Your record at the Academy is well known, Varna," he replied, "and they have watchers looking for such people. We know this because we have apprehended several over recent years, and your name has been prominent in their responses under questioning. And your performance in your assignments to date has indicated that you're likely to be prominent among the Warriors." He nodded, as though to a question that no-one had asked. "It's not a surprise that you were targeted, especially now when we understood the extent to which *Sirius* had been infiltrated. You were always a major threat."

Varna stopped herself before she responded with scorn and forced herself to consider what the old man had told her. And she realised that she had missed something.

"How have you experienced anything like I have," she asked with a challenge still in her voice.

"Well, perhaps not exactly the same as you, but enough for me to have some understanding. Long ago I was captured and subjected to torture and a sort of ritual humiliation. The Likudians seem to develop a liking for inflicting pain, especially those who are turned from the human path. They lack imagination, though, and so I can imagine the sort of thing you suffered." He paused to watch Varna's reaction, waiting for many seconds to continue. "I managed to escape after four years. Four years during which they asked me for nothing, sought no intelligence but merely tried to break me. They inflicted pain, sought to break my spirit. There was no subtlety, no sort of trickery to make me reveal any secrets. Just pain, fear and humiliation. It was that which allowed me to escape, for they could not envisage anyone remaining intact after that time."

Four years! Varna struggled to believe it. She had been held captive for no more than a week and this man had survived four years? She found that hard to believe until a whisper at the back of her mind caused her to think back, to remember the stories told in the quiet times of those who had been captured by Likudian sympathisers and the Empire agents. And of The Escape. There was only ever one referred to as The Escape.

"Rashi Kortuyen!" Varna breathed. "Why are you here?"

"I am Rashi," the old man said quietly. "I owed your father a favour and he asked me to speak with you."

Varna stared at this old man, a legend amongst the Warriors. She remembered the stories that so many thought were tall tales. Of the long imprisonment after Rashi had been taken, destroying most of his pursuers before being betrayed by members of his own team. It was now a familiar story to Varna. And of The Escape, when he somehow fought his way out of the torture chamber deep in an asteroid belt, stole a ship and made his way to a Union outpost more dead than alive. And behind him, in the Likudian outpost that no-one had known existed so close to Union space, there were no survivors. Rumours told of Rashi returning and taking his revenge in various ways. Other rumours spoke of a strange power that visited destruction on the enemies of the Union. Still others told of a ship that appeared out of nowhere and spirited the escapee away after visiting death on the Likudian outpost. Varna had always discounted the stories as being somewhat fanciful, and yet here was Rashi Kortuyen! For some reason she did not doubt his identity.

"How did you escape?" she asked. "And why do you owe my father anything?"

"The two are entwined," the old Warrior replied, smiling gently. "I did escape from my cell when the guard grew careless and allowed me to slip my bond. I managed to kill him with the implements which they had used to torture me, and stole his blaster. I shot my way out of the prison and stole one of their scout ships." He spoke laconically, the simple telling failing to hide from Varna's perceptive gaze the effect of old memories resurfacing, and in the moment he explained more. "I remember running through the station, using the blaster to cut down two who came upon me as the alarm was raised. There were two troops on the station, twenty of them in all, but they were stationed on the opposite side of the asteroid. I found where the torturers were quartered, just near the docking airlock, and killed them much faster than they deserved." Unconsciously, the gentle smile became a predator's grin, and Varna glimpsed the Warrior behind the old man. "And I made it to their scout craft. The controls were not that different to our own, which was a welcome surprise, and I managed to get away, broadcasting on all Union channels, although not really expecting to be heard by anyone who could help. I was trying to get away when the Likudians launched after me. They were much faster than my scout. The pursuing craft closed to strike range. But then my proximity alarm went off and a strange ship appeared, coming between me and the pursuers. It absorbed several blaster bolts and then just … destroyed them."

Rashi stopped and considered his words, staring at Varna but not really seeing her. Varna could almost see through the simple words, could almost see the small craft and its pilot expecting to be killed rather than escape.

"My father?" Varna asked, putting two and two together.

And getting five. Well, four and a bit.

"Not exactly. It was an experimental craft piloted by a Lieutenant Jord. He de-cloaked between me and the Empire ships. Absorbed their fire with screens they were testing, and returned fire with some sort of rail gun that should not have worked. That ship was just too small for it. There were three ships chasing me, and they were all killed in moments. I was taken aboard and found the co-pilot who had operated the guns was an Ensign Sancer. I told them my story. I thought they didn't believe me but they did. They just spun their ship towards that asteroid and told me to forget what would come next. And they destroyed it. Ensign Sancer fired some sort of missile that caused the asteroid to break apart,

then he fired that rail gun and targeted anything that looked man-made
- Empire-made - and tore them apart."

Varna stared. Her father? He had never even suggested anything
like that.

"And then that experimental ship grabbed my boat and jumped to
Union space. I was put back into the scout ship and told not to reveal
anything of that ship. They just took me back to Union lines and sent
me on my way, with a handshake and a wink. When I was located by
a patrol the scout ship's logs showed that I had somehow destroyed the
pursuers and turned back to destroy the Empire installation. I went
along with it. I guess I could have told the truth but there was no trace
- literally no trace - of that experimental ship, and I thought I could
better protect them. So I accepted what the ship's log said and became
a hero." He smiled ruefully. "This is the first time I ever told anyone of
this. Hopefully there are no recording devices here, but I'm pretty sure
your father has thought of that."

"Why tell me all of that?" Varna asked.

"I'm not sure," mused Rashi. "I was supposed to reassure you that
you're not alone in surviving what the Likudians do to us when we are
captured. To tell you that you did nothing wrong - and you did nothing
wrong, by the way - and try to get you to believe in yourself again.
Somewhere that went wrong."

Varna snorted. "So now what? Do I get re-assigned to some backward world to guard a latrine? While everyone tries to decide if I'm a
screw-up and best shuffled somewhere quiet for good?"

"Oh no, nothing that easy," Rashi replied, his gentle smile coming
back into play. "The right people have been made aware of what
transpired, and how you managed to uncover not just the one cell but
have helped to unroll a whole apparatus that the Likudians have been
operating within the Fleet, probably for decades. For every individual
who hates you for what you did there are many hundreds more who
applaud."

Varna absorbed that. While Rashi waited patiently, she took hold of it and turned it upside down and inside out, examining what Rashi told her from various angles. She forced herself to look from the outside, which she normally could do without conscious effort, but not at this time. She shuddered as she thought about being out there again, exposed to who knew what enemies from within the Fleet as well as outside it. She knew, recognised, that she had been damaged. The wounds that had been raw at a mental level were raw still. Time might heal many things, but some wounds stayed raw for a long time. Physical assault was but one of those, as were persistent attacks on one's self-belief.

Varna stalled in her thinking. The primary goal of her captors was to demean her, to strip away her sense of self-worth. The attack was at a basic level, a visceral level. But she had survived it and, somehow, someone had dealt with Wensor and his crude attacks. She doubted that it could have been anything she did, but she did survive what they had inflicted. She did also hold out against the more subtle and sophisticated efforts of Grinwell to damage her psyche. Was it enough? She sighed.

"I'm not sure, Rashi," she said quietly. "I can probably put up a facade but I know it won't hold. I don't know if I can go out there again."

"Yep, you've been injured, badly," Rashi said, smiling as Varna stared at him. "What, did you think I'd be one of the ones to tell you everything's okay? Well, it's not. It's not okay for you, it's not okay for the *Sirius* and it's not okay for the Fleet. So, as far as you're concerned, it comes down to your own strength. It comes down to what you want to do. Others have quit for less. No-one will think any less of you if you take early retirement and find a nice quiet planet where you can grow Distellian fire berries and make your fortune. Is that what you want?"

Once again, Varna turned her thoughts inward. She imagined herself growing Distellian fire berries - the craze *du jour* across human space - or anything else and couldn't do it. It just would not fit. She considered other things that may be options. Non-combatant counsellor? Maybe - she had the skills and the training, but just could not see herself in that passive role. Trader? Many ex-Fleet personnel took on the dangers of delivering the enormous array of trade goods needed around the rim of the human and allied worlds and again she had the requisite skills as far as she understood them. But no, that wouldn't wash either. She tried and discarded one potential occupation after the other. Finally, she thought about what she had uncovered, the festering rotten threads seeking to destroy the fabric of the Union from the inside, allied to the Empire agents who attacked from the outside. She considered the inescapable fact that the rot had spread further than she could have thought, even just in *Sirius* and its Fleet. And deep inside the spark that she thought had been extinguished was coaxed back to life.

"You're right," she said with a wry smile, the first smile she could recall since she had awoken. "I'm not cut out for Distellian fire berries. So, I guess I need to get myself back on the bike. *Sirius* will have to recover also and I may be able to help that."

Rashi again smiled the slow smile that Varna had come to like in the short time they had spoken.

"Oh, you need to get yourself back into the action, no doubt about that. But not on *Sirius*. When your father told me what had happened, and what he planned to do to get *Sirius* pulled back into shape again, I made a couple of calls." He paused for dramatic effect, causing Varna to roll her eyes, which in turn caused Rashi to grin. "You'll be transferred to another vessel, under the command of an old friend. *Starfire!*"

8. A Mission Reinstated

Serra walked into the gym and glanced around. There was only a single other occupant, a young woman who was single-mindedly pounding a punching bag into submission. Serra watched for a moment. The woman was working through a set of forms with which Serra was very familiar. Warrior-taught forms. It was the intensity of every strike that made Serra take notice. That she was skilled was evident. That she was fit was very evident. However, that intensity was eye-catching. Serra shrugged. There was nothing wrong with working off frustrations in the gym, and if that helped the Warriors - for the young woman also wore the standard workout gear assigned to the Warriors - then she was all for it.

Serra moved to the far side so she had free movement. She dropped her gear bag, split the seam and extracted a short sword. Carefully, she made sure the razor-sharp blade had its protective tip firmly embedded in the tip shield and that the equally sharp cutting edge had a thin protective strip along its entire length. Satisfied, the Grand Admiral removed her outer jacket, revealing her own fit figure clad snugly in all black gear. She started slowly, making sure she did not overdo anything. After all, it had been more than fifty years since she had done any of the exercises. While she was confident that the stasis chamber of her personal ship had all the requisite technology to maintain muscle tone, she did not wish to take chances. So, for the last few weeks she had been taking it easy, easing back into the old routines. Today would see the intensity ramp up.

The forms were very old and very familiar. Serra knew many different forms from many different cultures, having had unique opportunities to learn over the years. She slid into some of the oldest ones now, those with which she was most familiar. Like putting on a favourite pair of gloves the forms came back to her and she lost herself in the movement. It had been a long time but her body remembered and responded. As a thin film of sweat covered her body Mavin Serra moved from form to form, flowing, eyes closed. The sword was one with her in the forms. It was a focus that she could use and it moved and twisted, cut and thrust. But most of all it seemed to bend and flow, such was the skill with which it was used.

Standing back from her punching bag, breathing deeply, Varna noted the movement on the opposite side of the gym and watched. She did not recognise the woman. The forms being worked through were not familiar to Varna, although certain variations almost were. However, the skill level being shown by the woman was breath-taking. Never had Varna seen someone with such skill. As Varna watched the woman moved into a new set and her movements quickened. Spins, twists, jumps and turns were completed with eye-dazzling speed. And yet Varna had the feeling that this woman was not showing anywhere near what she was capable of. Varna started to turn back to her own training when from the corner of her eye she thought she caught a glow, but when she turned back there was nothing but the woman continuing at the forms. She shrugged and turned back to her own fitness training. Carefully, she brought up the image of Wensor in her mind and laid it on the punching bag.

Serra came to what she felt was a natural end of the form set for the session. She was breathing more heavily than she usually would have done and made a mental note to make time for her workouts each day. She would need all of her skills in the times to come. She wrapped the sword in its protective sheath and shoved it back into the bag, picked up her jacket and walked from the gym, noting that the young woman was attacking the bag again with ferocious intent.

"Admiral? The shuttle is lifting off now."

"Thank you." Serra turned to Jord after she acknowledged the communications officer's report. "We went a long way out of our way for these two, so I hope they're worth it. Any time lost could be costly. I don't know why, but I feel it deep in my bones."

Jord nodded seriously, his eyes glued to the monitor that showed the flight path of the approaching shuttle. A readout just above the projected flight path showed the distance between the two craft in rapidly tumbling numbers.

"These are two of the top ones you identified from your scans of the Warriors. We were lucky that they managed to complete their mission so quickly. Hopefully the time lost will be made up by the effect of having them on the team. Bluntly, they're the best at what they do."

"So their records say, which is why I am prepared to take the time. And they have the pre-requisites that I need. You were going to give me the full run-down on the team members. The parts the records don't tell. Now might be a good time."

"Yes, Admiral." Jord turned to Colonel Kiri. "Have Flight-Colonel Jalor and Sergeant Blaine report to the briefing room when they have freshened up, please. And find Major Barr and ask her to join us also."

He followed Serra from the bridge, entering the briefing room just as Serra finished ordering two coffees – real coffee, she stressed – from the Chief Steward. They discussed minor matters until the coffee was served.

"Ah," Serra sighed contentedly. "You know, Jord, I will never take real coffee for granted again. It seemed like no time at all while I was in stasis, but my body obviously missed the coffee. Now," she continued in her usual businesslike manner, "tell."

Jord sat back, cradling his coffee.

"I can give you their careers in a nutshell. Telling of the people will take longer. Careers first. Flight-Colonel Vinca Jalor, master pilot, able to fly anything but he also has exceptional insertion skills. He actually broke into the Empire's secure fleet facility and flew their experimental attack fighter out from under their best defences. Nothing like that was ever done before, nor since. First time he'd seen the controls. He led the defending forces when the Third Fleet ran into the Empire's Prime Battle Fleet after the Fleet defence commander was killed. Took his squadron straight through the attacking ships using tactics I still can't fathom and attacked the Empire fleet's flagship. Lost half his squadron doing it, but the Third was able to withdraw in good order when the flagship was destroyed. The amazing thing was that he kept half of his squadron intact. He's had a couple of other episodes where he pulled his ships through some tough situations and came out on top, became known as a tactical genius, quickly moved up to fleet level and became known for strategic genius.

"It was then that he moved into the Warriors. That was about ten years ago. We needed his skills to plan a mission to insert a team into a high tech area. His plan was unorthodox in the extreme, but it went like clockwork. Then we found that he had the skills required for a second mission he planned. He paired with Blaine on that one. They had to assist a planetary government overcome an insurgency fomented and funded by the Empire. Incredibly, between the two of them they did it. Brought the government forces up to date tactically, just about regenerated the local force's defensive skills. He actually led from the front in what he termed the final battle. The insurgents were badly broken with minimal losses to the government. He and Blaine were asked to stay, which is quite unusual, of course – usually the locals want to be rid of our people immediately to re-establish their own control, but Jalor seems to get trust almost instinctively. People like him. More to the point, people believe in him, implicitly.

"We've just now picked him up – and Blaine, of course – from their latest mission - they've been together for almost a decade now. This time they had to convince the local government to stay in the Union. Someone convinced the Assembly, which is their governing body, that the Union was trying to take over. It's the usual spiel repeated with variations for a very long time, but it seems to work on certain people. I know they succeeded, but I'm not sure how. We'll find out soon enough."

Admiral Serra directed a searching gaze at Jord. "Sounds like a super-man of some kind. Do you like him?"

"Super-man?" Jord laughed. "He'd hate that description. He's one of our best, but doesn't belabour the point. No fake modesty. But more of that soon." He left her second question unanswered. "As for Blaine." Jord grinned. "This one is easy. With the possible exception of our missing Champion, Weapons-Sergeant Argus Blaine is the most lethal person I can think of, with any weapon imaginable. He served in several campaigns around the galaxy drawing attention to his skills so fast that he was released from his nominal sector division for use in various units. He was – still is, in fact – asked for by name in ticklish situations.

"About thirteen years ago he joined an insertion team to provide specialist training to the Warriors on a range of obsolete weaponry still used at the target site. In the end, he went on the mission with the Warrior team. He's been with the Warriors since. He was paired with Jalor originally to balance field experience with strategy. They proved to work together very well. So, we left them together mostly.

"Blaine has all the qualifications to be a team leader but has refused each time. Says he's better taking orders rather than giving them." Jord shrugged. "All I know is that he's one of our best. Pair him with Jalor and they make a formidable team."

Serra held her coffee in both hands. She stared into its contents, lost to her own thoughts. Jord waited, patiently, aware the Admiral was reviewing what she had been told. Finally, she shrugged her shoulders in an effort to relieve muscles that had been held tense for an over long period.

"And you rate these two as the best in the fleet?" she asked quietly, still not looking at Jord.

"Probably by a fair margin. Jalor is certainly the best strategist, Blaine the best at weaponry. Jalor is no slouch with weapons, and I know he's been taking lessons from Blaine. Blaine has a pretty good tactical head, too. Combine them with Varna, and you will have the best all-round team, at least on screen."

"Tell me about Varna."

"Third member of your team. Varna Barr. Highly qualified. She joined us a short time ago after serving with *Sirius'* Warrior teams."

"A little unusual for someone to transfer from one fleet's teams to another, is it not? At least, it was in my day."

"It still is your day," Jord replied, amused. "But you're right. It is unusual. She's been through a terrible experience during and after her last mission, and we needed to get her away from the aftermath. Her father has just been appointed task force commander for the *Sirius* battle group and will have to deal with that trouble. You may recall him - Ensign Mika Sancer, now Fleet Admiral Sancer."

Serra nodded. "I recall him as a junior ensign. Without knowing this trouble, I suppose that is understandable, then. Easier on Mika, too. What is Varna Barr like?"

Jord paused, staring into his coffee cup. He considered Serra's question on several levels. Finally, he looked up and grinned wryly.

"First, bare facts. Rated a Senior Specialist officially, rank of Sub-Major - no, full Major now. Expert in a wide range of weapons and several forms of unarmed combat. Unofficially, she could be a rank higher except for a disciplinary infraction on *Sirius* that I think was fabricated. Nine missions to date, all of them successful. On the last, she protected the junior team members in a hot situation and apparently fought off a group of rebels alone after finding the team's number one had been suborned before being captured. The leader of the rebel faction was killed. Varna was tortured brutally and almost died. The traitor did die, supposedly at Varna's hand. He appeared to have tried to kill her while she was shackled and she somehow subdued him, even in her injured state, but he took a sword through the chest and had almost every bone in his body broken - Varna can't explain how, but the hearing was adamant that she was not at any fault in her actions. She's been on recovery leave since. She joined us while still on recovery leave and has refused to leave the ship. After her actions, security uncovered a large cell on *Sirius* of Likudian sympathisers. Varna was targeted by them during her recovery, it seems, which served to uncover even more, both in the *Sirius* fleet and elsewhere. May have saved many lives in the future." Jord's voice had remained even throughout the recitation.

"And the rest?" Serra asked, alert eyes holding contact with Jord. "What do you think about her?"

"I'm biased. I've known Varna since she was born. I served with Mika for the *Galaxy's* last patrol. And before that was when Mika joined our team and spent a few years with us. He's one of the few survivors of the second group. Varna's young, bright, undoubtedly good at what she does, but she doesn't mix in. Stands apart. Spends most of her time sharpening up skills that couldn't be sharper. Always professional, strictly correct in her procedures but willing to go outside the straight line if the mission calls for it."

"Sounds like she's trying to prove herself."

"Yes, she is," said Jord, slowly nodding her head. "At the Academy there was a rumour that she influenced the examiners when the results came out – she topped the class. When it was found she has a strong psi quotient the rumours became accusations. She was re-examined and did better than before. The results were confirmed. But the rumours persisted, even after she graduated. Her psi levels saw her given special training, which didn't help her a lot.

"Weapons, tactics, strategy, communications – she qualified for the lot, and all of them at the top of the list. By now no-one with any sense believes the rumours, if they ever did, but Varna keeps pushing herself. There's a suggestion that it has become a compulsion in itself. The episode unmasking the traitor and then somehow killing him did her few favours with his friends, although numbers of them have now been found to have been compromised also. It only became worse when her father was appointed to command the task force. Attempts to kill her in her own fleet! She was not told about most of them, I believe."

"Hmmm. What about Mika? Does he push her?"

Jord paused, lost in thought.

"Uh, sorry," he started, suddenly back with the Admiral. "I was remembering a five-year-old girl intently trying to cut out a perfect square using old-fashioned scissors. The intense concentration and determination were evident even then. Maybe," he mused, "there's no compulsion beyond a deepening of that same spirit." He shrugged, pushing the thought aside for contemplation at a later time. "As for Mika? No, no pressure. Mika's about as proud as a father can be. It wouldn't matter what she did. He's supported her, made no secret of it, but never used his influence either. But it will be easier on him for Varna not to be there as he takes the broom through *Sirius*. He's already started from what I hear. It won't be pretty."

Serra sat back. She toyed with her mug, absently tracing the crude painted lettering on its side.

"So, what do we have?" She held up her left hand, picking out fingers as she made her points. "First, a tactical and strategic genius who is also a master pilot, a weapons expert who makes the Seven Heroes of Jebarran sound like a bunch of pre-eds in diapers, and an exceptional psi talent who is good at everything she tries but who seems to have a chip on her shoulder. Sounds like an interesting group you and Denton are bringing together for me."

"Only me, I'm afraid - and you were the one who gave me this list of names, remember, although at some stage I would be interested in what made you pick the short list you did. But team composition is my job. Admiral Bard may disagree with my selections from time to time and he's never backward in letting me know about it, but it's still my call."

Serra nodded. "And you think they will work together? This is a mission that cannot fail."

"I know Jalor and Blaine will. Jalor specifically recommended Varna for her last mission and endorsed her being chosen for this one when I discussed it with him over the channel. And she received her first specialist chevron at Blaine's recommendation - she didn't know he was monitoring the mission, nor does she know he recommended her - after a campaign about four years ago. Yes," he smiled, "I think they'll go okay. They'll be here shortly."

"Then let's meet our super team. Seeing as we have no idea what we might find on the planet after this time, I can only hope they are what is needed."

A short time later the two men entered the wardroom, having come directly from the shuttle without being privy to recent events, nodding informal greetings to Jord and the woman sitting on an easy chair, who they each eyed curiously. Jord called the wardroom attendant to him, gave instructions for Varna to be found and brought to the meeting. Meanwhile he told Jalor and Blaine to help themselves to the bar. Neither needed a second invitation.

9. Team Two

Varna did not want to be found. She was in an isolated part of the huge vessel, sitting in a small nook in an oft-forgotten observation point, from where she could look out at the stars. She found it somewhat soothing and she could forget - almost - about recent events. She could see her reflection in the thick plexipane, and could *see* the shadow behind her eyes. Despite being reassured that her reaction was normal, she was not sure. While using it for some of her training impetus, Varna tried not to replay the scenes from her last mission. She tried not to remember the pain and humiliation that she had felt. She tried to block out just how helpless she had felt when she was held, tortured not for any information but for revenge and to cause damage. The taunting of her captors as she was stripped naked and shackled to a stone wall continued to seep into her psyche, to chip away at her self-confidence. Even as she tried to relax and work through the forms of meditation as she had been taught, they continued to come to the surface. That and the loss of innocent life had come close to breaking her.

And now, cleared for return to service by both physical and psychological medical experts, she continued to wonder if she was ready. In fact, she wondered if she would ever be ready again. She was not sure she could satisfy her own exacting standards once again. She ignored the persistent faint purr of her communication implant for the third time, knowing that she could never be completely out of sight on the vessel - her implant also included a location sensor - but wanting to just *be* for a while longer.

Finally, she stirred as a midshipman approached her and stopped close by.

"Sir," the midshipman said, "you are wanted in the Admiral's wardroom. Immediately, please." Calm, careful not to be accusatory, the midshipman stood with both hands clasped behind his back.

Varna had been in an ill temper for the last week, ship time, and the crew were aware that she had a hair trigger temper right now. They also knew some of her ordeal, but by no means all - and they knew that, too - so had cut her slack. But that had to end sometime, she knew, and that time probably was now. She took a deep breath, swung her legs out and stood in a single fluid motion and smoothed down her tunic.

"Okay," she said to the midshipman, "please let the Admiral know I'm on my way. I'll be a few minutes longer while I freshen up."

"Aye, sir," the midshipman replied, then spoke softly. "Major, if there is anything I can do to assist, please let me know. I would be honoured to help. We all would be."
Varna smiled wanly. "Thank you. I appreciate that. But there are some things we need to do for ourselves."

With that, she turned and walked away from her vantage point, steeling herself for she knew not what. She had tried to stay away from both Admiral Bard and Captain Jord, both of whom were friends and colleagues of her father and both of whom were worried about her. She had not come to any final conclusion about whether she would continue in the service or not, but she had decided to push forward as best she could. She had been out of touch with most of the ship's happenings since she arrived, deliberately, although she was aware of some sort of fuss and excitement that had occurred a little while before she joined the ship.

Varna quickly freshened up in her quarters, and then made her way to the Admiral's wardroom. As she entered, she took note of both the Admiral and the Captain, along with a woman of indeterminate age dressed in what looked like a seriously out of date uniform, although with no rank insignia. She looked familiar somehow but Varna could not place her. She also saw two field operatives - so she assumed them to be by their more casual ship clothing and equally casual attitude - leaning against a wall with glasses holding clear liquid. She was willing to bet it was not water.

"Admiral, Captain," she said as she entered, and nodded to the two men. She turned to the woman, seated in the Admiral's chair, and held out her hand. "Specialist Major Varna Barr," she said by way of introduction.

"Major," the woman said, with a smile, "I am very pleased to meet you. I knew your father a long time ago."

Varna nodded. Another old friend, she thought, hopefully not destined to ask too many questions about how well she was doing. Taking her cue from the other two men - she thought she recognised the taller one from somewhere - Varna moved to the small bar and poured a measure of Aparnian brandy into a glass, taking a sip as she turned back to the room.

"Well, I think seeing as we are all here, we can get started. Introductions are in order. Flight-Colonel Vinca Jalor," Jord gestured to the taller field operative, who nodded without changing his slouched position, "and Weapons Sergeant Argus Blaine." The shorter but powerfully built Blaine sketched a salute - so that's Blaine, Varna thought to herself, regarding the man who was a legend in the special forces world. "Specialist Major Varna Barr has introduced herself," Jord continued evenly, again gesturing, this time to Varna, who felt Jalor, Blaine and the unknown woman appraising her. Jord paused for effect, "I would like you to meet Grand Admiral Mavin Serra."

As he gestured to the still seated Serra, both men straightened and Varna slammed her glass to the bar counter. All were rigidly at attention, eyes fixed firmly on a spot beyond the wardroom walls in an eye-blink. Serra smiled in appreciation at the abrupt and total switch to professionalism. She started to feel better about the team.

"As you were," she said, standing.

The three Warriors relaxed. Jalor turned to Jord with a pained expression.

"Now that wasn't fair," he complained. "Sir," he added, turning away in mock disgust as Jord grinned broadly.

"Admiral, Flight Colonel Vinca Jalor at your service." Jalor held out his right hand, which was immediately grasped by Serra. "I can't tell you how pleased I am to meet you."

"Same goes for me, Admiral. Weapons-Sergeant Argus Blaine," the big man rumbled, shaking hands in turn.

"My father has told me about you," Varna said. "It is an honour."

"Now that makes me feel old," the Grand Admiral quipped. "And here I am not a day over…"

"Ninety-seven, Admiral," Jord broke in with a perfectly straight face.

"Thank you, Mr Jord," Serra answered with heavy irony. "Your complete honesty is admirable."

"Which is why you find my opinion so valuable, Admiral. I am following the advice given to me when I was a cadet ensign, quite some time ago."

"I must have been having an off day," she replied drolly. "Well," turning back to the other three. "Mr Jalor, you have a report?"

"Yes, Admiral." Jalor hesitated a moment. "May I enquire what your status is, Admiral? Operationally, I mean."

Jord answered. "Grand Admiral Serra has assumed command of *Starfire* and the fleet. Admiral Bard has assumed the role of fleet executive officer."

"Thank you, sir," Jalor nodded to Jord, then turned to Serra. "It could take a while. May I suggest we all have a seat?"

At Serra's nod, they all chose seats. When they were settled, Jalor began.

"Our mission was simple. Find out who convinced Bran's Assembly that the Union wanted to take over and allay those fears. It started well enough. The Assembly was happy enough to receive us and hear us out. But there was an undercurrent of unease. Some of the Union's recent actions have been questionable, like sending Task Force 5 into the Starmine Colonies to re-establish a Union-backed ruling council. Like posting interdict notices on so-called dissident commentators at Micra. Those were the two main examples known to the Assembly members. They didn't know of another half dozen or so instances that I can think of over the last twenty years and probably more I don't know of.

"But they were always directed at planets trying to leave the Union. I have never heard of a planet using those actions as justification to make the break. And in this case, the Union as a whole is lucky.

"Blaine and I were able to trace the rumblings back to the deputy leader of the Assembly. We found that he had allied himself to the military commander of the main continental force. Basically, after taking Bran out of the Union they were going to take over Bran. We could assemble the evidence fairly easily and timed our delivery of it to the Chief Minister and a number of Assembly members we knew were loyal. It coincided with a local festival. The Assembly was convened in emergency session and the deputy leader arrested.

"At the same time a group of Planetary Guards conducted a flash strike to capture the military commander and her associates. I'm pretty sure they were all identified. That effectively ended it."

"Casualties?" Jord asked.

"Only a handful on each side injured, a few dozen killed. Most of the killed were on the rebel side. The loyalist group was hand-picked and well-trained. The action was well-executed."

"Did you observe it?"

"No, sir. Blaine did. I was with the Assembly."

"Your opinion, Sergeant?"

"Professional, sir. They did their jobs well."

"I would not have thought Bran's Planetary Guard would have much knowledge of flash strikes," said Jord mildly.

"Ah, no, sir," replied Blaine. "But they learnt quickly."

"You were an observer only, Sergeant?"

"Yes, sir. I observed them learning quickly." Blaine gazed innocently at Jord.

"Hmmm. And the arrested citizens?"

Jalor smiled grimly. "Tried and executed, sir. All of them."

"The Union's policy is against executing dissidents." Jord's voice remained mild.

"They were tried for treason and murder. A little tenuous as no rebellion had actually occurred, but several Guards were killed while the rebels-to-be resisted arrest. And, after largely convincing the Assembly that the Union wasn't about to dictate to them, I didn't feel like trying to jump on them."

"Blind eye?"

"It seemed the best idea at the time," Jalor nodded.

"Okay. The diplomats can put together a mild protest, I suppose. I want the three of you available at 2100 hours for a prelim on the new mission. Sorry you won't have a break," Jord said to the two men, "but this is important. Varna, you're back on duty?"

"When you say, sir."

"Fine. 2100 for you, too. Dismissed then."

"One moment, Major," Serra spoke as Varna started to turn away. "Are you fully fit for duty after your recent ordeal?"

Varna stopped, taken aback by the question, that it was asked at all and so publicly. She quashed her own qualms as she turned to Serra, still seated, and gazing at her unblinkingly. Varna straightened as she said, "Fully fit, Admiral, passed so by all of the medical staff and I feel capable of fulfilling any mission on which I am sent."

"So, why did you have to leave your ship? That is very unusual and would only happen for a good reason."

Varna's eyes flashed but her voice was steady. "Is that mission suitable to be discussed here, sir?" she asked Serra.

"Jalor and Blaine are your fellow team members. I am making it a suitable topic. Make no mistake, Major. This is an important mission we are sending you on - critical in fact - and I don't want any team member who may not make it through."

Varna stared at the Admiral. "You need have no concerns about that, sir." She glanced at Jalor, who would be the team lead by virtue of rank. "I was on Mastic, a human planet in a small solar system in the Delta quadrant. We were trying to uncover what we thought may have been an Empire cell subverting the planetary government - which is what we found. The new Governor himself was the leader of the cell. In the process I found that my team leader had been turned long ago and was protecting the Governor. I think he knew I had my suspicions and caused an attack on the team. I was captured" - a faint shadow passed over Varna, noticed by Serra but not the others - "but when a rescue party came in I was in a bad way and the team leader, Wensor, was killed. By me, everyone seems to think. I'm still not sure how I could have managed to do so, as he had me pretty much unconscious and close to death.

"It took me a while to get back on my feet afterwards, and when I made it back to the ship there were a few of Wensor's old friends who made it clear they didn't want me around, even when the truth of his betrayal was made known. Some of them were found to be part of his cell. Then my father was appointed task force commander and it was decided I would be better placed elsewhere."

Jalor nodded. "Wensor, eh? Tallish, brown hair, hook nose, big opinion of himself?"

Varna nodded, surprised. "You know him? Knew him, rather." She grimaced.

"Yes, from my time in Fleet Strategic. He was under a cloud for some time. You were chosen as his second to ensure if there was something happening you would pick up on it." He looked to the senior officers. "I made a suggestion about that some time ago. Not just about Varna, although I recommended her, but someone who had a good nose for things." He turned back to Varna. "Did your psi skills come in there, do you think?"

"I've never thought the so-called psi skills are anything other than an innate ability to read people," Varna said, "no matter what others may think. I can read the small signals given off by people that show mood, nervousness, and so on. Sometimes I can almost feel what they are feeling, but I don't give a lot of credence to any sort of psychic powers. I guess some of that contributed to my suspicions and along with my proficiency in lip-reading, not some sort of psi magic, definitely confirmed those suspicions."

Jalor inclined his head. "That's a good skill to have. It may well come in very handy, in my experience. And Varna, in case you are in any doubt, that was a good job." Blaine just nodded.

Serra also nodded. "Don't write off those skills too readily, Major. This universe has some oddities still to be found. Okay, so as long as you are sure you are ready?" At Varna's nod she continued, "Then we will brief shortly. Dismissed."

"Mr Jalor, please wait a moment longer," Jord said as the new team members started to file out of the room.

Jalor nodded, waited until Blaine and Varna had left, then said, "Something else, sir?"

Jord nodded. "A couple of things Varna failed to mention. She was captured because Wensor sold her out. Also, she was tortured after being stripped and hung from manacles on a stone wall in a sort of dungeon. She was treated very badly. A serious effort was made to degrade her, to damage her spirit, both then and back on her ship. They wanted no information, no benefit, just Wensor's revenge."

Jalor's face had tightened as Jord described Varna's ordeal. "And still she managed to kill Wensor? After that?"

Jord nodded again. "And we don't know how, and Varna seems unable to tell us how. When the team got to the cell the door was open, Varna was collapsed on the floor against one wall and still in shackles. Wensor was against the other wall with a broken neck and most of his other bones in no better state, and impaled on his own sword. It looked like he had been flung against the wall."

"Varna doesn't look strong enough to overcome Wensor in the state she would have been in, and then to do that," said Jalor, considering. When Jord made no further comment, Jalor continued, "So, it's likely that she carries scars still. Also unsaid, I gather, is that Varna had not reported her suspicions to her ship? Like regulations direct?"

Jord smiled slightly as he said, "No, she did record her suspicions in personal logs and via tight beam to the fleet's security chief, and also stated that she was unsure if he was a singleton or part of ship-level conspiracy, or anywhere in between, so kept it to herself otherwise. A couple of Wensor's friends tried to attack her on that, but only made themselves look foolish. But you can see how a statement along those lines would not be taken terribly well in some quarters - another part of the reason for her to shift."

Jalor pushed himself from the wall where he had been leaning and said, "Well, she's very well credentialed, and I know Fleet has been watching her for some time. She obviously has courage and shows spirit and resilience. And seems to be right up our alley for what we're going to do, whatever that is," he concluded, looking at Serra.

She chuckled softly. "You'll find out soon enough. But about that decision not to stop the executions. Any more specifics on that?"

"No, Admiral. It was my decision and, as I said, seemed like the right idea at the time. Did I mention that one of those killed by the so-called rebels was the daughter of the former royal family? It brought the line to an end, and they were well loved by the people." Serra watched Jalor's face harden as he spoke, the bleakness of his expression and the haunted look in his eyes telling her that the princess had affected more than the planet's populace, which Jalor then confirmed. "You may as well know that while we were on Bran she adopted me as the brother she never had. We became close. I did not object to the assembly's decision."

"Understood, Mr Jalor, and thank you. Please accept my condolences. You may go now." Serra nodded to Jalor, who regarded her for a moment before bowing slightly and departing, face still tight.
Serra waited until the team members left, before sighing and shaking

her head. "It seems Varna Barr is not the only one to ignore the rules when needed. Their lives are hard at times, are they not?"

Jord smiled, or perhaps it was a grimace. "We look for the members of our teams to have initiative. We can't complain when they use it. Mostly, it's their own lives on the line anyway."

Bard had been sitting quietly during that exchange but now stirred.

"So," he said as he looked at his drink closely, "you're going to re-instate the old mission?"

Serra smiled and nodded. "Missed nothing, did you? Yes, there is a need. Over fifty years have passed and I need to know what has occurred."

"And there's something else happening that we don't know about, that we didn't know about when *Sunburst* dropped the original team." Bard looked at Serra, eyebrow raised. "Correct?"

Serra smiled wryly. "Correct. I will let you in on it at the right time, but for now I need you to trust that I know what I am doing. It may not seem like it from time to time."

Both men nodded and Bard answered for both, "No fear about that, Admiral. And when you're ready we'll be here to assist you in whatever you plan. I think I want to be in on this and I think it may be big."

Serra smiled. "It may well be the biggest thing you can think of, or cannot think of. I just hope things have not gone too far in my absence. So, I need to find out, which is what we will do. And our three Warriors are how we will do that. I don't particularly want to be too public about this."

Murk stumbled along the road. His weaving progress was hampered by the state of the road, which was not maintained - had not been for generations - and the fact that every few paces he took a swig from the jug he gripped in his right hand.

Murk was a hard man, not mean, not difficult, not even really angry any more. But he was hard. You had to be hard to survive in this harsh land of hard rocky ground where almost nothing grew but where many things existed that would bite, suck, sting and crush you to death. The rivers had dried to an intermittent trickle so long ago that the old tales of abundance were just stories told around the fire at night. No-one believed them to be anything except the imaginings of the Tellers, the wandering story-tellers who passed through every so often.

Very few people lived in this land now, although there were ruins that told of a different story in the past. Murk had found some of those ruins himself, or rather, he had stumbled upon them. They had been looted far in the past, so he obviously was not the finder of them. But the ruins made him stop and think that the story-tellers may be right.

The tales told of a time when this land was lush and green, growing fruits and flowers and grasses and all manner of things. Of rivers that ran full and swift, with fish for the taking by the people who had lived com-fortable lives in bright, airy dwellings. Those ruins once housed people who could be soft, because they had whatever they needed, whenever they needed it. Those people were healthy and full of life, not like any-thing Murk had ever experienced, and because of the abundance they had been able to devote large parts of their lives to art, philosophy and learning. In those tales the Tang people were looked to by the people of Ennaris as advisors. There had been members of the Tang who studied the stars, who understood how the world moved through the heavens - a fact that Murk wasn't too sure about because he didn't feel any movement.

The stories told of the time of the great destruction when the world changed, of great upheavals that caused the rivers to dry up, the fish to disappear and the land to wither and die. Many of the Tang died, and most of the remainder left for better places over the long cycles that followed. Until now when what remained was this dry, parched, arid wilderness where living was a day-to-day struggle and a man with any care for others, as Murk had been once, despaired. In Murk's past there had been a beloved life partner and child, a hard struggle to make ends meet that ended with both being taken from him during one of the periodic bouts of fever that swept the sparsely populated region and left it with even fewer people. Murk had weathered all of the hardships but the loss of his family had almost broken him. Aleesa had been the only one who could break through the hard shell that Murk, like most of the Tang people, had built around himself.

Murk was about ready to just lay down and let it end. He was not old, but he was toil-worn. His swords were razor sharp still, and the contracts continued to come, but he accepted few of them now. In this he was like most of his fellow Tang. He had nothing left to live for, and no-one who cared for him or for whom he cared. The jugs helped and even they were getting harder to find. Old Bolter would not last too long and his battered still and vats would fall idle in the near future. The Guardians only knew just what he put into his brews out here, but they kept the present at bay for a time.

Murk stopped and took another swig, having to tilt his head up to get at the last dregs of the almost empty jug. As he did so a bright light streaked through the sky. Murk watched it with dull, slightly unfocused eyes. The object crashed to the ground on the other side of a ridge to one side of Murk's line of travel. He lowered the jug and after two or three attempts managed to get the stopper back in. His thought processes, such as they were at this point, told him to investigate this phenomenon. He had heard of things falling from the sky and people had found strange bits of metal from time to time where they had done so. He might be able to salvage something, even just some sort of rock that he could sell to someone, somewhere. He could not think of who or where, but still he felt compelled to look.

He weaved towards the ridge. Looking around to locate himself, he thought that it would be the edge of the Vale of Tanga, the supposed home of the mythical being for whom the country around here was named and who gave his name to the people themselves, the Tang. The Vale once was reputed to be an unspoiled garden where peace and tranquillity reigned. Tanga had overseen that bounty, according to tradition, and helped his people to grow. Murk sighed as the alcohol worked on his emotions. If only that were so, he thought to himself. The Vale was nothing more than a bowl of misery, hard and dry as the rest of this benighted land with, he recalled, a pile of large rocks in the centre as its only feature.

After a couple of tumbles along his somewhat wandering path Murk made it to the top of the rocky ridge and looked down into the bowl. He stared, befuddled, at what he saw. There was the pile of rocks in the middle, just as he recalled, but he could not remember ever seeing them aglow, each rock pulsing a different colour. A small sward of green started from the rocks and moved out in a ring. It grew as he watched with his mouth hanging open and jug hanging from one hand, forgotten.

Murk had lost his mind. It was the only solution. He stared for a long time as the grass extended further and a small patch of the unyielding ground showed what Murk thought was a flower garden. Finally, he decided that if he was mad then he may as well go all the way. He started to make his way down into the Vale, finally getting to the level ground of the bowl itself, and stumbled towards the rocks. He could feel something coming from those rocks as he came closer, something that worked its way into his inner being. Without noticing, Murk dropped his jug as he came closer to the rocks. When he reached the edge of the green sward he stopped. He dropped to his knees to reach out and touch the grass, soft and pliable, long enough to wave slightly although there was no breeze. He could run his fingers through the grass, could feel the softness underneath where his memory said there should be rock and hard ground.

Murk did not notice the tears running down his face. Nor did he notice the man sitting on one of the rocks, idly swinging one leg as he watched Murk approach.

"Hello, Murk," the man said gently, smiling as Murk started, looked up and stared anew.

The man wore a simple green robe, belted with what looked like twined grasses, with sandals on his feet made from some sort of strange woody material. The man had dark skin, with black, curly hair and a heavy beard, trimmed to frame an open, smiling face. Murk struggled to his feet and tried to speak. On his third attempt he managed to do so.

"Wh ... who're you?" he demanded hoarsely. "What is all of this?"

"I am who I am," the stranger said enigmatically. "And this is the Vale of Tanga."

"But how can this be when there's no water?" Murk was sure he had died and gone to some strange place, but his natural intelligence was asserting itself, slowly, as the alcohol-fuelled fug receded, much faster than it usually did.

"Ah, now that is a good question," the stranger said, looking around. "There is much to be done to repair the actions of the last few thousand cycles. Water will return soon and the land will be restored. Come, I have a repast to share and I would like to learn more about what has transpired since I have been away."

Murk nodded, feeling the weight of despair lift without being aware of how that could be. Over the next half day Murk shared the simple meal of fruit, bread, cheeses and water - water, cold and fresh and sweet such as Murk had never experienced in these lands - and then he told the stranger of the hard life of the people of Tang, and such other news of Ennaris as he knew, often at second hand.

They talked and talked, with the stranger probing carefully. The conversation moved from the Tang as a people to Murk himself, and before he knew it, he was detailing his own life story, his losses and despair. The pain, the anger, the sheer desperation of life lived on the edge every day, of loss of love and loss of hope - for the first time Murk allowed it all to pour out, to be placed in front of this stranger. And he felt the pain lessening, the hurt that would never leave becoming more of a dull throb deep in his chest. This man seemed to have the ability to delve deep into Murk, and Murk responded as he never had to anyone before. And that day passed, as did the next and the next.

And so, Murk became the first of the new Guide acolytes of Tanga, Guardian of Ennaris, and as the gardens spread and the river was reborn and the trees sprouted and grew furiously he spread the word as given to him by Tanga. And as those stories grew the Tang who had been forced to leave started to return home. The Tang had changed dramatically over the thousands of cycles that Tanga had been gone. Those that survived were as hard as flint. The swords they wore were not fancy. They did not gleam for show, and nor were they decorative. The Tang had moved far away from their softer philosopher ancestors, and had become far less and far more.

The message Tanga wanted delivered was to bring the Tang together. And through the hard land of Tang and beyond Murk and a growing band repeated that message: the time has come! The Children of Ennaris have returned, as the old stories told. The people of Ennaris will be called to defend their homes against the ancient evil, and the Tang will be to the fore.

But above all of that was the simple message that meant so much more. Tang had returned! The Guardians have returned!

11. Landing

Drewflin was very still, perched near the sharp peak of a small hill. Light scrubby plants dotted the peak, with even more scrubby grass growing in tufts in the spaces between them. The heat of the twin suns beat down on the hill but Drewflin seemed not to be affected. From time to time he took a small swig from a water skin. Although he had been there for several hours, his attention had not waned. Nor was he visible to even the most careful scrutiny. An almost imperceptible shimmer may have been noticed by those who knew to look, but would have been attributed by almost anyone else to heat rising from the rocks that abounded on the peak. In any event, there were very few left who would know to look.

He sat immobile. His aged and lined face betrayed neither impatience nor expectation. His endurance belied his aged appearance. At times his eyes flicked to the sky to note the position of Lauris, the smaller of the two suns and the most convenient for time judgement. Mostly, his fixed gaze centred on the small dell a short distance from the foot of his hill and close to a flat, desolate patch of blackened ground formed as a perfect circle. According to the Prophecy, and indications picked up by the planetary defence sensors, it was about time.

His gaze sharpened even more as the air blurred a short distance away from the dell. Then, where there was long green grass surrounded by small trees and shrubs only moments before, three people stood along with a large carry bag. Drewflin sighed quietly and nodded, satisfied. Relieved!

Smiling slightly, he reached behind himself to grasp a small duffel, very old and of no particular colour, with an opening tied by a draw string. In moments, the draw string was loosened and a book extracted, all done while Drewflin's eyes remained fixed unwaveringly on the three below. The book was opened at a place indicated by a marker. The watcher's eyes moved briefly as he glanced at the book, now held in front of him. He nodded to himself and closed the book, returning his attention to the dell as the book was restored to the duffel. The book, the Prophecy, had been right, as it had always been once the events were imminent and could be interpreted.

Slowly he brought his right hand level with his chin, made a slight gesture and closed his eyes. He did not need the hand movement, of course, but habit had ingrained several gestures for certain uses of his gifts. His lips moved silently as he mouthed an incantation. His senses extended until he felt himself among the three. His sight and hearing now were acute enough to see and hear them clearly.

Using what he liked to think of as his mind's eye, the Mage examined the three new arrivals. The first, evidently the party's leader, was a dark-haired male. His face was pale, with dark eyes now blinking uncertainly, a long, thin nose and a tight mouth. The overall effect could have been to give him a pedantic look except for the alertness now coming into the eyes and stance. He wore a close-fitting one-piece jumpsuit, covering all but neck and head, hands and feet. Under the suit, his muscles were wiry and flat. Small pockets extended down the legs. His feet were en-cased in soft-textured boots. A belt, measuring about three fingers wide, was slung about his waist. The clothes and belt were a uniform dull silver colour, offering no reflections from the suns' light but standing out clearly in the green dell. From his belt hung a pair of mittens and several small black boxes, instruments of some kind. Also slung from the belt on the right side was a weapon, with the owner's hand hovering absently over it. Drewflin dubbed him "Black Hair".

The second member of the party was dressed similarly but, where the former seemed slim, this one's muscles bulged under the material of his suit. He had red-brown hair and darker skin, full lips and a slightly flattened nose. A fine scar extended from above his left eye to the hairline, lending him a vaguely piratical air that was softened by laughter lines around both eyes. This one, although evidently disoriented, had unlimbered his weapon and turned outward, preparing to counter any possible threat. A formidable and experienced individual, thought the watching Drewflin. He was given the name "Red Hair".

Now he turned his attention to the third person, a blonde-haired woman whose silver jumpsuit clearly displayed a full, though trim, figure. She had fine features, startling blue eyes and long, tapering fingers that held, rather than a weapon, one of the small boxes from her belt. She shook her head gently, seeking to clear her mind from the disorientating effects of transporting, and moved the box in an arc in front of her body, turning to cover all points of the compass. Her attention was centred on a small gauge on the front of the box. Occasionally, she moved a small slider. At a questioning glance from Black Hair the woman shook her head.

"Nothing," she said in a voice that was low and modulated.

Black Hair moved up to stand behind the woman. He signalled to Red Hair, sketching a circle in the air. Red Hair slowly moved outward in a spiral pattern, stopping at times to quarter the area in front of him. After a thorough examination of the surrounding area Red Hair slowly joined the other two. His attention remained on the surrounding area. The watcher silently nodded approval towards Red Hair, who he rechristened "The Soldier".

Black Hair moved ahead of the others, followed by the woman. The Soldier followed at a distance, eyes never still, watching the entire dell and its surrounds. The three slowly walked towards the blackened circle, The Soldier again leaving space between himself and the others.

As they neared the edge of the blackened circle, the three separated again, moving to points around the circle. The woman removed a second small box from her belt and held it with arm extended, studying the top of the box intently. The two men, meanwhile, were scouting the edge of the blackened area, seemingly comparing the blackened earth and the lush green grass growing immediately adjacent.

Drewflin's enhanced senses allowed him to see it all.

"No life forms other than birds and the small rodent-like animals noted in the scans." The woman's voice was tight, as though nervous tension was being held in check. And she sounded hesitant, as though the language was difficult. Her words were coloured by an almost imperceptible accent.

Black Hair answered, his voice betraying no accent, inflexions correct. "What radius have you used? It should be at least two klicks."

"I used two and then five," replied the woman as she continued to study the device.

"What do you make of the circle," Black Hair asked of The Soldier.

"Amazing," was the response, in a voice both low and thoughtful. "The edges are clearly defined, and the charred ground still shows minute traces of radiation, after all these years. But the grass right alongside is completely clean. I've only ever seen this in text books. But there's no doubt about it. This was done by a blitz mine."

"A blitz? Any hope of survivors?"

"None. The team wore standard issue personal shields, according to the ship's records. I don't know who brought the blitz along, but it was meant as a last resort device. I hope he took them all with him."

Black Hair looked at The Soldier, brows raised in a quizzical expression. "All of who?"

"Whoever was attacking, of course," said The Soldier calmly. "That's what I meant. It's a last resort weapon, only used when the enemy is in close and there's no way out. And its radius is determined by its explosion height. The destruction zone is like a cone, directed downward and out from the point of explosion. But it's very clean and quite precise. This burned out circle is all that remains. Everything within the explosion radius goes."

Black Hair replied thoughtfully, "I've heard of a blitz charge but never really understood how devastating they were."

Suddenly, the woman stiffened in her place and raised a hand in warning. The Soldier dropped to a crouch, then scuttled forward and rolled under a shrub out of the circle. Black Hair slowly rotated, hand hovering over his weapon, still on his left hip.

"Jalor! Varna! Down!" snapped The Soldier in a fierce whisper.

Belatedly, Black Hair - Jalor or Varna, the watcher set their names in memory - crouched and moved forward to the woman's position.

"What?" he repeated softly, eyes scanning as much of the country around the dell as possible.

"I sensed someone. Close." Drewflin raised his eyebrows and watched her closely as the woman moved her small black box in a short arc. "I think," she added uncertainly. "But the monitor shows nothing but birds and rodents, like before."

"Are you sure, Varna? It could have been a holdover from what happened here, couldn't it? Your empathic abilities may be reacting to an aura remaining." Jalor - the male, as the female was now identified as Varna - looked to The Soldier, who shrugged before returning to his survey.

Varna shook her head, less in denial than confusion. "I told you I don't believe in that. Anyway, after more than fifty standard years, any aura is gone, assuming such things exist. Or is not strong enough for that if it does exist. It is possible, of course. He was the Champion. But this seemed so strong and immediate. I've never experienced such a thing. It was what one of the instructors taught us could be felt if such did exist. And it was just a flash."

"Well." Jalor signalled to The Soldier and touched Varna on her shoulder. "We have to move. If someone is near we should avoid them, at least until we've blended in."

Cautiously, Jalor returned to the small dell and the carry bag, picked it up with his right hand and moved back to The Soldier's position. The latter was still crouched and wary. One at a time, with the other two keeping watch, all three stripped off their silver suits and changed into clothing modelled after the planet's native costume.

Their original clothing was collapsed to tiny volumes and inserted within pouches on their belts, which were themselves stowed in small packs. The weapons were broken down into components and secreted in compartments within the same packs. Jalor wore blue breeches, a billowing silver shirt, black calf-high boots and a peaked cap set at a rakish angle. Blaine – so The Soldier had been called by Varna to indicate she had finished dressing - wore similar but more conservative clothes of plain brown breeches and a shirt coloured a dull olive green. His boots were scuffed where Jalor's gleamed. Varna stood out in a brilliant white shirt, a black skirt that swirled as she walked, and knee-high brushed leather boots. She wore no headgear, but her hair was tied so it dropped down her back like a golden curtain.

Jalor led the small team back to the dell once again and extracted a belt from the pack. He pressed a small stud on the belt. The clearing shimmered once again and a long container appeared. Blaine and Varna opened a hatch on the top of the container. From it they took packs, a number of musical instruments, a long bow and a huge quiver of arrows. Varna extracted several short rods. Their original packs, containing their original clothes and weapons, were stashed inside the container. The hatch was closed and all three stepped back. Jalor touched a stud on top of the container, the clearing shimmered again, and the container vanished.

Blaine slung the bow over his left shoulder with the large quiver of arrows. Blaine took a stringed instrument, Jalor another. A flute went into Varna's pack, as did a small mouth organ, while a set of pipes was put into Blaine's pack. The short rods were attached to their belts to hang down the sides of their legs. Then, with instruments in hand, Jalor and Blaine led the way from the dell. Varna followed, stopping to look back at the clearing for a moment. Finally, she shook her head and followed the others.

Drewflin repeated his earlier gesture and again silently mouthed some words. His senses returned to normal. But still he sat near the hill summit, deep in thought. Throughout the time he observed the strangers, his body had remained still, although his face, to anyone able to see it, had shown a range of emotions. He frowned when Jalor brought all three together, nodded appreciatively at Blaine's caution and smiled when contemplating Varna and then showed amusement when the three dressed as minstrels in costumes well over a hundred cycles out of fashion.

He was still sitting on the hill long after Jalor, Blaine and Varna had disappeared.

12. First Camp

Their drop zone had been selected because it was where the original team had been inserted. That location had been preselected, from what Serra had told them, by a headquarters team because of its remoteness, based on preliminary scans undertaken by a Union ship that had been passing through the region and found the previously unknown planet. This was the same team that had been found to have been compromised by Empire agents shortly before the *Sunburst* mission. That mission appeared to have run into problems immediately, given the drop site was also the location of the residue of a blitz mine.

Surveys had shown that there were towns or villages at varying distances away, but none closer than almost two days steady walk for a Warrior team. There was a small road not far from the drop zone, and they headed for it after changing.

Jalor decided the team would spend three days getting the feel of the planet and their near vicinity, making sure that any effects of the transport were gone and that they suffered no ill effects from water or any foraged foodstuff. The weather was mild, which was expected given the latitude. The fact that the planet's wobble was vanishingly small, combined with its orientation to the twin suns, indicated that this climate was likely to remain fairly constant. Some small clouds wisped across the sky, which was a deeper blue than any of them had experienced before. Blaine, especially, had seen many different skies and the others accepted his judgement without question. But the grass was green, the rocks were rock-coloured and the bird life was reminiscent of many human-occupied planets of the Union, with the usual differences of plumage, size and colour. In fact, the similarities between this planet and Earth-standard were marked. That part of the detailed briefing was proving to be correct.

Walking the road was easy. There was a slight grade as the direction chosen appeared to be taking them into a mountainous region. The Grand Admiral had picked out what appeared to be a city as their initial goal, without telling them why that city was selected. It was the closest major centre to their drop zone, admittedly, but the Warriors were aware that the Grand Admiral was holding back something. Hopefully, it was nothing that would damage the mission. So, while the walk was easy, their attention did not drop away.

The surrounding countryside was interesting to all three Warriors. Trees abounded on both sides of the road. But these were not the tall, straight and almost evenly spaced trees of Earth's ancient forests that had been restored to what the public was assured was a realistic representation of the past. On this planet - Ennaris, they had been told by the Grand Admiral - and in this location many of the trees were tall but somewhat gnarled with thick bark of dark brown, standing alongside lean, straight trees with silver-grey bark and others with a peeling red-brown covering. Leaves varied from sharp muddy-green needles to broad blades of vivid green to long and narrow leaves that were a grey-brown hue. The trees were clustered in copses closer to the road, as though they had not always been there, while further away they formed a solid wall. Between the copses near the road were low shrubs of differing type, often of a grey-green colour, which also stretched to the tree-line. Blaine muttered an aside to Jalor and Varna that they would struggle to see anyone attacking from either side of the road, and all three sharpened their attention further.

They walked for several klicks and had moved appreciably higher in altitude as night fell. The two suns set about an hour apart. The smaller sun seemed to give out most of the light and set first, leaving a strange light that was brighter than twilight but dull in comparison to full daylight. When it was a hands-breadth above the western horizon and rapidly dropping, Jalor gave Blaine a nod and the latter turned them off the road, moving up a slight slope into the tree line. A dip in the ground that was surrounded by a stand of the tall, slim trees provided adequate shelter from unwanted eyes in Blaine's opinion and a cold camp was set as the larger sun was setting.

At the camp site ship rations were brought out and eaten, and the three sat talking quietly, discussing the world they had been dropped into. A short time after full dark, Jalor and Varna bedded down and Blaine took watch. He spent the time variously sitting, slowly walking around the camp site or crouching in place, listening to the sounds of the woodland that surrounded them. There was nothing out of the ordinary, he felt, even though he had never been to this planet before. The small noises were exactly what his experience told him would be expected in such a place. The scratchings, rustlings, cries and calls matched those found in many similar woodlands on many planets occupied by Union populations, and some non-Union.

After what he judged to be three hours or so, Blaine woke Varna. The latter came awake at a touch, eyes open and alert immediately. She sat and listened while Blaine briefed her on what he had noticed - nothing of interest - and then rolled himself in his small bedroll. She thought he was asleep before she had even stood, which elicited a small smile as she stood still and took stock of the space, turning in place slowly. No matter than Blaine had told her of the sounds, she needed to orient herself.

Varna had less experience than Blaine but she knew woodlands. Her original family home had been adjacent to a wood and Varna had spent a lot of time there with her mother as a very young child. After her mother's death - Varna shied from that thought - Varna had moved with her father to a different place, on another planet, where woodlands were plentiful and where she had developed a deep love for the tree-scape. Comments had long been made about the familiarity of many forms of plant life on planets around the galaxy which the Union found to be human habitable, and so it seemed to be here. The theory of the originators, the so-called parents of human-kind, were built on these similarities, and those of many forms of animals, insects, reptiles and birds. Nay-sayers merely pointed out that origin theories for many planets still proposed seedings from comets or asteroids hitting them and it was to be expected that similar environments would produce broadly similar outcomes. No matter what the theories said, Varna looked around and found much that was familiar. In fact, she thought, it *felt* familiar.

The trees in the immediate vicinity were a mix of something like eucalypts and pines, although those bark textures did not match when she carefully placed her hand on them as she slowly patrolled. But the leaves and needles were similar enough, the slight menthol and resin smells were similar enough, and the woodland floor had the same soft texture from the dropped leaves and needles so that the similarities were marked. The sounds she heard were those she would expect. As Blaine had done, Varna spent time being as still as she could make herself, listening to those sounds, eyes open and actively scanning even while she listened. It was a peaceful setting. Had she been there for leisure, Varna would have liked nothing more than to close her eyes and let the small sounds wash over her. But she was not there for leisure and her innate professionalism did not allow herself to lose attentiveness.

The sounds continued. Once a rush of wings was accompanied by a soft but shrill squeal a short distance away. At other times Varna could hear, quite close by, the unmistakable sounds of small animals making their various ways through the undergrowth, which itself was low and scrubby here. It was thoroughly unremarkable, just as insertion teams liked it.

She handed over to Jalor and rolled into her own bedroll when she judged her time to be up, and dropped off to sleep accompanied by the comforting thought that she understood this place and, even while dismissing any thoughts of her psi abilities having validity, she felt that no danger existed in the immediate vicinity.

Breakfast was more rations, although afterwards Blaine decided to do a spot of scouting and foraging, returning with a selection of berries and small roots. Jalor decided their camp location was good enough that they could spend a second day there as they became more accustomed to the planet, so there was no rush. Varna watched as Blaine reached into his pack and extracted a small leather-like pouch, from which he tipped two vials. They looked like they were made from some type of pottery, although she was sure they had been produced on *Starfire* from materials far removed from clay. He selected one and removed a stopper, then picked one berry from a small bunch and crushed it on a flat rock he had also picked up, and carefully measured a single drop from the vial onto the crushed berry. Although Varna joined with Blaine to watch intently, nothing happened.

"What is that?" Varna asked, still watching the crushed berry doing nothing.

"It's a sort of universal test for food safety. While you can never be completely sure, it tells you if the food being tested may cause you any grief when eaten. I always carry some with me. Picked it up on Urtliff years ago. It's never failed."

Blaine regarded the crushed berry for a moment longer, face expressionless, then picked up a second berry and popped it into his mouth. Varna started.

"But the test didn't show any reaction!" she said.

"No," Blaine replied, chewing thoughtfully. "And that's the right outcome. It would have produced some sort of coloured vapour if there was a problem." He grinned and handed Varna a berry. "Slightly tart but not bad."

Varna continued to regard Blaine with scepticism as she placed the berry carefully on her tongue and bit into it. The juices started sweet but tailed off to leave a slightly tart after-taste, with a vaguely furry feel on her tongue, while the skin dissolved in her mouth. Not what she would want to eat as the main part of a diet, but definitely something that could contribute. She took note of the berry to recall shape and colour.

Blaine repeated his test with a second type of berry, again producing no reaction. He and Varna tried this one and both spat the highly astringent berry out again. It took a long drink of water - from the *Starfire* supplies - to remove the taste. The third berry resulted in wisps of pale vapour rising into the air, and Blaine carefully separated out each of that type from the small pile he had made, along with the astringent one. Again, Varna took note of the two, noting especially the one likely to be poisonous.

The roots followed and for each Blaine cut out a section and made small slices, being careful to clean the knife after each one to remove cross-contamination. One slice from each he left solid, and he pulped a second of each, after which he applied a drop of his test liquid to each slice and small mound of pulp. The first root, giving out a pleasant smell and with an attractive pale golden flesh, produced a thick and oily vapour, while the other two - one with a crimson skin and white flesh and the other with a pale brown skin and slightly darker flesh - produced no reaction. The first was discarded and Blaine set to work to test cook the other two over a small fire that they had decided to risk in a cleared space.

Varna left Blaine to his work and moved to where Jalor sat, dividing his time between watching Blaine and Varna with a slight smile playing across his face and examining the surrounding woods. The noises of the forest were muted, possibly because of the presence of the three Warriors. Or perhaps because many forest dwellers came out by night. In any event, it was quiet enough that they could converse in murmurs. After briefly comparing the tiny portion of the planet with what they knew of other worlds, Varna took the watch from Jalor. The latter moved quietly to where Blaine was testing his cooked portions. The two started a murmured discussion, probably about where Blaine had gathered the berries and roots, Varna thought as Blaine gestured to several points of the surrounding terrain. She turned her attention from them and outward to listen for anything out of the ordinary.

The camp site's copse of trees had a smell somewhat like eucalyptus and were tall and thin with smooth bark and narrow, blade-shaped dark green leaves. The lower branches started at a point higher than Varna could reach while standing, which gave a greater impression of height. Intermingled with them were a small number of the thicker pine-like trees, with trunks that were knobbly and covered with thick, dark, gnarled brown bark that showed even darker stains where sap gathered. The pine-like trees had needles rather than leaves and contributed to quite a lot of the carpet of leaves and needles forming the forest's floor, with branches starting quite low. Beneath the slender eucalypt-types was a scrubby undergrowth, and Varna took note of the varicoloured shrubs with a variety of small leaves. Some had small spikes or thorns that the three strangers took care to avoid. There was a greater variety of shrubs here than they had seen along the road's edge.

Further from the camp, looking into the trees, Varna could see other types of trees, and a wider range of shrubs again. She could also see a small number of stems that probably belonged to tubers of some sort. There were no flowering shrubs or plants, she was surprised to note, although then again plants here may have different forms of propagation. She could hear a low and buzzy drone that sounded like bees, and realised that she had made an unjustified assumption that this Earth-like place would have similar natural laws to those of the many places that humans had colonised. She berated herself for a moment before putting it out of her mind and returning her attention to her surroundings.

Carefully, she tuned in to the sights and sounds of each section of the surrounding woodland. Following a practice that she had devised for herself long ago when exploring the woodlands near her homes, she divided the area into eight sectors that each represented about forty-five degrees of a circle centred on the camp. She turned her attention to each sector while maintaining general awareness of the entire area. It was a feat that others seemed not to be able to do effectively but one that she found to be almost second nature. She did not dwell over-long on any one sector and was able to do the eight sectors quickly, halting only occasionally to sharpen her attention to specific items. She was sure she had heard water from the sixth sector, which was down a slight slope, and she had identified what she thought might be a suitable defensible spot in the fourth sector, a group of large rocks that were hidden inside another copse of trees.

Blaine had finished with his cooking experiments and brought samples to Varna, along with a ship ration bar.

"Lunch," he said quietly, placing a small bark platter on the log Varna was using as a seat. "Try the mash before the cooked segments. I think the mash worked better. That brownish one doesn't look like much but it's more like a sweeter yam, while the white flesh has virtually no taste that I can find."

Varna nodded and sampled each, using fingers to scrape the mash from the bark. She nodded agreement with Blaine's assessments as she tried each of the root samples.

"I think I could hear water down there," Varna said, gesturing, as she started on the ration bar. "We probably should check that out also. And behind those trees up there is a pile of rocks that we may be able to use if we need to hide."

Blaine turned to look at the copse of trees some distance away, up-slope. He had found the pile of large rocks in his scouting after breakfast, but had not had occasion to mention it to Varna yet. Nor could he see the rocks from where they sat. And nor, again, could he hear any water.

"I found those rocks this morning," he said quietly. "They could be usable if we need to make ourselves scarce. How did you know they were there?"

Varna shrugged, as she had at other times on other missions when she seemed to be able to discern such things where others could not. "I'm not sure," she replied. "Something about the configuration when compared to the rest of the area. Maybe I could see something through the undergrowth when I was doing a sort of eyes and ears scan. Or maybe it was just the likely spot for such a thing."

"Pretty good," Blaine acknowledged. "And the water?"

"Oh, I can hear that pretty clearly," Varna said with a smile. "It's faint and some distance away, I would guess. It sounds like a small stream or creek, maybe going over some rocks."

"Hmmm. I'll check that out," Blaine said, looking in the direction Varna had indicated. "We could use a top-up. Can you hold the watch for a short while longer? I'll relieve you when I get back."

"Sure," she responded with a nod, handing him the bark platter as he stood.

Blaine had a quick word with Jalor, picked up one of the water flasks that looked like pottery, and then moved into the surrounding trees. He moved so quietly that Varna heard not a sound from where she was sitting. She returned her attention to the surrounding woodland, noting the small sounds. The light had a slightly different character, possibly because of the twin suns, and twin shadows caused some places that she had already examined to have a different look where the light made it through the canopy of trees.

She had just finished examining the area anew, taking note of the changes wrought by shadows, when Blaine returned, appearing from the trees with as little noise as he entered them. He lifted the flask to Varna and nodded to indicate that the water was where she had said it would be, then turned to Jalor.

"It checks out okay to drink, although I want to do a more thorough test. There's a small creek down there, about half a klick. How Varna could hear that is astonishing. I couldn't hear it until I was a lot closer. But the banks are pretty low and easy to navigate. The trees thin a little before you get there and there're a few game trails."

Jalor nodded as Blaine started the process of testing the water in the flask. He moved over to where Varna sat and squatted alongside her.

"Blaine found some game trails, so we should be able to catch something for meat. Are you okay with that?"

"I've had to do that before. I doubt we'll find protein farms on this planet with the technology they have, so we'll need something other than berries and roots," she replied, nodding.

"Okay," Jalor said, standing and looking in the direction from which Blaine had returned. "Meanwhile, I'll take a scout around and see where this stream is and what we might be able to find. I'm tempted to stay here another day, but then we'll have to be moving."

The team remained in place through the afternoon. Jalor took the watch from Varna after a while. Blaine had appointed himself the chief food procurer and tester, and made several scouting expeditions, returning each time with a selection of roots, berries and plants. By the end of the day, he had determined that a small number of leaves were edible, along with several more roots and a small number of berries and fruits. It was enough that the team could supplement their remaining ration bars. No animals had been captured with the simple traps Blaine had devised, but that caused no concern to the team. It was more likely they would bag some game during the night, when most of the woodland's animal inhabitants probably were active.

The following day followed a similar pattern, with the team taking the time to examine their surroundings. Jalor had decided the location was too good to leave as they acclimated. Two small rodent-like animals had been caught and Blaine expertly killed and prepared them for cooking. The team did move their site to be closer to the rocky mound, taking the time to remove any traces of their presence. The small fire had been built in a tiny pit excavated by Blaine and it was filled and scattered with leaves and needles sourced from various spots at a distance from the camp. Blaine declared himself satisfied and they settled into a depression between the rocks.

As they prepared for the third night Varna was looking forward to a sleep and was grateful when Jalor opted to take the first night watch. She was feeling out of sorts, she had told Jalor, fuzzy almost rather than ill. During her previous sleep period she had been woken by strange almost-dreams, snatches of which she could recall but of which she could make no sense. A large tree stood in a clearing, glowing faintly. A pile of glowing rocks sat in a peaceful green sward. A dark cavern glowed with what she described as a malevolent red-orange light. An old man regarded her thoughtfully.

She realised those images, and others that she could not recall, had been running through her sleep and gradually becoming more insistent. The result was that she slept poorly and she knew that she would have to do something about that. She settled in her bedroll and initiated the breathing exercises of the Treffantic meditation that she found was most effective at draining away stress and tension, relaxing the psyche. Sleep came as she dropped into the meditative state, a deeper state than she had experienced since arriving on this planet. But, if anything, this opened her to the strange images even more.

Almost immediately, a rapid and bewildering procession of unfamiliar scenes and strange faces swept past her. Presences seemed to batter against the edges of mental shields that she could not recall raising, that she had raised instinctively. Those shields she had been taught by an old shaman who maintained the ancient practices of her forebears who traced themselves back to the African continent on Earth. From there originated tales of beings of power who lived among the people and taught certain selected ones in the ways of Treffantic philosophy. But the shields were inexpertly raised and Varna proved unable to hold back the rapidly increasing volume of images.

Now, though, the flood of images was accompanied by sounds that swelled into a roar that swirled and flowed. Varna felt herself being inundated, overwhelmed. She struggled to hold the tide back. She tried to rebuild the shields and failed. Like Anduric silverfish darting to nip and nibble at a carcass, Varna felt the sights and sounds flashing into her, flaying her, tearing pieces of her away. She tried to curl herself into a tight ball, the better to hold off the attack, but was unable to hold off the bombardment. She rocked and twisted in a last effort to stop herself coming apart, of being lost in the storm that was driving into her, through her.

She awoke suddenly to Jalor shaking her with concern etched on his face. For a moment she stared at Jalor, not quite understanding what - who - she was looking at as the experience, the dream, failed to recede. And then she was able to push the edges of the terror away, which allowed her to grip down hard on her inbuilt strength, the resilience that she thought she had lost but that had enabled her to overcome - largely if not completely, she thought - the events of the recent past. She took a deep breath and exhaled evenly, setting herself into a different relaxation routine that took a couple of seconds to initiate.

"I'm okay," she said with a quaver in her voice. *Damn*, she thought, *maybe not so okay.*

"You didn't look okay. You looked like you were fighting something, or being attacked by something," Jalor said, frowning. "And you were whimpering."

"It was a nightmare," Varna replied. "I think. It was pretty scary, not something I've experienced before."

"You think? You mean there may be something else?"

"It felt like some sort of force that attacked me. No," she thought for a moment, "not really a single attack but a wave that just rolled over the top of me. Like it wanted to get my attention but just got too big and wanted to get too close but was made up of lots of tiny little things that wanted parts of me. I can still remember it, clearly."

"Dreams fade fast, don't they?"

"So I've been told, and it's usually been my experience. Which may mean there is something." Varna shook her head. "It's silly, but the clamour for attention, the invasion of so many things trying to force their way inside me, it's like something one of my instructors tried to teach me when I was just a child. She taught me how to raise shields, and I tried to do that but failed. I wasn't strong enough."

"Or practised enough," Jalor said, sitting back on his haunches.

Blaine moved into sight, having done a brief circuit around the camp and its surrounds. He shook his head to indicate that he had found nothing of note.

"We're planning on moving on after tonight, but we can make a start now if you want," Jalor suggested. "It may be the site of the camp, or something in the vicinity."

"Or something in the water, or the air, or my imagination," Varna replied sourly. "No, let's stay to the plan. Perhaps it was a one-off and this is the end of it."

"Well, see if you can get some sleep, then. Blaine, change of rotation. You relieve me now and then wake Varna when it's time. In the morning, we'll be on our way."

Varna nodded wearily, appreciating the opportunity to sleep while not being too sure she wanted to. She settled herself again and closed her eyes, willing herself into a transitional routine preparatory to entering one of the meditative states that she knew could be used to enter sleep. For peace of mind, she also gave a part of her meditation to the Treffantic shields, something that she had not practised for a long time. The time seemed to be right for them to be practised again. She slowed her breathing and faded into a semi-trance, where she was aware and yet not, asleep and yet not. She allowed herself to drift on the edge of full sleep for a short while, testing the dream-scape for attackers and finding none. With a mental sigh she lowered herself back into sleep, or as much as she could allow.

And found the swarm had reduced to a bare few of the myriad things that tried to breach her fresh shields and failed. Varna kept her attention on them even as she sought the rest that she knew she needed until, at the far edge of her consciousness there was a flare of brightness and the things, the almost-presences, fled. The brightness did not move closer, and Varna did not feel at all threatened so, with her shields intact, finally she slept.

She was awakened by Blaine while it was dark. Their tiny fire had been allowed to sputter out during the night. The pitch dark was relieved only a touch by the light of one of the moons, peeping out from the side of a cloud bank. It was enough for her to see the outline of Blaine's shape as he briefed her for her watch, and asked if she felt able to take it. Having assured him that she was fine, Varna moved carefully to a spot where she could see the whole camp site, although as the moon slid behind the clouds again the deep black of almost total darkness enveloped her.

Given there was no watching to do, she decided to use her other senses. Hearing was the primary alternative when on watch, she had been told repeatedly in her training, along with smell, and it was to hearing that she turned now. Holding very still, she strained to extend her perception of sounds as far into the dark as she could. The sounds of the forest, with which she now felt more familiar, came and went, seeming to drift on the faint breeze. She heard the now familiar *skreet* of some small animal as it was taken by a larger predator - she assumed it would be larger. She heard snufflings closer to the camp as something, probably a sort of pig-like creature Blaine reporting glimpsing, used its own sense of smell to examine the ground. There was the whirring of night-birds as they passed by. Insects chirped and called. A small variety of noises and sounds rose and fell. There were none that caused any anxiety, but were heard and assessed by Varna. Of smell she could detect nothing other than the faint resiny smell of the tress in the immediate vicinity.

Opening her eyes briefly, Varna was able to make out vague shapes and outlines as the moon was out from behind the cloud, enough to see movement if there was any, she thought. But that lasted only moments as the clouds slid back in front of the pale light source and darkness returned. So, she closed her eyes again and concentrated on extending her senses. Hearing and smell, she thought again. She tried once more to push those senses to their greatest extent, slowing her breathing and making it shallow, looking to drop her heart rate to remove any possible distractions. For a few moments she thought that she could hear some-thing from a long distance, almost like she could feel it. It was a large animal of some sort pushing through the undergrowth, but quite a distance away.

The feeling only lasted a short time, and was replaced by a throbbing behind her eyes. Perhaps she had pushed too hard, she thought, and gave up trying to do anything other than monitor the camp site. In any event, it would start to brighten to dawn soon. She sat back against her selected tree and tried to use one of the techniques to reduce headache via light meditation. In the three days they had spent in this location they had seen nothing to concern them, and she expected nothing more now. Sure enough, the sky brightened in the east and once it became bright enough for her to see clearly, she woke Jalor, picked up two of the now empty water flasks, and made her way to the small stream that she had pointed Blaine towards on the first day.

She returned to find Jalor and Blaine both up and looking fresh, while she felt a little groggy, probably from trying to push her senses past what they could do. Having taken the opportunity at the stream for a general clean-up, she should have been feeling more alive. Instead, she moved more slowly than normal as she tidied the spot she had chosen for her bedroll and settled her pack. She accepted a small platter from Blaine and ate the fruit, berries, nuts and some sort of greens that they had found to be tasty and seemingly nutritious, but she had to force herself to eat the lot.

Still, with the first of the two suns still low in the east, and the second, larger one just poking its head up behind the first, the team was ready to move. Blaine took the point and Varna followed, with Jalor trailing slightly behind. One last look around the camp site and Blaine pronounced himself satisfied, and then led the way from the camp.

Far away, sitting comfortably in a tree that glowed ever so slightly, one who the people of Ennaris knew in their myths and legends as Fernis sensed the movement and knew the three were moving. The woman showed promise, but Fernis had felt the need to intervene. She had to learn her way, however, and such intervention could not be the norm. But for now, he would maintain his watch.

13. Eresh

The small city of Kushnel stood on the southern shore of the Bitter Sea, the great body of water that had drowned the land and now formed the divide between the northern and southern continents of Ennaris. Kushnel had started as a small fishing port but, as one of the few sheltered and safe anchorages, grew rapidly once coastal ships were constructed by a local warlord long ago, and again when the larger ships that could span the new inland sea came along with the rise of merchant princes. Now, it was the largest of the five southern cities. On the inland side of the city, within its own huge compound, stood the great Temple of Eresh.

The floor of the Temple teemed with people, all of them trying to get close to the offertory bins so they could place in them their offering of food and goods. All sought to invoke the help of Eresh, the god-like Guardian who met the dying and transported them to the wonders of paradise to celebrate a life replete with good works and gifts made to her name. Each of those making offerings were welcomed by a priest, usually one of the junior priests, who accepted the offering, provided a blessing and placed what was offered in one of the bins provided for the purpose. There were bins for various foods, jewels, coins and other assorted offerings.

Watching over the happenings on the temple floor, seated on a pedestal raised well above and looking down on the milling throng, was High Priest Azgarb. He enjoyed watching his bounty grow. His corpulent body was wedged into his stone throne. There was a pitcher of the finest wine and a bowl of sweet treats on a small table alongside his throne, and crumbs spilled down the front of his robes, which were made of the finest materials available. He watched the proceedings avidly, noting the foods provided that would furnish him and his confreres with their evening feast, the wines that he would enjoy. A frown creased his brow at what was obviously an ordinary wine delivered in offering - that could go to the junior priests who still believed the rubbish about serving the people. He snorted, causing some of the crumbs to shift and flow as his bulk moved and shook. Once he was one of those but he quickly learned better, taught by the high priests and senior clerics who preceded him.

The Temple of Eresh had been dedicated to continuing works thought to have been close to the heart of the Guardian Eresh, she who was the friend to the sick and dying, to the poor and the hopeless. Temple legend had it that, even before the rebellion's disastrous end, Ennaris had not been as idyllic for all of its citizens as the stories told, and Eresh had sought to assist those who were less fortunate. Azgarb snorted again. His experience of people was that they were poor because they did not work hard enough. Those who were sick were merely a drain on society and the sooner they were gone the better, so he had quite some time ago decided to give them little sympathy. No, his sympathies lay with the rich and powerful of the land, especially here in the rich coastal province of Belgrith. The Temple provided them support and, in turn, they protected the Temple from those who would accuse it of being too worldly, of not holding to the will of Eresh. Azgarb chuckled at the thought of all of those who truly believed in Eresh and the Guardians, those mythical beings of Ennaris' deepest legends. Oh, they probably were based on real people back in the mists of time but they were long gone now. Still, the believers provided the means for Azgarb and his sort to live comfortably, so they could have their beliefs.

His gaze sharpened and Azgarb's petulant mouth pursed in irritation. He was watching Resta, a young priest newly raised, who was walking through the crowd assisting those rich and poor who wished to make an offering. Resta was an example of an overly pious, self-serving type, constantly asking why the Temple was not doing more for the people, taking as little of the food offerings as he could and wanting to donate leftovers to the poor. *How did I allow this one to be raised to the priesthood*, Azgarb asked himself, *and what do I do with him?*

He saw Resta talking with a woman dressed in little more than rags, carrying a tiny bag that contained a few precious food items. A child in a small barrow accompanied her. The child was obviously ill and wasting, probably from lack of food as much as illness. Azgarb felt no pity for the woman nor the child - they were not worth his attention as the High Priest of Eresh. But Azgarb's disdain turned to rage when he saw Resta return the food packet to the woman. He laid his hand on the child and clearly raised a prayer to Eresh for intervention. Azgarb gestured to his security head.

On the temple floor, Resta spoke gently to the woman, soothing some of her fears for her child, who had been born and raised in an environment that could only turn out poorly nourished and sickly children. There was no help from civil authorities and the temple that should be helping them was under the control of a venal and cruel high priest. All Resta had were words, words for the woman - her name being Anya - and words for Eresh to help however she could.

Now Resta watched as the temple guards closed in, trying to remove the food parcel from Anya's hands. They were shocked when the young priest, who was usually gentle and kind to all, knocked the guard aside before he could reach the parcel and then stood between Anya and her child and the guards.

"Hold!" Resta cried aloud, enraged. "You are in the Temple of Eresh and will not handle her people so. Stand back and stand fast. Your behaviour is the opposite to that required to live by the word of our Lady, Eresh."

"Ha!" the senior guardsman laughed at the young priest. "Who do you think you are," he sneered, "to be telling the temple guards what to do? We take no orders from you or your type. Now, *you* stand back or face the consequences of your actions."

The young priest, faced with four guards, held his ground gamely. Laughing evilly, one of the guards drew his sword, looking forward to having some fun, only to have his laugh die as he found himself surrounded by the mob of poor people, many of whom had also experienced the rough edge of the temple guards' ridicule. He felt a blade point sticking into his side and started to sweat. The other guards looked around at the mob. They then looked over the mob members' heads to where the wealthy had started to leave the temple, leaving the guards, the bullies, to their fates. Suddenly uncertain, the senior guard looked to where Azgarb was struggling to the temple floor from his raised throne, alarmed at the turn that had so suddenly been taken.

Waddling along, sweating profusely from the unaccustomed exercise, and with his huge girth requiring the help of multiple temple guards to make it down the steps to the temple floor, Azgarb was muttering angrily and frowning. This usually had the effect of causing people to pay some form of obeisance, for an angry high priest in the temple can bode no good. Now, however, such obeisance was lacking. Azgarb, while picking up on the anger of the poor and peasantry at the actions of the guards, ignored it entirely, sure in his safety in his own realm.

Azgarb reached the knot of people. Resta bowed to him but did not retreat.

"My lord high priest," Resta said, "thank you for doing us the honour of making your way from on high. I am sure you will agree that there is no need for any sort of commotion." Resta smiled, gesturing to the widening crowd of poor. "There is sufficient food raised for some time to come now, so we do not need to take from the very poor when all they need is prayers for their children."

Azgarb sputtered, outraged. "You have no right to make such a decision," he shouted. "Gifts of food and goods are necessary for the priesthood to function and you do not turn it away."

Resta deliberately took a long look at Azgarb's enormous figure, easily making up more than two normal men in girth. The high priest resembled a very fat ball with eyes and flailing hands more than a man. The onlookers picked up on his hint and laughed aloud.

"I am sure the priesthood is fed adequately," he said dryly, as Azgarb's face turned beet red. "And it is our bounden duty to assist these people, not profit from them, as in the days of the rebellion when Eresh and her Guides helped the people to survive." His voice was mild but carried clearly through the temple, which had suddenly gone quiet.

Azgarb's raspy breathing was clear. His outrage grew still, fed by fear at what he was hearing and the realisation that he had been left alone by those he considered to be his friends, for apart from the guards the only supplicants left were the poor, and there were many of them in Kushnel.

"Priests are not here to cater for every little thing wanted by every poor person who comes along," he spluttered. "We are here to revere Eresh and her works in the past, to remember them and prepare for her return, as the scriptures state will be the case."

Resta made a show of turning to read the inscription high on the wall behind the altar, stating that the temple was for all, poor and rich alike, healthy and sick, and that it would offer help to all without favour or discrimination. He turned back with one eye raised in question. Azgarb now wanted this to end - how had it come to this? - and signalled to the senior guard who drew his sword and clubbed the young priest to the ground with the sword hilt.

The four guards were grabbed and held tightly, their swords wrested from the two who had drawn them. Behind the crowd the rest of the temple guards rushed forward, drawing their own swords, preparing to cut down the crowd. Several of them grinned at the opportunity so offered.

Suddenly, behind the altar a bright light flared out, brilliant in its intensity. All activity immediately ceased on the temple floor as the glare receded to show the statue of Eresh against the rear wall, glowing from within. There were gasps of awe, and not a few of fear, as the face of the statue turned to look at the crowd. The right arm rose and all swords and knives from the guards, as well as several of the crowd, were torn from their owners' grasps or lifted from belts, then rose in the air to hover over the assembly before being gently placed in a pile behind the altar.

The statue spoke. "Azgarb, who are you to speak for Eresh? Who are you to stop my followers from doing their works of good? By whose authority do you condemn my people to poverty and ill health when you should be helping them. *You* are not my high priest."

Azgarb stood with his mouth wide open, staring at the impossibility before him. There must be some trick, some sort of foolery. Behind him the people were on their knees, while the guards were held immobile, unable to move.

"Begone Azgarb! Leave this place and never return. Take your bullies with you. You are outlaw from this time on." The statue pointed to the door of the temple. "Begone!" she roared, and Azgarb and the guards scrambled to the exit, tumbling down the steps to the road surface.

The guards ran from the temple, watched with interest by many. Azgarb tried to run but was unable to do so, stumbling in their wake. Aware that something strange was happening but not sure what, more and more people crowded into the temple. All of them came to a halt, awestruck, as they saw the blazing statue.

Eresh stepped from the stone of the statue, which returned to its original dull state, although many watching thought its visage and countenance were softer, more kindly.

"Resta," she said as she glided towards the priest, who was standing once more with Anya and her child. A trickle of blood ran from a cut over his eye. "Heal my child, Resta."

Unsure, because this was not what he had been taught could be, Resta stared at Eresh, who now was a woman floating before him with kindly eyes and a soft smile.

"Trust me in this, Resta," she said. "It is part of your destiny, to be the first of my new Guides."

Startled, Resta stood for a moment then nodded slowly. It felt right, somehow. He had always been able to help the injured, people and animals, to heal faster, or to recover from illness more easily. How, he could never understand. It had been an easy decision to join the temple, to seek to help even more of the sick and poor. Now, without really understanding what moved him, he stepped to the side of the barrow where Anya's child, a young girl of around four cycles named Benya, huddled with her eyes wide and staring. He held out his hand once again and placed it on Benya's head, not really understanding.

Relax, Resta, he heard in his thoughts. *You will understand in due course. For this, you are my instrument.*

Around his hand a glow formed, growing to envelop his hand and moving down Benya's body. Limbs, which had been crooked, straightened, and her stomach, which was swollen from lack of suitable food, smoothed. Her skin lost the dullness of illness and even her hair looked healthier. After a dozen heartbeats the glow faded, leaving Benya standing in her barrow with eyes even wider and staring in adoration at the young man. Anya gasped with joy as much as shock at the transformation, and the crowd was silent, awe-struck at witnessing this miracle.

"Know this," Eresh said clearly. "Resta is my Guide. There are no more priests, no more high priests. This building is a temple no longer but a place for healing and contemplation. Know also that the time of Prophecy and story has arrived, and the Children of Ennaris walk this land, here to help save all from the old evil arising. The Guardians return. *I* have returned. Spread the word to all that the people of Eresh will stand against this evil."

14. Varna

The Warriors moved steadily, although not quickly, making their way through the woodland in the same direction as before. While the city was quite a distance to the north-east, the scans from *Starfire* had shown a village to the south-west of their landing site. The road had moved somewhat east of north after leaving the vicinity of the circular dead patch where the original team had perished. Now, Jalor decided to look in on that village. His memory of the scans was that their original road would take them away from that village. So, leaving the road, they travelled through a small valley that Jalor thought would lead them to what the scans indicated was a road of sorts.

Once again, the terrain and vegetation took on almost familiar traits, especially now that they had spent some time here. Blaine was like a ghost, making no sound at all that Varna could hear, and she knew she had good hearing, even without trying to enhance it. Varna felt like she was blundering through the scrubby undergrowth in comparison, although she knew she left almost no trace, and that Jalor was the same. But the throbbing had returned, along with a dull ache behind her eyes that caused her to squint a little. It was full daylight now and there were occasional glaring reflections from something on the other side of the valley. After two of them had speared into her eyes, Varna called a halt and quietly pointed them out to the others.

Blaine, who had not noticed the flashes, frowned thoughtfully as he tried to locate what may have been reflecting the light. He raised one eyebrow to Jalor in question and, when the latter nodded, swung his pack from his shoulder, and moved off. Jalor touched Varna on her shoulder and gestured to her to stay put. Nodding, she twisted to look around and found a suitable place to wait, with shade from a small copse of trees and a few rocks that could be used to duck behind if needed. Gratefully, she made her careful way to the rocks and sat. Jalor maintained a watch a short distance away.

With a start, Varna awoke. Guiltily, she realised she had drifted into sleep while waiting for Blaine to return. The throbbing behind her eyes seemed worse, if anything, but she tried to push it behind her, which was largely unsuccessful. Shading her eyes, even though she was in shade still, she tried to work out what had woken her. Jalor remained watching the spot where Blaine had disappeared, as well as the general area, but that was not it. Thinking back, she realised it was as though something had tapped her, although there was nothing and no-one near apart from trees, rocks, a few birds in the trees and what looked like a tiny lizard-like creature standing perfectly still on a rock and staring at her. It was joined by a second lizard-thing, and then a third. Unknown to Varna, above her in the tree small branches swayed and bowed slightly as the number of perched birds swelled. Some were calling but most were eerily quiet. In the undergrowth, tiny rodents peeked their pointed noses out and stared, while larger creatures made their careful way towards the small group of rocks in which Varna sat.

When Blaine returned Jalor stood out from the tree against which he had waited, and then stepped back into the shadow again. It was enough and Blaine joined him after making a roundabout way through the undergrowth.

"I found what was reflecting," he said as he squatted against the same tree. "They're some sort of rock or stone blocks, perfectly smooth cut. It has a sort of glassy feel to it, and the sunlight really does reflect off it. If I had to guess I would say they were manufactured. And they're big, mostly buried from what I could see but still taller than me."

"Manufactured? Are you sure?"

"No, but it's what it felt like," Blaine replied. "You had to see it to understand. When I say perfectly smooth, I mean perfectly. Like glass.

Sharp edges and no wear, and yet they look to have been tossed to where I found them. They were not in anything like a wall, just individual blocks scattered around. A couple did have scorch marks on the back surfaces though. There were others where the smooth face was away from us."

"What do you think?"

"Not sure," Blaine said. "Think of an old stone block wall hit by a rocket blast or some other sort of projectile explosion. The rocks get blown apart. I'm thinking that's what this looked like."

"Recent?"

"Not likely. The reason we could see these I think is that some sort of fire went through here not too long ago and burnt away the surrounding vegetation. But they look to have been where they are for a very long time."

"Could the fire have given them the scorch marks?"

"I don't think so. It looks old, like it has penetrated deep into the blocks. Whatever caused it was strong, real strong. And long ago."

"Okay, so nothing for us to worry about but another fact to consider. The scans *Starfire* ran showed fairly reasonable building techniques in stone, about what you would expect from a pre-industrial civilisation, but nothing that could make perfectly smooth surfaces."

"Or manufactured blocks of that size," Blaine agreed.

"So, part of what the Admiral warned us was likely to be a puzzle." Jalor considered briefly. "But it's nothing for us to worry about," he repeated, "so we'll keep moving. We can get a bit further and have a break. I want to make the road before nightfall."

The two men turned to Varna and stared. She was seated with her back against a rock, eyes open but with a glassy look, obviously not seeing. Ranged around her were an array of forest creatures, all quietly watching her. Birds of various sorts, sizes and colours sat in the tree above her. Dozens of small rodents and larger furred creatures fanned out beside and before her. The small lizard-like creatures had been joined by larger ones on the rocks. In the undergrowth, Blaine thought he could see shadows of larger creatures.

"What the...?" Jalor said and, before Blaine could stop him, took a step forward, stepping on a branch that snapped loudly.

In a moment, the space around Varna was empty as the creatures scurried into the undergrowth and the birds took flight. The lizards dashed off the rock. Behind Varna something large crashed through the undergrowth as it moved away. Varna blinked, her eyes regaining life. She shook her head, as though to clear it.

"What happened?" she asked in a shaky voice.

"Just what I was going to ask you," Jalor said, his tone grim.

"What were you experiencing just then?" Blaine asked in a mild tone. "You appeared to be in some sort of trance."

"I think I may have been," Varna nodded, shaking her head again. "It was like the last time, with a whole lot of things trying to get to me. But this time they seemed to be trying to make contact, and there were not as many of them."

Blaine nodded while Jalor just stood and looked at Varna thoughtfully, then turned and looked around the terrain, at this strange land that was so familiar to them all and yet seemed to be having some sort of an impact on his team member.

"Do you feel like moving?" Jalor asked. "I'd like to try to make that road before nightfall today, and I think we have a way to go yet."

Varna nodded and rose, stretching as she did as though after a long sleep. The three moved away, Jalor in the lead and Blaine telling Varna what he had found of the reflective blocks, the speculations he and Jalor had made and then of finding her surrounded by the animals and birds. Varna said nothing as she thought back to what she had been feeling, as though there were many somethings trying to make contact with her. Her headache had returned, though, and she put her attention on her surroundings and their trek through the rocky valley, eyeing the tree line just above them and the valley floor below them.

After a hurried stop for a light meal of fruit and some of the greens, the team set off again, but this time Blaine ranged further ahead. They should be getting close to the road, Jalor thought. He watched Varna carefully, for the latter was starting to move as though tired and worn, even though this trek should have been little more than a stroll for the three Warriors. Jalor was considering options, not just in terms of trying to locate potential enemies such as the Empire agents, but also the possibility that the planet was by no means benign, no matter how Earth-like it seemed.

The road was little more than a wide track, ragged on the edges and with the centre hard-packed but rutted as though by many hard wheels. Blaine stopped the others and gestured to them to wait behind some screening trees while he made his careful way to the road and examined it. He waited, listening, before waving them forward. Once on the road Jalor pointed to the right and the team moved off immediately. The light remained strong although the day was coming to an end, and he wanted to be part way along before stopping for the night. By his reckoning, the village should be no more than a day or two away.

Blaine rummaged in his pack as he walked, attention never wavering from his surroundings. Without breaking his watchfulness or his stride he pulled out what looked like a short stave inside a made-to-measure scabbard, and attached it to his belt on one hip - one of the rods Drewflin had noted. A large wicked-looking knife went on his other hip in its own sheath. He slung his pack back to his shoulder and glanced to Jalor, one eyebrow raised in question. The latter shook his head with a wry smile and reached into his own pack for a similarly scabbarded stave, which he duly attached to his belt. Varna shook herself into greater awareness, pushing the weariness and headache aside to follow suit.

It was only a short distance along the road when those precautions proved to be necessary. Rounding a bend, they found three men engaged in stripping a fourth person who was lying prone at their feet. One of the three glanced back and called to his fellows on seeing the Warrior team come into sight. Immediately, the other two left what they were doing and, with wolfish grins, the three spread across the width of the road and started towards the team.

Ordinarily, Jalor would try to avoid conflict, especially this early in a mission. But these were obviously a band of criminals and, given the way they approached, were not likely to allow them to walk away. Each had drawn a short-bladed sword in their right hands, and one carried a knife in his left hand. Jalor glanced to Blaine who merely nodded in response. A glance told them that they faced inexpert opponents. Blaine positioned himself to confront the bandit holding both sword and knife. All three Warriors unlimbered the short staves and separated to provide fighting room. On Jalor's muttered command they stopped walking and waited.

Two of the bandits were grinning broadly as they approached, but the third bandit's matching grin slipped as he realised the three victims appeared to be anything but afraid. Still, he thought as he continued his approach, short sword swinging lightly in his hand, none of them had real weapons now and if all they had was those little sticks then there was little to worry about. He and his fellows had moved into this territory only recently and were experienced in dealing with travellers, most of whom had little defensive training, no matter how uncon- cerned these ones tried to appear. Although, he thought uncertainly, these three didn't seem to be making any sort of effort to appear to be unconcerned. They actually *were* unconcerned!

The trio were almost in range and he was about to voice his fears when the little sticks became something else. Each of the supposed victims did something and those sticks grew into some sort of long staff. The two men stood with their staffs held upright and still. The woman - and he was now aware that she was a real beauty - moved her staff gently back and forth. The bandits hesitated slightly as the victims now appeared to be less helpless than they had seemed to be but moments earlier.

Blaine took the battle to them. With a single step forward and slightly to the side he opened the angle and forced his opponent to turn to face him, putting him slightly out of position and changing his balance. The bandit snarled and swung the sword in an arc from top left to bottom right, which usually exposed his victims to the thrust of his knife as they tried to counter. This time, though, the sword encountered the staff and, rather than cutting or breaking the wood, the sword rebounded and the knife stroke ended before it started. Blaine swung his battle staff - a weapon usually carried by Warriors in the field - in a short, sudden counter that struck the knife hand. The pain of the strike on his exposed hand caused the bandit to release the knife, which dropped to the road. And Blaine did not stop. The staff's swing was reversed and the angle changed. Before the attacker was aware of the change of direction Blaine's staff clattered into the rib-cage that the sword swing exposed and then a further reversal resulted in a hard strike to the head just above the left temple. The bandit dropped.

Jalor dealt with his attacker with little more fuss. A wild swing, that was no more effective than his fellow's had been against Blaine, opened the bandit to a counter and Jalor responded with a sharp horizontal strike to the neck, breaking it with a sharp *crack*!

Varna, despite still suffering the effects of whatever was assailing her on this planet, went into a series of moves that she had used to great effect before. As the third assailant, he who had been less sure, approached she started to twirl her battle staff. Faster and faster it turned until it was a blur, a disc that formed an effective barrier. Once, twice and then a third time her attacker sought to stab through the spinning disc, only to have his sword brushed aside. To both right and left his fellows had been dealt with far too easily and he realised that they had taken on the wrong opponents. Still, he also knew that he was unlikely to be treated leniently given the usual fate of bandits in most parts of the region so he renewed his attack, looking to charge through the spinning barrier and bull the woman into submission. That failed. The staff stopped spinning suddenly and, before he knew it, he had been struck with the blunt end in his chest with all the apparent force of a hrss's kick. Pain blossomed from the point of the strike and he could do little other than stop. The staff spun again, this time in an arc that struck with devastating force to the exposed head. The bandit's life of crime ended.

The three Warriors stood and surveyed the wreckage. Three bandits down and dead, the latter quickly confirmed by Blaine, and a fourth person also dead, also confirmed by Blaine.

"Well," Blaine said as he joined the others after checking on the bandits' original victim, "first contact went well!"

Jalor nodded and shrugged. "Looks like this planet is not all that peaceful, after all. Let's get this cleaned up and we can let someone know about it when we hit the village. Varna, are you okay?"

The latter was directed to a pale-faced Varna who was swaying slightly, using her still-extended battle staff to hold herself upright. She nodded but Jalor was far from convinced.

"Well, you sit yourself down somewhere and we'll take care of this," the team leader said.

Within a short time, the three bandits and their victim had been transferred from the road to a small gully Blaine had located a short distance off the road. Blaine also gathered the weapons of the three bandits and their victim, along with what he assumed was small quantities of the local currency from the bandits and a much larger quantity from their victim. Thoughtfully, Jalor examined the piles of weapons and currency.

"We'll share out the bandits' weapons, which don't seem to be too poor, quality-wise, and their money. It's likely the weapons were taken off previous victims so don't be surprised if someone recognises a sword or knife. It's unlikely any money will be recognised."

"We can return any weapon whose owner claims it," Blaine nodded. "But I like the idea of being armed with something more local."

"And we take the victim's stuff with us also, along with what looks like some documents. I doubt they would last too long here. It looks like a lot of money, based on volume and weight if nothing else." Jalor poked his finger through the pile. "Gold, silver and copper or bronze. If this follows the usual law of averages the gold will be the most valuable, then silver and the bronze will be the smallest amounts. This guy carried mostly gold and silver."

"You know," Blaine said, "the fact that he was carrying all of this and didn't have any significant protection tells us that this actually is a peaceful area. If it wasn't, then I would expect him to have guards or be part of a caravan."

"Likely," Jalor conceded, then gathered the coins into the leather purse the victim had carried and tucked it into his own pack. "This adds a bit of weight," he muttered.

Blaine and Jalor now each wore short swords and Jalor sported the bandit leader's knife on his left hip. Blaine had found a smaller knife on one of the bandits which he placed in Varna's pack. She was unwell to Blaine's eye, so he was reluctant to add more to the weight she had to carry, but he also knew she would not want to be coddled over much. Still, it was Blaine who bundled the victim's higher quality weapons and strapped them to his own pack. They were much better armed than they had been, but also more encumbered.

With a quick glance around the site of the short but deadly fight to make sure nothing was left behind, the trio started to walk again. Blaine once again took the lead position, while Jalor took up the rear. Varna, obviously suffering some kind of ill effect, wavered between them, striving to walk in a straight line but failing. Jalor maintained as much of a watch on her as he did on the surrounding landscape, which was changing slightly. The scrubby and rocky woodland with its blend of tall pine and eucalyptus-like trees was becoming more a forest with large, thick trunks that were reminiscent of Earth's fir trees and the scrubby undergrowth was becoming thinner.

As the day wore on, the road dipped lower and lower. The fir-like trees now dominated and the three walked through a sort of corridor with tall straight trees to each side. Undergrowth was far less visible than it had been at their previous camp-site. Birds of many varieties and colours flitted from tree to tree and branch to branch, seemingly keeping pace with them, chattering and squawking as they did so.

Blaine stopped at a point where the road dipped and turned, waiting for the others to catch up. As they did, he pointed to where a number of thin smoke trails rose into the now early evening sky. No buildings were to be seen but it was obvious that a small town or village, or a large establishment of some sort, was amongst the trees.

"I would guess that's the village," Blaine said. "Probably can't see it because of the trees. Maybe a little too far away for today, though. And we'll want to get there in daylight rather than full dark."
Jalor nodded, as he watched the smoke trails.

"Let's find somewhere to bed down," he said. "Off the road, if we can find somewhere in this forest."

Blaine just shrugged off his pack and deposited it at Jalor's feet. With a glance to left and right, he headed into the forest to the left, which was slightly higher in elevation. Varna sighed, moved to the same side of the road and sat, using her pack as a backrest. She closed her eyes, trusting to Jalor to maintain watch, and fought to regain composure, to resist whatever was affecting her. Her eyes were heavy and she felt like she was pushing through a thick mental fog. After having been able to push away the earlier effects during the fight, she suffered them even more now. The heavy, sluggish feeling had closed in on her increasingly as she walked. By the time Blaine returned with news that he had located a suitable spot slightly behind them and in the forest, she was almost oblivious and only roused with a great effort to move to the spot Blaine had selected for a night camp.

They had only moved a relatively short distance before Varna gasped and stopped, both hands holding her head in pain. Jalor hurried back to her - she was third in line of march - while Blaine took one look at her and went on guard, in case of what he had no idea.

"Varna, what is it?" Jalor asked quietly, also watching the forest through which they had been moving.

"Oh, it hurts!" Varna exclaimed, accompanied by a slight moan. "It's been growing all day. It feels like something is trying to climb inside my brain, but like a battering ram. It's like I had a couple of days ago, a constant battering but it's also like being surrounded by a thick fog."

"Some sort of psychic attack?"

Jalor was concerned, and more convinced than ever that his team member was being targeted by something. He needed his team intact and functioning for this job. And he had a feeling that Varna would be a key. Several hints had been provided by the Grand Admiral during their briefing, and it was obvious that Mavin Serra knew more about this planet than anyone had thought.

"Don't know." She was trying to breath slowly, calmly, and Jalor recognised the attempt to establish a meditative state.

He considered options and decided that, if she was suffering to the point where meditation was needed, then it was time to stop. Jalor made a hand signal to Blaine and the latter moved out up the slight slope to lead them to the camp spot. Meanwhile Jalor took Varna by one hand and guided her after Blaine. The three came to a small sheltered hollow soon after. Jalor sat Varna against a smaller tree. Varna's eyes were closed and she was sweating slightly as she fought whatever was attacking her. Blaine started to set up the camp.

Jalor stood over Varna, feeling helpless. Not a great start, he thought. In his mind he played back the briefing from Serra as he watched Varna struggle against whatever was attacking her, wondering if he had missed any hints.

15. Briefing

The briefing with Grand Admiral Serra had taken place on the day after the introductions.

"This is a planet unlike any you have seen before," Serra had said to the team, with Admiral Bard being the only other person present, and he seemed surprised at the tone of the Grand Admiral's voice, which was tense and hard. "The first team was given little preparation time, as I am afraid you have been. I had reason to believe there was no time then, and after more than fifty standard years the position cannot have become easier. That team was responding to reports that this planet had been infested by the Empire, with Empire ships having been identified at long range during a brief period when the planet was accessible. It seems to be so again, based on scans taken very recently by a scout ship from this fleet." To their surprised looks she nodded and continued, "Yes, there is a planetary shield of some nature that hid this planet and it seems now to be intermittent."

Bard noted mildly, "This is the first I heard of this, Admiral."

"There's more, I'm afraid." She paused, looking down before lifting her head, almost defiantly, and holding eye contact with the team, one by one. "Ennaris, which is what the inhabitants call this planet, is very old, and had an advanced civilisation before Earth's humans had come down from the trees. That civilisation was destroyed thousands of years ago and the remnants are now very slowly moving through an intermediate civilisation level, literally dragging themselves up again. My concern is that the Empire may make this a colony planet, and that

I cannot allow. I will not allow it! This planet is too important to the galaxy to allow that to happen. You need to trust me on that, because you will not find anyone else who knows of it.

"Your mission, therefore, is two-fold. You are tasked with locating any indications of the fate of the first team, especially Clay, and then determining if the Empire is occupying the planet or any part of it. If they are, then try to get us word however you can, and do whatever you need to do to disrupt their plans. Use your initiative. Your usual weapons probably will not work once the shield comes back down, so consider more medieval weaponry. You will be dropped in the same coordinates as the original team. Questions?"

Jalor glanced at Blaine and Varna, then nodded. "Do we have anyone on the planet who can assist? You suggested we may be able to locate someone during our first briefing."

Serra hesitated. "There may be a small number and they may make themselves known to you, but you cannot count on that. They may all be gone - my contact could not say for sure."

Varna was toying with a small ornament as she said, "What about the people, language, culture? Do we have any ideas?"

"You will have the same language program as the first team had. There may have been some language drift but it should be minor if anything. There is a common language with some small regional dif-ferences, so you should experience few problems there. The cultures of the planet have diversified and you will encounter a variety depending on how far you need to move around. I'm afraid you need to work through the regional differences as you find them." She noticed Varna's ornament and frowned. "Varna, may I see that, please?"

Varna shrugged and handed it over. Serra held it in one hand as she examined it, shocked.

"Where did you get this?" she asked, slightly breathless.

Varna thought back. "Someone gave it to me when I was very young. Actually, he left it with my father. I was only an infant at the time. Dad gave it to me when I turned ten, which is when he was told it should be done. I've had it ever since. Dad was told that I should keep it with me and I've done that. I like to hold it when I'm bothered by things. Just doing that seems to help for some reason. I have no idea what it is. I was told to keep it ..."

"Close against your skin." Serra finished, her gaze still on the ornament, shaped as a small bird in flight. "It is an Aldenthrush," she said. "It is an ancient design, handed out very rarely and only to specific people on special occasions."

"Well, I don't think there was a special occasion for me. Just someone visiting my father when I was young."

"Do you have any memories of this person?" Serra asked.

"Not really. Impressions that I'm not sure are real or not - tall man, soft voice - nothing more than that. I was playing and paid no attention. I thought he was a nice man and had an odd fancy that he sort of glowed in the light." She paused. "Come to think of it, it was at night." A shrug. "Oh well, childhood memories can't be trusted really."

"Perhaps they can," Serra said as she handed the ornament back to Varna. "Keep this close, child, for I believe you will be vital to this mission. It seems there are things occurring that I don't know about also."

Jalor returned to the present as Blaine quietly made preparations. He glanced about and nodded, approving of the location. Blaine quickly put a fire together, using some dried moss and grass, and a flint he took from his pack, to spark a small flame which he nursed into a fire.

"No-one around, it seems," he said to Jalor. "The forest is quiet but we're still not overly familiar with the animal and bird life here so I'm not too sure if this is normal or not. How's Varna?"

"Meditating," Jalor replied. "She told me up on the ship that she practices about five different forms depending on what she's trying to do. One of them helps her to overcome pain and keep going. I'm guessing that's what she's doing now." He looked around their camp site. "There's not much we can do right now. I just hope she can work through this or we'll be in a bit of trouble. Serra thought she would be a key for some reason."

Blaine nodded. "Yes, there's more to this than we've been told." He grinned wryly. "Of course, there's always more than the ground team is told. I think tonight and tomorrow morning we use the last field rations we brought and then tomorrow I'll go hunting unless we head to the village. Do you plan to stay here a while?"

"Tomorrow we go to the village if we can. After that it depends," Jalor replied. "If Varna recovers enough, we move on. Otherwise, we may stay for a further day or so. I'll get the rations on if you take another sweep around?"

Blaine nodded, rose and moved into the bush soundlessly. Jalor shook his head. He would never be able to do that, he thought to himself as he reached for his pack. Then he busied himself with the rations, secure in the knowledge that Blaine would find any dangers.

The night passed uneventfully with Blaine and Jalor splitting watches, something they had done on many occasions. In the morning Blaine prepared a simple meal of wild berries, nuts, some greens he recognised from their previous camp and the last of their ship rations.

Jalor changed his mind about heading to the village. So, for the next two days the small team remained in the same vicinity. Blaine located what he thought was a better spot for the camp, and so they moved to the new location during the second morning. Varna was half-guided and half-carried. This site was a small open patch among a jumble of large rocks atop a small hill that was leaning against a cliff face. There was good cover and protection afforded by the rocks, but also visibility in three directions via the small hill. The fourth direction was blocked off by the sheer cliff rising about forty metres above them, which Blaine reasoned would at least cause problems for someone coming at them. A small stream meandered from a tiny opening in the cliff and through the clearing to provide water, running down the hill and into the woods.

The weather remained fine and balmy for the two days. Some small game animals were caught and formed the basis for hot meals. The lack of any more ship rations caused no concern for Jalor - they would have had to dispose of unused rations before encountering local people, anyway.

Varna had roused during the first morning, although she remained groggy. She maintained a schedule of meditating at times through each day, which seemed to help. Jalor had several discussions with her about what could be causing her condition, from oddities to the planet's magnetic field or some sort of atmospheric disturbance to which her psi senses were reacting. While Varna had little or no faith in the existence of such senses, she could not discard the thought that something about the planet was affecting her via those psionic attributes. She tried to stand - sit - watch on the third night, but could only get part way through her shift when she had to call Blaine to relieve her. The next morning, she was morose, apologising to Jalor and Blaine for failing at one of the most basic team functions. Neither saw a need to find fault in Varna's behaviour.

Jalor decided to remain a further night, despite having no rations left and the game being somewhat scarce. Varna was awakened by Jalor for her watch - she had insisted she should try again - and found the night sky was brilliantly clear, a deep black bowl broken by myriad stars blinking high above. She had the ever-present fuzziness that made it difficult to concentrate, but forced herself to relax in an effort to relieve the feeling. The night seemed so tranquil and she found herself listening intently to the small sounds. Although she had never actually visited Earth after her mother's death, she had heard that it was like this, large parks with trees and brooks, night birds hooting and calling, small animals rustling through the undergrowth at the edge of the clearing and further away. Ennaris' smaller moon was just peeping above the horizon to start a fast transit across the heavens. And the night – or something – called to her deep inside.

Surprisingly, Varna felt the disorientation fade a little, and she felt better than she had for the last few days, which was promising.

This was not her first planetary drop by any means, and the effects of transportation normally were gone after a few minutes. But better or not, she still felt ... unbalanced, as she described it to herself. Her senses were abuzz. She imagined that she could feel the creatures in the surrounding wood, could sense the trees patiently awaiting the morning sunrise – sunrises, she corrected herself. The stream in the near distance, the rocks surrounding the small party, the planet itself - all seemed to clamour for attention. Was there something here? Was something trying to take root in her mind? Was it possible that there truly were those psionic senses people seemed to believe she had?

Varna stubbornly sat her watch, struggling for focus, striving to hold attention on her surroundings, to ensure that she was aware of any approaching people or creatures that may cause harm. But her attention was diverted time and again, without her volition, and she found herself afloat amongst the sensations, trying to remember the lessons learnt so long ago when her psychic potential was first discovered, even though she dismissed it at the time and had done so many times since. She recalled being advised not to force any contact, but to be aware and ready to either protect or respond. She thought back, far back, to the lessons about psychic defences, but having never experienced what she thought of as a psychic experience, no matter what others said about her latent abilities, she had never really practised the defences. She knew the forms, of course, one of which was the shields she had used a few nights before. But the others ranged from shields to basic forms of defence and attack.

And so, this time she let the sensations come to her. She felt a thrill of excitement and a tingle of fear as she truly was able to recognise individual threads after a time, rather than the inchoate mass seething across her consciousness that she had been experiencing so far and that had so overloaded her senses. Excitement won out. She struggled again briefly, knowing that she needed to maintain watch, but she could see - could *feel* - nothing inimical in the vicinity and surrendered to the sensations.

She fell into a trance that was beyond anything she had experienced before. She found her senses expanding further, racing from sensation to sensation. She was able to make sense of individual sensations but she had no overall frame of reference, and so she moved from one to the next, seemingly without volition. Here a flower, there a small insect like a honey bee, a night bird that somehow felt her pass and offered a trill in greeting. She moved faster, and faster still, leaping wildly now, drinking in all she could find, touching, feeling the lives of birds, plants, animals but now knowing them as gradations of psychic colours - she never realised that colours existed like that.

Still faster she moved and she tried to slow the onrush. She couldn't. She recognised that she had lost control, if she ever had it. Excitement turned to fear, and fear then verged on panic. There was no way for her to stop. Her psychic sense was being drawn in and driven by the planet, or something on the planet, and she felt herself losing her own sense of self. She felt herself flying apart, dissolving into the swirl of psychic energy that now seemed to reverberate to the depths of her being. Panic became terror. There was no stopping, no halting this head-long rush into she knew not what.

Suddenly, her onward rush was arrested by a sensation, a presence, so bright, so vivid, that she was blinded, psychically, and wrenched back into her own body. She woke from her trance with a start, breathing raggedly, her blood rushing through her veins urgently. Her heart pounded heavily. Her head ached fiercely. But at the same time, she felt less disoriented, lighter, more focused than at any time since landing. It took a short time for Varna to regulate her breathing and calm herself. She did not notice the fading flare from her Aldenthrush beneath her tunic. She judged it almost time to hand over to Blaine anyway.

Struggling to her feet, Varna tapped Blaine for his watch, gasping a quiet explanation of what had happened to her, apologising again but stressing that she was sure there was nothing nearby to cause danger. Blaine merely nodded, no questions asked, and settled in to watch for the rest of the night while Varna moved to her place, settled down and sought sleep, which took a long time to come. The ache inside her head grew again, and her sense of well-being evaporated. When she slept finally, it was poorly.

After the third night, Jalor decided it was time to move on again. The three team members were more accustomed to the light of the two suns, which in itself was unusual enough. They recognised the normal sounds of the forest surrounding their small rock-bounded clearing and were starting to understand which plants were useful or not. Through more careful trial and error, they found additional root and leaf plants that were edible, and a new wild fruit that was sweet and delicious, as well as others that they decided were better avoided. Their clothes now had a lived-in look and both Jalor and Blaine sported stubbly beards.

Their sparse equipment and belongings were packed - in reality they were not fully unpacked at any time - and they were walking out of the rocks soon after the first sun announced the break of day. The small village was not far away, Jalor was sure, and that was their intended destination. There they would find food and should be able to start their mission in earnest.

Varna struggled to maintain the normal pace of march, so their pace was held back to help her. Jalor continued to monitor her while Blaine ranged ahead and behind, ensuring they were not surprised. She had fallen into a sort of fugue in which she hallucinated while remaining aware that it was happening. As she haltingly described it to her companions in a break during the early afternoon, it was as though something was trying to communicate with her, to get her attention, trying to touch her - more than once she had flinched as though being touched - and she was becoming more and more worn as she tried to maintain some form of equilibrium. She did not want to lose control again, and feared the consequences should she do so. She had been close to losing herself, she felt. At each of the frequent stops she attempted to meditate, with which she had only minor success, and as soon as she had to move again the struggle began anew.

The village appeared in the near distance and the small team stopped to survey it. Two rows of cottages stretched along the sides of the narrow road, which was slightly wider where it passed through the village. Blaine's expert eye noted the attempt to defend the village. Two carts were parked across the road where they could be drawn together and he could see men on the far side watching them warily. A little further along the road, probably around the centre of the village, more men stood and talked, each holding a spear and several with stubby swords.

"This village is scared of something," Blaine said. "Let's be careful."

Jalor nodded shortly. His own eyes had not stopped scanning the village, taking in many of the same details Blaine had seen, but also noting the relative lack of smoke from the short chimneys that stuck above each roof.

"Well, if there's something out here to scare them then we may be better in there anyway," Jalor said. "And we need to see if there's anything we can do for Varna."

With a shrug, Blaine led the way towards the two carts, holding his arms wide in what he hoped was a demonstration of peaceful intent. The others followed close behind. As the team approached the men standing guard, one stepped forward, raised his hand in the universal signal to stop and opened his mouth to speak.

Varna stopped abruptly. She stood in the middle of the track, unmoving, eyes wide open, mouth moving. Jalor had moved two further paces before noticing that she was not with him, and called Blaine back. Varna was staring back along the road, into the forest to their right, her entire being caught up in the struggle. Finally, amid the jumble that was assailing her psychic senses, she realised there was a warning of danger approaching quickly, and the warning was urgent, to run, to hide. With a wrenching effort she broke free of the voices.

"Danger coming," she croaked to Jalor. "Must hide. From there," she finished, pointing into the forest where a small game trail emerged to cross the larger path that they followed.

Then she collapsed at Jalor's feet.

"Captain to the bridge!"

Jord arrived moments after being summoned. He took a look at the main screen and then short-range and long-range scanners. A bright object was clearly visible, far away, on the main screen but there was nothing on either scanner.

"Ideas?" Jord asked the bridge crew. "Mr Rork?"

"Nothing on the scans, no matter how I tweak them, sir. But based on what we can see on screen I expect it will pass close to the Fleet." Rork scratched his head. "It's the same sort of energy ball. You can see it fluctuating."

Jord nodded and bent to press a stud on the console in front of him.

"Grand Admiral to the bridge, please," he said calmly. "Communications, inform the fleet that at this stage we do not expect hostile intent of this object but to stay alert. And don't get in its way," he finished dryly.

Serra strode into the bridge, repeating Jord's actions of a short time before in viewing the screen and the scanners.

"The object has become noticeably brighter in the last couple of minutes, Captain, Admiral," Rork said from his station. "It looks like it will pass close to the *Jescu*."

"Get that ship moved aside," Serra commanded, then nodded as the destroyer powered up main engines and moved several kilometres without the command being given. "Good, well done!" she said approvingly.

"Here it comes," Rork said quietly.

A flash of light that almost blinded the main forward image receiving sensors sped past *Starfire*, on a direct heading for Ennaris.

"Stand down," Serra said. "That was the second, was it not?"

"Yes, Admiral," Jord replied.

Serra nodded, staring at the screen as the bright object disappeared around the curve of the planet. She shivered slightly as she did so, which Jord noticed.

"Cold, Admiral?"

"No, Jord. Seeing legends come to life is a little staggering, though." She smiled at his uncertain expression. "No, I haven't lost it yet. I want to be called to the bridge for each one of these events, please. There will be a few more."

"Aye, Admiral," Jord replied, watching as the Grand Admiral walked slowly off the bridge.

In a remote part of Ennaris' largest ocean, where no-one but the creatures of the sea were witness, the bright ball of energy came to a hover just above water level and then gently submerged. There was no loud sound, no reaction as it entered the water, just a light growing dimmer as it moved deeper into the ocean's depths. The ball came to a stop where the sea floor was split by a deep trench, and then slowly moved to one side of the trench, where the light revealed a cavern dug deeply into the side of the trench. The resultant bench formed a sort of entrance portico.

The cavern lit as the ball entered and with a flash the ball of energy was replaced by a swimming woman. Her blonde hair, long and wavy, spread in a fan around her head as she swam. Long legs kicked power-fully as she swam to a side ledge where she climbed from the water. She was tall and willowy, sheathed in a sheer but opaque material from the waist down. Small wings extended from her feet. Stopping, she looked around the cavern, seeing the accumulated detritus of the ages during which the space was untended. With a wave of her hand the wrack that had been cast into the cavern, and the dust and salt rime from the waters, shifted to form a small pile on the floor and was then swept by unseen forces into the water.

The woman walked to the ledge where the water lapped gently, crouched and extended one hand to lay it on the water as she sent out the call. Standing once again, she took another look around the cavern before diving into the water once more. The sheath extended past her feet and formed a single large flipper. With a kick she dived through the opening back into the ocean.

She looked around herself and rejoiced at being back in her own waters. For a time, she frolicked with the various fish that were attracted to her presence, the many and varied colours of the fish producing a submarine dance of eye-watering beauty. She stilled. The fish likewise ceased their dance and as though with a single mind moved away. But they did not flee, for they knew they were safe.

The woman floated serenely near the sea floor as she was surrounded by the huge predators of the sea, enormous mouths filled with razor teeth. Beneath her were great sea crawlers with massive tentacles and nipping claws. All came to a halt at a respectful distance, leaving the woman in the centre of a great sphere of creatures. Finally, pushing through the assembly came the leviathans, with even the huge predators making way.

One leviathan approached close to the woman and very gently bumped his great nose to her own. His skin showed signs of great age, with odd gnarled bumps and protuberances, scrapes and scratches, lines and scores. The woman gently rubbed the great head so close to her. Most of the sea creatures were unable to do much more than bask in the warmth of her presence, but the leviathans were not most sea creatures.

Mind to mind she apologised for being away for so long, an apology that the leviathans accepted without assigning blame.

"Where are my Sea Guides?" she asked, mind to mind once again in the way of the leviathans.

"Alas, this one is the last," responded the old leviathan, great sadness transmitted with the words. "The others were unable to sustain through the ages and have gone to the halls. They all died in service of the oceans, either during the rebellion's end or after."

The woman hung her head sadly. It was worse than she expected.

"However," and now the leviathan expressed joy where there had been sorrow, "in recent cycles we have seen gifts returning to the calves. I have begun to train a new generation and several near readiness."

"You have done well, Ooshmin," the woman said. "Your trainees must be made ready, for the time is close. The Children have returned."

"As have you, Ana," Ooshmin returned, satisfaction oozing across the link.

"Indeed, and my brothers and sisters will return also. We must prepare for the final battle." She turned in a circle to look at the creatures surrounding her, most of them unable to follow the discussion that had just occurred. "But there is time for us to enjoy before we get to work."

And so saying, Ana, Guardian of the oceans and seas of Ennaris, sped into the midst of the many sea creatures and played as she had not done for eons. And for those who could hear, the oceans echoed with the joy released.

17. Dimming Hollow

The villagers stared as the creatures emerged from the wooded slopes almost five hundred metres away. Jalor bent swiftly and lifted Varna, slinging her over his shoulder unceremoniously as he turned towards the village. The creatures were like nothing he had seen before and he did not doubt that they were what this village was afraid of. Still, it would be safer in the village than standing in front of it. The villagers were stirring to push the carts across the gap left between them as Blaine reached them, holding the gap open for Jalor and Varna to enter before helping the villagers to close it.

Not, Blaine thought as he looked around, that the carts would be much help. Nor would the villagers be much help.

The villagers were terrified, staring at the approaching creatures with wide eyes. Blaine sighed as he looked around quickly, seeing the fear that blanketed the villagers. All but one, an older man, who charged from one of the cottagers carrying a bow and a small quiver of arrows. The older man shoved aside one of the villagers who continued to stare at the approaching creatures and shouted.

"Wake up, all o' ya," he cried as he fitted his first arrow to the bow. "Get yerselves ready to fight, damn ya. You too," he snarled at Jalor and Blaine, "if ya don' wanna die."

Blaine was now able to make out some of the features of the band approaching the gate. They did not hurry, nor did they deviate at all. It was as though they knew that they would overwhelm the villagers and so there was little cause to move faster. The deliberate approach was having a profound effect on the villagers, Blaine thought. Even with the older archer cajoling them, and the imminent arrival of this group obviously intent on attacking, the villagers seemed unsure of what to do. They remained gripped by fear.

Jalor moved into the village with Varna where a young woman took her from him in front of a neat cottage. He returned to Blaine's side. The creatures were about fifty metres away and spreading apart, presenting a line. Of uniform height, they moved rapidly with an odd loping gait. There were ten of them. Each was shrouded in a crudely made hooded and sleeveless garment that extended only to their waists, below which was a type of kilt - more of a loin cloth - made of what seemed to be the same material. Heads were hidden inside the hoods. Heavily muscular arms led to large hands that ended in what were more like claws than fingers, each with sharp nails. Their feet were more akin to hoofs, hard and hornlike. In fact, Jalor realised as he stared at the oncoming line, they *were* hoofs. Weapons - crudely made swords, spears or pikes, wicked-looking notched knives - hung from their belts or were carried in hand. To Blaine's eye the weapons seemed unwieldy and clumsy, but the attacking force showed intent and seemed to be all muscle. In his experience, crude and clumsy weapons wielded by a strong man would kill as easily as refined weapons. Not that these seemed to be men. Blaine glanced to Jalor as he took his bow from his shoulder and grabbed a handful of arrows from his quiver.

The old archer released his first arrow, which flew straight into the chest of the nearest attacker. The man released a short laugh of satisfaction that became a grunt of disbelief as the arrow shattered. His second arrow fared no better and the man swore bitterly. Meanwhile, Blaine lined up the first of his arrows and let fly, his target no more than thirty metres away now. The arrow, created by *Starfire's* chief armourer, punched through whatever armour the creature was wearing beneath the hooded cloaks. The creature fell. Blaine grabbed a second and third arrow, notched and released them a second apart. Two more attackers fell. The attacking force closed up again, now no more than twenty metres away.

"We won't stop them all," Blaine said to Jalor, "not with arrows at least."

He released another two *Starfire* arrows in quick succession, downing two more of the remaining seven attackers. The older man whooped as he continued to fire at the strange group. One of his arrows penetrated what must have been a small gap in the armour, bringing a sixth to a halt, although it did not fall. Blaine's next arrow finished it off.

Jalor, meanwhile, grasped his battle staff and extended it to its full length.

"Fall back," he told Blaine.

"What?" Blaine asked as he reached for more arrows from his quiver.

"I said, fall back. You have the one weapon that seems to stop them. I doubt swords or spears will. But the rest can keep them busy while you mop them up."

Blaine nodded and started to walk backwards as the first of the remaining attackers reached the blockade and merely reefed one of the carts aside. Blaine's arrow took it just below the neck and it fell. The remaining three charged through the gap now opened. The first swung its crude sword at one of the men who tried and failed to defend himself. The sword crashed through the scythe he held and cut through his torso almost completely. The creature died with another of Blaine's arrows through its head.

The remaining two snarled, the first sound any of them had made, and charged at the small knot of men standing staring at the dead villager. Lifting a wicked looking pike one of the creatures drove its point into the belly of one man while the second raised its sword and chopped at a second man, only to have the swing interrupted by Jalor's staff and diverted. The pike-wielding creature was Blaine's next victim while Jalor now found himself the target of the remaining attacker. Even while he was taking evasive action from the huge overhand swipe of that crude sword, Jalor took in the bone-like plate that covered the chest and torso to the waist. The creature's hood fell back and Jalor almost stared at the head. It was vaguely and disturbingly human but with some sort of animal's snout and what seemed to be short tusks protruding from its mouth. Small black eyes stared at its intended victim with what Jalor could only describe as intense rage. Jalor's training kept him from concentrating on the sight too much, as he focused on holding out the wild swings of the now enraged attacker.

"Jalor, drop!"

Jalor heard Blaine's command and immediately thrust himself back and down to one side, trusting his partner implicitly. Above him he heard the sword swing through empty air with a swoosh, followed by the quiet *twang* of Blaine's bow and the thud of the arrow's impact. Rolling away from the attacker, Jalor looked up to see the arrow extending through the creature's right eye and out the back of its skull. The creature collapsed backwards, spread-eagled.

Carefully, Jalor stood and looked around. All of the strange attackers were dead, as were two of the villagers. The remaining villagers, obviously at a loss about what to do, stood and stared at the bodies. The older villager walked up to Jalor swearing.

"Bedamned useless thing, yer nothin' but a piece of firewood," he complained as he neared.

It took Jalor a moment to realise the man was talking to his bow, held in one hand and being regarded with disdain as the man walked. He looked up to Jalor, who stood a head taller, and nodded greeting.

"We're in yer debt, we are," he said to Jalor, turning toward the approaching Blaine to show that he included both in that greeting. "I'm not sure what would 'ave 'appened had you not been 'ere. Likely the same as 'appened over to Kilik's Reach a few days back."

"This is happening elsewhere?" Jalor asked as he watched Blaine tip one of the creatures onto its back to examine it more closely. "Is it common?"

"Aye, it's been 'appenin' aroun' and about," was the reply. "Kilik's Reach had no-one left alive. All twenty-seven of 'em slaughtered. None o' the killers were found. They just killed everyone an' left. If all they 'ad was the same bow as me I can see why."

"It's not your bow," Jalor said. "It's the arrows. They seem to have some sort of bone chest-plate that your arrows can't penetrate."

The older villager looked from Jalor to the nearest dead attacker, the one Blaine had turned over, then to his bow and back to Jalor. He nodded.

"But yer friend's arrows could do fer 'em," he said, as much question as statement.

"It must be the type of wood we use," Jalor said, thinking rapidly, "or maybe the way they are treated as they are made."

For an odd moment he wondered what the reaction would be if he said they were made of exotic materials in a Lightship possibly still in orbit around the planet, and shook his head to clear the thought. Maybe what was affecting Varna was affecting him, too.

"They're all the same," Blaine said as he walked up to Jalor and the old archer. "They all have a strange mix of hu..., er, men and some sort of pig or goat-like creature." He paused to gather his thoughts again as what he said was "scroffer" for pig and "kussar" for goat, an effect of the translator pushing unknown words into his language centre that he usually did not even notice. "They have what seems to be a natural armour covering back and chest, wrapping around to cover their upper arms also. It extends like plates down their torso and becomes a sort of extra-thick hide for their upper legs. The lower legs are like those of a kussar also with hoof-like feet. The hands have claws rather than fingers. All male, if that means anything, and more manlike in that regard than animal. Oh, and their blood is black."

Jalor nodded and thought for a moment. Around him the villagers were emerging from hiding and a small number stood around the two dead men, one of the women keening and grasping the body of the first man to fall.

"Who's in charge here," he asked the older man.

"In charge? Why, no-one," the man replied. "We're free men, not subject to anyone. We look to the Faero" - the word translated to Jalor and Blaine as overlord - "but we're free. But Korza was probably the leader."

He gestured to the first dead man.

"Well, someone needs to get started on clearing this up in case there's another attack. Blaine, see if you can grab some of these men and drag these things out of the village. Looking at them I think burning will be the best bet but I doubt everything will burn." He looked back into the village. "I left Varna with a woman in the village. I'll check on her now and then give you a hand."

Blaine nodded and turned to walk away, stopping when the old man spoke again.

"I'll help yer," the old archer said. "Name is Giffin, by the way. Was a member of the Faero's guard for thirty cycles, I was. Never seen the like of these afore."

"Jalor and Blaine," Jalor said, pointing to himself and Blaine.

"Blaine, Jalor," Giffin said, nodding. "My thanks again, Jalor. Blaine," he continued as the two men walked towards the first of the dead creatures, "can I trouble yer for a look at those arrers of yer. I seen lots of different ones an' always thought mine were pretty good but nothin' like them."

Giffin's voice faded as he and Blaine headed away. Jalor smiled at Blaine having to deal with the garrulous Giffin and started towards the cottage where he had left Varna. He nodded politely to the few villagers who watched him pass. It was a small village and he thought there may be as few as fifty and probably no more than a hundred villagers. The small cottages ran down each side of the small road, some with short paths running to the door, others with the door opening directly into the street. Most were maintained, neat and tidy, and the ones that showed wear and tear seemed to be showing age rather than being ramshackle and uncared for. Thatched roofs abounded and walls seemed to be made from heavy timber logs with gaps caulked by mud or plaster of some sort. Small windows set into the log walls had shutters. Most windows were closed still in the aftermath of the attack. Doors were of wood. One or two opened doors showed that they were hung from some form of pegs that seemed to act as hinges, although one or two older ones were hung with what looked like leather straps.

Five cottages down the road was the one where he had left Varna. He had quelled his misgivings in leaving his team member in the care of an unknown person by rationalising that she probably would be safer there than where he and Blaine would be taking on the attacking force. Still, he was anxious to make sure she was safe.

The wooden door opened and the woman with whom she had left Varna appeared in the doorway.

"Have they gone, then?" the woman - Mansela she had called herself - asked.

"All of the attackers are dead," Jalor replied quietly.

"Thank the Guardians," Mansela said, relieved. "Your friend remains unconscious. Please come in."

Mansela stood to one side as Jalor nodded his thanks, stooped slightly and entered the cottage where he could stand straight again. His head almost brushed the beams that crossed the single room and supported the roof structure. The bottom of the thatched roof was about a metre above his head when he stood in the centre of the room. Like most of the villagers Jalor had seen, Mansela was a little shorter than he was, although she was taller than Giffin.

Varna was laid out on a small pallet bed, on what looked like a straw-stuffed mattress laid on a low wooden platform. She had been covered by a colourful blanket and her pack rested alongside the bed. Jalor's own pack accompanied it, as he had left it behind before hurrying back to assist Blaine and the defenders.

"Has she regained consciousness at all?" Jalor asked as he knelt beside Varna.

"No," Mansela said as she sat on a stool by a small table by the door. "She muttered something I could not understand but has not awakened. I sent my son for Ansela. She's my sister and has learned the healing lore. She may be able to help your friend."

Jalor was about to demur when the door opened and another woman entered, accompanied by a boy who Jalor thought may be no more than five or six years - cycles, he corrected himself to local usage - of age. While younger, the woman showed strong resemblance to Mansela and was already talking as she entered the cottage with evident familiarity.

"What problem do ye have sister, that caused Mondas to make me come so quick. Oh," she said, stopping just inside the cottage as she saw Jalor still kneeling by Varna's side, "not for yerself, I take it."

"Indeed not, sister," Mansela said. "This is Jalor and the young woman is...?"

"Varna," Jalor supplied to Mansela's raised eyebrows.

"Varna," Mansela repeated, nodding and drawing the boy to stand by her. "This is my lad Mondas."

"You're one of them that saved the village from the strange creatures." Ansela said, nodding. "You have our thanks, and more. What's wrong with her?"

"I don't know," Jalor said evenly. "She has been suffering from something for the last few days." Jalor considered how much to say and then decided to follow his instinct that said he could trust these people. "She said something about feeling like a lot of things were trying to attack her, or at least to get inside her mind. I know it sounds strange, but that's what she said."

Mansela and Ansela shared a look. Mansela nodded, then stood and pushed the door shut before returning to her seat. She drew Mondas to her again, then nodded once again to Ansela.

"I have heard of something similar from time to time," Ansela said carefully, staring at Jalor intently. "I may be able to see what is causing it but I need you to stay still and don't interfere."

Without waiting for Jalor's response, she knelt on the other side of the bed beside Varna. Carefully, she examined Varna's face for several seconds and then gently placed her right hand on Varna's forehead, closing her eyes as though concentrating. Her eyes flew open and she gasped, eyes wide as she turned to Mansela and then to Jalor.

"Is something wrong?" Jalor asked, worry shading his voice.

"No, not wrong," Ansela said in wonder, turning back to Varna. "Not wrong at all. Just, unexpected."

Ansela took a deep breath and placed her hand, which was shaking slightly, back on Varna's forehead. She held it there for a long while, eyes closed firmly and lips compressed. After a few moments Ansela started to perspire, tiny beads appearing on her forehead and it was obvious that she was determinedly holding herself in place. Jalor glanced to Mansela in mute query, and Mansela shook her head to indicate she did not understand what was happening.

Finally, Ansela took a deep breath and removed her hand. She opened her eyes, sat back on her haunches and watched Varna. Jalor could see a little colour returning to Varna's cheeks. He had not realised that she had gone so pale, and relief flooded his face.

"What is it?" Mansela asked her sister.

"An awakening, but she's blocked," Ansela said. "But the strength I sense is ..." Ansela stopped, lost for words.

"What is an awakening?" Jalor asked, looking from Ansela to Mansela.

"It is a gift coming awake," Ansela replied, watching Varna carefully. "I'm not surprised that she's having such trouble, as usually gifts manifest when children are quite young and then develop. I've never heard of a gift coming this late."

Jalor sighed. So, Varna was being affected by something on this planet and it triggered something in her. He thought of the reports of strong psionic traits that never seemed to be acknowledged by Varna. Maybe that was it. Maybe not. He shrugged to himself. Whatever it was, he had to find a way to deal with it.

"You must make sure no-one around here knows she has a gift, whatever it may be," Mansela said to Jalor, her expression so intent as to cause Jalor to pause a ready assurance.

"Why is that?" he asked.

"With that question you prove that you are not from here," Ansela said, "or you would know that those with gifts have been hunted for thousands of cycles. You would know what an awakening is, even if only from tales told by the travelling Tellers."

Jalor stared at Ansela for a long moment and then smiled ruefully. Undone at such as early stage by something so simple. The two sisters shared a brief look and then both turned to Jalor.

"Where are you from, Jalor?" Mansela asked quietly. "How do you not know of these normal things?"

"As you say, we are not from here," Jalor said carefully. "In fact, we come from a place quite a long way away and have come looking for someone. This," and he gestured to Varna lying on the bed, "was not what we expected."

Mansela nodded and held up one hand as Ansela was about to ask further.

"You have assisted our village when you did not need to do so, and for that you have our thanks. We'll keep this to ourselves," she said looking to Ansela, who nodded shortly. "But do not speak of it to others until you reach the Faero's citadel. There you may find answers to Varna's condition. The old ways are not completely forgotten at the citadel. Those with gifts are not banished nor are they attacked, few though they are in these days."

"And how can I be sure that you will not report this?" Jalor asked, looking Mansela squarely in her eyes.

Mansela smiled gently, but it was her sister who answered.

"Because we are of the Blood!" Ansela declared, quietly but fiercely. "And the Blood remembers its oath!"

Jalor was about to ask further when the door was opened and Blaine thrust his head into the room. He took in the tableau presented in a moment, Varna lying on the pallet with Ansela by her side still, and Jalor standing with Mansela and Mondas. Nodding to the two women, he looked pointedly at Jalor.

"Jalor, we may have a problem," he said quietly. "You need to come with me, now!"

Jalor nodded. Blaine had no dramatic leanings and rarely if ever exaggerated. Whatever it was, it was important. He looked to Mansela who nodded.

"Go with your friend, Jalor from a long way away," Mansela said with a smile. "Ansela and I have some small skill with healing and we have some herbs and tinctures that will help Varna. It will take another day or more for them to work, in any event."

Jalor considered, looking at Varna lying helpless on the bed. If he left her here there was no guarantee that she would be safe. Then again, in most assignments Jalor found himself having to trust someone and he thought he had developed a pretty fine sense of knowing who that would be. He felt he could trust these two women, even though he had known them for a very short time. He nodded shortly, decision made.

"I trust you to take care of her," Jalor replied to Mansela, earning a warm smile. "But we may have to leave shortly, so anything you can do to help will be appreciated."

He took one last look at Varna, then gathered his pack and quietly opened the door, glanced outside and then exited the cottage. Blaine was waiting for him, holding his bow.

"What's the emergency?" he asked.

Blaine turned from looking back towards the simple blockade that had been reinstated at the road into the village and nodded. He turned toward the end of the village.

"Apart from Varna, I think we've found Shadows!"

18. Morrig

The Great Desert swept almost from the west coast of the southern continent to the east. It was unbroken except by a narrow strip of green that inhabited the banks of the great river Negra that cut through the smaller continent from the heights in the south to the great bight that separated south from north. For days on end a traveller seeking, for whatever reason, to move through the desert itself would face wave after wave of sand, which was constantly shifting, constantly moving, always treacherous for those unaware. The three riders were not unaware.

Riding the huge derhrss, which was able to survive without water for many days, the three were swathed head to feet in flowing robes of a muted colour which, combined with head-dresses that covered all but a slit where eyes and upper nose were visible, kept the suns' extreme effects at bay. Accustomed to the desert, Elmani kept a careful watch which was second nature, and not just to make sure the desert did not reach out and grab them unaware. Caution was required also because, with his two companions, Elmani was chasing down a band of raiders who had preyed on an isolated settlement and preyed specifically on families with children. The families had been slaughtered.

The loss of community members was always painful, but the loss of the children to these strange creatures created outrage throughout the desert. Elmani had visited the settlement as part of his regular rounds not long after and had immediately started a pursuit. Knowing the desert, he was confident of chasing down these attackers who, from reports, were ill-prepared for the conditions but who had headed directly into the heart of the sand ocean.

For three days now, the companions had travelled and seen small signs here and there, difficult even for the experienced to identify, that told Elmani that he was on the right path. But he had found no signs now for a day. There seemed to be something unnatural about these people who would head into the desert on foot and maintain a consistent lead like this. He decided that they would check one final oasis before heading back, no matter how much he wanted to catch them and deal out justice.

Elmani called a stop, holding up one hand. As he turned to speak with his companions, he noticed something from the corner of his eye. Something was embedded in the sand of the next sand ridge. Signalling for caution, Elmani indicated that he had seen something. All three dismounted and carefully moved down the slope of the ridge where they had been riding, low enough so they were not visible to watchers. They then crept up the next slope, watchful, careful where they stepped. Elmani signalled again and the other two faced outward while Elmani moved up to the object.

It was a horn, sticking out through what seemed to be a black helmet. Carefully, Elmani brushed away sand to uncover the face of one of the beasts, snarling in the rictus of death. The helmet was actually a bony skull cover, he noted. A wound was evident as he uncovered more of the body where a sword had hacked into one arm. Elmani recalled that one of the survivors spoke of a defender who had managed to score on an attacker before being overwhelmed - this must be the one injured. It appeared as though it had just dropped dead and was left where it fell. Elmani considered. What he had heard of other attacks was that the attackers burned their dead before leaving, although there were few dead usually. Perhaps they needed to be at a specific place and so hurried on. Perhaps they did not notice this one missing. Or perhaps they were close and planned to return to retrieve the body and dispose of it soon. The oasis was only a short distance away, after all.

Elmani decided to leave the body where it lay. It was less than a quarter of a day to the Morrigonar, the Oasis of Morrig. The day was moving towards the sudden night so characteristic of the desert lands, so the three moved back to their mounts and located a suitable camp site some distance away, where they made a cold camp, set a guard and slept. For the entire time, none of them spoke.

The next morning all three were up and moving at first light, circling the oasis to approach it from above a rocky ridge. They arrived before mid-morning, again leaving their derhrss to their own devices, and crawled to where the rocky ridge overlooked the oasis. The remains of a camp-fire could be seen, as could nine of the beasts, but there were no guards that they could see. The camp was situated near the old ruin, a structure that had been built in times long forgotten against the water's edge and somehow remained intact. Tradition said that it was built by the sect of Morrig in the days after the rebellion, or perhaps before it. El-mani was not so sure of that, but the water of the Oasis of Morrig never failed - it was the only oasis where that could be said - so who knew.

It would be suicide for the three of them to attack the camp, no matter their motivation for vengeance - justice by another name - but all three settled in to wait for an opportunity. Across the middle of the day they watched, enduring the heat of the suns and the sand, hoping for a chance to destroy some or all of this band. They appeared to be waiting for something, and were in no hurry to retrieve their fallen fellow. El-mani had signalled to pull back from the ridge and the three had started a quiet hand signal discussion about whether to attack or not when, with a flash, a bright ball of light dropped from the sky into the oasis. The three scrambled for the ridge again, to see the nine standing and staring at the structure, which was now opening. A glow emerged from the gaps as the stone walls rose outward with a loud groan to show that the structure was a small pavilion.

Inside the building, on a divan of truly ancient design, sat a single figure. The figure stood in one lithe movement. Dressed in the traditional ancient garb of the desert warrior, the woman - obviously a woman - wore a figure-hugging one piece garment, sand-yellow in colour, but without the weapons belt. A knife sheath was on each calf and she wore a head-dress, with the face open. Slowly, she walked from the pavilion into the sun, staring at the nine beasts without fear.

Startled, the nine creatures now growled on seeing a single person and, with a guttural cry, started to move towards her in a shambling run. Elmani and his companions had already shed their bulky robes, revealing themselves to be dressed in similar garb to the woman, but they were armed. Leaping down the ridge Elmani yelled to distract the attackers from the woman, drawing a wicked scimitar as he did so. His companions imitated his actions. They knew they would be too late, for the beasts were almost on her and they redoubled their efforts, calling to her to run.

Their calls died out and they stumbled to a stop as the woman held out both arms. Her eyes flashed, and fiery bolts streaked from her hands to strike every one of the attackers, destroying them in moments.

Elmani was the first to recover and he stepped forward, bowing deeply. The woman's eyes softened as she watched him.

"Lady," he said humbly. "I am Elmani, and I greet you on behalf of my people."

"Thank you, Elmani," she replied. "And I thank you and your friends for seeking to save me at what would have been the sacrifice of your own lives. It would appear the corruption has begun to spread once more, so our return is timely. Are you prepared to assist me in what I must do?"

"We have seen your power, my Lady, and now see your great beauty, but confess that we have no knowledge of who you are. The, er, pavilion has never been seen opened in our lifetimes or many lifetimes before us. In this place where the water never ceases, and which is a known haven for the people of the Great Desert, we thought to hunt down those who had attacked and slaughtered defenceless men, woman and children, but we had no thought of stumbling on one such as yourself."

Elmani watched the woman, waiting, one eye raised in ingenuous query, so that she laughed.

"Nicely said, Elmani. I'm sure you can move people easily, and such we may well need. I am Morrig, and this is my Vale."

"Oasis," said Elgray, one of Elmani's companions, the first word he said during the long chase. Usually he went months without saying anything at all.

"What?" said Morrig and Elmani together.

"It's the Oasis of Morrig, not the Vale of Morrig." Elgray shrugged. "Just saying."

"Well," Morrig said with a happy smile, "then it's my Oasis. And I have returned with my fellow Guardians to assist the Children of Ennaris to defend this planet. We must bring the various people together as they were, long in the past. It's time for the people of the desert to come out of their isolation. And you three are going to be my right hand."

She looked at the three of them expectantly, as Elmani and Elyard both nodded.

"Hands," Elgray said. "Not hand."

19. Beast Men

Shadows! Jalor stood still for a moment and then gestured to Blaine to explain. In response, Blaine waved him forward and started to walk back to the blockade. Jalor fell in beside him.

"Apparently, while we were defending this village there was a hunter out in the forest. You need to hear what he has to say."

They approached the small group of men standing near the carts that had been wheeled back across the road. Jalor recognised all but one, a tall middle-aged man holding a long bow in one hand, with a short sword on his left hip and a long knife on his right. His free hand was pointing back into the forest.

"Over there, by the second ridge," he said to the listening men as Jalor and Blaine reached them.

"Hilva Nem, this is Jalor," Blaine said. "Would you repeat what you told me, please? Jalor, Hilva Nem is a hunter and was out when we were attacked."

Hilva Nem looked at Jalor, did as quick an assessment top to bottom as Jalor had ever experienced and nodded. Jalor felt the man's piercing green eyes had read deeply into him in that one moment.

"Aye, I'll repeat it," Hilva Nem replied in a deep voice. "I thank you for what you have done for Dimming Hollow. It's a small village and not much known beyond this region, but it's our home and valued as such."

"We could not abandon a village to such as those creatures, whatever they were," Jalor said. "But please, tell me what Blaine thinks is so important."

Hilva Nem's green eyes twinkled as he smiled. "Aye, captain. Nay," he continued as Jalor opened his mouth to speak, "I've seen my share of captains and if one such as Blaine defers to ye then ye be the captain, right enough. Anyway, I was out lookin' fer an aylah, fer there's bin reports of a white-tail or two lately and our stocks of meat are run a bit low. I tracked 'er for a bit and found a good hide where I could see 'er eatin' and was about to take my shot when she startled and bounded away. Somethin' made me stay where I was and lucky it was too," he said emphasising the last with a nod, "because a moment later a troop of ten creature-men walked past. I couldn't see 'em all that well but I'll bet they were the same as what Giffin described 'ere."

"Another lot?" Jalor nodded.

"Aye," Hilva Nem nodded. "Not likely to be the ones who attacked 'ere. But Blaine seemed right interested in the one who followed along. Weird it was, all covered in a black robe that went from hood to feet. Only there didn't seem to be feet. It looked like this one just sorta floated along. Anyway, they went past an' I stayed where I was for a bit, but then curiosity got the better o' me and I follered 'em. They made a sort o' camp a way further on. The, uh, creatures were carryin' bags and emptied 'em. They," Hilva Nem swallowed and his eyes turned haunted, "they were bits of people, arms an' legs an' such, and these creatures just set to an' started eating 'em. I got away then, couldn't stay an' watch that."

"Ate them?" Jalor looked from Hilva Nem to Blaine. "Cannibals?"

"There's more," Blaine said, turning to Giffin. "Giffin, tell Jalor the other thing you told me."

Giffin nodded, glancing uncertainly around the small group but then started.

"Well, you see there's a number o' farms aroun' 'ere, been 'ere for a long time handed down and aroun' families and such. Some of those farms have been attacked by somethin' in the last few tendays and there's bin no-one found left behind. I'm thinkin' it's these kussar-men things bin doin' that attackin'. Thing is, it's like they's choosin' which ones to go fer, as there's others that were left."

"What sort of pattern are you thinking, Giffin?" Jalor asked.

"The Blood! They's after the Blood, I'm thinkin'," Giffin said, nodding to the group. "And I'm thinking they's after those with young'uns."

"The Blood!" one of the other men exclaimed, one who Jalor recalled had frozen when the attack started. "Old wives' tales. The Blood ain't nothin' any more. That was in the old days. Now it's just people takin' the name. Next, you'll be sayin' the gifts be returnin' and the Dark One's comin' back."

Giffin nodded.

"Aye, Grellis, and what I'm hearin' the gifts do be returnin'. The Tellers be tellin' the old stories again and the gifts be returnin'. And the Blood is bein' hunted by these things." Giffin nodded again, agreeing with himself. "I tell yer these things be huntin' the Blood. Because the Blood is what the stories all tell will save Ennaris when the Dark One comes again."

"Why would they come 'ere, then?" the man named as Grellis asked in disdain. "Yer bein' crazy. And them's just stories, anyway."

Realisation struck and Jalor turned to Hilva Nem, who had turned to look into the village when Giffin was talking.

"They're okay," Jalor said to the hunter.

Hilva Nem glanced at Jalor, his deep green eyes studying the Warrior before nodding.

"If these creatures be killin' the Blood then the Faero needs to know," Hilva Nem said. "And there're families out there that'll need help. We're likely the only ones who know. We need to warn 'em."

Grellis scoffed again. "The Blood be gone, I tell ya'!"

"The Blood is not gone at all, Grellis," Hilva Nem said, turning to face the man. "I am of the Blood! And the Blood remembers the oath. We are ready, we are always ready to defend Ennaris, to defend the likes o' you against the Dark One or any others who come. I have others of the Blood out there who need help, but," and he turned to face Jalor, almost apologetically, "if there's a chance these creatures may come back, I must stay here."

Jalor nodded understanding. Mansela and Ansela were of this Blood, as was Hilva Nem, and that meant Mondas was, too. Did Mondas have one of these gifts? Were the Blood the allies the Admiral mentioned? They sounded like some sort of warrior class and if they were being hunted by these creatures, who seemed to be in alliance with the Empire agents, then they needed to be helped. Jalor came to his decision and started to issue his orders. Blaine smothered a smile. He had seen this Jalor many times, the tactician and strategist coming to the fore in times of stress and need and taking charge where there was a gap.

"Blaine, give Hilva Nem a dozen of your arrows. Hilva Nem, these will stop the creature-men where your normal arrows shatter on the bone plates they wear. If there is one of those cloaked ones that seem to float, everyone else concentrate on that while you take care of the creatures." He paused while Hilva Nem nodded shortly and Blaine started to pull shafts from his quiver. "Giffin, I need a map of the farms where the Blood live, especially those with children."

"Aye, captain!" Hilva Nem nodded.

"Aye, captain!" Giffin repeated, as he turned and trotted away. "I can have that fer ya in a snap."

"Aye, captain!" Blaine parroted, returning the glare Jalor turned on him with a smile.

Jalor shrugged. So much for a cover story that made the team non-military. If it hadn't been blown by him with the two women, it certainly had been now.

"The rest of you men make sure those barriers are in place and better than they were before. Keep an eye on the gaps between the cottages, too. Hilva Nem, Mansela and Ansela are looking after a friend of ours. She became ill but they think they can help her. Please tell them that we will be back shortly." Jalor looked around the group that had had stayed still, staring as the stranger issued orders. "Move!"

Jalor and Blaine watched as the troop of ten creatures trotted by. Hidden in a dense copse of aspen-like trees, they had heeded the warnings given by Hilva Nem and carefully located the hide not far from one of the trails leading from where the creatures had stopped to eat their grisly meal. This trail led to the farm closest to the stopping place, and Jalor made a guess that it would be first. He was relieved when they heard the war-band, as he had started to think of the groups of those things, moving along the game path, making no attempt at stealth, and he and Blaine were able to position themselves to view them as they went past.

The band were identical in appearance and dress to those that had attacked the village. Of uniform height, they moved rapidly with an odd loping gait that Jalor had not noticed during the attack. They did not speak and passed in single file along the narrow trail, turning onto the main path heading away from the village and moving to a faster trot. Following the troop, seeming to float just above the ground, was a Shadow, those nearly invisible enemies that the Union fought in space and on the ground.

Both hunkered down further, just in case. Shadows they had met and battled before. They were sworn enemies to the Union and in many ways the Warriors had been formed almost three hundred years before to combat them and the inimical influences they caused wherever they turned their attention. Shadows were thought to have some sort of extra-perceptive senses. They were thought to be able to sense the presence of Warriors, but this one did not pause in its journey.

The Shadow changed things. While they had been warned that such was possible, their mission to observe and locate had just changed character and took on more of the second part of their instructions. They had to disrupt whatever plans were under way and buy as much time as they could. Without the need for discussion, they waited a short time to ensure there was no following party, then moved forward to take the same path as the Shadow's war-band. Before too long the band took another game trail off the road. They appeared to have a definite destination. More interesting, they seemed to know their way around, which indicated there were sympathisers or spies somewhere. Jalor and Blaine followed quickly, alert for signs that their presence had been noted.

Jalor judged that they must be close to the first farm. The two Warriors increased their pace and in a short time reached the edge of a small clearing, obviously the farm, with a cabin in the centre that was now under attack. The cabin was well built, sturdy and squat, and the occupants were attempting to defend themselves. Arrows shot from wall openings were reaching out to strike the attackers, but while some were missing many bounced off the body armour under the hooded garments. The fight had just begun but it was obvious that it would be over quickly - there were only two defenders that Jalor could identify, based on the fact that arrows were being fired through only two arrow-slits.

For Jalor, there was no debate about getting involved. The presence of the Shadow was reason enough. Besides, the mere fact that more than ten attackers assaulted the one small cottage was something neither he nor Blaine could watch without intervening. Blaine quickly extracted from his pack the light but tough bow-string and strung his bow in a single smooth motion. Moving out into the open, he tipped his quiver of arrows to the ground, while Jalor grasped his staff. The first intimation the attackers had of trouble was when Blaine's shafts, fired with a rapidity that always left Jalor marvelling no matter that he had seen it done before, took the three closest from behind. The *Starfire*-wrought arrows easily pierced the bony armour that withstood the defenders' wooden shafts. The remainder continued trying to break into the cottage, oblivious to the damage caused to their fellows.

Jalor stood alongside Blaine as he released the arrows, each dealing death to a target before, with a slight frown, Jalor directed him to target the Shadow, which had now noticed them. Blaine obliged, sending two fast shafts - both in the air at the same time, such was the speed with which Blaine notched, aimed and loosed them - at the Shadow. Now under fire, the Shadow dodged. It succeeded in avoiding the first shaft but was unable to avoid the second, which pierced the centre of the flowing robes. As usual when a Shadow died, the jet-black robes collapsed as the life force expired.

Immediately, the remaining seven attackers stopped their attack, shaking their heads as though emerging from some sort of daze. They turned toward Jalor and Blaine and, with a series of grunts, lumbered forward, Blaine loosed two more shafts - two more attackers down, five to go - before dropping his bow and drawing his recently acquired sword. Jalor extended his battle staff as they prepared to meet the beast-men.

The two Warriors separated, Jalor meeting the first of the remaining attackers with his staff, ducking a wild swing that would have sent his head tumbling and stabbing the shaft hard where he judged the upper armour plate to end. Relieved, he watched his attacker halt and bend double. The staff cracked again, hard, over the hooded head, and the attacker went down. Blaine ran past the fallen attacker and on the way helped himself to the crude sword that had been dropped, before launching himself at the oncoming attackers with both weapons moving constantly. The creatures assisted by charging directly at Blaine without trying to coordinate between themselves, thus allowing him to deal with each in turn. Having examined the bodies at the village, Blaine had determined that there was a weakness under the arms, where the armour did not seem to provide coverage, and behind the knee for the same reason. The thighs should also be vulnerable, but they were thickly muscled and covered with some sort of tough hide. The first two opponents were down within moments, one dead with the crude sword still extending from the wound beneath its arm, and the second having been effectively ham-strung as Blaine had slipped beneath the wild swing. That one he left for later, to meet the third. In short order he had dealt with that one also, but not before having to evade more wild swings. These creatures were not skilled but they were strong and, when Blaine clashed swords with this one, the force almost unbalanced him and left a deep notch on the sword's blade. Still, skill won over brawn and Blaine slipped through the wild attack to run his captured sword through this creature's torso under the arm. Once again, the sword was left in the wound as the creature collapsed, leaving Blaine without a sword.

Jalor's attacker had managed to get back to its feet, realised it had no weapon and grabbed hold of a sword dropped by one of its fellows. The team-leader was alternately attacking and defending massive swings of the sword. Blaine had lost track of the last one. He turned to his left at a noise, to find a sword raised over him and starting a downswing, too fast for him to counter. But then the downswing broke and the sword dropped from a now lifeless hand, as a sword point appeared through the bony chest of the final attacker. The cottager grunted as he heaved his sword back out of the body, using one foot to provide additional leverage, after which the body dropped to the ground with a clatter of what sounded like body armour.

Blaine looked to the one he had hamstrung to find that it was pinned to the ground, a long spear protruding from a point just above the kilt.

With a final crack Jalor smashed the staff over the attacker's head, drew back and pressed a second stud to extend a thin blade from the staff end, which he then drove as hard as he could into the side of the attacker, retracting the blade as his target shuddered and lay still. Jalor leaned on his staff with the blade now hidden again, breathing heavily, as Blaine checked each of the band to ensure they were all dead, and then set about retrieving his shafts. Like those he had used at the village, none of them had suffered damage in slicing through the armour, and Blaine made a mental note to thank the *Starfire's* master armourer, whose team had manufactured them. In short order, he had returned to Jalor's side.

The cottager gestured to the cottage, then turned to bow to the two Warriors.

"I thank you," he said formally, the words coming to the Union Warriors through their translator implant with a faint burr. "We would have held out for but a very short time had you not intervened."

Jalor nodded acknowledgement as Blaine turned at a noise. A woman and child, a girl aged about seven years - cycles - old, were crossing the field, the woman shielding the girl from the carnage as best as she could, while the girl struggled to see as much of it as she could.

"We were asked to help by Hilva Nem and Giffin from Dimming Hollow," Jalor said quietly as he looked around, "but we have other reasons to join in as well."

"Aye, well you did seem to know what you were doing," the cottager rejoined. "My name is Almin Bor, and this is my own heart, Magwyn," he continued as the woman and child joined them, "and our daughter Aldar."

Jalor introduced himself and Blaine by name, describing themselves as travellers from a long way away.

The woman bowed her thanks, while the girl's eyes shone in excitement. "Can I see an arrow? Please?" she added belatedly, with a look at her father. "They went right through where ours hit and broke."

Blaine smiled and extracted an arrow - one that had not travelled through one of the band of attackers, and handed it to Aldar. Almin Bor - the Warriors were to find that, like Hilva Nem, he was always given his full name, as were others of his people - was as interested as his daughter, and took it from her after a moment, running his hand along the shaft.

"This was not made around here," he said. "This feels like some sort of metal, but yet not."

He looked at Blaine enquiringly.

"No, not from here," said Blaine. "And not metal. Just a different kind of wood from where we hale, very hard and strong."

"Yes, well, if you say so," Almin Bor rejoined, a nod and a smile telling Blaine that his story was accepted but not necessarily believed. "It is remiss of us not to offer you refreshments, although I would like to get rid of all this." He pointed to the bodies littering his field.

Jalor considered, agreeing to help tidy up the field but then having to move on. "But we must return to a friend who is unwell in Dimming Hollow. If she awakens without us there, she'll be concerned."

Magwyn looked up. "Husband," she said. "We have discussed this and now is the time. We should go to the Faero with these goodsirs, if they are going that way." She glanced at Jalor and said, "We are not the first to be attacked, but I believe we are the first to survive. We know of two other families who have been killed, obviously by a large number of men."

"I'm not sure these are men, exactly," Blaine said, drawing Jalor's attention to one of the attackers, whose hood he had drawn back to reveal the same bestial face, with the same snout rather than a nose dominating piggish features, and fangs that were more like short tusks emerging from the wide mouth.

Jalor studied the face revealed, his gaze moving down the length of the body that Blaine was systematically stripping of its garments. He had missed the opportunity for any close examination at Dimming Hollow, for they had left as soon as a map could be produced By Giffin. From the waist down to the hoofed feet the body was more humanoid than beast, obviously male, but above the waist was a mix of humanoid and what seemed to be elements of some sort of animal. Hair that was more like a pelt covered the shoulders and strong arms, running down a barrel chest to a stomach region that would have rippled with muscle when alive. On the torso and back was that thick layer of a bone-like material that appeared to be natural armour plates in place of skin. And there were those hoofs and claws.

"Not someone to take home to visit," Jalor said.

He noticed that both Almin Bor and Magwyn were studying the revealed body, the latter in no way disturbed by the near naked male form as he would have expected from what seemed to be a largely agrarian society. Even the young girl was studying the body with interest.

"Very strong and, from what we have seen, very aggressive," Jalor said to Blaine. "But they were being controlled by the Shadow, I'm guessing.

Did you note that they were released when the Shadow died? They were only grunting as some form of communication."

Blaine nodded. "Let's get rid of these and we can discuss that later," he said. Gripping one leg, and without ceremony, he began to drag the body to a bare patch closer to the forest. "We can burn them here where it should not damage your fields," he said to Almin Bor.

It took some little time to create a mound of the dead attacking party. Their weapons, those crudely wrought swords, spears and pikes designed to tear more than stab or cut, were collected and thrown into a small shed attached to the cottage, and the bodies burnt. The Shadow's robes were also cast into the fire after a careful search that yielded nothing.

Finally, they were ready to depart. Jalor had agreed to have Almin Bor and his family accompany them to the next farm rather than back to the village. Almin Bor was a fighter, that was obvious, and his sword looked to be old and well used - he claimed it was an heirloom and had been passed down from a noble forebear - while both he and Magwyn were at home with bow and arrows. What was more important, his sword and spear had pierced the inbuilt armour of the strange creatures. Blaine issued to both a small number of his precious *Starfire* arrows.

Leaving the field to head back into the forest, Jalor noted that none of the family looked back to the farm, almost as though that was a detail of the past. Jalor would find that to be characteristic of the Faeronar, the people of the Faero as they styled themselves. It was even more so a characteristic of the Blood, who were a subset of the Faeronar. They were a hardy and self-reliant people, he thought, and he was looking forward to meeting more of them. Blaine and Almin Bor had struck up a friendly relationship, each recognising a fellow warrior. Almin Bor, it turned out, had some form of military background, and he looked the part. Apart from his sword, Almin Bor carried his spear, slightly longer than he was tall, that looked very serviceable and his long bow. He had taken the time to retrieve and don a combined breastplate and back-plate, both worn over a suit of mail that came to his elbows and knees.

Aldar was quiet and composed, carrying a small pack easily and holding a walking staff as though accustomed to it, while Magwyn had arranged to pack what food could be carried and without asking distributed it among the men, carrying her own load just as easily, her own long bow in hand.

The party took very little time to walk to the point where the game trail met the road. They walked without talking, eyes constantly shifting from close to distant.

20. Trance

The world receded as she collapsed. With her last conscious effort Varna reached into herself, trying and failing to stop whatever was closing out all her external perceptions one after the other – touch, smell, sight, sound – until she seemed to be nothing but consciousness floating in a void, black but not dark, close but infinite in breadth, neither cold nor warm. That feeling of something just outside conscious thought remained, an annoyingly persistent buzz that was now almost identifiable and, in this state, was not debilitating. And somehow, however she was able to do it, Varna had held back the final descent into complete unconsciousness. Moreover, Varna now knew that she recognised the feeling, but from long in the past.

So, she stopped struggling against whatever it was and accepted that something was affecting her. With a deliberate decision she ran through the final forms of meditation and plunged deeper into herself. She surrendered to her unconscious, freed herself from the constraints that bound her to the waking world. She found herself hovering on the brink of the memorising nodes, those spaces and places that she had been taught about but had never been able to access, no matter how often she tried. And yet here she was and here they were. The stories that she had been told were of people losing themselves in their own memories, or going mad when they recalled things they had sought to forget. Varna knew she avoided certain memories, but put that down to a healthy defence mechanism, of not wanting to relive those bad memories.

However, it appeared that whatever was happening needed her to remember things. Perhaps it was for the best. She felt no pressure to plunge into her memories, and yet was sure that was what she was meant to do. With a mental shrug, Varna closed down her psychic perceptions - the ones she had not believed in, she thought ironically. It was something that she had not tried to do for a very long time. She had failed repeatedly back then, which strengthened her belief in their non-existence. Perhaps it was something she had to be in deep trance to do, as she was now. She savoured the knowledge that she did, actually, have those sorts of powers, although she had not consciously used them. Whatever was affecting her wanted access to her memories, or wanted her to have access to her memories. She tried to puzzle that out once again but the trance state seemingly was not conducive to such thought processes. So, given that she had been unable to stop whatever it was from getting her here, and given that she seemed to have some form of control, she pushed herself over the edge of the well of memories. So intent was she in being aware of what was happening that she failed to notice the quieting of the mental buzz. With some excitement and no small amount of trepidation, she opened herself to her deepest memories as she had never been able to do during her training, no matter how the instructors tried to induce her to do so.

Sights, sounds, feelings, aromas so evocative as to induce clear memories of people, places and events floated past in a slowly gathering parade. Recent memories, clearly defined and closer to the surface, were encountered first, were passed as she moved further into the past, her own past. Varna noted them as she fell past them – the landing on the planet's surface, the meeting with the legendary Grand Admiral, the initial resistance by the crew on her transferring to *Starfire* and the subsequent thawing when both Admiral Bard and Captain Jord welcomed her warmly to the fleet's teams, then deeper down to the moment when she informed her father that she had decided to leave *Sirius* to be seen to be her own person. And past that to her last mission with *Sirius* when she revealed Wensor as the traitor and exposed him only to be captured and tortured. She shied away from that memory before exploring it too deeply. She still did not know how she had done what they said she did, and was not sure she wanted to know yet. It seemed whatever was affecting her did not need to see it yet either and allowed her to skip past.

She sank deeper into her past. It was not an actual decision, but it just felt like the right thing to do. She accelerated her rate of descent, skipping several missions and other Fleet events that she was sure had no bearing. She kept moving backwards, flipping through events like she was reading a holonovel backwards.

She stopped.

Varna found herself observing a scene she had tried to push away, to forget completely. Of course, that was impossible to do and she knew it, but she had tried. She suffered anew, alongside a younger self, as she was accused of using psychic powers to cheat her way through her Academy training. The accusation itself she could take in her stride. She had been accused of cheating before and knew it was prompted by a mix of fear and anger – fear of the possibility that someone could get inside your mind and anger that the accuser had failed, or not achieved as well, while she excelled. But this one hurt because of the accuser. He – Varna could not bring herself to think his name – had avowed devotion and love only days before, declaring that he found her supposed psychic powers to be neither disturbing nor worrying. And she had believed. She could still feel the shock as she realised that it was he who had accused her of cheating. She was not to know until later that the charge was dismissed immediately, although she was made to re-sit the exam with added safeguards as proof of no psychic tampering.

Deep in trance as she was, Varna felt herself growing numb as the betrayal was once again laid out before her. Subsequent history was to vindicate her claims of innocence to such an extent that an apology was made by the Commander of the Academy. But that brought no surcease of the pain of betrayal, nor the anguish that became a burning flame of hatred that, for the first and only time, had focused her will to a needle point and allowed her to push a probe into her accuser's mind. Ironically, she thought now, that should have proved she did have such abilities, and yet she had not made that connection at the time. For there, rather than the gentle, kind and understanding person she had allowed herself to love she found an ugly mass of jealousy, hatred and sordid ambition. In a single thrust faster than thought itself she had stripped bare the contempt in which Falar - so she truly could think his name and not quail - had held all others, herself included, and the lust for power that had led him to turn traitor. The shock at finding that he was an agent for the Enemy at such a young age was observed and played back, but seemingly had no power to damage her any more.

With a mental sigh, Varna released herself from the node point associated with that memory. This was not what she sought, although there was a feeling that it was linked somehow. She re-entered the stream of memories and continued pushing back, into her late teens, seeing faces she remembered, minor embarrassments, early experiments with intoxicants, sex and their interrelationship. But they were not what she sought either.

She stopped again. Even floating in the sea of her memories, Varna was amazed as she watched her father discuss her progress with both her tutor and another person. Because it was a very early memory, the faces were fuzzy, indistinct. Her tutor, an early one with a strange name – Srina Bell, she recalled with a little effort – had always praised her and told her she would be strongly attuned to people. But now the other person turned to her and held one hand out over the young Varna, and she felt herself floating again, drifting serenely without concern. This was what the older Varna now recalled, the same sensation of drifting, of being observed by a power that she could not describe.

Almost, almost she could discern the face of the person but the details never quite came to her. She could almost hear the voice but, again, not quite, as though her memories had been fogged. But she could distinctly hear her father thanking the person for paying a visit and for the gift and making assurances that all care would be taken for yes, she was a special child.

Then she felt a warmth envelope her as the person turned to go, replete with love and ... hope, she thought. The person turned back and lifted one hand as though in benediction and now Varna could hear a thought that came to her from him, for she now realised the visitor was a man. *Child,* the thought was also fuzzy but Varna fought to hold clarity, *we will meet again for the time is coming when the children must return.* And the stranger was gone.

Varna floated for a time as she replayed that memory, but without any further clarity. Then, rather than go further into her childhood she started to pull back. Back through the early years, through her teen years, struggling with the feeling that she understood what people were saying and thinking but not being sure how or why, having been told repeatedly that true psychic abilities did not allow that - and she did not believe in them, even then. Again, she passed through the experiences at the Academy, this time merely filing the unpleasantness away - she had dealt with that. Back through her training and first assignments until, again, she arrived at the last mission with Sirius.

She was about to avoid this episode again but something made her stop. She fought with an instinct, an urgency that she needed to deal with this finally, to remove this piece of baggage from her life. And the more she fought the stronger was the pressure to investigate further. She bowed to that pressure.

Once again, she was on the planet Mastic watching Wensor, her team leader, dealing with the local magistracy, who had the dual role of law maker and judiciary. It had been Varna who had discovered that the previous Chief Magistrate was an agent of the Empire and had placed a number of co-conspirators in positions of influence across the magistracy, ousting the previous magistrates, who themselves had been corrupt and had been gouging their own people shamelessly. It was the public outrage at the level of corruption displayed that allowed Angfor Tusk to assume the Chief Magistracy on the death of his predecessor. Now Wensor was conducting an interview to establish how far the Enemy agents had been able to infiltrate. Varna relived that mission.

Varna was troubled. Wensor said all the right things for the situation. He expressed outrage that the Empire had been able to act under the noses of the local Union representative, but he seemed less concerned than he should have been. Varna, as second to Wensor, had suggested that the Union representative should also be scrutinised but Wensor had vetoed that idea. The other two members of the team had seemed surprised but, being quite junior and relatively untried, did not voice an opinion. And Wensor had requested someone else as second for this mission, which indicated reservations about Varna, although none were raised when her place on the team was confirmed by the squadron team coordinator.

Varna also had discovered that Wensor had not informed *Sirius* of the findings on the planet. She had seen him operate the small transmitter but his voice and demeanour were not quite right. She felt that something was wrong there and had taken the opportunity to check the transmission logs only to find that no transmission had been made.

Now Varna watched as Salit Kurn, the Union representative who had not recognised that the Empire was suborning the magistrates and sundry others in the planetary government, approached the interview and was invited by Wensor to take a seat. Again, she felt a wrongness, an indefinable frisson at the fringes of her mind that she had learnt to interpret as tension and fear. It was coming from the group involved in the interview. Varna should have been included in that interview also, as team second, but had been excluded with the explanation that Wensor wanted her to be free to move through the small city and watch the interactions of the inhabitants, using her supposed psi skills to pick up under-currents. She had agreed and left almost immediately, but did not just wander through the city. Instead, she had arrived at the tavern ahead of Wensor, wearing a simple disguise that shielded her face, ordered a drink that she had repeatedly stated she hated and some food and settled down to wait.

Wensor had never really understood Varna's abilities, she had thought. What he did not realise, what many people in the Union did not realise, was that the supposed psi talent was not mind reading, even if it existed, nor was it some form of magic. Magic! In this day and age!

Varna had snorted to herself as she thought about it. Most people did not realise that in many cases the 'talent' was more about paying attention to the subtleties of body language, shifts in linguistics, attitudes and other keys. And Varna was very good at all of those, as well as having these occasional feelings – and her feelings had never been wrong. She had one now.

So, with some trepidation, she knew not why, Varna had turned her full attention on the three in the interview. Angfor Tusk seemed composed, where Salit Kurn was uncertain and scared to the point that his whole being almost quivered. Wensor she could not read easily, as his back was to her, but his tension was obvious, too. Varna was able to make out the words from Salit Kurn and the responses from Angfor Tusk – her ability to read lip movements, even in a less familiar language – was another talent Wensor ignored. But Varna always sought to get a good understanding of local languages. She was very good at learning new languages quickly, where Wensor relied on translator programs. She realised that Salit Kurn was entreating, almost beseeching, some form of protection.

"But how do we make sure of this?" he asked Wensor.

It was Angfor Tusk who responded. His lips were tight and, Varna now realised, he was experiencing enormous tension even though his demeanour was studiously unconcerned. "I think the team will have to uncover a small cell of renegades acting to undermine the magistracy," he said. "The renegades will attack and in the subsequent affray only Wensor will emerge intact. A shame! Such promise snuffed out from the three who perished!"

Wensor said something, hands extended as though in query and Angfor Tusk responded again. "I think you will have to take me into custody to make it look good for the rest. You can say that you are holding me in the magistrate's cells and the team can be accommodated above them. I have hidden entrances through which the assault team can pass. Let that be tonight, Wensor."

Wensor nodded and said something else that Varna could not make out. Salit Kurn nodded, rose to his feet and bowed to Wensor while appearing to pointedly ignore Angfor Tusk, and departed.

Floating in her deep trance Varna experienced once again the feelings of anger, of fury, that she had felt while watching the meeting, and some uncertainty in that she hoped Wensor was playing a deeper game. The trance muted the fury but she was now able to recall minute details previously missed – the two men lounging near the door who followed Salit Kurn out of the tavern after a final glance around the room, the glances and nods between Wensor and Angfor Tusk as Wensor stood and moved toward the door.

As soon as she could do so without making it seem like a deliberate move, Varna had tossed back the drink without grimacing, which took some effort for it really was vile, pushed the remnants of the food to one side and stood to leave, throwing coins on the table as she did so. The serving woman had appeared from nowhere and scooped the coins into her apron pocket, searching for change and then bowing to Varna in gratitude when the latter indicated to keep the change. As she reached the door Varna had felt Angfor Tusk move up behind her so she stepped to one side as she exited and bent to retie her boot laces, even though they were tied already. She peered under the hood of her cloak, worn up as many did in this town, and watched as Angfor Tusk gestured to a man seated across the road. The two men met in the centre of the road and turned towards the seedier end of town. Varna took note of the second man and then headed back to where the team was based on the edge of town.

She reported to Wensor that she had been moving around the city and could get no real sense of anything out of the ordinary, although she did report having seen Angfor Tusk leaving a tavern. Wensor nodded.

"Okay. Well, maybe I'll get better luck this evening. Right now, I think we'll pick up Angfor Tusk. You two" - pointing to the other two members of the team - "come with me. Varna, the city has some sort of holding facilities beneath the magistrate's building. I want you to check them out and make sure they're secure. Apparently, there's accommodation above that we can use while we await a hearing, although I'm not sure who we can see as being unbiased here."

Wensor picked up his sidearm, replacing his nondescript cloak with the Union cloak from his pack. The other two team members did likewise and all three exited the room. Varna, meanwhile, merely sat and thought. Then, using a private code, she called the security chief of *Sirius*. After speaking for a short while, she picked up her own Union cloak and swung it around her shoulders, attached the neck chain to its matching clip as she did so, then left the building. A well practised quick check told her that her small bird ornament remained in place, under her clothes on a fine chain.

The magistrate's compound was typical of the local buildings. It was constructed as a square, with an entrance through a set of main gates leading into the internal courtyard. Varna arrived at a time when she estimated that she should have been just ahead of Wensor in escorting Angfor Tusk to his cell. Her arrival separate to the team had not been expected, she thought, so she decided to sow some doubt. On her arrival, Varna had been shown to a small office opening onto the courtyard – all rooms opened to the courtyard, she noticed as she crossed it – where a short, tidy woman received her. Varna identified herself as a Warrior of the Light, which was unusual in itself for those who knew the workings of that organisation, and stated that she was in advance of the main force and wished to see the holding chambers. The woman exhibited some consternation that Varna did not try to allay. Sometimes it was more useful for people to act on their own assumptions. Varna was taken across the courtyard to a set of doors, where the woman left her. Inside the doors, a flight of steps went down, with another going up, probably to the accommodation. Varna waited for a moment, trying to decide if this was a trap. It probably was, she thought. Finally, she decided to go down and check the cells anyway.

She had reached the bottom of the stairs when the attack came. She had expected some sort of attack, so her reaction time was good. Her blaster was in her hand without thought and she fired repeatedly, as much to create noise and confusion as to do damage. Above, she heard confused noises, either a fight of some sort or many people running around. It was likely that she had precipitated unplanned actions, she thought as she continued to lay down a withering fire that covered her attackers as much as the walls and ceiling. Hopefully her actions meant the two junior team members would be safe from Wensor's plan, but she could not know. She had the two immediate assailants down when a new assailant crashed a cosh over her head from behind. She was unconscious before she hit the floor.

Varna regained consciousness fully, but kept her eyes closed. She was part sitting, part hanging from manacles against a stone or brick wall, the metal of the manacles cutting into her wrists painfully as they took her weight. She was naked - oddly, her chain and bird ornament remained - and when she opened her eyes to a slit, she saw her clothes thrown in an untidy heap on the floor against a side wall. She could see the barred door on the facing wall, so she reasoned that meant she was against a side wall of the building, but below ground. Was this one of the holding cells? Slowly she worked her way around her limbs and muscles but apart from a splitting headache and pain to one side - she guessed she had been kicked when unconscious - she did not seem to be hurt further.

How long had passed? A small square of light showed against the far wall, obviously from a window set high above her head, so it was daylight still. The attack on the team may not have started yet, or it may be over.

She was thinking of ways to get out or to get word to her team when a key scratched in the lock and the door was flung open. Two men, dirty and unkempt and holding hard wooden staves entered, sneering at her as they did. One walked straight to her and slapped her face, rocking her head from left to right. She tasted blood.

Chuckling, the two walked away, leaving the door open. Just as Varna thought a mistake had been made Wensor walked through the open door. He stopped a short distance from her and smiled, relishing the position.

"So, little miss high and mighty all bound and trussed up, eh? The boys are drawing lots for the order when they have you tonight. Thought you'd like to know that the betting is you won't last more than the first five."

Varna spoke for the first time. "Why are you doing this?"

"What, this? Taking care of my friends here or making sure you have a good time?" He chuckled again. "Well, it doesn't matter much that you know. I've been a double for years so this is just another assignment here. As for you, that is pure pleasure. I want your daddy to know what happened to you and for the Fleet to know what happened to the golden girl, she who has all of the gifts and is better than the rest." He sneered.

"What gifts? And why my father?" Varna sought to keep Wensor talking.

"My secret," Wensor snarled, taking a short length of something - Varna recognised it as some sort of bone cylinder used by the people of Mastic to roll their bread dough - from his pocket and wordlessly launching a series of blows on her arms, legs, body. Varna grunted with the effort of staying quiet, not giving him the satisfaction of hearing her scream. Finally, as she struggled to maintain consciousness through the pain, Wensor stopped.

He left, this time closing the door behind him. Varna stifled a groan and tried to make herself more comfortable. The pain caused another involuntary groan. Tears leaked from her eyes and ran down her face. She tried to think of ways to escape but nothing came. She felt helpless and completely vulnerable. The beating and Wensor's certainty that she would suffer conspired to undermine her innate self-confidence, which she knew was one aim. There was no-one she could call on, now. She feared her two team-mates, who were too young and inexperienced for this mission and what they would face, had been killed. And all because she had deliberately walked into a trap and allowed herself to be caught.

She was unsure how long she was held. Her efforts to maintain some sort of awareness of the passing of time failed with repeated bouts of torture, threats and physical attacks. She was beaten with batons and staves, fists and boots. The pain could not be denied. The men constantly told her of the sexual assaults she could expect. She was urinated on and forced to both urinate and defecate in place. After what she judged was the third day, but may have been the fourth, fifth or even the sixth, she was sure that she had some broken bones. She was black and blue over much of her body. Still the beatings came.

She tried to block the pain, using some of the techniques she had been taught for moving into a semi-trance state, but the waves of pain did not allow that. She lapsed into a semi-conscious state in which she lost the remaining sense of time passing, or of any sounds. So, she was unaware of the battle that erupted above when the *Sirius'* Marines suddenly stormed the compound, reacting to the warning she had given several days before, thereby saving the two captured and imprisoned junior team members from being murdered. Nor of the explosion when the Likudian sympathisers triggered an explosive device that resulted in many innocent deaths.

The first change she became aware of was when her door was flung open and Wensor charged inside. He was carrying a laser carbine in one hand and, strangely, his ceremonial sword in the other. He was sweating profusely and snarling incoherently. Varna came to, mostly, as he jammed the sword under one arm and wrenched one manacle open, allowing her to slump unevenly to the floor before scoring her skin with his sword. Standing over her he raised the carbine and brought the stock down deliberately on her leg. Varna felt the bone snap and she screamed, as Wensor raised the carbine again and smashed down on her other leg. Varna screamed again as she *pushed* him away with everything she had in her, trying to make him stop, to get away from her. She whimpered in extreme pain and terror, almost losing consciousness after the second blow. She was unaware of Wensor being picked up and flung across the room to collide head first with the stone wall and start to slump to the floor, his neck and many other bones having been broken by the hard impact. But she could see it now. The remnants of her awareness held enough for a buried memory to be called forth. The sword had followed, skewering him with such force that it pierced the stone and held the former Warrior in a half-slumped position. Oddly, she also now recalled a fading flare of light, another tiny detail that she had not remembered previously. And then she had lost consciousness entirely.

When Varna regained consciousness, she was in the *Antilles'* sick bay, with both legs encased in healing gel pods and bandages covering much of her upper body. Over the next week she learnt how her message to *Sirius* had resulted in Wensor's Warrior cohort being sidelined in favour of Marines, resulting in the compound being invaded. Marines being marines, not many of the defenders survived to surrender. Varna was located by a sweep team, one of whose members recognised her and called for immediate medical evacuation.

Caught up in replaying the scene before her, and being unable to direct her view away from the sights and sounds of her past, she lost control of her memory stream. Events now started to rush past her again in a confused mess, reminiscent of her experiences of the past few days. Before she could panic, though, Varna was startled by a sudden bright flash. Abruptly, her headlong rush through the past was halted. At first, she failed to notice the presence awaiting her as she sighed mentally and pulled back, thankful for being stopped, however it had happened.

Suddenly, she realised she was not alone in her thoughts. She felt that there was someone or something hovering near her. In panic, she tried to escape, not knowing how to do so or where to go. The presence exuded calm, however, and made no attempt to interfere with her in any way. Rather, it was as though the presence was waiting for her permission. Even in the depths of this trance, she felt ashamed of her panic. She knew the experience with Wensor and his band of Empire sympathisers had crushed her confidence but the sheer panic she felt surprised her. She attempted to pull herself together.

Who are you? She thought as clearly as she could, thinking that the presence may not speak Standard, then dismissing the thought as probably irrelevant.

Yes, I understand you, Varna Barr. The voice was gentle in her mind, and Varna inexplicable felt warmed by it. *I am sorry to have startled you, but you were losing yourself in your vision and I felt it best to intervene. You have been long awaited, child. You have suffered greatly and your experiences have caused you to be unsure of yourself. You have no reason to doubt yourself.*

Varna held herself as still as possible, mentally. She *saw* that she was in a vast space, with grey mist swirling about but no apparent breeze. The ground was solid and yet insubstantial. She wondered if this was some sort of breakdown but fought against that thought. Some remnant of her true, innate strength bolstered her. She still felt that the presence was close by, and she wished the mist would clear. With that thought some of the mist slowly swirled away, to reveal a figure, a man, tall and lean, wearing archaic robes of white trimmed with brown. White hair flowed past his shoulders. A long white beard extended half way down his chest. The man looked like everyone's expectation of an avuncular wizard. All he was missing was the pointed hat, Varna thought to herself.

In a blink the figure wore a pointed hat. Mild eyes continued to regard Varna who, to her surprise, found herself laughing at the change.

So, you can listen into my thoughts too? Varna was still somewhat overwhelmed, but a little more relaxed after the moment of amusement. *May I ask who you are?*

My name is not yet for you to know, he replied. *Not because of any concern I have about you knowing who I am, but because it is not your time to come forth just yet. That will come soon enough, and we will assist you to do so. You must go to the Forest of the Guardians and seek the Tree.*

Help how? Varna thought, becoming a little dreamy.

We will help you to bear your burden, my child, the figure replied gently, and with a smile that melted Varna's reservations. *You have been unprepared for your role on Ennaris. We will help you to adjust, in preparation for the times to come. You will recall this meeting in time, but for now just remember the Forest of the Guardians and the Tree. Go there as fast as you can!*

The mist swirled back over the figure and Varna felt herself drifting away, wishing that she could keep hold of the feeling of warmth and safety that had accompanied whoever that was. She fell out of the dream.

Varna woke.

21. Ogun

Ogun was elated. There was enormous satisfaction in reviewing his achievements with his latest client world, which was progressing well now after being almost wiped out by the bedamned Andorethi far in the past. He also was elated at the long wait being over. He missed Ennaris, missed the world he had helped to create and the people who most resembled his own. Helping these younger client worlds to evolve was satisfying, and he knew that he would do more of that in the future. However, Ennaris was the world that he and his companions, who had been given the charge so long ago by The One, saw as home.

He flashed across the vastness of space as a solid ball of energy. Across many skies, some of which he had helped to recover from disasters, or from aggressors like the Andorethi, he was seen. He knew it but did not care. To his knowledge, none of the people on those worlds would understand what he was, not for a very long time, if at all. So there would be theories established by scientists, legends created by the superstitious, perhaps new religions founded by those looking for something in which to believe. So be it.

He was one of the less passive Guardians but understood the need to allow these worlds to develop, even though assistance was needed in most cases. As the Guardians' people were assisted in times long past in their own home in another distant galaxy.

He was looking forward to revisiting old grounds on Ennaris, of being part of the community of Guardians again, even if only for a relatively short time. A short time for the Guardians would still be many, many lifetimes of the Ennarisi, of course. He was looking forward to helping the descendants of the survivors, after he and most of the Guardians had been made to leave Ennaris soon after the rebellion. Frustratingly, he still did not understand why that was the case and Odruf seemed unable or unprepared to explain the reason.

His reflections were broken as his extremely fine senses took note of activity in the space above Ennaris. Two fleets of space-faring vessels were holding station. Warships, he noted at closer inspection, even though he was far away still. His thought narrowed. One of the fleets was full of Andorethi and several of their subordinated peoples, all of whom had been influenced to savagery rather than enlightened civilisation. They had much to answer for, as did those who supported them.

The other fleet comprised - if he had eyebrows in this state they would have shot up - Ennarisi. He was unsure how that could be, given the interdiction on most advanced technology. On closer inspection though, no, they were not Ennarisi but human. Now that was a turn up. He had heard from his fellow Guardians that the humans' - Ordorethi in Ennarisi terms - had made it to space but he had not expected such a fast progression and spread through their sector of the galaxy. They must have made a real jump over recent times. He had not bothered to take much note of them and their progress, but the *rate* of progress seemed a little too fast. They did not match the Andorethi fleet's fire power and numbers, though, so may have some trouble.

He felt something and his focus narrowed to a specific ship and he smiled to himself in recognition, as much as a ball of energy travelling at almost light speed can smile. And he pondered.

On *Starfire* Jord once again called Serra to the bridge. The tracking stations were fully manned as the fleet kept close watch on the Empire fleet, which had arrived in the vicinity only a standard day before and seemed to be very slowly positioning for an attack. The Union fleet was out-gunned badly, Jord knew. The newest Empire dreadnought provided massive fire power that surpassed anything the Union had in the vicinity. Even *Starfire* would be defeated in an extended engagement. Without the dreadnought, the Union forces would have the edge and probably could hold station to support the team on the planet. He knew Serra would not budge this time.

And now there was another of the energy balls approaching, which is why Serra was here. Again, the main screen could see the ball approaching at huge speed, but the sensors showed nothing.

"Admiral," Rork called out from his tracking station. "This one has made a slight course correction. Still on course for Ennaris but taking a slightly longer route if my calculations are correct. And heading for the Empire fleet I think."

Serra merely nodded. "Weapons cold," she instructed, even as she watched the Empire fleet reposition and start firing all their guns at the energy ball. "I have a feeling," she muttered to Jord. "Pull our ships away from the leading edge. Get them back."

The orders were relayed and Jord looked at Serra, who now had a small smile playing across her face. "Admiral, you know what these things are, don't you?"

"I believe I do, Jord, but I may be wrong. I don't think we have anything to worry about, and even if we did fire everything we had it would have no effect. Hold station, everyone," she called out to the bridge crew. She continued to watch.

For Ogun, a warrior Guardian whose particular interests included such subjects as volcanoes, quakes and other things that make loud bangs, he now had in front of him a force of beings for whom he had developed a particular antipathy. Andorethi and their subordinate races had caused massive death and destruction on world after world across their sector of the galaxy and, obviously, were seeking to expand. They would not do so on Ennaris if he had his way.

The ball of energy flashed past the screen of Andorethi ships, ignoring the plasma bolts, anti-matter charges and rounds fired from rail guns, some of which were poorly aimed and shredded other Andorethi ships, which he thought was amusing. He probably should not take part in this, he thought. Not deliberately. Then, with a thought he formed into a spear of solid energy, smashing through the heart of the Andorethi dreadnought with enormous force.

The crew of *Starfire* watched, stunned, as the Empire flagship broke up. The explosions that erupted throughout the vessel were much more than could be explained by any sort of space battle on a vessel of that size and power. Serra smiled broadly and laughed aloud, prompting questioning looks from Jord and others of the crew.

"In joke, Jord," she said lightly.

Because she could have sworn that she heard a disembodied voice say "Oops!" as the energy ball, a spear no longer, sped on its way towards Ennaris.

22. Rendezvous

Two hours into the trek from Almin Bor's and Magwyn's farm Blaine called a halt. Looking from Magwyn to Aldar and then Almin Bor, he put one index finger to his lips in what he hoped was universal for quiet and gestured for them all to move off the track on which they been walking. Almin Bor raised a single eye-brow in query, to which Blaine gestured with his head to the right. With a nod to Blaine and then to Magwyn, Almin Bor led his family from the track into the scrubby undergrowth and crouched, out of sight. Very faintly, Blaine heard the unmistakable sound of a sword being drawn from its sheath. He smiled faintly before turning to Jalor.

With a couple of hand signals Blaine and Jalor moved to the other side of the trail, away from Almin Bor. Blaine had his captured sword in hand, along with his knife, while Jalor held his battle staff, yet to be extended. Both crouched behind similar scrubby undergrowth, several metres apart, and waited.

After a few minutes Jalor heard very faint sounds that sounded like a small group of people moving towards them on the same path. More of those strange creatures? More bandits? Straining his hearing as far as he could, Jalor knew he would never be able to estimate how many people there were but he knew that Blaine would already have done so. The man was a master at any trail work. He turned slightly to Blaine and made a mute query.

In response Blaine held up four fingers, followed by a rocking of his hand back and forth a few times. So, four people but not completely sure. Good enough. If there were only four it was unlikely to be another troop of those creatures. Unless they had taken losses, of course. Jalor continued to crouch, noting that Blaine had laid his sword down and now held an arrow notched and ready to fly, the bow held parallel to the ground.

From around a slight bend came a large man, dressed in leather trousers and sleeveless shirt, well-muscled arms bare. He stepped carefully, with a long bow similar to Almin Bor's held with an arrow ready to fly, short sword at his right hip. A large pack was slung over his back and he carried it with ease. His eyes moved back and forth, up and down as he scanned the area in front of him. Behind him came two children, walking quietly and carrying small packs, followed by a woman with another bow held ready to shoot. The woman wore a simple breastplate but no mail, and she also had a sword hanging from a belt on her left side.

The man stopped and, instantly, the two children and the woman did the same. Both bows moved to cover the area. Jalor watched intently. Something must have given them away, some indication that others were here. The man stood completely still, eyes moving but nothing else. The tension in his body was plain to see but yet he held himself still, making no sudden moves.

From the other side of the trail came a bird call, short and soft, and then again. The man relaxed, as did the woman, and turned to where Almin Bor now stood and pushed through the scrub. Behind him came Aldar and Magwyn. Both Almin Bor and Magwyn had their own bows ready for use, but their bows held no tension. The small family on the trail waited, quietly. Only when Almin Bor had reached the man and reached out his right hand so the two men clasped hands around each other's forearm did either speak, and it was Almin Bor.

"Belka Min, well met," Almin Bor said quietly, eyes scanning the trail behind them. "Are you being chased?"

"Almin Bor," Belka Min acknowledged. "We're not sure. We saw smoke from Asbor Jin's direction and with the recent attacks thought it better to move first."

"Good move. Are you all well? Sindelar, it's good to see you again." The latter to the woman who had moved to join the two men, shepherding the two children with her.

"We're well, captain. Where do you go? We planned on joining with you. Your farm is better defended than our own." The woman looked to Magwyn and nodded greeting, but her eyes continued to scan the surrounding forest.

"We and our new friends were coming to your farm to warn you," Magwyn said.

"Friends?" Belka Min queried.

Almin Bor smiled and gestured to where Jalor now stood, followed by Blaine a moment later. Sindelar stared, chagrined, as the two Warriors joined them. Belka Min snorted.

"Where were your tracker skills then, Sind?" Belka Min demanded, although with a laugh in his voice.

Sindelar had no answer beyond a sharp tap to Belka Min's bare head with the tip of her bow. Almin Bor chuckled.

"Jalor, Blaine, this is Belka Min and Sindelar, with their children Bimlis and Tris. Sindelar, believe it or not, is one of the best scouts the Faero's guard ever had. Or was," he said with a sly grin.

"I'll still track you down any day, captain," Sindelar retorted. "I would have worked it out if Belka Min had not been making so much noise up front."

"Well," Jalor said to Almin Bor. "If we're not going to Belka Min's farm, where next?"

"Asbor Jin was on the list," Almin Bor said with a shake of his head. "We can only hope that he managed to get away. If he did, he will meet at the rendezvous. There's only one other nearby, and they are two days travel away."

"You refer to Grestal Pin, I take it?" Belka Min asked.

"Aye. Have you heard anything from him?"

"He had some beasts he was taking to the citadel for sale a tenday ago," Sindelar said. "They may not have made it back to their farm yet."

"If they do then they'll have to pass the rendezvous point. We'll put the signal out and they will see it." Almin Bor considered. "No others are within easy reach except Sandyn. We should make towards the rendezvous and wait. We can swing past Sandyn's farm when we leave, if he does not come here."

"I'm anxious about Varna," Jalor replied. "I'd like to get back to Dimming Hollow soon."

"And what and where is this rendezvous?" Blaine asked?

"I understand," Almin Bor replied to Jalor. "As for the rendezvous, the Faero's guard has a number of rendezvous points around the plateau to act as meeting locations. If there is an attack then the Faeronar know to make for one of them. We leave signals in known locations and we always check them as we pass."

"We left our signal out when we left the farm," Belka Min said, nodding. "Any of the Faeronar who see it will know what to do."

"What about those who are not Faeronar?" Blaine asked.

"There are few in these parts who are not Faeronar," Almin Bor explained. "And many of those know the signals and the rendezvous also. They will come."

Jalor nodded. He would have to leave Varna in the village and trust that she would be safe. At least Hilva Nem was there and he seemed to be capable. Jalor said as much to Blaine.

"Hilva Nem?" Almin Bor and Sindelar glanced to each other and laughed quietly. "He's more than capable. Hilva Nem was my sergeant during the Escar campaign fifteen cycles ago. He's one of the best bowmen on the plateau."

"Why do you laugh?" Blaine asked, recognising the sort of easy familiarity that comes with serving in the same unit.

"He also has perhaps the foulest tongue of anyone I ever served with," Almin Bor replied with a smile. "I've seen the toughest men quake before one of his tirades. He was legendary for his insults, very inventive."

"He seemed quite mild and even tempered when I spoke with him at Dimming Hollow," Jalor said, to a snort from Sindelar.

"Wait till you see him angered," she said. "Or hear him!"

"Time is passing," Blaine said. "We should make for this rendezvous of yours and see who turns up."

"This way," Almin Bor nodded.

He glanced to Sindelar, who merely nodded and moved past the group, hand brushing Belka Min's in passing.

"Sindelar will take point," Almin Bor said. "Magwyn and Belka Min will take the centre."

Blaine smiled and said, "Jalor, perhaps you and Almin Bor can talk tactics and I'll take the drag."

"Drag?" Almin Bor asked.

"Tail end of the column," Jalor said. "It's a very old term from our home."

"Ah," Almin Bor replied.

The small column moved up the trail, back towards Almin Bor's farm.

The rendezvous proved to be off the main trail - they passed the trail leading to Almin Bor's farm without more than a glance - and up a hill via a winding route. Sindelar directed each to take a slightly different path so a firm track did not appear and so the group moved up the hill in a staggered formation. Blaine was astonished at the composure of the three children. When he commented on it to Belka Min he merely shrugged and said "They are of the Blood", as though that explained everything. Blaine was starting to see a pattern with these people of the Blood. Things that needed to be done were done. Complaints were not voiced, even if they were felt. Resilience was a quality that was valued as much as expected, as was the perfection of the skills one had. Blaine liked what he was seeing, like calling to like.

At the top of the hill the thin trail ran into a long and low wall of rock, a cliff-side for a steeper hill perhaps. Almin Bor and Sindelar signalled to stop and they walked carefully to a point that looked no different to any other part of the rock face and disappeared. Looking closely, Blaine thought he could, in fact, make out some slight change in the rock. Sindelar re-appeared and gestured to them, waiting as first Magwyn and Aldar and then Belka Min and the other two children moved past. Blaine waited as Jalor moved almost silently past. He maintained a watch down the hill and to left and right where the trail ran past. Sindelar gave a glance that Blaine recognised as an instruction to stay where he was, and then moved back down the hill, returning but a short time later.

"Obscuring the trail?" Blaine asked quietly as she moved to stand by his side.

"Yes, and placing the signal," Sindelar said. "Come."

She turned and led the way to the wall. Here, a passage came out, narrow and tight, parallel to the rock face. It seemed only to go several arm lengths into the rock but Sindelar disappeared around a corner and Blaine realised that the passage was merely the start of a tunnel. He nodded to himself. Already, this place had a ready protection, for this passage could be held against normal attackers for a long time by only a few people, given the level of weaponry he had seen so far. The passage opened a little after the initial turn, and it wound into the rock, twisting and turning. Pale light came from some sort of devices placed high on the wall, spread far enough apart that it remained a wan light. The trail trended slightly downhill. After what he thought would only have been a minute or so of walking, faint light appeared in front of him and the trail took one last turn and opened into a natural bowl. Sindelar disappeared from view.

Blaine stood on the rim of a large open space, literally a bowl with a small lake in the centre, rising to what seemed to be a natural ridge of rock surrounding it. Blaine guessed he was looking at the bowl of an extinct volcano, and the tunnel probably had been left by a lava flow that pushed out and escaped. The slope was covered by tall thin trees and grasses with long stems waving in the light breeze. The light was failing by this time and he struggled to make out the further side that was in shade. Nevertheless, a better natural hiding place Blaine had not seen in his years of service. To the right, nestled against the rocky ridge was a building, and Blaine watched as Sindelar strode to one of two windows in the front wall and spoke to someone inside.

Slowly, Blaine made his way down and across the slope, meeting a faint track that led back up the slope to the building and down in the direction of the lake. As he walked, he noted that some of the trees bore fruit and that what he thought was long grass looked like some sort of grain crop. He was nearing the door of the building when Sindelar turned from the window with four wooden buckets. Turning she tossed one and then a second to Blaine, smiling when he caught them one in each hand as though it was something he did every day.

"Come," she said as she strode past him again. "We will need water and that means carrying it up from the lake."

Blaine shrugged and turned again, following the former scout as she headed down the slope. He caught up with her half way down as they walked through a small grove of trees that were in flower, with some of the flowers having set small fruit.

"What is this place?" Blaine asked Sindelar. "And how long has it been used?"

"This is the primary rendezvous," Sindelar said. "It's called Holpenvalk, which in an older form of Ennarisi means something like a vale of hope. It's been known to the Faeronar for thousands of cycles and I have no doubt was known to our forebears long before that. The Faeronar maintain the plantings you see here, and we tend it on a rotation. The store up there has enough supplies to support a thousand people for at least a year."

"That little shed has so much storage?" Blaine turned back to where he could just make out the structure through the trees.

"It goes into the rock a bit," Sindelar laughed.

Blaine found himself enjoying this woman's company. Everything he had seen her do on the trail had been done with quiet efficiency, with no wasted effort and no uncertainty as to her role. When she had called a halt to listen to something the column had halted immediately, and when she called them forward again there was no hesitation from any of them, which indicated a depth of trust in her judgement and skills that Blaine appreciated. This was a no nonsense people and he guessed that lack of competence would be called out rather than glossed over. Sindelar obviously was good at her job.

"Here we are," she said as they approached the lake. "The level's a little higher than the last time I was here, which is good, but not too high. Sometimes you can't do this without getting soaked."

Sindelar walked into the water but it did not reach even half way up her boots. Following, Blaine saw that she was walking along a narrow stone pier that had been extended from the shore into the lake.

"Is this used for a boat?" Blaine asked as he followed her into the pier.

"Yes. There's a small row boat back in the store house also. The lake has some fish and we catch them at times. It gets overstocked if we don't harvest it occasionally. But it also means we can collect water from further in. Keeps any mud and muck out of the way."

She bent and with practised ease pushed each bucket into the water, rising again with full loads. She squeezed past Blaine as he approached the end of the pier and did likewise. Together, both started the walk back to the store house. Blaine walked easily with his burden, but a little more than half way back Sindelar called a brief halt. Placing the buckets on the ground and using her boots to stop them from overbalancing, she rolled her shoulders and stretched her back.

"Out of practice," she said in explanation. "We have a well just near the door of the house on the farm. You get spoiled not having to carry water very far."

Blaine nodded. After a short rest, Sindelar rolled her shoulders one more time and then bent and lifted the heavy buckets with a fluid grace. The two walked the rest of the way in companionable silence.

Entering the building, Blaine followed Sindelar to a stone cistern placed against one wall and emptied each bucket into it. The cistern was only a quarter full, but the small group would not need more before morning, Blaine thought. He turned to look around the room. A lamp had been lit at the back of what turned out to be a large room, giving out a surprising quantity of even light. A table stood along one wall with stools stacked on its top. The floor was stone, expertly fitted and obviously well maintained. The interior walls were - interesting.

Walking back out the door, Blaine gave the building a more detailed examination than he had when bringing the water in. He pursed his lips in surprise. The shed was not made of wood, as he expected, although there were wooden planks attached to it so it looked like it had been. Rather, beneath the wood was a smooth surface, seemingly not ravaged by time. It looked to be similar material to that which lined the inner walls. The windows were open, with shutters that would close across the opening, but again the shutters were made of the same smooth material with planks attached such that when closed they would seem to be made of wood.

Blaine walked back into the building and ran his hand down the inner wall. He looked up to see Almin Bor watching him and smiling. The former guard captain walked over.

"Most first-time visitors ask the same question. And we give the same answer. We don't know what it is or where it came from. The best guess anyone has ever had is that it was from before the rebellion. Stories among the Faeronar say that when the first users of this hide-out arrived, they found a neat stack of these materials just here, on this platform of what looks like stone." He paused while Blaine bent to run his hand along the flooring. "No, it's not stone. And no, we don't know what that is either."

"And the lights?" Jalor asked as he joined them.

"Lights?" Blaine asked.

Jalor grinned, pleased to have noticed something that his usually eagle-eyed team mate had failed to see.

"The dim lights in the passage way and this one at the back are all artificial."

"Something many people don't recognise right away," Almin Bor said mildly.

"We've seen something like it before," Jalor replied easily.

"We should stay here for a day, to give the opportunity for anyone else to come," Almin Bor stated.

"That's another day away from our friend," Jalor grimaced, glancing to Blaine who shrugged. "Still, we'll see this through."

Almin Bor nodded, as though the decision was a foregone conclusion, which Jalor thought it probably was.

Magwyn and Belka Min had put together a basic but hearty meal from the stored supplies. A large kitchen of sorts was at the back of the structure, which Jalor found slightly odd until Belka Min explained that the smoke from the fires was drawn up through tiny fractures in the rock and dissipated above the rim of the bowl. From the outside you would never know anyone was in there with a single fire going, he told them.

Exploring further, Jalor found that the huge store-room was carved from the rock behind the structure, and it was well stocked and obviously well maintained. In fact, the space carved into the wide rim was where most of the accommodation could be found. Jalor could imagine quite a large number of people living here for extended periods. Of course, this could only work if there was no aerial transport, in which case it was horribly exposed.

"We'll take turns on watch during the night," Almin Bor told the group as they finished eating. "Sindelar will show you where the watch station is and where to look for signs of concern." This latter had been to the two Warriors. "We'll be here tomorrow night also, but then plan to head to Dimming Hollow the following day. If he has not turned up, we'll detour by Sandyn's farm and gather them up, too."

23. Teller

Varna woke fully, as she usually did, and laid quite still and with eyes closed while she worked out where she was. She was on some sort of mattress, probably made of straw. The small sounds were nearby so there was someone else in the room, wherever that was. She did not get a sense of danger, but that meant nothing.

She thought back to the last thing she remembered, other than the strange dream. The three Warriors had been approaching the village. She recalled that she was struggling to maintain pace with the others and was looking forward to being able to sleep for a time. They had approached the village and she had felt bombarded with what she felt were warnings, and the urge to hide from whatever was coming. And then nothing except the dream.

So, she must be in the village. Varna guessed that she collapsed and Jalor found somewhere to stay while she slept it off. Carefully, she tested her arms and legs and felt no constraints. Then she took note that, while she still felt that strange fuzzy sensation, it seemed to have retreated a little, for which she was grateful. She felt better than she had for a couple of days, in fact.

Cautiously, Varna opened her eyes a slit and looked around as far she could see without moving her head. That was not very much. She was in a small cottage of some sort, with white walls of some sort of plaster or stucco and a thatched roof. The bed she occupied seemed to be against one wall. The sounds came from somewhere behind and to one side. Slowly, she turned her head towards the sounds, only to find a young boy sitting on a stool, staring at her.

"Ansela," The boy called.

The sounds stopped. Varna turned her head further, eyes open fully now, and saw a pretty young woman walk to her side, smiling down at her.

"Hello," the woman said. "My name is Ansela. You're in the cottage of my sister, Mansela, and her heart, Hilva Nem. And this is Mondas. Your friends left you in our care while they sought out local farm holders."

Varna nodded and tried to sit up. She managed the feat but her head was swimming and she had to steady herself with one hand.

"Don't be too concerned about that," Ansela said with a smile. "I believe you are going through an awakening, quite a bit later than most, which is why it is affecting you more than usual."

"Awakening?" Varna said, puzzling out the meaning.

"Yes. Usually, of course, the gifts show themselves when we are children, but you seem to have come into yours now. That's very unusual. I've been able to dull the effects but can't stop them entirely, I'm afraid. I'm not strong enough to do that."

Varna nodded without really understanding. She could still feel the effects of this awakening, whatever that meant in reality, but, as she thought when she awoke, it had receded. Still, now she was in a strange cottage with people she did not know and she had no idea where Jalor and Blaine were. She would have to trust their judgement that it had been safe to leave her in the care of these people. The dizziness had passed by now and Varna decided to try to stand. That lasted a very short time as the dizziness returned in a wave and she dropped back down onto the mattress, deciding to lean against the wall instead.

Ansela smiled and said, "It's likely to affect you for some time, I'm afraid. Apparently, back when the gifts were not seen to be trouble, there were people who could help others to go through this sort of thing. But we don't have them any more."

"I guess I'll just stay here, then," Varna said, holding her head very still, "and try to regain my strength. Once Jalor and Blaine get back, I'm sure we will be on our way."

"It's likely," Ansela said. "Mansela and Hilva Nem should be back soon and they may have news. Hilva Nem has reorganised the village's defence the way Jalor suggested, so hopefully that holds off those creatures if any more come."

"Tell me what happened, if you can, please?" Varna asked. "I collapsed at the gate or barrier. I'm alive, along with you, so I guess that attack failed?"

"All thanks to your friends," Ansela said, and launched into a description of the fight and the aftermath, as she had received it from Hilva Nem.

"So, the arrows bounced off some sort of armour?" Varna asked when Ansela had finished.

"Or they just broke up when they hit it. Hilva Nem said it is some sort of growth on their skin, like a heavy plate at front and back. Only your friend's arrows could penetrate it. He left some with Hilva Nem in case of another attack. Oh, and Giffin managed to wound one of them with an arrow that snuck in between a gap in the bony armour, but he said that was a lucky shot."

Starfire's arrows, Varna thought to herself. They would have been made of a composite of some sort, likely similar to what the Lightship's hull plates were made of.

"At least there are some vulnerabilities," Varna replied. "I'm glad my friends could help."

Ansela brought a mug of something to Varna.

"Here. This is a bit of soup, but I have added some salvis. It grows well around here. This should help you sleep for a while longer. I'm guessing a little here but it's likely the effects will be a little less with more sleep. It may allow the awakening to proceed more easily."

Varna took the mug and after a dubious look into the contents decided she may as well drink it. She started to feel drowsy almost immediately and lay back in the bed after handing the mug to Mondas, with her thanks. She was asleep as soon as her head hit the mattress.

She awoke to a bright dawn streaming into the cottage via an open kitchen window. A different woman was working in the kitchen area and she turned when she heard Varna stirring.

"Hello," she said warmly. "Ansela told me you had woken yesterday. I'm Mansela, by the way. That lump over there", and she pointed to a fur-wrapped pile to one side of the door, "is Hilva Nem. Mondas has gone to get some water and should be back soon."

Varna nodded, realising that she was sleeping in someone's bed. Given that Hilva Nem was sleeping by the door, she assumed it belonged to him and Mansela, or one of them.

"I'm sorry for taking one of your beds," Varna said in a low voice. "I should be okay to sleep somewhere else."

I hope, she thought, as she experimented in sitting up. That worked. There was a little bit of dizziness but it seemed to pass okay. Now for the biggie. Varna pushed herself to her feet, more than half expecting to find herself back on the mattress in short order but no, she stayed standing. She was not quite steady, so there were effects still, but she was upright at least.

"Well, definitely better," Mansela said with evident satisfaction. "And don't you worry about using the bed. You're not the first and you won't be the last. Ansela will be along soon. Come, sit at the table and we'll get something to drink."

Mansela moved to the back of the cottage where a small fire burned in the hearth. An iron kettle was hung over the flame. She picked up two mugs, gave them a cursory examination for cleanliness and carefully, using a cloth hanging by the side of the hearth, she swung out a kettle that was hung over the fire and poured a measure of whatever was in the kettle into each mug. She handed one to Varna, now sitting uncertainly on a stool at the table and then sat in a second stool.

"And don't worry about Hilva Nem, either. With the odd goings on he's taken to sleeping across the door for the last couple of nights." She took an experimental sip of her mug, made a slight face and reached for a small clay jar. "Nothing like a mug of das in the morning, but it can be a little bitter."

Varna watched as Mansela spooned what looked like honey into her mug and gave it a thorough stir. Varna took an experimental sip of her own mug. Coffee of sorts? No, something related possibly and it was quite bitter. She followed Mansela's example and added the sweetener before taking a second sip. Much better.

"So, how're you feeling? A little wobbly, I bet," Mansela asked.

"Wobbly, yes," Varna replied. "A little dizzy still and I don't feel like I'll be dancing any time soon. But it's an improvement on what I was experiencing."

"Good, good. I expect Ansela told you a little and you probably have more questions. Well, if you can hold off for a bit, I can probably get you better answers to most of your questions. We have a friend who arrived in the village last night and he's about the most knowledgeable person any of us know about the gifts and such."

At that moment the door swung open and Mondas entered, struggling to carry a wooden pale of water. He carried it across the room, being careful not to spill any and lowered it to the floor alongside the hearth. At the same time Hilva Nem stirred and rolled over, saw the two women sitting at the table. He made a performance of sniffing the air.

"Yes, yes, the das is on," Mansela said in mock exasperation. "Get yer lazy bones up and pour yerself a mug. Mondas can have a half mug today. I'll have the food done when Ansela gets here." To Varna she continued, "Ansela usually brings some greens or berries or such. She goes into the wood early to get the freshest ones before the animals feed on them."

Mondas gave a cheerful smile and reached for two mugs. As Hilva Nem poured from the kettle, still attached to the hook that hung it over the flame, the boy carefully held the mugs steady.

"I warned her against that," Hilva Nem said as he settled at the table, turning to Varna. "Well met, Varna. I'm Hilva Nem. It's been our honour to assist you and yer friends, after what they did for the village."

"Hilva Nem is the village hunter," Mansela said with obvious pride shining through. "He's the best archer in the village, or any village for some way around."

"Hmmpf, not while that Blaine is here, I'm not," Hilva Nem said with good humour. "From what Giffin told me he shot nine times at those things that attacked us and killed nine of 'em. Giffin got that lucky shot to stop one but none of his arrers even scratched 'em otherwise." Hilva Nem gestured to where his bow and quiver stood by the door. "Blaine left me with some o' his shafts. Never seen anythin' like 'em. Perfectly straight, arrer head can't be told apart from the shaft an' the flights are from no bird I ever seen."

Varna nodded, thinking fast. "We have some master craftsmen that make high quality bows and arrows," she said. "I'm glad they were able to help. I know I was no help."

"Ah, never mind that," Hilva Nem said. "Mansela tells me yer goin' through an awakenin'. That's pretty special but don't be sayin' anythin' much about it outside o' this cottage. Most people in these parts remain afraid o' the gifts." He snorted. "As though it's the gift that is evil. None of them listen to the stories careful enough. Was people that went bad not the gifts. Anyway, better for yer to say nothin' about it to anyone else. Oh, except Flin. He should be along in a bit and he'll probably give us some stories tonight."

"He's here now," Ansela said as she pushed the door open and entered, followed by a tall, much older man who had to stoop somewhat to fit through the door.

The cottage was crowded now. As Mansela stood to take a travel pack from the newcomer, Ansela made herself at home with a mug of das.

"Flin!" Mansela welcomed the newcomer as she stood and hugged him. "It's been too long!"

Hilva Nem likewise welcomed Flin with a firm right arm clasp. Varna winced at the firmness of the clasp for someone who appeared to be quite advanced in age, but Flin seemed to experience no ill consequence.

"Mansela, Hilva Nem, well met to you both," Flin said heartily. "Hello Mondas. You've grown from the last time I saw you."

Mondas gave Flin an inscrutable look that told everyone that he had no memory of seeing this man before. His parents laughed at their son's expression.

Flin turned to Varna and bowed from the waist, the movement imbued with a certain elegance that surprised Varna. She gave him a nod in return. The older man sat the table, accepting a mug of das from Ansela.

Mansela smiled and said, "Flin is a travelling Teller. He stops by on occasion and spends time with us. Well, with Ansela, truth be told."

"As a friend," Ansela said quickly, to a smile from Flin. "But a good friend."

"And a friend to the Blood," Hilva Nem said softly.

"Well, it must have been three or four cycles since I was here last," Flin said to Mansela. "What news from the bustling centre of Ennaris that is Dimming Hollow?"

"Ah, let me think," Mansela said with a wry smile. "Giffin had an ingrown toe nail two cycles ago, and Herdis broke his arm falling off a log when drunk. That was one cycle ago." She made a face like she was thinking hard. "That's about it."

There were chuckles all around at the acknowledgement that little changed in the small village.

"Except for the fact that we were attacked by some sort of strange creatures two days ago," Hilva Nem said into the mix.

"Strange creatures?" Flin asked, one eyebrow raised.

"Some sort of odd mix of man and animal, mostly seemed to be kussar. But they had a strange bony armour on their chest and back, and their skin was tougher than anythin' I've seen. They had terribly made weapons but were almost impossible to stop." Hilva Nem shook his head.

"If it weren't for Varna's friends, we'd all be dead," Mansela added soberly. "Our arrers just bounced off them or broke. Only Blaine's arrers could stop 'em. We lost two men to them as it was."

Flin's attention had sharpened when the blend of man and kussar was mentioned. He looked from Hilva Nem to Mansela to Varna and back to Hilva Nem again.

"Do you have any of these creatures that I can see?" Flin asked.

"We burned 'em and buried what was left. I guess we could dig 'em up but I'm not sure you'd get too much." Hilva Nem considered. "I could get Giffin to draw one fer yer."

"I have a better idea," Flin said as he drew his pack towards him from where Mansela had put it near the door.

He rummaged through the pack and finally drew a small book from it. He flicked through the book and found a loose page that he extracted and laid on the table. On the page was drawn a rendering of a creature, half man and half something that to Varna seemed to be between a goat and some other beast. The image showed it glowering. The sheer strength of the creature was evident even in the drawing.

"Is this what they looked like?" Flin asked.

Varna, not having seen the creatures, picked up the page. She struggled to contain her surprise when she felt the unmistakable feel of plasfilm or something very similar. Certainly, it was nothing that this planet should be able to produce.

"Aye," Hilva Nem replied. "That's pretty much what we burned. There were ten of 'em. Is that one of yer special drawin's? Or did you get that done just recently?"

"It's one of my special drawings," Flin replied, distractedly. "It's called a ghazrak. And you say one of Varna's friends was able to kill them? Using what sort of arrow?"

Before Varna could find a way to stop him, Hilva Nem stood, took two steps to where his quiver sat against the wall and pulled one of the *Starfire* arrows from it. He handed it to Flin as he sat again.

"This is one o' Blaine's arrers," he said. "They cut through that armour like it weren't there."

Flin turned the arrow over in his hands, feeling the material. His expression was neutral.

"The workmanship of this arrow is exceptional," he said. "Is this ... er ... wood normal where you are from, Varna?"

"Pretty much," Varna replied, as though it was an everyday discussion, and decided to turn the tables back on the Teller. "But I've never felt anything like this."

She handed the drawing back to Flin. He nodded as he put it back into his book, which Varna thought had more pages of the same material.

"It is a drawing on a sort of paper from before the rebellion," Flin said, to gasps from Mansela and Ansela. "We have forgotten how to make this sort of material."

"But that's over five thousand cycles ago," Hilva Nem said. "I've seen some of yer pages before but never guessed you had anything that valuable."

"Valuable?" Flin smiled gently. "It is the image that is important, not what it's drawn on. Those creatures were thought to be long gone. I will need to take this news to the Citadel. The Faero must know of this."

"Aye, that's a good idea," Ansela said. "But you remember I asked you to have a look at Varna here. I'm sure she's goin' through th'awakening. I've done what I can do but she had suffered somewhat fer it. I thought you could help." Ansela turned to Varna. "Flin has a knowledge of many things from the old times. And his skill with herbs is like nothin' I've ever seen. If anyone can help you get past this it will be Flin."

"Awakening?" Flin looked at Varna in surprise.

"Aye," Ansela replied with a nod of affirmation. "You know I understand that sort o' thing, Flin, an' trust me when I say that Varna is sufferin' from a delayed awakening. I thought you might be able to help her."

Flin looked at Ansela, eyebrow raised.

"With, you know, some o' yer herbs," Ansela replied, staring Flin in the eye, one of her own eyebrows raised in mimic of Flin.

Varna followed the exchange. She was sure there was an undertone of something, some knowledge that these two shared and to which she was not privy. That was confirmed, to her at least, when Flin smiled wryly and nodded.

"I will see what I can do," the old Teller replied.

"Herbs?" Varna asked. "If this is some sort of weird condition how will herbs help?"

"Fact is, we don't have much other than herbs and traditional remedies for some o' these conditions. And some people understand 'em better than others. Flin is one who does." Ansela shrugged. "Stories, including those that Flin tells, are that long ago, before the rebellion destroyed the land, we could have cured pretty much anything using some sort of machines, but that was then."

Flin nodded. "Indeed, Ennaris was a much different place then. But we do what we can do now. I will have to gather some fresh herbs to supplement my dried ones for this. It's not a cure, mind. It's more something to dampen the effects. If you come to gifts late the effects can linger for many tendays."

"Ansela said she had never known of this before," Varna said to Flin. "Have you?"

"Not for a long time," Flin said. "Unfortunately, the people of Ennaris, in their ignorance, sought to stamp out the gifts after the rebellion and they very nearly succeeded." His expression turned grave. "Many good people died during those dark days. Many gifts were lost that could have helped Ennaris recover from the damage done. And since then, signs of gifts have been hidden in fear of their discovery resulting in persecution once again. So, we don't see many gifts very often and strong gifts much less than that."

"And these gifts take several different forms?" Varna asked, curious.

"Many and varied," Flin replied. "As many variations as there are people with gifts. Each person may have different strengths in gifts, differing combinations of gifts with different strengths between them, or no gifts at all."

"What causes them?"

"We're not sure. Even the very old traditions were not sure. There was speculation that it was something to do with the planet's rotation or magnetic profile or such, but no-one seems to be sure."

"The Guardians," Mansela put in.

"Guardians?" Varna asked.

"Beings of legend," Flin said smiling. "The mythical beings who caused Ennaris to be formed as you see it today, or rather, as it was before the rebellion. We have many stories of the Guardians and how they created Ennaris from near to nothing, how they made the Ennarisi the leading beings of the galaxy. They are entertaining stories."

"The Guardians are real," Mansela maintained. "The old Guides and Mages were the helpers of the Guardians and made Ennaris a paradise." She sighed. "I would have liked to see that."

"It was a paradise compared to today," Flin agreed. "But it had its own problems, as the rebellion showed. The Guides and Mages worked for the good of Ennaris, but it was those Mages who sought power for themselves who were the cause of the rebellion's damage, also." He shook his head and grimaced. "So many good people died and Ennaris regressed to almost no civilisation at all."

"Well, perhaps that's a story fer tonight," Hilva Nem said. "Meanwhile, work awaits."

"And I'll search out those herbs," Flin declared. "I will return before the evening meal. We can tell some stories, sing some songs and I will see if I can ease the effects of Varna's awakening before we retire for the night."

24. Kunas

In an eyrie high above the world, perched on the peaks of the highest mountain range on Ennaris, called the Peaks by most although known as the Torish Range on ancient maps, were the homes of the great Rocs. These massive and highly intelligent birds had been friends and companions to the Ennarisi for such a long time before the rebellion and its disastrous aftermath that so greatly changed Ennaris, but they had since become nought but legend and myth among the remainder of those people, with the exception of the few hardy souls living close to and on the mountain slopes. In being forgotten they had, themselves, become lost and aimless. No longer could they share in the tasks of keeping Ennaris safe for its inhabitants. They continued over the long cycles to train for war and patrol the skies based on established habit, but the young Rocs were restless, as young ones always are, and wanted more than merely to hunt the mountain voles and watch the suns rise and set. Over the endless cycles since the rebellion, the Rocs had withdrawn almost completely and they were less for it.

Their numbers had been in decline for many cycles, and some had thought the Rocs would die out. They had consolidated their eyries from five to one. In recent times, however, more fledglings had hatched and the hopes of the Rocs had lifted.

Ar-kunya was perched on his usual ledge overlooking a dizzying height, reflecting on the sad history of Ennaris since the time of the rebellion. Far below, his sharp eyesight could pick out mountain glims, with their woolly coats and short horns, leaping from ledge to rock to ledge as they foraged, while further out across the peaks the occasional

Roc would leap into the air, plummet towards the far distant ground and rise in the thermals, sometimes clutching a prize but often just for sport. The joint leader of the Rocs was considering recent events of which he had heard rumour from the people of the low lands, for despite being forgotten by most the Rocs had continued to maintain an interest over these long millennia. A waning interest, it was true, which was one of the problems to be addressed. The rumours told of a battle being fought in the near past by strange beings but with no survivors being seen, and of half men-half beasts roaming the land more recently, of old tales being revived and old prophesies being remembered.

Rocs live to a great age but none now alive were alive during the rebellion, nor were there any who knew those who had been. However, all knew the stories of the Rocs who swept down from their heights to rescue the people as their land crumbled and burned around them, of the heroic battles as the Mage Guides and the non-Mage Guides attempted to halt the destruction and, when that proved fruitless, to limit its extent amid great losses to themselves. The Rocs remembered those who fought and perished alongside the Council of Mages. Of the Roc warriors who fought the demon-spawn that had been created by the rebels. Of those who had flown with Ennaris' greatest Battle Mage as she and the remnants of the Council tried and failed to halt the destruction, even while defeating the rebel Mages. So many Rocs perished in those battles, fighting alongside their Ennarisi friends. To have been forgotten after that was painful for most Rocs, although they were aware that their former companions had forgotten many things. The Rocs, however, did not forget.

Now Ar-kunya could feel change coming. The prescient quality of the Rocs produced agitation among the flocks but also evoked anticipation, of what no-one could say. Sitting on his ledge, Ar-kunya contemplated what might happen should that anticipation prove to have no grounds. The young Rocs, he was sure, would degenerate and their society would fracture, despite the natural discipline which had been built into them over the eons of working with the Guides and Mages.

He had used the current feeling that something was about to happen to tighten their training, to return to some of the old disciplines in preparation, but for what? Without a goal the gains would be short-lived. Ar-kunya contemplated an uncertain future for the Rocs.

A brilliant flash caught his attention. Something streaked through the atmosphere of Ennaris. It was very high but coming close. Ar-kunya was seized by a sudden impulse and sent out the telepathic call for an urgent session, a call that reached all Rocs and directed them to attend the meeting ground immediately. Such a call had not gone out in the memory of the oldest living Roc. The flashing light disappeared among the tall peaks but there was no sound of impact, no detonation telling of a space rock or something else crashing to ground.

At the meeting ground a short time later, Ar-kunya and El-arwe, his mate and joint leader, perched on the ceremonial stone, waiting for quiet from the assembled Rocs when a glowing ball rose over the rim of the bowl in which the meeting ground was set and moved towards them. Several Rocs became alarmed and moved to intercept the object - retreat did not enter into the thoughts of a Roc - but were stopped by Ar-kunya. He examined the ball of light closely and then, with a gesture to El-arwe, jumped from the ceremonial rock to stand on the floor of the meeting ground. She followed him.

The light mounted the stone, flared very brightly and faded to show a massive Roc. It was sleek and jet black, and stood upright facing the assembled Rocs. None present had ever seen Kunas but all knew instinctively that it was he, the Guardian who included all of the birds of Ennaris under his protection, all those of the heights and eyries, of the skies and all those who inhabited them. Every Roc bowed in submission. Awe caused wings to shift and feathers to ruffle.

At last, Ar-kunya thought jubilantly. *At long last.*

Kunas looked over the Rocs assembled before him. He knew none of them, of course, for his old companions were long gone. He felt a pang of loss, even though he knew it would be so. But he also saw into the hearts of those around him, and knew they were strong, as willing to protect as those Rocs of old, even though many of them were impatient and uncertain.

My friends, he sent to them via the telepathic channel all Rocs shared, I have been away for too long, and for that I am deeply sorry. Know that it was not by preference but by necessity that we had to leave the Ennarisi to their uncertain fate. Your ancestors suffered with the ground-dwellers and the water-dwellers. But I see that you have held true through the ages. Now the time has come. The Guardians return. The Children of Ennaris have returned, as was foretold. Your time is at hand to return to the ken of the Ennarisi, to provide assistance and guidance, to foster once again the friendship that held sway so long ago. Prepare, my friends, for your aid will be greatly needed. We prepare for the final battle.

The Rocs swelled with pride. Their wings were held outstretched. They overlapped and filled the huge meeting ground with a riot of every colour imaginable. Ar-kunya and El-arwe joined with their flock mates as they lifted their heads and the battle cry of the Rocs rose into the skies of Ennaris, such that once caused the strongest enemies to quail. The great hook-beaked belgars heard the cry and wondered, for they had never heard the like but their racial memories made them tremble with joy. The black caws, those ancient friends of evil, heard the cry and wondered, and their racial memories made them tremble with fear.

Yet Ar-kunya was troubled still. For in the past when the Rocs went to war, they were accompanied by the Alnar-kun, the battle Mages who fought from aback the Rocs, forming formidable pairings.

The Mages of Ennaris were decimated. Where would the Alnar-kun be found?

Be at ease, Ar-kunya, Kunas sent to the Roc co-leader. You will do battle with what you have, and whether you have the Alnar-kun or not, the Rocs of Ennaris will fight well.

Ar-kunya acknowledged the rightness of that sending. After such a long time, the great Rocs, ancient and steadfast friends and allies of the Ennarisi, were united in their determination and would give a good account, with or without the Alnar-kun. The Guardians were return-ing. The last battle with the ancient evil was coming. The great Rocs would be ready, as they always had been.

25. Reunion

The slight motion alerted Blaine. He was about half way through his shift at the entrance to the passage way when he saw the slight movement almost half way from the road to the cliff. He had been watching carefully in the dark, with the wan light of the larger moon, Varis, casting just enough light to create faint shadows. It was also, he realised, just enough light to allow him to see when those shadows changed. He had been told where to look to see movement, locations where refugees or attackers would have to pass in order to reach the cliff passage.

Slowly, Blaine moved back in the small alcove in which he had settled about one hour earlier. He reached for the pull rope and gave it two tugs, then moved back towards the entrance, easing his sword from the scabbard, very slowly to make sure there was no noise. He held the sword at this side, point down, blade stretched along his leg. Straining his eyes, he thought that he could make out several figures making their stealthy way to the entrance, moving with the surety that told Blaine that they knew their destination. That probably meant they were refugees, but Blaine was too experienced to make any assumptions and waited without making his presence known.

The first figure reached the top of the slope and was at the edge of the cleared area between the last of the shrubs and the cliff face. Sindelar had explained to Blaine and Jalor that a stretch of about twenty paces depth was kept clear of vegetation along the cliff face. Blaine watched as the figure crouched and stayed motionless for a long time. Blaine nodded to himself, approving. Whoever this was he - or she, perhaps, but Blaine felt the figure was male - knew what he was doing. The figure put one hand to his mouth and made a sound like a warbling bird song. Blaine relaxed. That was the signal Sindelar had taught him. Blaine waited for a count of five, scanning along the slope to the road in a single look, and then stepped from the alcove into the moonlight, and back again.

Immediately the figure rose and gestured behind him. Blaine was sure the figure was male now. He moved quickly but with no noise to the cliff wall and waited. From the undergrowth at several parts of the vegetation line figures moved, adults and children. Every adult carried a weapon, as did many of the larger children. As the first reached the passage Sindelar stepped out, having been summoned via the pull rope, and shepherded the newcomers into the passage. Blaine counted twelve newcomers, then thirteen as the first man made his way to where Sindelar stood still, clasped arms silently and entered the passage. Sindelar turned to where she knew Blaine stood and nodded before she, too, entered the passage. Blaine settled down again to watch.

Morning saw greater bustle around the shelter as the larger number of people went about getting fed and preparing for the day to come. Blaine had handed over to Belka Min after his stint and awoke to find Almin Bor and Jalor discussing the day's activities.

"So, we stay for a short while in case there are stragglers and then head for Dimming Hollow," Jalor was saying as Blaine walked to where the two men stood, just under the small overhang at the front of the shelter.

"Aye, I think that's best," Almin Bor replied. "With Welkis and Formel and their families we have a sizeable party. Too large to be unnoticed now. But it gives us greater strength also."

"Are they fighters?" Blaine asked.

"Every one of the Blood is a fighter," Almin Bor replied, the slight edge to his statement reflecting pride in his people. "But Welkis was in the Guard and Formel's Jilnar was in Escar's foot army." The twist of his lips indicated what he thought of that army. "But she's one of the better ones, almost as good as Magwyn in a fight."

"Magwyn?" Blaine asked, surprised.

"Every woman and man of the Blood learns to fight. All develop one or two primary skills, usually sword and bow. Magwyn is a good archer but I have never seen her defeated with the knife." Almin Bor's voice again reflected pride.

"Why are the Blood so prepared for defence or battle?" Jalor asked. "It's obvious that great effort goes into being prepared, but for what?"

"The Prophecy," Almin Bor said.

Seeing that meant nothing to either Jalor or Blaine he smiled and shook his head.

"Your cover story needs work, wherever you're from," Almin Bor said wryly. "Everyone on Ennaris knows of the Prophecy. It's said Goroth will come again and Ennaris will join behind the Faero for the final battle, for the life of Ennaris and the galaxy. And the Blood will be called to lead the final attack." He nodded emphatically to himself. "And so, we will be ready."

Jalor considered for a moment, glancing around the bowl at the activity under way. Some were preparing food. Others were starting the process to tidy the bowl. Several were making minor repairs on the pier in the lake. Children were helping or playing, but none were making any noise to mention.

"So are the Blood and the Faeronar the same?"

"All of the Blood are Faeronar," Almin Bor said. "Not all Faeronar are of the Blood."

Jalor nodded his understanding. So, the Blood were a subgroup, proud and, he expected, quite fierce when provoked, but peaceful otherwise. The inherited dedication for the whole subgroup to hold themselves in preparedness was nothing he had encountered before. But then again, he was fairly sure this entire mission would be like nothing else either. There were huge gaps in his understanding of the situation, and he was fairly sure the Admiral dropped the team onto Ennaris knowing that they would be forced to puzzle it out. Certainly, their cover story had not lasted any time at all, and yet Almin Bor for one seemed to take it in his stride.

"Tell me, Almin Bor," Jalor asked after a moment, "who would be able to tell me more about what is happening across Ennaris?"

"That would be the Tellers," he replied. "Another thing all Ennarisi would know, by the way."

Almin Bor waited, eyes never still as he surveyed the bowl, moving from rim to lake and to the far rim, then back again.

"When we can tell you we will," Jalor said. "I appreciate the trust you have demonstrated given you just met us."

"You have fought for and protected the Blood, and we do not forget," Almin Bor said, rising easily. "But make no mistake, Jalor, if you seek to damage Ennaris or the Faero you will be fighting the Blood."

Almin Bor moved to help one of the children who was struggling up the slope with a bucket of water slopping over the top. Jalor turned to Blaine, who returned a lop-sided grin. He liked these people and he did not want to fight them.

The party was prepared to move out of the bowl when the warning signal rattled - it was a simple device of a stoppered clay jar with pebbles inside - and another couple appeared at the opening. At the signal the older children had gathered the younger to one side while their parents dropped travel packs and placed hands on their variety of weapons. They all relaxed when one of the figures waved and the two started down the slope.

"Rengis Kar and Ursil," Almin Bor said to Jalor. "They are from the side of the plateau close to the farthest edge." He gestured back in the direction of his own farm. "They must have set out before we did."

The newcomers arrived at the small bench in front of the shelter and dropped their own travel packs. Rengis Kar proved to be a tall, strapping, younger man with dark shaggy hair and beard, while Ursil was a shorter woman, lean and blonde.

"Almin Bor," Rengis Kar exclaimed, holding out one arm to be clasped. "We saw your signal and came as fast as we could. You're just packing up?"

"It's good to see you both. You must have left your farm three days ago to be here now," Almin Bor replied as he returned the arm clasp. "Did you see any others?"

"Aye, we did. What with the attacks on the outer farms we decided we could not protect our place. Especially as Ursil is with child," he said with a smile, causing a round of congratulations, hugs and pats on the back to ensue.

When he had a chance to speak again, he grimaced.

"We saw smoke from near Asbel's farm and there was no indicator at his trail. We didn't investigate, though," he continued to nods from the group. "Gril and Sebol had their signs out, so I'm assuming they managed to get away. I expect we'll find them at the Citadel. Welkis and Formel are here. I saw your signs." This to nods from the two mentioned.

"Asbor Jin may have been attacked," Almin Bor replied bleakly. "Belka Min saw smoke over that way, and we saw no sign. It doesn't mean they're dead though. We'll pick up Sandyn when we leave here, assuming they're okay. Meanwhile, we can spare some time while you refresh yourselves, but we'll have to move soon."

Soon meant a very short time. Rengis Kar and Ursil had a quick meal and were ready to go in a quicker time than Blaine had seen from professional soldiers. The group now numbered twenty, with eight children in that number, most very young. As Almin Bor had laid out, Sindelar led out followed by Jilnar, then the main body of the group with the children in the centre and most of the adults led by Almin Bor ringing them. Rengis Kar and Blaine brought up the rear. Jalor walked behind the group of children.

The troop made frequent stops at what Blaine thought would be hourly intervals, mainly to give the younger children the chance to rest. None of the children were carried, with the exception of Jilnar's babe in arms, and she was passed from adult to adult as they travelled in the main group while the others all maintained a watch on the children and the passing country-side. The walk was uneventful, though tense, and by the mid-afternoon they had reached a trail that Almin Bor said led to Sandyn's farm.

After some debate it was decided that the group would wait and Almin Bor, Magwyn, Jalor and Blaine would make the short detour to the farm and bring them out if they were still there. The rest would be in a small meadow a little off the road further in the direction of Dimming Hollow.

The clouds thickened as the group climbed up a small heavily wooded ridge and then down the other side, pausing at the crest to take a careful look around the land below. It was a wild landscape, with knife-edge ridges marching into the distance ahead of them. To the left there was, far away, a range of mist-shrouded mountains, the crests invisible in the gloomy light. Probably in the clouds anyway, Jalor thought. At a long distance to the right, he could see what looked like a bare patch in the forest, with a splash of yellow.

"The citadel," Almin Bor said when Jalor pointed it out. "We are about four days march to there from here directly, but the way we go it will take a tenday at best."

Nodding, Jalor gestured for Almin Bor to lead the way. Before mid-morning they arrived at the farm of Sandyn. Here, instead of a free-standing cottage as they had found at Almin Bor's farm, they were faced with a palisade of logs, shaped to points at the top and embedded in the earth. A single gate provided access and when they approached, they heard a dog - or at least an animal that sounded like a dog - barking.

"Whatever you want, we don't need, so move on," a harsh voice called from inside the gate.

"Sandyn, it's Almin Bor. Open your blasted gate and let us in. These are friends."

"How do I know you're Almin Bor?" Sandyn challenged. "Anyone can say that."

"You lame-brained son of a yog-farmer, open the damned gate before I kick it down and hang you from your own wall," Almin Bor shouted.

"Well, you sound like Almin Bor, alright," came the reply from inside the palisade. "I guess I can take the chance."

The gate was opened to reveal a heavyset, muscular man with a shock of red hair and a bushy ginger beard framing a round face. He was wearing a leather jerkin and held a broadsword to his side, ready to bring it up if necessary. After the party moved inside a heavy timber was replaced in the brackets to each side of the gate.

"Where's the other one?" Sandyn asked suspiciously, having clasped forearms with Almin Bor in greeting and now looking around the group.

"Here," said Blaine, standing behind Sandyn. The latter started and then glanced at Almin Bor and shrugged.

"Well, at least I know you're not with those black ones that have been killing people," Sandyn sighed. "How did you get in?"

"I scaled the wall," Blaine replied blandly, "and just waited till you opened the gate."

Sandyn glared at the small dog-like creature who subsided, embarrassed it seemed, to the ground. "That wall is higher than two grown men," he growled.

"Yes, it is." Blaine left it at that, but his meaning was clear. If he could get over it so could others.

"Sandyn, we've come to get you to move. You know there've been attacks. We think they're targeting the Blood." Almin Bor scratched his head. "You know the old gifts are returning and these people don't want them to. And they're not quite men."

Jalor cocked his head to look at Almin Bor at mention of the gifts, but the latter was frowning at Sandyn.

"Aye, Captain, I've been thinking of moving but haven't been too sure. What made you pack up and leave?"

"Being attacked in my own home," Almin Bor said bitterly. "If it was not for Jalor and Blaine, we wouldn't be here to tell the tale."

"You beat them off? I've heard they don't quit." Sandyn still was not completely sure of the strangers.

"They killed them all," Almin Bor said softly, nodding as Sandyn rounded to stare at him. "Ten of them."

"Where are you heading?"

"The citadel," Almin Bor replied. "There's a group that met up at Holpenvalk. They're waiting for us in the small glade just up the road toward Dimming Hollow. We'll go there and then the Citadel. And we need to move. We can be fairly sure there are more of the creature-men around. We stopped by another farm between our one and here and found tracks, made after the fight at our place."

"Well, that sounds grand," Sandyn said, "and I've been preparing, but I have a problem."

"Magnor?" Magwyn chimed in for the first time, looking to the cottage. "I'll see how she is." She moved off without awaiting a reply.

"Magwyn's sister," Almin Bor explained to Jalor. "She is with child and it has been difficult. Can she travel?" This to Sandyn.

"We may have to carry her. I'm not sure the hrss will be any better than walking." He shook his head worriedly. "And, of course, we have Andry and Eldry."

Jalor experienced a sinking feeling. A pregnant woman with difficulties travelling and, he assumed, two more children. "How old are your children?" he asked.

"Three cycles and five cycles," Sandyn replied.

"Okay, how ready are you to go?" Jalor reclaimed his calm demeanour with an effort.

"If Magnor is okay and we get the kiddies ready then we can go almost immediately. Snout is good on the trail, even if not so good at knowin' when someone comes over a wall." He glared afresh at the dog-like animal, and then sighed. "Let's just put a food pack together. It's almost done anyway."

Jalor accompanied Sandyn and Almin Bor to the house, while Blaine looked around the enclosed compound. There was a competent look to the buildings. It was obviously quite old but was in good repair. The gardens were lush and packed with fresh herbs, vegetables and what looked like fruit trees to Blaine's alien eyes. He was standing there when Eldry, the five cycles old girl, stepped from the house and started to walk through the garden, hands trailing along the leaves of the plants, caressing the fruit trees.

Sandyn and his heavily pregnant wife, Magnor, accompanied by the rest of the group hurried from the house, with Sandyn carrying a small boy. Moving to join them, Blaine still watched Eldry as she moved around the garden, touching each and every plant, herb, bush and tree.

"Saying goodbye, she is," Sandyn said sadly. "Many of them will not make it through the time we are likely to be away but she's trying to give them strength to get through."

"Is she speaking to them?" Blaine asked, intrigued.

"Aye, that she is, and they like it." Sandyn smiled at Blaine's raised eyebrows. "'Tis true, the plants respond to her speaking to them and singing to them. I never seen the like. 'Tis her gift."

Eldry finished her farewell and moved to join the small group. Sandyn pulled the gate to and manipulated a lever through a slot. Blaine heard the log slip into place.

"Not that it will stop too many of those black bastards," Sandyn said, "but it may keep the wild animals out in the meantime."

It was late afternoon when they re-joined the road and immediately Blaine held up one hand. Pointing to the road surface he commenced a careful scrutiny of the road in both directions and then the surrounding woodland. Jalor took one look at the road and turned to Almin Bor. In the dust of the road were tracks that were not made by normal feet, and there looked to be a group of them. Blaine pointed in the direction of Dimming Hollow.

"The glade," Almin Bor muttered.

"No more than ten ahead," Blaine said. "We can catch them up."

"Not with Magnor like this," Sandyn said. "Can you stop them?"

"With Blaine's arrows we can," Almin Bor replied.

"Then go," Sandyn said. "We'll follow and await you further up the road."

Almin Bor glanced to Jalor and then nodded. Blaine drew five arrows from his quiver and handed them to Sandyn.

"These will stop those creatures, but you need to hit them as high in the chest as you can. Your bow can't put the same weight behind them as mine so you may not be able to penetrate as easily."

Sandyn took the arrows and examined them, eyes wide as he felt the smooth shafts and strange flights. Meanwhile, Blaine counted the remainder of the arrows and handed another five to Magwyn.

"I'm told you can shoot," Blaine said.

Magwyn nodded in mute answer and took the offered arrows, fitting four of them into a small quiver that hung at her side. She held one in hand, already slotting it to the bowstring.

With a nod the four started a steady jog up the road. Blaine and Almin Bor kept a watchful eye on the surroundings as they ran. They quickly reached a point where the tracks milled around and Blaine pointed to the side closest to the meadow.

"They stopped for a moment and then headed in," he said.

"Smell," Almin Bor replied. "They could smell them."

Blaine nodded and led the way into the undergrowth, following the trail of damaged brush and trampled ground cover. The attackers made no effort at stealth but blundered through the underbrush in a straight line, lending credence to their ability to somehow sense their prey. Smell seemed likely, Jalor thought.

They were almost too late.

The line of ten half-man creatures were lumbering towards the small group on the far side of the small meadow. The men and women of the party were standing in front of the children with weapons in hand. Belka Min and Rengis Kar were firing arrow after arrow but Jalor was sure they would do no good. The two men came to the same conclusion, dropping their bows and drawing short swords.

Blaine skidded to a stop, bow in hand. Magwyn separated from him, sprinting to the left to provide a different angle. Blaine's first two shafts were on their way before she stopped and lined up her first. Blaine's third and fourth were sent while she aimed and let her second fly. The first two of Blaine's shafts found their targets at the base of the skulls of the leading creatures. His third lodged in the shoulder and the fourth penetrated the back plate of his target. It staggered the creature but did not stop it. Magwyn's first speared through the heavier muscle on one hip and caused it to collapse, while her second bounced off a back plate. She gave a muttered oath and picked up her quiver to dash forward, moving closer so the arrows arrived with more force.

Their counter-attack served the purpose, however. The lumbering charge faltered. Two were dead and three more wounded, one unable to move. The rest turned to see where the attack came from. One of them gave a grunted command and the two other wounded with one unwounded continued to move towards the defending group. The other four turned back. Blaine sent one more arrow into the back of the uninjured one attacking the group. It would not kill but might slow the creature enough to give the defenders an edge.

Almin Bor had moved across to stand with Magwyn. Two of the creatures resumed their charge, this time at Magwyn and Almin Bor. The other two ran at Jalor and Blaine. Magwyn took careful aim and fired at one when only twenty paces away. Her shaft penetrated deep into the chest and the beast crashed to the turf. She reached for the second last arrow as Almin Bor stepped in front of her, sword and long knife held firm and steady. The second attacker raised its crude sword and brought it crashing down. Almin Bor held his own sword, forged long before he was born, and turned the attacking swipe to one side, causing the creature to turn slightly also. Quick as a striking slither, Almin Bor's knife dashed in and out of the attacker's side where the breast and back plates left a small gap.

Behind him, Magwyn slowly scrambled backward, bow in one hand and the last two *Starfire* arrows in the other. The creature was enraged at being stabbed and swung its sword in a continuous barrage. Lack of form was more than made up for by sheer aggression and power. Almin Bor stepped back and away from Magwyn, moving in an arc. He could barely turn the attacks, such was their ferocity. He knew if he tried to block one the power of the strike would be likely to break through, so he tried to turn that power against his foe. With a grunt of effort, the creature swung on overhand stroke that slid down Almin Bor's blade, glancing off his shoulder's chain mail and staggering him. He went to one knee to hold balance. The creature roared and lifted his sword for the killing strike and faltered as Magwyn's arrow punched through the bone chest armour, a little off centre. Almin Bor pushed himself forward, thrusting his sword up and into the gap Blaine had described between the chest armour and the thicker muscle of the lower thighs, where the creature's short kilt began. The creature dropped its sword, grunted again and fell to the side, dead.

Almin Bor nodded to Magwyn and looked to Jalor and Blaine. One of their two beasts was down with two arrows sticking out from its head. Jalor was picking himself up but seemed mostly unhurt. The second was swinging hard and fast at Blaine, who was barely holding his own. Blaine's captured sword was of reasonable quality, especially compared with the thick and blunt blade wielded by his opponent, but it was not of the quality of Almin Bor's. With an effort Almin Bor heaved his sword from the side of the dead creature and stood. He ran towards Blaine, marvelling at the man's ability to slide around or slip to one side of the attacker's lusty strokes. Once again, brute force and aggression made up for lack of skill, and Blaine was forced to defend rather than launch any form of attack. Blaine flicked a glance to Almin Bor who held up his sword. Blaine nodded, ducked a wild swipe and gestured with his head to a vague point behind him. Understanding, Almin Bor dashed five metres behind Blaine and thrust his sword point first into the turf, then backed away with long knife in hand.

Magwyn sprinted towards the small group of defenders. The wounded creatures had, indeed, been slowed enough to be engaged by the more experienced defenders. Magwyn slowed, worked rapidly through a set of breathing exercises learned many cycles before to slow her heart beat. She slotted the last of Blaine's arrows and let it fly at the nearest of the attacking creatures, which was engaged in an enraged onslaught against Welkis. Her shaft caught it under the arm raised to strike and punched deep into the creature, which shuddered and collapsed. Black blood gushed from the wound.

Welkis glanced to Magwyn, nodded shortly, then turned and ran his sword through the creature fighting Rengis Kar, looking for and finding the same spot where Magwyn's arrow entered. Both men turned to see Belka Min standing over the prone body of Formel, defending desperately from the enraged attack that seemed to be characteristic of these strange half man, half beast attackers. The two men separated and came at the creature from both sides, both stabbing their swords in the side gaps between the armoured plates. The creature staggered backwards a pace before falling, taking both swords with it.

Blaine, meanwhile, had backed away from his attacker. The latter blindly followed, grunting something unintelligible to Blaine. He suspected it was some form of challenge, but may have merely been an expression of the ever-present rage. Blaine's sword was badly notched, showing its relatively poor construction. It held together still, which surprised him, but would not last for much longer. He felt the hilt of Almin Bor's sword at the back of his leg and spun. With one swift movement, Blaine shifted the captured sword to his left hand and grasped Almin Bor's sword, pulling it from the ground. His spin took him slightly out of the line of attack and the creature was put off balance as it swung a huge downward strike. Blaine caught it with both swords crossed but, instead of backing away as he had been doing, he stepped to the right, taking his opponent further off balance. Two lightning-fast strokes followed. With the first Almin Bor's blade sliced through the creature's left thigh. As it reacted to that injury, Blaine stepped in and thrust the other sword upwards through the lower jaw and into the brain. The sword shattered as it met the hard bone of the upper skull, but the damage was done. The creature collapsed.

It was a sombre group that joined Sandyn and Magnor on the road to Dimming Hollow. A rough stretcher had been constructed, on which was laid Formel's body. Jilnar walked alongside the stretcher, one hand resting on Formel's arm. The older of their two children, bewildered at what had happened, was carried by Magwyn, while the babe was carried by Ursil. The men of the troop took their turn carrying the stretcher front and back.

The walk to Dimming Hollow was slow, in part owing to Magnor's advanced pregnancy. Both Welkis and Rengis Kar were injured. Jalor had been clubbed aside by one of the creatures who were intent on attacking Blaine, and sported a nasty bruise and cut to his side, as well as possible concussion. The injuries had been bandaged at the site of the battle while the creatures' bodies were gathered and burned.

Consequently, after a later start than planned and the battle and its after-effects, the group arrived at the outskirts of Dimming Hollow as night was falling. At a cry from one of the watchmen, the villagers emerged from their cottages, took one look and swarmed around the newcomers. The children were carried into cottages while the uninjured shared sighs of relief at their arrival. Ansela arrived with a tall old man in tow and both set about working on the injured. Formel's stretcher was taken up by villagers and carried away, to be held somewhere safe until he could be farewelled.

Blaine watched as Jalor's wound was dressed by Ansela with the old man assisting. The woman knew what she was doing. The wound was cleaned, slathered with some sort of poultice by the old man, whose hands seemed to hover for a moment over the wound, and bound with fresh bandages. Jalor had been the last, insisting on Welkis and Rengis Kar being treated first. Ansela was finishing up as Varna walked up to Blaine.

"How is he?" she asked.

"He'll be fine, I think," Blaine replied. "It was a glancing blow, more a shove than anything else. They were trying to get to me to stop the arrows, very single minded. More to the point, how are you? It's good to see you on your feet."

"I'm better but from what I was told it's likely to be temporary. Ansela, that's who was tending to Jalor, has some sort of gift that no-one talks about. Flin, that's the older man, is a Teller, a wandering storyteller, but also some sort of herbalist or something. He has herbs for everything. Between the two of them they managed to get me up and about."

Blaine nodded as Jalor gingerly stood, thanking both Ansela and the old Teller. He made his way over to Blaine and Varna, walking carefully and slowly.

"Okay?" Blaine asked.

"Just peachy," Jalor replied with a grimace.

"Headache bad?"

"Actually, I don't feel much of a headache. I guess it can't have been a concussion after all. The wound already feels itchy. Flin - that's the one helping - put some sort of herbal compound on the cut and it seemed to feel better almost straight away." Jalor paused. "Actually, it does feel far better than I would have thought."

"Well, apparently Flin will be giving some stories tonight," Blaine said. "It might be good for the people here. They've been through a bit in the last few days."

Jalor nodded.

"We've been offered an old cottage, over near Ansela's," Varna said. "Two rooms. It's been empty for some time but the village has maintained it as a sort of refuge. The others who have come in will stay in a couple of other cottages, or with friends. I think most of them will be at the story telling tonight, from what Mansela told me. It may be interesting to hear some of them."

26. Stories

Despite the recent events, or perhaps because of them, the evening became a strange form of celebration. A fire had been built in the middle of the road that bisected Dimming Hollow, at a place where the houses on each side were set a little further back than those that stretched along the road in each direction. Blaine had been told that this represented the town square, a standard inclusion in the better Ennaris towns that the speaker knew about. Admittedly, he only knew about a small number, but they all had their squares and this was Dimming Hollow's. Given the almost fierce pride with which the statement was given, and the fact that the speaker was Rekbas, the villager who brewed a form of potent red ale that Blaine was imbibing at the time, he thought it prudent to merely nod.

Almost the entire village was at the event. The newcomers had been cared for and most were in attendance. Rekbas provided small barrels of his ale, which was universally regarded by those who knew such things to be among the worst they had tasted. However, it was dispensed and enjoyed liberally. A variety of foods was brought out, each villager contributing something from larders or gardens. Hilva Nem had proven his hunting prowess with the delivery of what looked to Blaine to be something like an antelope, although with a squared face, shorter legs and a long bushy tail. The meat was roasting on spits around the edge of the fire, being tended to by several men who had been testing Rekbas' ale for a little while. Parts of the meat were overcooked in places where the spits had been abandoned in the general rush to help the injured and bereaved, but no-one minded that.

Wooden plates and bowls were handed around. Jalor, Blaine and Varna found themselves in the middle of the action, with Jalor resting on a small bench surprisingly easily given the wound he had incurred. Welkis and Rengis Kar appeared to be much better than expected also. Perhaps their wounds were not as bad as was thought, Jalor thought to himself as he watched them walk to the spits and back to where they were sitting, stiff and sore but far from as bad as he thought they would be. Perhaps he would look into those herbs.

It was after everyone had eaten enough to satisfy their immediate appetites, drunk enough ale to induce a form of mellow, and when the fire had diminished to a bed of brightly glowing coals that Giffin stood. Swaying slightly, he made what seemed to be a formal greeting and request for a Telling.

"My friends," Giffin said, "the last days have been difficult. We welcome new friends who helped us to defeat a vicious and horrendous foe" - nods to Jalor and Blaine - "and then helped again when our neighbours needed it against more of those abominations. We have suffered loss in those encounters." He paused and all those assembled nodded pensively. "But we are Faeronar and we will not allow these beasts to destroy our spirit. And at the time when we needed to have those spirits raised, we have an old friend return. I request our friend Flin, the best Teller of Ennaris, to provide us with a tale."

He bowed to the old man, carefully lest he overbalance, and sat back on the log that had been dragged to the fireside. The old man nodded pleasantly.

"Thank you Giffin. Yes, this village has been through much in a short time. So, what to Tell," he mused.

"Tell us about the rebellion," a small voice piped up.

"No, let's hear the story of Antylas and Grefmin," came a counter request.

That was followed by a confusing clamour of shouted requests which were delivered with good humour. It was as though the shouted requests was part of the ritual, Varna thought. In fact, she thought as she considered further, it probably was.

"Oh, I think the full tale of the rebellion is a little too long for tonight," Flin the Teller said, waving a small pipe around that Varna was sure had not been lit a short time before. "Hmmm, let me think. There were some good suggestions, but I think I may tell the story of Marjory, the last and greatest of the Battle Mages of Ennaris. She who saved Ennaris from the worst of the effects of the rebellion."

"But the damage still happened," a surly villager, deep in his cups by this time, muttered.

There were various shushes and glares directed at the speaker but the Teller did not seem to mind.

"Aye," Flin replied gravely, "the damage still happened. But it would have been much worse, and Marjory's actions allowed some hope, as the Prophecy says." He paused, gathering his thoughts. "Marjory was young to be a Battle Mage. This was the time of Ennaris' greatness, with all manner of wonders being created by those with many and varied gifts. But even so, the Council of Mages was full of old men and women, and old men and women are set in their ways. Change comes hard to them."

"How old?" The question was thrown to Flin from the far side of the bed of coals.

"You ask that every time, Triskol," Flin said to general laughter, "no matter which story I tell."

"Well, you never answer," came the reply.

"Very well," Flin said. "The Archmage at the time, Belthars, was around ninety thousand cycles old, but the oldest of them all was Halfgar. No-one was ever sure of his age, but he had been around for longer than anyone could remember, and the oldest of the Mages at that time other than Halfgar was Korlis. And Korlis estimated his own age to be one hundred and ninety-six thousand cycles."

"How can you possibly know that?" Triskol asked again.

"Because the traditions say, that's why," Flin replied. "If you don't believe I know the answer, why did you ask the question?"

"Well, you never answered it before," Triskol said to more general laughter.

"Well, I have now, so you need a different question," Flin said with a smile. "Anyway, as I was saying, the Council was largely populated by very old men and women. They had their own concerns, of course, and the work of the Council took up a large part of their time. As a result, they were usually seen by the younger Mages and Guides to be out of touch. Recognising this, Belthars decided to bring some younger Mages onto the Council. One of those was a young woman. Marjory. She had been the leading student of her generation at Resgalar, which is where the academy for Battle Mages was located. Her abilities had astonished the teachers and she was rapidly given greater responsibility. She was reputed to be one of the most powerful Mages ever seen. Halfgar, who claimed to have seen more of them than anyone, made that claim. He also had something like a gift of foresight and declared that she would save Ennaris."

Flin smiled, looking inwards as though in remembrance.

"Imagine that! This young Mage, not quite five thousand cycles of age, being declared the most powerful and a future saviour."

"Five thousand!" Triskol spoke up again. "How is that young?"

"Triskol!" Flin glared at the man, to no effect, and sighed dramatically. "An age of five thousand cycles was young by Mage standards. Non-Mages lived to be many hundreds of cycles of age at the time, as a result of the Mage gifts and advanced technology, don't forget. But back to Marjory. She had been placed in charge of building special devices that protected Ennaris, far more advanced than anything we can build now. She had designed very advanced machines made from special materials that we no longer know how to make. She had visited other planets, other worlds!"

Flin paused and looked around. Most of the listeners were rapt, eyes wide. This was as much a story of Ennaris' former greatness, something they heard about in small snippets, parts of stories or references in ancient songs. The thought of these special people struck wonder, even though they were reputed to be tainted. And the idea of going to another planet! Amazing! Flin made eye contact with Jalor, held it for a moment and turned back to the gathered listeners.

Well, Jalor thought, that was significant in some way. But how?

"When the time came to bring the young Mages onto the Council," Flin continued, "Marjory was the logical choice to be one of them."

"What was she like?" a small voice asked from near the fire.

"What was she like?" Flin gave a sad smile. "Ah, child! She was among the most beautiful of the women of Ennaris. She was tall, almost as tall as me, with thick black hair that she would let fall down her back, tied only with a single clasp behind her neck. She stood straight and looked at the world directly. She was loving and gentle to her family, she doted on her young son, and she was generous to her friends. She did not shirk her responsibilities, even though they took her from her family for long periods, and she was the greatest Battle Mage Ennaris had ever seen. Her power! Oh, her power shone through like a torch in the dark of night."

Flin paused again, looking over to the small girl who had asked the question, eyes shining in the reflected light from the coals.

"And she was wise. When she spoke in the Council the old ones listened. She worked to make sure the old traditions were honoured, but also sought to bring many things up to the modern standards. Many changes she championed, some simple and some difficult to achieve. She used to say that the difficult things were why the Mages were here, for the simple things could be done by anyone. And she got the difficult things done."

"She sounds like some sort of wonder woman," Mansela said.

"Wonder woman? She was direct, forthright and very intense when she needed to be. She could be uncomfortable to be around at times, while at other times she was a joy. Her Mage powers were advanced, very advanced, and she knew many things beyond the arts of battle, war, attack and defence. But when the time came, she was resolute and firm and those who made of her an enemy learnt their mistake.

"For the time did come. Goroth, one of the Council Mages, refused to accept blame for events caused by rogue Mages under his control and rebelled against the Council, claiming that the old men and women were out of touch and needed to be replaced by those with a better understanding. Of course, those would be Goroth and his minions. That rebellion ultimately caused the devastation. The Tellers tell many stories of the destruction of Ennaris over the short period of almost two cycles. All are true. The might and greatness of Ennaris were destroyed and most of the population with it. Ennaris lost billions of people, more than you can ever imagine. Many times more than the number of people left on Ennaris. Great cities, that lit the planet when seen from so high up in the sky that everything is black, were no more. Works of art of such beauty that it made grown women and men cry were destroyed. So much learning, so much good, all gone. The Council and the loyal Mages and Guides fought and died against the rebels, seeking to protect the ones who remained. Belthars and most of the Council members were killed as they tried to save this planet and its people.

"At the end, only a handful of Mages survived on each side. Marjory and her helpers confronted Goroth and his minions to end it once and for all. The place was not far from here, in fact."

"What of the Guardians? Did they not do something?" Giffin called out.

"The Guardians?" Flin smiled gently. "The Guardians of legend are charged with protecting Ennaris. They are not charged with saving the Ennarisi. That is our job! All of us! We are the ones who must decide what we do. We are the ones who must take responsibility against those who seek to take our freedoms, our safety, our lives. And that's what Marjory and her companions did. And in what was intended to be the last battle, Marjory led the remainder of the Mages of the Council and overwhelmed Goroth and his force. And do not be misled by tales of how easy that was. Goroth was himself a Battle Mage and he had two other Mages of strength with him. Marjory was the sole Battle Mage remaining from the Council. Goroth thought he would win easily. He taunted Marjory and her friends with the damage he had wrought, using weapons of such destructive power that parts of the land would take thousands of cycles to recover, and some has yet to do so.

"Marjory stared down Goroth and refused to yield. And then Goroth called down the most powerful weapon Ennaris had ever made, one never intended to be used on the planet itself. It was on a great ship that sailed between planets and was made to protect that ship from others who may seek to harm it. And Goroth called that great ship to come down from the space between worlds and attack. The ship's weapons were made of energy, like great arrows made of light rather than wood and iron."

Jalor and Blaine exchanged glances. A ship-based main energy weapon used in the confines of a planetary atmosphere would be devastating. The people sitting around the fire could not understand what that may mean. Did this Teller even understand? Likely not. These people had no idea about energy weapons, given the state of their civilisation. Jalor, Blaine and Varna did.

"And so that great ship turned its weapons on the place where Marjory and her friends stood. The great weapon fired continuously. And Marjory withstood the great weapon with her own force, joined with that of her friends. And finally, when the great ship's weapon could not fire any more, Marjory retaliated."

Jalor imagined the scene of a main energy weapon being discharged continuously within the atmosphere. It would overheat the ejector but not until it had emitted a massive amount of directed energy. How did one person withstand that?

"Marjory called the defences she had devised to destroy the ship, which fell into the deep oceans. And then Marjory drew the power from her friends and attacked Goroth. After a mighty battle between the two Mages, Marjory was victorious. Goroth was defeated and his two chief minions fled. Goroth was captured and taken to a place where he was locked away, for the Council Mages did not kill enemies without trial. But the cost was enormous. The amount of energy released by Goroth and the other attackers, and by the defenders as they tried to turn it away, caused Ennaris to buckle and tear. The land heaved and rocked. Much of the land was forever changed. The ocean rushed in where there had been no ocean before, and the land collapsed in many places. The remaining cities and towns crumbled and fell. And many people died. So many people died."

Flin stopped. He looked around the gathered people, many of them staring into the embers as they thought their own thoughts about the times described, the battle fought, the woman who had defended the planet. And the damage caused by that battle.

"Many died," the Teller continued, "and many continued to die. The few remaining Mages and Guides did what they could to help. Aye," he said, holding up one hand, "I know the common stories say that the Mages and Guides caused the destruction, and those rebels did do so, but those few who were left tried to save as many people as they could. They used their gifts and tried to save the land. And they died also. Some because the people took out their anger on them, believing them to be the cause. Some because the work took all of the energy they had and demanded more. Some because of despair. Many Ennarisi died because, as Ennaris degenerated into anarchy and lawlessness, the stronger ones preyed on the weaker. Some because diseases that were easily dealt with before now could not be treated well. Ennaris was decimated. But in the depths of despair there was a message of hope. For Halfgar, who had the gift of foretelling, was seized by inspiration and wrote the Prophecy before he, too, died trying to ensure that the destruction wrought by Goroth would not recur. And that Prophecy says that Ennaris would take its place alongside the people of the stars when the Children of Ennaris returned. But it also said that Goroth would return, and there would be a final battle to decide who took Ennaris into the future and what sort of future that would be."

The silence when Flin stopped speaking was broken by Giffin again, who said, "And when does this Prophecy we've been hearing about for all our lives come to pass, Flin? For most of us, Goroth is a story told in the old tales and you say he will come again. How do we know when Goroth will return?"

"Among other things, the Prophecy tells of lights in the clear night sky when the Children of Ennaris return," Flin said. "Of the appearance of fell creatures that attack and destroy without reason. Perhaps," he said as the villagers looked to each other, "perhaps these creatures you have been attacked by. Who knows."

"And the lights?" Giffin asked.

Flin paused, looking around the gathering and then pointed to a section of the night sky above the distant peaks that Almin Bor said surrounded the Citadel which would be their destination when they set out again. As one, all turned to look where Flin pointed. Dimly, Jalor could make out pinpricks of light. As he watched one of the pinpricks flared and died, followed by another and a third. Jalor's mouth went dry as he turned to Blaine and Varna in turn. Blaine nodded, while Varna's jaw set. The pinpricks that flared and died were ships.

The fleet was under attack.

27. Pio

They were a small group, although they had started as a much larger one. They were deep in the forest and being hunted, stalked, by strange creatures that seemed to be half men and half some sort of beast. Two men and three women remained of what had started as a group of twelve, members of the roving Quatoz people.

Usually, they lived their lives in their own ways, staying away from large towns and cities, only making their way to smaller towns when they needed something they were unable to hunt, gather or make for themselves. They were comfortable travelling the length and breadth of the double continents of Ennaris, camping as they wished in their large communal tents. Many of the more staid people of Ennaris did not understand their ways. Many rumours described rites and practises that either did not exist or that twisted what did exist and that led to them being viewed with suspicion and, in some cases, dread. They were not always welcomed. They were sometimes shunned and driven away.

They were most at home in the forests, though, those remnants of the huge stands of timber that once cut a swathe across the centre of the northern continent below the great grass plain. This one was a favourite, with its huge trees, spreading boughs, the sparse undergrowth and large spaces between the trees that seemed like halls in some great mansion. They enjoyed the solitude, peace and tranquillity of being in these places, with the birds and small animals to provide background noises. The few aggressive large animals they knew to avoid and, all in all, they lived their lives contentedly.

Now, though, peace had become nightmare and death had visited this break-away band of a traditionally peaceful people via a danger that none had expected or seen before. And so they were running, leaving their camp far behind in panic and fear. The five remaining Quatoz were the youngest, the most agile, those with the greatest endurance. Two others had tried to fight but were overwhelmed without real effort by their attackers. Another had fallen when unable to maintain a pace and was killed where he lay. A fourth had tripped down a gully and broken his neck. The final two had just disappeared and their whereabouts or even if they lived were not known.

It seemed to Rayga, the oldest of the five runners, that they were being herded. She could hear the group of attackers behind, coming at a shambling run, beating the shrubs and trees as they went to keep the pursued moving. She and the others were aware of shadows in the distance to both sides, closing in on them inexorably as they tried desperately to get ahead of the pursuers, all the time moving deeper and deeper into the forest. For so long a refuge, it was now to be their end.

Suddenly, the runners came to a large open space, with almost no cover bar some rocks on the far side. In the centre of the space was a large circle of blackened ground, with a tiny grass circle in the centre of the black. The unlikelihood of this being natural flashed through Rayga's mind even as she moved out from under the trees.

The beaters were moving up fast, forcing the five further into the open. At the same time, two other groups of the same horrible half-beasts emerged from the forest on each side. The three groups of attackers started to converge. The five found themselves in the blackened space, and then they clustered at the small green spot in the middle of the clearing. Rayga experienced despair, knowing that she would die here, and with no understanding of why that was the case. She saw the same expression on her friends' faces, tears rolling down their cheeks as terror took hold.

The half-beasts surrounded them now, staying back and slavering, grunting, slowly closing the circle and enjoying the fear they evoked. All five produced knives, even while their terror took root, although they knew that their knives against the roughly fashioned swords and spears facing them would not help at all.

One of the beasts looked up as a flash appeared in the sky, its gaze then followed by all of the attackers. They stopped and cowered, while the five looked on uncertainly. A bright ball of energy sped from high in the sky to hover over the heads of the five. The half-beasts howled at the light and broke for the trees. Bright, hard beams speared from the ball of light and every one of the attackers was incinerated in a moment.

The ball of energy settled to the ground near the five Quatoz, before fading to show a man standing before them. He looked around at the clearing, knelt to feel the ground and frowned.

"This is a place of great pain," he said quietly, "but also one where hope was kindled." He looked at the five, who were standing still, knives held in fists, staring at their deliverer. "You may put away your weapons, for I have a higher task for you to undertake."

With a start, Rayga glanced at her knife and then sheathed it, as did the others.

"Who are you?" she managed to say, without her fear causing any quaver in her voice, how she was not sure. "We are grateful for your aid, and for our lives, but never have any of us seen such before, either you or those things."

"I've been away for a long time," the man said to her, addressing them all. "My name is Pio. I do hope my name has not been forgotten, despite the length of time away."

"Pio? The Guardian?" Rayga stammered a little this time. "We've been hearing stories of the Guardians for some time now, and the tales tell that you made the forests of Ennaris. But we've also been told that the Guardians are not real, are symbols only."

"Oh, we are real," Pio said with a smile. "And I helped the forests to grow. I did not create them. Creation is for someone else, I'm glad to say."

"Why are you here?" Rayga said, calming down slowly. The rest were content for her to take the lead in the conversation, but they were hanging on every word.

"Because the legends are coming to pass," Pio said, "and the time has come for the Guardians to return to Ennaris, at last. The final battle for this world is not far away, and I need your help to prepare your people, even those who think I am but a symbol."

"Legends? Which legends?"

"The Children of Ennaris have returned and they prepare to lead the Ennarisi against the great foe of the rebellion. It's time for divisions to be healed, and for dissension to cease. At least for a while," Pio said with a quirk of his lips. "And you are to be to the fore of my effort to help. Come, there is much to do."

And so, with awe and not a little trepidation, the five young Quatoz people began their lives of service to Pio, Guardian of the forests of Ennaris.

28. Attack

The attack came suddenly. After the unexpected destruction of the dreadnought the Empire fleet had held station. They still outnumbered the Union fleet by a significant margin but the Union ships now out-gunned the Empire. While no-one was lulled into any sort of false sense of security, the logical thing to do was to hold station. The new enemy commander seemed to have different ideas.

Without warning, four ships accelerated from the edges of the Empire line, two at each end. As they did so four other ships at each end repositioned and opened fire at long range on the nearest Union vessels, all four targeting the same Union ship at each end of the line. In moments two of the Union vessels were adrift.

Jord ordered the fleet to lay down protective fire. Energy bolts criss-crossed the space between the fleets, usually doing little but making defensive shields flare. Some missed and dissipated far behind the Union ships. Two Union destroyers changed their patrol routes to intercept the accelerating Empire ships, now passing by the drifting edge pickets. There was no way those ships would be able to stop until they were far past the Union fleet given their vectors and momentum.

Serra appeared on the bridge, taking in the scene in moments. Bard was moments behind her.

"Jord, those ships will be suicide runs." Bard turned to Kiri, who had been sitting in the command chair when the action started and had stayed there. "Kiri, evasive for those ships out there. Fire everything at those ships."

Serra watched as the two Empire ships each abruptly altered their vectors to pass between two Union capital ships. In each case one was a carrier. The Union ships poured heavy fire on the two Empire ships. The damage inflicted was huge as energy and plasma weapons pounded the two ships. The engines winked out as the weapons fire became too much for their systems to bear, but momentum carried the ships still. The Union ships were manoeuvring away from the oncoming ships, while maintaining their rate of fire. But it was too late. The two Empire ships exploded in huge fireballs, creating shaped fields of debris that sped outward from the point of detonation like shrapnel. The Union capital ships on each side bore the brunt of the attacks, while those further away received damage of varying severity. Shields of the closest ships had no answer to the volume of reinforced plating and other metal and composite materials that bombarded them, and buckled. The debris impacted along the near sides of the Union vessels, stripping away weapon and communication pods and puncturing the thick plates in multiple places.

Damage reports came thick and fast. Escape pods launched from three of the four Union ships. The fourth launched no pods, continuing to accelerate away from its previous position, trailing a cloud of oxygen through the perforated hull. It was outside the Union lines when its main fission reactor lost containment and the ship exploded. For a period of three heartbeats a tiny star existed just beyond the line of ships, before collapsing to reveal a small field of debris. The blast had been so intense that almost nothing was left, most of the ship and its crew having been obliterated.

Serra stared at the main screen with her hands clenched while around her the *Starfire* bridge crew coordinated rescue efforts. Five ships were damaged and one lost with all hands, for the cost of two of the lesser Empire ships. The abrupt nature of what happened would have its own aftermath for the crews of the ships of the fleet. More especially, however, was the fact that their available fire-power had been reduced. This was a new tactic for the Empire and that was disturbing in itself, for the enemy did little that was new. Now, having succeeded once, it was likely they would try again. Perhaps, having the dreadnought destroyed would prove to be a double-edged sword if it allowed a less hide-bound officer to take charge.

"Admiral, *Dekros* and *Quasar* report extensive blast damage to their fighter bays. The bays closest to the blast are basically gone and the control systems will make it hard to manage the others. Both lost quite a few stingers. *Dekros* has flights on patrol. They'll recover to *Starfire*." Jord paused and considered. "*Triell* has repairable damage but it will take some time. Both *Hittar* and *Lokar* had shields and engines knocked out during that opening salvo. Both are adrift and we'll launch tugs to haul them to the back of the fleet."

Serra nodded shortly.

"I've never known any Empire tactic like that," Jord continued. "That's worrying. I'm guessing it was aimed at our fighter force, and that's taken a bit of a hit. But it also leaves them with a sizeable advantage in ship numbers."

"It's not large enough yet for them to do much about it, though," Serra said, "at least not based on what we used to have to deal with. No, I think that was opportunistic. The fact that it worked will embolden them, though, so we have to be ready for repeat attempts or other actions that may be out of the ordinary."

Jord nodded, watching Bard move from station to station, stopping at each for a quiet word with the operator. Many of them would be shaken, although all had seen combat. He glanced to Kiri, who was passing orders by voice even while her fingers danced across the pad in front of her. The colonel's face was tight, but Jord was sure that was rage rather than stress.

"Let's hope the team is doing better."

The morning after the story telling proved to be overcast. A blustery wind caused clouds to scud past overhead. Jalor and Blaine stood with Hilva Nem at the barrier where the battle with the creatures had taken place. Almin Bor made his way to the small group.

"Sandyn and Magnor will stay here for the birth," Almin Bor said without preamble.

Jalor nodded, relieved. Magnor would be a liability if they met any more of those things.

"Jilnar will stay here, too," Almin Bor continued. "The rest will be coming with us to the Citadel. Formel's sending will be this morning and then we can be on our way."

Jalor nodded again, not knowing what a sending might be, but going along for the sake of his battered cover. *Shattered cover, more likely*, he thought as Almin Bor turned and walked back into the village.

"How long does a sending usually take here," Blaine asked. "Without meaning any disrespect for Formel, but we don't want to be spending too many nights away from some sort of shelter."

"The sending will take the morning," Hilva Nem replied. "We'll need to gather some more wood, first."

Blaine nodded, rubbing his hands together against the chill wind.

"I'll help with that," he said. "I didn't know him for more than a day or so, but he was a fighter. That much I do know."

"I'll check on Varna," Jalor said.

Jalor found Varna being tended to by Ansela and Flin, the latter mixing some of his ever-present herbs in a mug of hot water while the former gently rubbed a salve into Varna's temples.

"Are you okay?" Jalor asked quietly.

"Yes and no," Varna said. "I'm still a little dizzy, but it doesn't feel anywhere near as bad as it did. Flin tells me if I can make it to the Citadel there may be someone who he knows there who can help me more, one of his friends. If it is this gift thing, we'll need to find out what it is. He seems to think the same person at the Citadel may be able to assist there also."

Flin paused mixing his herbal concoction to look over and nod.

"Ansela is of moderate power in her gift. I know someone who may be in the Citadel who is a little more practised at easing the symptoms of a range of effects like this. It has been a long time since he has had to do so, but it's not something that goes stale. I can't guarantee Varna will get to the Citadel without being overwhelmed again, though, so I think I'll come with you."

Jalor regarded Flin steadily for a moment, considering.

"We'll be moving pretty fast," he warned.

"Oh, I think I can move pretty fast," Flin replied blandly. "At least as fast as the children you will have with you, at any rate."

Jalor glanced to Varna who just shrugged. Nodding thoughtfully, Jalor turned to Ansela.

"This gift you have, Ansela, how did you come by it, and how can Flin tell how powerful you are in it?"

"I was born with the gift, of course," Ansela said, looking at Jalor in surprise. "But it came on me when I was about five cycles old. I had no-one to teach me, although Flin passed on some of the old lore from the old stories. I can feel that there are limits to what I can do. I can feel that there is a lot more that could be done than what I can do, and I told Flin about that. The old lore says that those with gifts are able to sense the level of their own power. I know I don't have a lot of power. I have more than some, and less than others. But there are no others near here, I think."

"No," Flin said to her, "there are no others with the healing gift this side of the Citadel plateau, unfortunately."

Ansela nodded.

"There's a need for more healers," she said to Jalor while continuing to knead Varna's temples gently. "But, if I'm what we have, then I'll do the best I can do."

"And you know that for sure?" Jalor asked Flin.

The old Teller carried the mug to Varna and handed it to her, nodding as she took a sip, grimaced and took another. Absently, Flin placed his hand on her head and looked at Jalor.

"Yes, I know that for sure," he replied. "I am a friend to all with the gifts, and all know that. There are old stories that tell much about how the gifts were used, and I pass them on where I can do so. I know many of the ones for gifts of healing and caring for all manner of plants and animals, less for other gifts. But the people seek me out for those tales, so I tend to know who has gifts."

Jalor gazed at the Teller as he busied himself putting his leathern packets of herbs back into various pockets in his travel pack. Something, but he was not sure what, seemed to be missing, or wrong. Off, he thought to himself. Flin seemed to be genuine and yet there seemed to be something off. He could not put his finger on it. He decided to leave it for now, but he would keep an eye on the Teller.

Meanwhile, Ansela declared that she had done all that she could do, and started to pack up her ointments, vials and herbs, placing them in her own pack. Varna thanked her warmly as she continued to sip at the herbal drink. Jalor thought her colour looked better, which could only be good, so for now he would hold his concerns to himself. He gave his thanks to Ansela also and then exited the cottage, waiting for Varna in the chill wind. His pack included a thin hooded cape which would keep him warm, but for now he would leave it where it was.

The sending was a sombre affair. Formel's body was placed on a low bier of wood, with dried grasses liberally woven through the branches. Welkis gave a short speech extolling the virtues of his friend and a flaming brand was touched to the base of the bier. There must have been an accelerant used, Jalor thought, as the wood lit with a whoosh and Formel's body was hidden by the wall of flame. In a surprisingly short time, the bier was reduced to little more than ash. Jilnar was led away by a group of women from the village, sobbing inconsolably.

With little further ado, the group that would go on to the Citadel gathered their various packs. Muted farewells were said, Ansela handed Varna a small vial of ointment to rub into her temples, and the group set off. Once again, Almin Bor set the order of travel and Jalor fell in beside Blaine at the back of the group. Flin was nowhere to be seen, Jalor noted with a frown, but then shrugged. Three days to go before they would arrive at this Citadel that seemed to be central to these parts. Perhaps having Flin and his herbs along would have been useful, after all. Hopefully Ansela's ointment would suffice.

Varna awakened with a start. Jalor was crouching over her. The group had made an early camp in a small clearing that was within a copse of trees, away from the road they had been following, and Varna had fallen asleep immediately. Lifting her eyes she saw Blaine at one side, watching something over her shoulder and starting to move. Almin Bor stood by Blaine, looking perturbed. Magwyn and Aldar were sitting by the side of the fire preparing some sort of root vegetables. Struggling to sit up, assisted by Jalor, she turned to see Flin sitting on a log, regarding them all steadily.

Jalor nodded as she came awake, eyes searching out Blaine who was circling through the woods to look in on those left on watch. He turned to Varna, raised one eyebrow and quietly asked, "Are you okay?"

She sighed and nodded in return. "I fell into another trance of some kind." She paused. "I'm sorry, Jalor. It's like whatever it was has been waiting for me to come back out on the road. It's like the one I had before. I was literally reliving whole stages of my life. I thought I was exercising more control this time, but it overwhelmed me again. And then something, or someone, snapped me out of it again. It was a whole lot more real than anything I have experienced since we arrived here."

"Well, something affected you," Flin said before Jalor could respond. "I tried to awaken you but without any success at all."

Jalor moved to a position in front of Varna, facing Flin. How had he made it through the watch that was set? An old man had slipped through experienced sentries, from what Almin Bor said of the men and women with them, and was now sitting quietly on a log with his back against a rock, hands resting lightly on his knees. A nondescript pack rested at his feet. Flin exuded calm. Almost against his will, Jalor relaxed.

"You may need to move your camp, Jalor," Flin said quietly. "I'm surprised Almin Bor allowed a camp here. It may not look like much, but this was part of the site of Goroth's final battle, when Marjory and the Mages finally succeeded in capturing him at great cost. It has been suggested that the residues in this area are more potent than almost anywhere on Ennaris. From what Varna has said I do suspect she is experiencing an awakening of gifts. But this may not be the best location for it."

"Was it you?" Varna breathed. "The bright light, was it you?"

Flin frowned. "Bright light? I'm unaware of any bright light, I'm afraid."

"What light?" Jalor asked as Blaine rejoined the group and shrugged.

"I was out of control again," Varna concluded, "and whoever or whatever snapped me out of it, it was like a brilliant light that just stood there and stopped me."

"And you think it was Flin?"

"Yes and no. I get the hint of the same sort of colours about him."

Flin raised a single eye-brow. He stood in one fluid motion that belied the aspect of significant age and walked over to the others.

"Colours? You can sense my aura?"

More intrigued by the man's excitement than anything else, Varna nodded. "At times," she said. "But only in flashes. I can't seem to catch hold."

"Hmmm. Perhaps a reader," the old man mused to himself, momentary excitement quenched. He appeared to ponder what he had said before shrugging and returning to his log. "Well, time will tell. And no, I did not intervene in any sort of way with whatever happened."

Jalor looked around the small group. All except the Teller looked to him for the lead, even Almin Bor, despite the fact that the latter had sorted the marching order. Jalor sighed to himself - this mission had not gone well at all.

"I thought you were planning on coming with us from the village," Jalor said, watching Flin closely. "I assume you know everyone here? Then you know they know how to keep a watch. How did you just walk in here?"

"Yes, of course," Flin said, nodding to Almin Bor, who returned the nod. "Well, I do know how to move through the woods, you know. One learns many things on the road. And I didn't want to wake everyone, although that seems to have happened. I must admit I thought I had fallen into a tale when I found Varna tossing and turning like that, perhaps the one about the Red Rider and her quest for the magic gourd."

"Ooh, I like that one," Aldar said before being shushed by her mother.

Flin smiled. "It is a favourite. Perhaps later, eh? Anyway, this is close to one of the spots I have used as a shelter on my travels, so I know it well. There is a cave back there a way," and he pointed vaguely off to the right, "and I was heading there when I realised that you had chosen this spot to camp. I decided to come on in. There are particularly unfriendly hapthars in this area, but also the odd slither at times, so the company will be welcome."

"Hapthars?" Varna asked, glancing around.

"Oh yes." Flin smiled. "Four legs, big snout, huge tusks and very ugly, at least to those who are not hapthars. They make very good eating but are very hard to catch. And you really don't want to have one come upon you unaware."

"Well, it's now dark and we're set for the night. Despite what you say, Flin, I think we may be better staying here for the night. Almin Bor recommended this clearing and I'm not sure if there's another nearby." Jalor nodded to Blaine who tapped Almin Bor and the two men stepped out of the clearing, starting to gather more wood for the fire.

It was later, after food had been prepared from the various packs of the party and supplemented by additional herbs and treats provided by Flin, drawn from his own pack. Varna, after appearing to have a burst of fresh energy on awakening, had drifted off into a dull hazy state, and ultimately been bundled up in a cloak and fallen into a fitful asleep. Flin regarded her steadily for a short while before turning to Jalor.

Flin asked about the fights with the strange creatures. The story was told and Flin, evincing all the curiosity of a professional story-teller, asked question after question, concentrating on the actions of Blaine especially, who started to feel uncomfortable under the barrage of questions about how he came to have such skill in weapons, for a traveller. Flin regarded him unblinkingly, not as a challenge but with steadfast interest.

"I guess I'm just well-coordinated," Blaine said. "And I get lucky sometimes."

"Lucky, yes, I can see where that would be helpful when you are travelling." Flin laid slightly more emphasis on the last word. "And Varna appears to be coming into some sort of a gift at a much later age than I have ever heard of," he remarked mildly, turning to Jalor, eyes sharp under bushy brows. "And I have heard of quite a few in my time."

Jalor was unsure about what to say to Flin and so shrugged his shoulders. Flin pointed to his pack.

"I have my herbs that seemed to help. I'll make some up tonight and again in the morning. Some stay-awake may come in useful for the journey tomorrow, and I'm sure I have some in there. And, of course, she has Ansela's balm."

Jalor, reflecting that he barely knew any of the people with whom he was now travelling, was non-committal. "Maybe. The ointment and your herbal drink do seem to help. She was meditating a bit also and that helped somewhat."

"Her colours are funny," a young voice piped up.

Flin sat upright and turned to look at Aldar, sitting close to the fire. "What was that, Aldar? Colours?"

Aldar looked to her mother and, receiving a smile and a nod, stood and walked over to where Varna lay, muttering slightly in her sleep. "Yes, her colours are all cloudy and that's making her sick. She needs someone to fix her colours. Can you do that?" Aldar finished, looking at Flin.

"Er, I'm not sure," Flin said, taken aback. "I may have some herbs that can do that, but we will wait for the morning to let Varna sleep for a while."

"I know you can help Varna," Aldar stated with finality. "She's very pretty and her colours are really beautiful."

With that statement the girl walked over to her mother, laid down near the fire and relaxed into sleep. Jalor, amused, watched Flin who, after staring at Aldar for a few moments, sighed, shook his head and also settled himself for the night. Jalor looked to Almin Bor and Blaine who held up one finger - he would take first watch - before nodding and settling down for the night.

In the morning the small group bustled around. Blaine had been relieved by Almin Bor. Jalor had been surprised to be woken for his turn by Magwyn, who had relieved Almin Bor, but said nothing and merely took his place until morning, when he started to gather additional fuel for a fire. With Varna still suffering the ill effects of something, he thought they may have to wait some time. But he recalled Flin's warning that they should move. How much he should trust the Teller he was not sure, but at the moment he was open to almost anything to explain what was happening.

A small meal was prepared with Flin adding some sort of ground dark coloured seeds to the pot of boiling water. The others welcomed the addition, which proved to make some form of coffee-like brew. He poured a measure into a metal mug for himself while setting out additional mugs to make it clear the brew was communal, took a sip and visibly relaxed.

"No day starts as well without a mug of brall," he said.

Magwyn scooped up mugs and poured one for herself and Almin Bor before also sitting near the fire and sipping appreciatively, followed by several others. She nodded a thank you smile to Flin, who nodded back. Flin took a few more sips and then pulled his pack over to him, reached in and extracted a small packet which, after being laid on the ground and opened, revealed a range of herbs, seeds and some small nut-like objects. He sorted through them, and pulled forth a small bundle of herbs.

"Ah, this is what I want," he said to no-one in particular, putting the herbs in the palm of one hand and crushing them thoroughly with his other palm. An intense aroma reminiscent of lemon myrtle wafted across the clearing.

"This is keep-awake," he said to Jalor and Blaine. "It grows in the mountains to the south. Many people use it when they need to stay awake for extended periods, but it has other properties. Maybe," and he looked to Aldar, "just maybe, it will help with colours."

"What are you going to do," Jalor asked.

"Just hold this under her nose. The aroma is quite strong and should get through whatever is bothering Varna. It may be better than the tea. It's not a cure but we may be able to travel on towards the citadel for a while." He nodded. "If not, we will have to rig up some sort of carrier for Varna, I expect."

Flin arranged the crushed herbs on his palm and then, placing one hand very gently on Varna's head, held the other under her nose. With a slight moan, Varna awoke. She snorted, sending crushed herbs flying and causing Flin to sit back and laugh.

"Well," he said to Jalor, "that seems to have worked, at least for now." He smiled to Varna and picked himself up, brushing herbs off his hands as he moved to where Blaine was rebuilding the fire.

Jalor nodded. "How are you feeling?" he asked Varna.

She grimaced but then realised that she only felt a shadow of the debilitating fugue she had experienced once again the night before. But it was a sizable shadow. She smiled and tried to rally. "I feel much better. Almost as good as new. And hungry. Did I eat anything last night? Was it only last night or did I go for a longer period again?"

"Only since last night, and yes you ate but not much. Breakfast soon." Jalor looked over to where Blaine was preparing a hearty if somewhat confused breakfast from the available ingredients. "If you can figure out just what our master cook is doing."

"I heard that," Blaine retorted. "Come take over for yourself and see what you can do." He did not mention that he had no idea what some of the ingredients were, and was doing what every good mission team member did when in doubt - a stew.

Varna smiled at the exchange. "I need to be caught up," she said to Jalor quietly. "I missed a lot of what was said last night."

They were interrupted by Aldar running up to grip Varna's hand. "Your colours look much better! I knew he could do it."

Varna looked a question at Jalor who grinned. "Aldar told Flin that your colours were all mixed up and confused. Apparently, your colours are very pretty."

Varna smiled to Aldar. "Thank you, Aldar."

Flin turned to Almin Bor. "These attacks. You and others appear to have been targeted specifically."

"Others have been attacked recently," Magwyn stated flatly. "Including my friend Alwin. She and her children were killed a week ago and, before he died, her Frelred said they were strange creatures all in black." A single tear slid from one eye but Magwyn remained steady in demeanour. "There have been rumours of others being attacked further out."

Almin Bor nodded, moving to her side in support. "Frelred was a good man. He provided for them better than most. He fought and died to protect them, as we have done since the world was broken, and will do till it ends." Determination shone through Almin Bor's words as he looked around the gathered group. "We will protect our families, our children. And when the time comes, we will protect the Faero, as we did in the past. We are the Blood," Almin Bor stated quietly, but pride and deep spirit reverberated through every word, reflected in the sharp nods of those gathered around the fire. "We were the first and we will be there when the last trumpet blows. Every person of the Blood knows his or her place in this world. We are taught our history and that of this world from the moment we are born. Every man, woman and child of the Blood will fight to their last breaths to protect those who attack or demean us, who hold us in contempt or who fear us. When we are called once again, as we will be when the Children return, we will stand with the Faero to return Ennaris to its place and remove the evil."

"And your children are the cause of the fear?" Flin asked, watching Almin Bor and Magwyn closely. "The children are showing signs of the gifts, are they not?"

"Aye, that they are," Almin Bor said. He looked to Aldar, shaking his head gently. "After so much time the gifts are being seen again. Our Aldar has been taught to say nothing of it to others because of the fear that is caused, even among those at the citadel. Some fear it is fell sorcery. Many have forgotten their history but we do not."

"And the others who have been attacked. Their children are also gifted?"

"Aye, they are," Magwyn said, a lift to her head. "The Blood is regenerating, as the Prophecy said it would when needs must. You told of the signs last night. The time foretold must be getting close."

"And someone is now trying to stamp that out," Flin said to no-one in particular. He paused, deep in thought. Jalor and Blaine exchanged thoughtful glances, as Flin stirred once again. "And there are many more of the Blood living in small holdings like yours. And in villages. Those may have not yet have been warned or gathered."

"Probably quite a few," Almin Bor replied. "There are at least six families within walking distance of us, and some villages that have remained intact over the long cycles. We have stayed within call of the citadel."

Varna stirred, having listened spellbound. "Who, or what, is the Faero?" she asked.

Almin Bor turned to her. "The Faeronar are the people of the Faero. Our tradition tells that the Blood, the old Blood, once ruled the whole country but were dispossessed long ago and gradually pulled back to the citadel. It is of great age, having been built in the last years of the Golden Age as a refuge for the Blood during the ancient wars that broke the world. The Faeros lead us as they led the whole land in the past. The Prophesy says the Faero will lead us again as we fight the evil and regain our place."

Flin cleared his throat to get attention. "Well, that's not completely accurate, I'm afraid. The Faero did not rule as much as made sure things worked, but that was across the whole planet, not just one country." He smiled as Almin Bor's eyes opened wide. "Yes, that's right, the whole planet. It's more latterly that the role of the Faero was identified with military responsibilities, although there was a bit of that from the start. What is not well understood is that the Guides, the group of gifted and non-gifted people who helped make sure things were done right, in many cases were drawn from the Faeronar. Not completely, mind you, but there were many."

"The Guides!" Almin Bor snorted. "Our tradition, and your own stories, tell us that it was the Guides and Mages fighting against each other that caused such great destruction, leading to much of the land being damaged and made unliveable. You said as much at Dimming Hollow. And then they left us to our own resources." He repeated his sound of disgust, throwing both hands in the air. "How many died, how many were left with nothing? How many women and children were killed or died in hunger? The traditions tell of bands of outlaws roaming the land, taking what they wanted when they wanted it, not being stopped except where local lords grew the ability to do so."

"Much of that is true," Flin said quietly, nodding. "But not all."

"The Guides were charged with protecting the land and the people. They were the ones we tried to turn to but could not because they were not to be found! Where were your precious Guides then, story teller?" Almin Bor glared at Flin as though he was the one responsible.

"Dying," said Flin quietly, with such grief in his voice that Almin Bor halted his tirade and stared at the old man. "Yes, Almin Bor, man of the Blood, of the Faeronar, the Mages and Guides were dying in those early days, as I also said last night. When the battles were done, there were but a double handful of the truly gifted left. They tried to reduce the damage across the world but it was too great, far too much damage had been done. Several of them exceeded the amount of power they could draw and use and so died. As I said, others died when the people rose against them, blaming them for the result of actions by rogue Mages and Guides who tried to usurp the leadership of the planet for their own selfish ends, to take power and wield it to their own benefit. Until there were too few and the damage could not be contained."

"And you know this how?" Almin Bor asked, subdued. "Our traditions have been passed down from family to family, in ancient tales and a few precious volumes of memories by those who lived near to those times. Are you saying our traditions are wrong?"

"No, my friend, not wrong at all. But they tell the tale from a perspective, and there were other perspectives. We have our own traditions, and they also tell of the destruction, the fight to survive, the fight to live and reclaim as much of civilisation as possible. And the failure of those who were asked and who tried to help. We record the deaths of those who stood up to the aggressors, and those who were killed by the angry mobs. And we have the traditions of the glories yet to come, when the Children of Ennaris return to fight the evil in our midst, and to return this planet and its peoples to their rightful place in the universe."

Almin Bor, Magwyn and Aldar were transfixed, as were the others gathered. Jalor, Blaine and Varna exchanged wary glances. Reclaim their place in the universe? Flin had said something similar at the village. What did that mean? Almin Bor seemed to have similar thoughts?

"What place in the universe?" he asked, staring still at Flin, whose gaze had softened as he spoke, had become less focused.

"What? Oh, that is another tale for another time, I think, the story of the Prophecy of Halfgar, oldest of the Guide Mages." Suddenly he turned to look at Aldar, gripping her mother's hand. "Aldar, you told me about Varna's colours being all mixed up. How are they now?"

"Still mixed up but not as bad. They kind of look misty, like something is covering them up." Aldar looked at Varna and smiled. "They will be very pretty when they are fixed up."

Varna smiled and shook her head. "Well, I am feeling better. Not completely well, but better. I think I can move."

Flin again glanced to Aldar. "So, does everyone have these colours?"

"Oh, yes," Aldar replied quickly, then glanced to her mother for reassurance, receiving a nod in return. "Well, almost. Those bad men had no colours, but everyone else does."

"So, what colours do your mother and father have?"

"Father's colour is blue, like the way you feel sitting around a fire on a cold night. But when he tried to stop those bad men, his blue became like the ice over a lake." Blaine, recognising the warrior mentality being described, looked to Almin Bor and nodded slightly, one fighter to another, the latter sitting straight at the acknowledgement. "Mother's colours are apricot and rose but there was red when the bad men came. I think she was angry."

Magwyn smiled to her daughter. Angry, Varna noted, not terrified.

"And Jalor and Blaine?" said Flin, a slight grin aimed in Jalor's direction.

"Jalor is yellow like the sun and black like the night," Aldar said. She seemed a little troubled. "The black seems to shift around over the yellow. I've never seen that before. Blaine is brown but with golden bits shining through - that's also unusual. The gold was shining brighter when he fought the bad men." She looked at Blaine, who winked at her, causing a smile.

"And Flin?" Jalor said into the sudden quiet, smiling disarmingly to Flin.

"I'm not sure," Aldar said hesitantly. "He is grey like the dark rocks but sometimes there are bright white lights, like the grey is hiding something."

"Yes, well," said Flin. "And Varna we already know has many colours. Have you seen anything like that before?"

"No," the little girl said. "They are all the colours, swirling around. Not so muddied as before but still not as bright as they should be." She let go of her mother's hand and walked to Varna. "But they are getting more muddied up again."

Varna nodded, wincing. "Whatever you gave me is wearing off," she said to Flin. "My head aches and the fuzzy feeling is returning."

Aldar nodded. "Her colours need to be fixed," she said, and without ceremony reached out to touch Varna's temple with the palm of one hand.

Varna stiffened and her mouth opened in a soundless scream. Jalor leapt to his feet before Flin held out a hand imperiously, blocking him from going to Varna. Blaine, watching intently, held his ground. Varna slowly closed her mouth, eyes widening as Aldar removed her hand.

"There," Aldar announced. "That's better! Now the colours are a lot brighter." She moved back to her mother, who was watching her with a combination of awe and pride.

Flin stared, gaze switching between Aldar and Varna, back again and then again.

Varna swallowed, looking to Aldar. "Wha...," she stumbled, "what did you do? The headache and fuzzy feeling are gone. Oh," she said in delight, looking around, "I can see so much more clearly."

"I fixed your colours," Aldar said, in a matter-of-fact way, as though explaining the obvious to a slow adult. "I couldn't do it all because there was something stopping me." She smiled shyly. "I hope you don't mind."

"Mind? That was a great gift you gave me," Varna said, walking over to give Aldar a hug.

Flin watched on. "Gift? Yes, I suspect that it was." He considered his words before turning to Jalor. "I think it is imperative that we search out the remaining families and take them with us to the citadel."

Jalor regarded Flin for a long moment before replying. "I thought the objective was to get to the Citadel as fast as possible."

Flin waved away what he saw as a minor objection. "Nevertheless, it's obvious to all that you and Blaine are warriors" - he ignored Varna's exclamation at being excluded, although Blaine grinned - "and most warriors of honour are unable to see innocents suffer. Do I need to remind you that it is the children they seem to be after?"

Jalor chuckled despite himself. "You've not really made the case that it is the children being targeted." He held up a hand to forestall Flin's next words. "But I agree it's likely. And I didn't say we wouldn't search them out, merely that it was not my plan. Plans change." He looked to Blaine and Varna, both of whom nodded, then around the rest of the gathered men and women, receiving more determined nods. "So, let's go get the others."

30. Larger Group

Seventeen people. That was the count as they broke camp in the small clearing and prepared to move out. It was too large to move stealthily, even though the children continued to be more disciplined and better behaved than Jalor had ever thought could be the case. Almin Bor's thought had been to move through the woods, staying off the paths. There were no villages that needed warning in the immediate vicinity, and he was sure that he would be able to locate the three farms that were between Dimming Hollow and the Citadel. Jalor, however, merely shook his head. Pointing to the obvious signs of occupation of the small clearing by a reasonably large group. They were signs that could not be removed effectively.

"If we're in the trees and some of those things come upon us, we'll have a worse time," Jalor told Almin Bor. "Even though we may be able to move through the trees without too much noise, if they find us there, we can't stand easily. That and the fact that Blaine's arrows are our best weapons, and the trees will limit their effectiveness."

Almin Bor considered and nodded shortly.

"Aye, it makes sense. It seems to be wrong, though, not to take the cover."

Jalor nodded in sympathy. "Really, we'll make what is likely to be a slow dash to the Citadel. We take the road and move as quickly as we can. We get to the farms and get back on the road fast. I think it's the only way."

The group formed up as they had before. Sindelar led off, scouting far enough ahead that she would be able to warn them of anyone coming. The children walked in the centre, led by Almin Bor and Welkis, with Rengis Kar and Ursil trailing. Varna walked among the children with Aldar, who seemed to have adopted her, and Magwyn. Flin walked behind them, followed by Jalor and Blaine, the latter staying further back and acting as rear guard.

The morning passed uneventfully. Varna was able to keep pace, revelling in not feeling the debilitating lethargy, headaches and overall lack of well-being that she had experienced since landing. She could feel it lurking at the back of her consciousness, like an untamed creature waiting to pounce, but for now she was mostly free of it and able to pay attention to her surroundings.

Towards midday the group came upon the path to the first of the farms. Considering what available cover existed, Jalor and Almin Bor agreed that it would be best for everyone to stay together, so as a group they turned onto the path.

They had walked the path only a short time when Sindelar held up one fist and the group immediately stopped. Looking around, Jalor indicated the bush to one side of the path. The adults in the centre each picked up a child and moved off the path, picking their way carefully but quickly into the undergrowth where they crouched. The children stayed quiet and Varna found herself both marvelling and shaking her head at the thought that children needed to be brought up with such an awareness of ever-present danger, real or imagined.

Almin Bor waited in the path, sword in hand, Welkis by his side. Blaine had moved to the side opposite to that where the children had been taken, standing behind a bushy shrub where he could see the path and step back if necessary, or be seen and act as a diversion to lead attackers away from the others. He stood easily, an arrow nocked and ready. Jalor held his staff, not yet extended. Looking around, Jalor realised he would have to get another sword soon, if for no other reason than blending in. He snorted to himself. While Blaine had made him learn how to handle a fighting sword - not the ceremonial ones that the military forces still had for some reason - and while he was quite handy in Blaine's opinion, he still felt that he was a novice compared to the Weapons Sergeant. Still, it did seem to be the weapon of choice here and he had passed the one obtained from the bandits to Blaine to replace the one shattered during the last fight.

A thin warble came from the path ahead and Almin Bor and Welkis both relaxed slightly. They did not sheath their swords, Jalor noted, but they did stand slightly less tense. Four men walked around the bend and gestured to Almin Bor, who walked forward to greet them, clasping arms one after the other. They wore a uniform of sorts, black leather jerkin over black shirt and heavy trousers, with black boots. Over their shoulders were cloaks, also black, with a crest. Each had a sword and long knife hung from a broad leather belt, also black.

After a brief discussion Almin Bor gave a peculiar whistle. Within a few seconds Sindelar loped back around the bend, joining Almin Bor and the four men. All four turned back to where the others awaited them.

"It seems Jelnis Dil and Hornesh have already gone," Almin Bor told Jalor. "These are four of the Faero's guard and they have been doing the rounds warning everyone in the near area. Jelnis Dil's farm is unoccupied, but there are strange prints around the cottage. No sign of a struggle, luckily."

Jalor nodded.

"Where is the next? Have they already visited that one?"

"They gave the warning to Trellar and Freltis already. That would have been our third stop. In fact, they've given warning to six farmsteaders in the last day. All are on their way to the Citadel already. So, we have Girslit to go. His Bresla died two cycles back and he has three children. We can be at his farmstead before dark falls."

"Let's see if we can make better time and be there and gone before night falls. I'll feel better if we can choose our site for the night." Jalor looked back along the trail, eyes moving restlessly across a landscape that still was foreign to him, no matter the familiar look to much of it. "Will these four stay with us?"

"Aye, they'll accompany us to the Citadel. We can use the extra swords. They're good men in a fight."

"We may well need them," Jalor agreed. "Let's move."

The children were brought back out and the journey continued. The pace was increased and the younger children were carried by a succession of the adults as they struggled to walk as fast. Sindelar was joined by one of the guards as she scouted the way ahead, and two of the guards fell back to join rear guard duties with Blaine, who nodded companionably and then placed them where he wanted them. The fourth, who proved to be a rank akin to a corporal, moved back and forth along the order of march, sharing quick words with the members of the group. The people in this region appeared to be well acquainted with each other, Jalor reflected. Was that just being companionable as part of a cultural subgroup, or perhaps as part of a trade and collaboration group, or were they always on a war footing?

The addition of the four guards gave the group a more aggressive feel. Blaine would drop back every so often to check their back trail and then catch up to the others. The guards were surprised the first time he did that, but became familiar with the tactic. As they walked Blaine explained some of the techniques learnt over many missions about checking back trails. He quickly became accepted by all of the guards as a sergeant of sorts, especially when Almin Bor looked to him for updates.

Varna felt more alive than she had since landing on this planet. The forest was different enough to anything she had experienced that she found many things to examine, even while continuing to pay attention to her companions and maintaining a watch on the areas through which they moved. It was such a strange feeling. She felt that she was seeing things that she had never seen before, a depth of vision that she had not noticed in other situations, on other worlds, including her home world. Trees were of varying shades of green, but she could almost see the life pulsing through them, sap moving under the bark, small worms and bugs burrowing in the gaps in the bark, or crawling along branches.

Tiny though they were Varna fancied that she was able to see them clearly, or nearly so. It was amazing! So much life that everyone ignored because it was out of sight, too small to be noticed. But there they were, existing each in its own unique way, each with its own means of surviving.

The birds continued to sing, songs of joy in the sunshine, trills of satisfaction in having caught the crawler, hoots and calls of caution at these large ones moving swiftly through their midst. Varna found herself listening to the birds, hearing them as they called to each other in different voices. She could tell one from another, where previously they had all merged into a sort of avian background noise. She could tell which birds were warning others of the approach of dangerous strangers, and which were not afraid even so. Almost without volition she sent out reassuring feelings, and in response she felt waves of welcome as the birds reacted. All around the small troop of Ennarisi and humans, bird life erupted in a dazzling display of aerial acrobatics, causing the children and some of the adults to stare at the sight. Without conscious thought, Varna held out one hand and a small bird, bright of plumage and with a shrill *tweep* as a cry, launched from its tree and landed on her hand, hopping to maintain balance before making the short flight to land again on her shoulder. A second bird, larger and with a more aggressive stance, did likewise, so that Varna now had a bird on each shoulder. Blaine, behind Varna, watched in fascination as a third and then a fourth bird likewise perched with the other two. All were tweeting and whistling as though having a conversation with Varna.

Varna, meanwhile, had fallen into a kind of marching meditation, listening to the birds and the surrounding forest and finding nothing to threaten them from the myriad bird-life and the animals that were avoiding them. The twin suns were moving through the day and shadows were starting to lengthen when the party reached the edge of the trees. As they emerged from the forest the birds each gave a farewell cry and flew from Varna's shoulder, the first one giving her a tiny peck on her neck before doing so. It was enough to rouse Varna and she self-consciously glanced around, seeing Blaine watching her.

"Okay?" he asked, with a smile. "Your friends had to go?"

"They belong in the forest," she said in response, shrugging as she did so.

"You need to keep paying attention, though," Blaine said seriously, "even if you are feeling better now."

"We were in no danger," Varna said to Blaine. "The birds would have told me." She smiled at Blaine's raised eyebrows. "I know how that sounds, but it's true. The birds and animals had no fears other than us stamping through their world."

Blaine nodded thoughtfully but even as he did so there was an urgent hoot from within the forest and the birds disappeared. Blaine looked to Varna and she nodded.

"Something or someone is coming. Danger!"

31. Sentinel Tree

Blaine and Sindelar returned from a forward scout and conferred with Jalor and Almin Bor, who had moved up to join them. With a few gestures, a couple of nods and several significant glances around them, a decision was made. Blaine departed again, this time back in the direction from which they had come, while Jalor announced that they would find a quiet camp site and stay there for the night. Sindelar led the way down a slope to the left of the track. Most of the rest followed confidently, familiar with the terrain and the path being taken. The four guards waited watchfully on the road while Jalor made his way to where Varna and Flin also waited.

"The track ends just a little ahead, and then there's open country for quite a long way," he said quietly. "If the second group of those things happened on us in open country, and if they are more numerous than the first lot, then we would be in trouble. So, we'll wait here for a bit and find somewhere we can defend."

"Almin Bor and Sandyn know of a place?" Varna surmised.

"Yes, some large rocks down there. Apparently, it slopes down and then rises a short way and the rocks are on top of the rise. Almin Bor has a good head for defence, I think, and he thinks it can be defended if the numbers are not too great. And he seems to think Blaine can do anything in that regard."

"Almin Bor is a shrewd and reliable judge," Flin said carefully. "Do not let the farmer on display lull you. He was one of the best military leaders of the Blood at a very young age, before meeting and wooing

Magwyn. He can be trusted with any sort of secret, and will reserve judgement."

So, Varna thought ruefully, it's not just Flin who doesn't believe their story. Ah well! Varna and Flin followed the same path behind the others, catching and shepherding Aldar ahead of them. The children remained quiet and calm. It was amazing, Varna thought to herself yet again, how these children already knew how to be quiet when it was needed. Her respect for these 'people of the Blood' continued to grow.

They reached the bottom of the slope and followed a faint trail upwards, to come out in a space half-way up a small hill. The top of the hill was crowned by huge rocks, with the largest one near to them split down the middle as though struck by a giant axe. Varna stayed on the outside while Aldar and Flin followed the rest into the opening. She waited with Sindelar for Jalor to reach the rocks and all three turned to face where the trail exited the scrubby woods.

"Can you two do a scout around these rocks? Let's see where we may have problems if they attack us here."

Jalor thought he could see where their former track ran, and hoped he would be able to see anyone moving on it. Varna and Sindelar nodded and moved off, dropping packs just inside the crack in the rock. Varna unclipped her staff from her belt but did not extend it. Sindelar had her sword in hand. Almost soundlessly, Varna started a patrol around the rocky outcrop, taking note of how the vegetation seemed to have been cleared to a regular distance down the slope. Meeting Sindelar on the far side, she could find no other entry points to what she knew would be a small cleared area amid the rocks. Impressed, after only a few minutes the two women were back to report to Jalor.

"It's a good location. No other entry points and this cleared zone goes all around. I think this is a well-used vantage point," Varna said as she joined Jalor.

"It is," Sindelar confirmed. "We have a few of them around the plateau. They're places where we can retreat to if needed. They haven't been used for a while but like Holpenvalk we keep them maintained."

"I thought that may be the case. Both Almin Bor and Sandyn suggested this spot before we left Dimming Hollow. This is the ideal sort of spot a group could use as a fall-back if needed. Another rendezvous point or a last stand."

Varna considered for a moment, thinking about these simple redoubts scattered across this high plateau in preparation for something. But what?

"Blaine?" she said after a moment.

"Scouting," Jalor replied, dividing his gaze between where he thought the track was and the trail leading to the rocks. "Assuming there are some of those creatures coming, and that he can do so without too much danger, he'll try to reduce their numbers. If they follow the same pattern as the first lot there will be about ten of them with a Shadow."

Varna gasped.

"Shadow? You've seen them here?"

Jalor frowned, realising that with Varna's unusual condition and the hustle and bustle that had occurred neither he nor Blaine had ever mentioned the Empire agent that Blaine had killed.

"Sorry," he said to Varna, grimacing, "when we had the fight at Almin Bor's farm there was a Shadow involved, potentially as the leader. I've had no chance to give you the full story since, and you were out of it at the time."

"That may mean we're facing some form of telepathic enemy, then," Varna replied thoughtfully, waving away the apology.

Sindelar looked from one to the other, surprised. Telepathic? And Jalor and Varna obviously knew about these people also.

"Damn," Jalor said, mentally kicking himself. "I should have thought of that. If that's the case then they may be aware we're here, or that someone is who can fight back. Our arrow shafts can pierce that strange armour of those half-men where the local ones shatter, and that will have been noticed. If that was passed on before it was killed ..."

He left the remainder of the sentence unsaid. From the timbered slope arose a warbling bird cry and Jalor shifted stance.

"Blaine will be here soon," he said to Varna, who raised an eyebrow. "That was a Valerian Honey Sucker. Not too many of them around here, I'm betting. But it means trouble also, otherwise it would have been a Deltan Manitor."

Sindelar was confused again but held her tongue. She had never heard of either of the creatures Jalor named, and she had a good working knowledge of many of the creatures of Ennaris.

Only a moment later Blaine emerged from the tree line, moving rapidly to the rocks.

"There are twice the number of those creatures, about twenty of them," he reported. "But they're herding five children - no parents. And they're close. And Jalor, two Shadows."

Jalor nodded.

"How close?"

"A few minutes only."

Jalor called for Flin, who appeared moments later accompanied by Almin Bor. He rapidly filled the storyteller in on the situation.

"The children again," Flin said grimly. "They're seeking out the next generation of the Blood. We must save them if we can, Jalor."

Almin Bor just nodded.

"I thought you might say that," Jalor replied. "But it will take all of us to make that happen. Blaine, Varna?" At nods from both, he continued, "Then let's get this happening. Almin Bor, I plan on leaving Magwyn and Sindelar here with the other women and children, and the rest of us will take the fight to them. Okay?"

"You can try to leave Magwyn out of this but will find yourself with a war on two fronts if you do," the farmer said with a grim smile. "And you know she shoots a mean bow," he said meaningfully, nodding to the bow slung over Blaine's shoulder, "especially with your shafts. That frees you up to fight also."

Magwyn materialised behind Almin Bor and nodded.

"I would avenge my friends," she said quietly but fiercely.

Jalor hesitated a moment and then acquiesced. In no time at all they had explained the situation to Sindelar, who agreed reluctantly and moved to guard the crack in the rock while the rescue party, led by Blaine, headed at a rapid clip down the slope and into the trees. As they went, Jalor explained the strategy he had worked out. Reaching the path, they turned left and made good pace to where the path opened to the grassed area Jalor had sought to avoid when stopping for the night.

Varna was left in the tree line, with Magwyn seeking her own place to one side. The latter carried Blaine's bow and the quiver of shafts from *Starfire*. Blaine had told her not to miss or she would have to go find any lost shafts and she had just sniffed at the suggestion, smiling as she walked away. About one hundred metres outside the trees Jalor paused the party. There was a slight dip in the ground, sufficient to shield them from sight for a few moments. All crouched into the dip, staying low. Neither Jalor nor Blaine could see where Varna or Magwyn were.

A short time later, Blaine signalled as the half-men emerged from the trees and started to cross the open space. The five children were towards the rear, with two Shadows gliding along with them. Flin made a half-growl when he saw them, an expression of disgust as though he recognised them.

"Ghazrak!" Flin snarled.

"You know these things?" Jalor asked quietly, watching the creatures that now had a name as they stalked into the opening.

"I do," Flin replied tightly. "They are an attempt to replicate the devil-spawn, luckily a poor attempt. It would seem Grensor did not perish after all. We thought as much."

Jalor glanced to Flin. The old man had a glint in his eye, a hard expression on his face. The storyteller was replaced by ... something. Later, he thought. Jalor waited until the whole party was in view.

"Now," he said and they all stood. Flin was in the centre with Jalor and Blaine on his right, Almin Bor on his left and the others ranged on either side.

Flin merely stood without any weapon evident, while the others carried swords. Jalor and Blaine had their telescoping staffs attached to their belts. Blaine held his captured sword easily in one hand, as did the rest of the party. The first of the advancing half-men - ghazrak - yelped when they stood and the whole band stopped, bunching slightly, looking around suspiciously for others. Only fools would take on a band their size when there were only eight of them, so there must be others. Finally, after a grunted discussion and with some waving of one hand, the band spread out slightly and started to advance on the men in a rough and unruly line. Two of the band held the children back just outside the tree line. The Shadows drifted after the main force.

The larger force was only thirty metres away when the first of Magwyn's shafts reached out from hiding and drilled through the neck of one of the stragglers. None of the main group noticed the rear-most one fall, nor when a second straggler followed. When a third fell with a gurgled cry, though, several of them stopped to look back, which resulted in a fourth being felled.

Not bad, Blaine thought to himself, given they were about eighty metres away and Magwyn with an unfamiliar bow.

The number of attackers were now fourteen plus the two Shadows - one Shadow, Blaine amended as one of them fell to Magwyn's fifth shaft, the robes fluttering to the ground as its spirit faded - and two of the half-men turned back to locate the archer. To provide further distraction, Blaine and Almin Bor each stepped toward the attackers, swinging their swords in a display that would have had Blaine's old sword master gritting his teeth.

But it achieved the goal. The remaining Shadow still held back two ghazrak to guard the children and did not notice Varna steal from the gloom beneath the trees. Relying on what she now knew of the children of the Blood, Varna put one finger to her mouth in the universal symbol for quiet and gestured the children to move behind her, while she moved toward the guards. As the first guard turned and saw her she pressed the stud to extend the staff, and then a second stud that released the blade embedded in the staff. The first guard went down with a thud. Varna needed to retract the blade and then struggled to extract it from beneath the fallen body, which gave the second ghazrak enough time to whirl and advance on her.

Deftly she swung the staff in a blocking move, before twisting it so that one end thudded into the guard's head, where it joined its neck. That had no effect beyond causing it to shake its head and grin evilly. Varna sighed, knowing this could get difficult now. She found herself hard pressed to keep the half-man at bay, as it kept trying to bull into her. One advantage, though, was that it had forced the fight into the trees, out of sight of the main battle, which meant its fellows did not see what was happening. But that was scant comfort right now, Varna thought as she felt the wind of a particularly vicious sword swing that she diverted at the last second. This was not going to work much longer.

Varna noticed the children had gathered on one side, so she moved in the other direction. Suddenly, as her attacker slightly over-balanced following a wild air swing, Varna retracted the staff and skipped back several paces, bending over to give the impression of being winded - okay, so it was not all impression - and watched as her assailant managed to re-balance and, with a roar, charge at her with sword raised high for a cutting downswing. Judging her moment, Varna hit both studs and planted the extended staff firmly in the ground so the ghazrak impaled itself on the extended blade. Its eyes opened wide and with a final gurgle it collapsed, drawing the staff to the ground also.

Once again Varna struggled to extract the staff's blade and then had another struggle to extract the staff, but at last it was done. She looked for the children and found them in a tight knot, all five staring at her, obviously afraid but watchful. Again, Varna was struck with the spirit of these people, realising that these children may have seen their parents killed in the last day or so. Varna extended the blade again to wipe off the black blood and then retracted the staff and hung it from her belt. Only then did she move over to the children, the oldest of whom was about the same age as Aldar and the youngest about the age of Eldry. Again, she raised one finger to her lips and gestured to them as she moved deeper into the woods. She knew they would be missed and wanted to find somewhere more defensible.

Meanwhile, the two ghazrak who had diverted to look for Magwyn were the ones who noticed that the children were missing. They moved to investigate and found their dead comrade, with signs leading into the wood. With a couple of grunts, they followed the signs into the trees. Varna could hear the two coming through the trees, making no attempt at stealth. Shepherding the children ahead of her, Varna found herself being drawn to a large clearing that she was sure had not been there before.

In the midst of the clearing was a large tree, with a truly enormous trunk and branches that extended half-way across the clearing in each direction. The huge trunk appeared to have been split open at some stage and a sort of chamber was revealed as she came closer. As she silently directed the children to the tree, Varna was dismayed as her old fuzzy feeling made itself felt again. She felt rather than heard a roaring in her head. Not again, she thought, and not now! With great effort she guided the children into the tree's cave-like opening, placing herself at the opening to guard them for as long as she could. She held the staff with the shaft extended but the blade hidden still, struggling to maintain focus.

She felt a warmth creep over her, even as the pressure inside her head seemed to increase. Whispers were forcing their way through, offering words intended to comfort her and holding her still even as the two half-men emerged into the clearing. With some confusion, Varna saw them looking around. Obviously, they were also confused at the existence of the clearing and great tree, but somehow missed seeing her standing in front of the tree. In fact, they both looked directly at the tree, at her, and their gaze moved on. She was watching still as first one and then the second were killed by arrows, and then Magwyn emerged from one side of the clearing, moving to the tree in the centre. She frowned at Varna standing still in the tree's opening and pushed through to find the children in a small group against the back of a surprisingly spacious area.

Varna could feel her blood pulsing through her veins. She could hear her own heart beating. She was unable to move, even when Magwyn pushed past her into the tree's interior chamber. She still could not move as she heard the sounds of battle move closer and saw the remaining Shadow and two half-men back into the clearing. They also looked around and again did not see her. Following them were Jalor and Blaine, both taken aback at seeing the clearing, but continuing to concentrate on their prey. Behind them came Almin Bor, and then Rengis Kar and Welkis. Varna could see that Jalor was injured, and his movements were more sluggish than those of Blaine, who advanced on the three relentlessly.

Blaine now wielded two swords, although one obviously had been taken from one of the half-men, and he was grim-faced as he moved further into the clearing. All were now well underneath the overhanging branches of the tree. The two half-men suddenly lunged at Jalor, who managed to avoid the attack by leaping back awkwardly, and Blaine closed the small gap to stand with him while the attackers drove hard with energetic if unskilled moves. Almin Bor tried to flank the band, and one ghazrak followed him, dividing its time between the injured Jalor and the threat posed by Almin Bor. The Shadow watched closely, with strain evident even through the usual ground-length robes covering a not quite corporeal body. Finally, Blaine disposed of one of the half-men and turned to defend Jalor, whose face now was ashen and who was forced to step back from the fight. As Varna watched the Shadow drew with insubstantial hands from under its robes a long, wickedly gleaming knife. It moved towards Jalor, who now was tottering to one side of the ongoing fight between Blaine and an increasingly desperate ghazrak.

The lethargy retreated. Varna felt almost a physical lifting of the pressure in her head and, shaking her head in an effort to clear the remnants, she lifted the staff, stepped out from the tree trunk, pushed the second stud and drove the blade through the Shadow.

With an audible sigh - Varna had never heard a sound from any Shadow in the past - the robes collapsed over the staff and extended blade. At the same time Blaine ended his battle with the last attacker, sweeping both swords in opposing arcs to simultaneously knock the half-man's sword aside with one while driving the other through the middle of the torso.

With a sigh of her own, Varna retracted the blade and staff, and ran to where Jalor had slipped to kneel. She caught him as he toppled over, blood staining arms and legs.

"Children?" he asked.

"Safe. All safe," Varna replied, easing him to lie on the ground.

Jalor smiled, closed his eyes and let the encroaching blackness take him.

32. Flin

The four guardsmen burst from the forest into the clearing, staring in shock at the tree that dominated the space. Almin Bor waved them over wearily. After a short discussion, they were brought to the group under the tree. All four showed signs of injury but all held themselves erect.

That evening the group decided to stay in the strangely comforting presence of the enormous tree. After Flin made a close and thoughtful examination, the dead ghazrak were dragged away - no easy task as they were very heavy - and a small fire was kindled beneath the overhang of the tree. Sticks and twigs for a cook fire were gathered from the forest - by unspoken consent the great tree was not touched, although the children were bedded down inside the space opened by the rent in its side.

Flin spent much time with Jalor, cleaning and tending to wounds in his left arm and leg with a herb poultice and simple bandages. Varna thought she saw a faint glow around Flin as he worked, but she could not be sure. Jalor seemed to be more comfortable when Flin had finished, though. The other injured were given some of the peculiar herbal treatment that Flin dispensed. Varna was sure she saw some sort of glow from time to time as he attended the wounded. But the effects of whatever assailed her, whether trying to be of help or not, were gathering again, and she retreated to lean against the tree as she sought the relative peace of meditation. She managed to sleep somehow, but awakened without being refreshed, and with the effect of the awakening gift - or whatever it was - continuing to creep over her. Even Flin and his herbs were unable to effect any improvement and she resigned herself to struggling on.

Jalor was resting, reclining beneath the tree in the clearing. Blaine had made the journey to bring Sandyn, Sindelar and the children from their hide-away. Varna had explained to the group how they had found the tree and moved the children into the opening, with Magwyn having exhausted her arrows, and how Varna had been unable to do anything but stand and watch until the last moment. Also, how the half-men had seemed to look right through her as they came out to locate the children and again as they retreated from Jalor and Blaine. Flin was troubled. Standing beneath the tree he could tell it was very old but could sense nothing special about it, beyond the central chamber and, of course, the fact that the tree probably should not exist.

"The tree sounds as though it's what was once called a Sentinel Tree. I have never seen one but recognise it from descriptions. Halfgar used to remind the Guides that Sentinels were placed to provide safe havens, to protect those in peril."

"Placed by whom?" Varna asked as she walked around the tree with the storyteller.

"The Guardians," Flin said, with a quirk of his lips.

"You seem to be troubled by thoughts of the Guardians," she replied, carefully not looking at Flin as she ran one hand gently over the bark of the tree.

She could feel nothing now, and only had faint and uncertain memories of what happened from the time of reaching the tree to killing the enemy agent.

"The Guardians," Flin mused. "You know, I have defended the Guardians for my whole life, telling the old tales, ancient tales, working to meet standards defined thousands of generations before I was born. Many people over the long history of Ennaris have believed the Guardians to be real. But the Guardians are an ideal. They are mythical beings who led the earliest Ennarisi out of the mire and into intelligence, provided us with principles that have been maintained over an unimaginably long time. The oldest tales tell of the Guardians battling to save Ennaris, to protect it from all sorts of perils that the ancients didn't understand and so presented them as all-powerful beings, well-intentioned and always looking out for us."

"We have similar legends," Varna said.

"And then after a while the Guardians no longer appeared to the people and those legends waned." Flin sighed. "Sometimes, I would sit out under the stars and wish that the Guardians could be real and that they would appear and resolve our problems for us." He laughed shortly, bitterly. "Of course, that did not happen, even during the rebellion that caused the destruction of our world, so why would it happen now?"

Varna was surprised at the storyteller's bitterness about the Guardians' lack of support.

"Perhaps the Guardians represent something of a higher order, like your better instincts. That was one interpretation that my people put on the old legends." Varna smiled. "And perhaps they are tales told to make people feel better, that they are not alone in the universe, that even in the worst of trials someone cares, even if that someone doesn't actively take part. And perhaps, also, just to make sense of things that are not understood."

Flin nodded, sighing.

"Perhaps all of those things are correct. Certainly, by ascribing higher order considerations and making them an authority by whom our principles were developed and who delivered them to us, the Guardians are out of reach and thus unchallenged. Even those who rebelled did so knowing they went against the principles of the Guardians, so deeply were they ingrained in all Ennarisi, but they also believed that there would be no consequences from the Guardians."

The two stood for a moment, sharing the peace under the tree. But time continued to pass.

"Come, Flin," Varna said gently, "we must move on."

She moved back to the group that was breaking camp.

"Yes," Flin said to the tree after Varna had left, resting his forehead against its rough bark. "But I do wish they were real. If the Children have truly returned then we will need all the help we can get."

The group cleaned the clearing as well as they could. Jalor was surprisingly better than Varna had expected and was walking with the aid of a crude crutch.

As they reached the cover of the forest Varna turned back. The tree seemed to waver slightly and she could have sworn she saw a figure standing in front of the opening in its side. Shrugging, and gathering her strength to battle against her strange lethargy and fatigue, she turned back and entered the forest. Blaine again brought up the rear.

When the small group crested a rise and Varna looked back to search for the clearing, she could find no trace.

As they walked the story of the battle was told. There seemed to be some confusion about how Flin made his way through the thick of the battle, using a sword that none had seen before that seemed to be able to disable the ghazrak. It seemed that the battle advanced with Flin darting in to cause enough damage that the others could finish each of the creatures off. The two that had backed into the clearing had, in fact, followed the Shadow when it retreated.

"You recognised those things?" Varna asked.

"I did," Flin replied, looking around the gathered group. "They are ghazrak. They are fell creatures made by Grensor, or if not him then one or more of his acolytes. But I fear they were made by Grensor."

"So, what are they?" Blaine asked. "And who's Grensor?"

"Grensor was one of Goroth's lieutenants. He was a gifted geneticist and was quite a medical pioneer. He developed some very important techniques for overcoming several illnesses, better than those that had been used for a very long time, but he strayed to the dark arts. Originally, he sought to make better soldiers, but as he was drawn deeper and deeper to the forbidden lore his experiments took terrible forms. Ghazrak are inspired by what are commonly called demons. But they are constructed from men and a blend of different creatures. Their bodies are altered in awful ways."

"You mean, he takes these creatures and cuts them up?" Almin Bor shivered as he asked.

"No, a geneticist makes changes at the level of the body's cells," Flin replied. "A cell is the smallest part of what makes your body. And each cell can hold enough information for your body to rebuild itself. Grensor made those cells different enough that he could grow the ghazrak. However, I do believe that he melded together parts of different creatures, including men, so there may be some truth in answer to your question."

Varna glanced to Jalor and Blaine in turn. Both raised eyebrows. A simple storyteller explaining the basics of genetic engineering. Just another story? Or was Flin something quite different.

"How do you know of these creatures?" Varna asked. "None of the others seem to know anything of them."

The gathered members of the party agreed, head shakes occurring all around.

"Some of the oldest stories tell of them," Flin replied dismissively. "We usually don't tell those tales. They are too unsettling."

"I can understand that," Blaine replied as though it was of secondary importance. "Did you notice anything different when you examined them? You spent quite some time before we burned them."

"They do seem to have some differences," Flin replied carefully, "at least to what the stories say."

"The stories describe them in a lot of detail then?" Blaine queried.

"Enough that I could tell there were changes," Flin replied looking steadily at Blaine. "The armour is thicker than the old ones are described as having, and they appear to be more heavily muscled. They all seem to have some sort of horn. Some of them had two. In the old stories there was a single horn, and often it was filed to a point and used as a last resort weapon."

"How many were there back then?" Jalor asked. "Were they easy to make? Were there thousands, hundreds, hands-full?"

"There were hundreds," Flin said. "From what I could gather for every specimen that worked there were many that failed. And it needed a strong power source. If Grensor or someone else has managed to recreate these things, they must have some of the old technology also."

"Power source?" Almin Bor asked, trying to follow the conversation and feeling that he was missing something important. "Like a fire and bellows, or hrss-driven pump?"

"Something like that," Flin agreed, "but much more powerful. Remember, at the time of the rebellion Ennaris was far more advanced. They had ways to make light or energy that we are unable to recreate with our current skills and abilities. I fear Grensor has managed it."

The group moved on, moving faster than before. They reached the final farm, sitting in an open field with the inevitable cottage in the centre, a barn on one side. The signs of a struggle were everywhere, with damaged fences, overturned farm wagons, implements strewn around the yard.

Blaine looked to Jalor and nodded towards the cottage and barn. Jalor held out one hand, the other still gripping his makeshift crutch, halting everyone while Blaine went on alone. He entered the cottage, exiting after only a short time, and then moved to the barn. After a longer time, he returned, grim-faced, shaking his head. Almin Bor stalked to the barn and entered, accompanied by Flin, both returning with fixed expressions. Almin Bor glanced to each member of the group and without words started back towards the road. The rest of the group, with the children, followed wordlessly, as did the guards.

Flin stepped close to Jalor.

"Go with them," he said quietly. "The citadel is almost two days at our current pace. I will catch you up shortly."

Jalor searched Flin's face. The calm mien of the storyteller was gone - in its place Jalor saw implacable intent, a barely held fury. He hesitated. Finally, he just nodded and started hobbling after the others. Varna followed and Blaine trailed behind, constantly searching the woods where they ended at the field boundaries.

The group was silent as they moved along, with their pace being held back by the children and the injured. They had been moving for about two hours, Varna estimated, when behind them there was a loud clap and a bright flash. Varna whirled about to see a pillar of smoke rising from where she estimated that the farm was located. Blaine grimaced and exchanged looks with Jalor - anyone in the vicinity would be alerted now, especially any more of the invading forces.

In a remarkably short time Flin caught the group, his expression still forbidding.

"Something else your stories teach you?" Jalor asked dryly.

Flin glanced at him.

"Something like that," he said shortly, then sighed. "I could not leave them like that, especially the children. And I left a message for those who may return. They have declared war on my people, and war they will have."

And who are your people, Flin?" Jalor asked quietly.

"They are all my people, Jalor. And I will not fail them again."

It was not too far further along before Flin paused, turned in the road and looked back. The others also stopped and turned, caught by something in Flin's demeanour. In the distance, from the last farm, there came another flash followed by a rolling thunder that lasted for several heartbeats and then faded away. Flin stared but his sight was elsewhere. Finally, he turned and seeing everyone else looking at him, gave a frosty smile.

"They went back," he said. "They will not harm anyone else."

Flin started to walk down the road again. After exchanging glances with each other, the group followed. Blaine passed by Jalor, standing in the road looking back to where Flin had done whatever he had done - Jalor decided he did not want to know, although he knew he had to find out - and snorted.

"Storyteller. Yeah right! And I'm a Drakonis dung fly!"

33. Lak

The steppes of the eastern part of the northern continent were harsh but, for those who knew its secrets, far from barren. Here the people had split apart into clans after the rebellion's devastation, those who were left and those who sought shelter over the ensuing cycles. Water was scarce if you did not know the land but, for those who called the steppes home, the pointers to food and water were clear. The clans only took what they needed, leaving plenty to regenerate and for others who were in need to take what they needed. They had survived in a loose confederation since shortly after the rebellion, at times making war on other clans, and at other times assisting former enemies to survive sickness, drought, fire. Peace had now existed for many cycles.

Occasionally, the clans came together in a great gathering. The Gathering it was called, and all knew which gathering was meant. Here the clan leaders would discuss conditions, would settle disputes great and small, and would make decisions that warranted their attention in council. So it had been for many lifetimes, and few doubted that it was a good way.

Also at the Gathering were contests of skill, for while clans fought amongst themselves - and occasionally those fights became heated and hurts were taken - rare was it now that a true clan man or woman was killed or seriously injured at a Gathering. Children were rare amongst the clans and they were prized. Thus, child-bearing aged people of the clans were protected to the extent possible, in accordance with the traditions and laws of the clans. The contests were the clans' way to ensure that the old skills were retained, without the need for warfare.

The killing skills, the defensive skills, the quiet stalking to infiltrate a camp. For the Prophecy, known by all the people of the clans, said that they would play a major role when the Children of Ennaris returned. And they were to keep themselves ready.

None alive truly understood the directive but those traditional tales, handed down from mothers to daughters across the ages, from fathers to sons, and repeated at gatherings around the communal fires, told of Lak, the Guardian who loved the great open spaces, and her final instruction to the survivors of the rebellion's end that they must hold themselves ready to defend Ennaris when the time came. The clans' predecessors, ever combative in approach in the highly civilised world before the destruction of the rebellion, interpreted their instructions after that event to mean that they must build battle skills and hold those skills at their peak. Battle skills became a way of life, and the people of the clans of the steppes became a byword for fighting skills and courage. One did not pick a fight with the clans and expect easy victory. Several had tried over the cycles. None had succeeded.

The Gathering was also the time when the young passed through their tests and became men and women in the eyes of the clans. They would then leave their parents' tent and join that of the younglings, where their instruction would deepen and they would determine where their individual skills lay. And so it came to pass that Horint was riding alone across the steppes. He maintained a sharp lookout, for it was not unknown for those of another clan to try to disrupt the trial, partly in jest but partly to ensure the trial truly tested the candidate. And at times to cause humiliation, for despite the clans surviving together and taking part in a community of the steppes people, there were those who maintained jealousies about hunts won, or who undertook stealthy escapades to bring ridicule on the clan that failed to detect the stalker, and at times just because of personality differences.

Luckily, to Horint's knowledge there was only a single clan being difficult at that time, and the elders were discussing what that clan was doing, as it had not yet attended the current Gathering. That was unheard of and presaged problems, so the other clans thought. For if one clan broke apart and betrayed the ways of the steppes dwellers then trouble would follow. Horint was aware that the elders, his own father included, were even considering true armed conflict as a possible outcome, a thought too horrible to contemplate after so long without open warfare. Horint, even while he turned over these thoughts, was also paying attention to his surroundings.

He became aware of a noise coming up from the rear. Horint tensed, gripping his spear and shield tighter while using his knees to turn his mount, the better to face any danger face on. However, there was no-one and nothing in sight, except the long grasses waving in the light breeze that usually blew across the steppes. Puzzled, Horint continued to watch. His mount stood perfectly still, awaiting the subtle orders that Horint had been taught from the time he could hold onto a rein and straddle a hrss. It came to him then. The sound was coming from above him!

Horint looked into the sky, shielding his sight from the brightness with the hand holding his spear, in time to see a bright bolt of light blast across the sky. It was past him before he knew it. Horint tried to follow its path as it plunged over the ridge nearby and impacted with a great *whoomp*! The young man was shocked into immobility, but only momentarily, for the steppes people were of hardy stock and preferred to face dangers head-on. Besides, whatever it was had come to ground in the Eye of Lak and Horint had been warned about entering that domain. So, of course, he was curious about what it held, and this seemed to be a good opportunity to find out.

Kicking his hrss into motion, Horint guided it to the point where the rocky ground rose above the steppes and formed the ridge that encircled the Eye. He dismounted and ground hitched the hrss, confident that it would remain exactly where he left it for as long as needed.

He scrambled through the broken rocks that legend said were thrown up long ago by some sort of massive explosion and crouched so as not to expose himself to the skyline. Carefully, he peered through a gap in the rocks. His breath left him in a rush, for sitting serenely on top of a small pile of rocks was a beautiful young woman, and she was looking directly at him! Where had she come from? How could she be there? She had no hrss and Horint was aware enough of his powers of observation to know that he would not have missed seeing a hrss moving across the steppes.

But Horint saw something else, too, that caused him enormous concern. Behind the young woman - she really was very pretty, Horint noted - a sand viper, most deadly of a large number of deadly slithers, was moving in her direction. It must have been disturbed by whatever the object was that came down from the skies. He stood and tried to warn the woman, waving his hand in a gesture to move away. But the young woman merely smiled and waved back, gesturing for him to approach her. The slither moved closer.

Horint ran down the slope, or tried to. Dodging sharp rocks, hurdling smaller ones, slipping and sliding as the looser shale-like stones moved under his feet, he drew his sabre as he ran. It would be touch and go, he thought.

"Move!" he shouted as he reached the floor of the Eye and started across smooth level ground. But the woman merely stayed sitting. The sand viper was almost to her. She calmly watched Horint race across the intervening ground. Horint reached her just as the sand viper raised itself to strike. He decided he did not have time to use his sabre and settled for shoving her out of the way, only to feel the sand viper strike take him in the back.

He cried out as he hit the ground beside her but, even though he knew the sand viper poison was already working its deadly way through him, he forced himself to his feet to kill the viper before it could strike again. He stood and swayed, trying to locate the slither while he could, but failing to do so. Finally, he fell to his knees, feeling with despair the growing numbness that he knew was the sand viper poison killing him. And then it was not. The numbness quickly receded and then faded away completely. Horint stared in confusion as the young woman stood and reached out to help him to his feet.

"I thank you, my protector," she declared. "I'm pleased to see that the clans have remained true over all this time, and that self-sacrifice for others remains in your blood."

"Who are you?" Horint stammered.

"I am Lak," the woman replied. "Stand, Horint, and stay with me. The time has come for the clans to prepare. The time has come when your preparations during the long wait will be tested. For the Children have returned and the Guardians are coming home."

Horint, wondering that this beautiful young woman could be a Guardian, *their* Guardian, *his* Guardian, took a moment to realise what she was saying. Then he prostrated herself before her, face pushed into the dirt. But she grasped him by the arm and lifted him effortlessly to his feet.

"No, my Horint," she said softly. "Neither you nor your people have need to pay obeisance to me. I am not a god, and I definitely do not want worship. But I do want the clans to be ready for what may come. Accompany me now, Horint, as my right hand. We have much to do."

Over the next two days the group maintained a wary but steady pace. Each night saw them find a protected spot that one of the former militia members knew. The first night after the battle of the tree, as they called it, there was a stand of trees with a small rocky barrier ringing a clearing within, obviously man-made and well used. The second night it was the peak of a small hill with an indentation where the children were placed while the adults slept in a tight ring around them. On both nights guards were maintained.

On the morning of the second day a couple of men stumbled into the tree camp, exhausted. Each had wild eyes and carried various wounds. They were the sole survivors of a guard unit that had encountered a troop of ghazrak. Calmed down by Sindelar under the sharp gaze of Almin Bor, they told a story of coming upon the creatures as they were feasting on something that proved to be arms and legs of people. The guard unit had attacked and been thrown back, doing little damage to the half-men as their swords and spears could not penetrate the armour plates at front and back.

"They're unbeatable," one of the guards gasped.

"No," Sindelar said. "They can be beaten. But you have to know how."

"There's a gap in that armour under each arm, and again below the chest plate," Welkis continued. "But it takes more than one of you to take that stroke. And you have to leave yourself open in doing so."

"Except that Blaine's arrows can break through the armour," Magwyn continued, gesturing toward the Warrior. "And his bow can shoot them harder and further than ours."

"So, there are ways and means," Almin Bor said, "as you have always been taught. You're exhausted but we must continue. Take a short time for food and drink and then join with us. We go to the citadel."

"Aye, captain," the second guard said. "I'd reckon these things are heading there, too. And we came across sign of others too. Don't know how many but at least two more groups."

"At least thirty, then," Jalor said, standing, "and likely more. How strong is this citadel?"

"It's never been taken," Almin Bor said. "And the Faero maintains a strong Guard there."

"Not any more," the first guard said with a sour twist of his mouth. "Intika took most of the guard out to find and warn the people. Then Creely sent the remaining guards out in small groups to warn people about these creatures. There's no-one of the Guard left there now."

"All of them? If they've been running into these things in small groups then we may have lost a lot of the Citadel Guard," Almin Bor commented with a worried frown.

At nightfall of the second day the number swelled again with the discovery of a third guard, from another patrol, limping determinedly in the direction of the citadel. The march stopped again as the newcomer was treated, given some water. Varna watched Flin take some herbs from a pouch by his side, carefully separate out some seeds and then mix it into a mug of water. He stirred it with one finger and Varna could have sworn she saw steam rising from the mug. Flin handed the mug to the injured guard and then without ceremony tore open the guard's trousers, displaying a nasty gash. Another handful of herbs was gathered from his seemingly inexhaustible pouch and Flin considered them thoughtfully.

"Andry," the story teller called to the knot of children and protective adults who were preparing for the night's camp.

Andry and Magwyn walked to the group. Flin held out the herbs, a collection of leaves and stems.

"Andry, I understand that you can help plants to grow strong and tall," Flin asked.

Andry glanced to Magwyn who nodded. In turn, the girl nodded to Flin, who crouched beside her in a fluid motion.

"Well, that's excellent news," Flin said. "Now, I gathered these herbs several days ago and have been trying to keep them as fresh as I could. But I probably need them to be a little fresher. Do you think you could try to make them a little fresher for me?"

Andry looked at the herbs in Flin's hand and then turned once more to her aunt. Magwyn smiled and nodded once again, glancing back to the group who were watching proceedings. Meanwhile, Andry reached out but, rather than take the herbs in her own hand she gently placed her small hand over them while Flin continued to hold them. She concentrated for a time and Varna could see little difference. Flin, who had watched her closely, smiled and gently laid his free hand on Andry's head.

"It's okay, just relax. See how the plants all have their little veins. They carry tiny little bits of nutrients - like food - for the plants, even after they have been harvested. See if you can just help the leaves to take that food from the veins and use it to freshen up just a little."

Andry looked into Flin's face and nodded once again. A determined look came over the girl and she concentrated anew. Varna was sure she detected a faint glow from Flin's hand that still rested on Andry's head. Magwyn gasped as the furled and withered leaves gained colour and slowly unfurled. Andry kept concentrating and the leaves continued to open, their skins firming and deepening in hue. Varna thought she could almost see the leaves absorbing the nutrients that remained in the veins, which paled as they lost their contents.

"Thank you, Andry," Flin said gently. "You can stop now. Magwyn, Andry will be hungry, I expect."

Andry lifted her hand from the herbs, staring at what she had accomplished. She turned to Magwyn with a huge smile. Magwyn smiled back, pride in her niece warring with wonder as she also stared at the herbs. Mother and niece walked back to the waiting group, where the adults made a fuss of the girl and her accomplishment. Fear of these gifts did not extend to the Blood, it seemed. Varna turned to Flin and noted a single tear run down his cheek, which he brushed away before turning back to the injured guard.

"This will hurt," Flin said conversationally as he ground the fresh herbs between his hands until they almost formed a green paste. "But you will be able to walk again soon."

Again, Varna watched closely as the old Teller pushed the paste directly into the wound. Again, Varna was sure she saw a glow surround Flin's hand and the angry red of the wounded flesh faded. The guard tensed and grimaced, holding in the pain, but as the red faded from the wound he relaxed.

"You'll be a lot better by morning," Flin said. "Have something to eat and drink and then get some sleep. That's usually the best remedy."

The guard nodded gratefully to Flin, who stood and started to walk towards the camp preparations. Varna followed.

"How did you know about that? What Andry had to do?"

"You learn many things wandering Ennaris," Flin replied with a sideways look at Varna. "But I also knew a boy who could do the same thing a long time ago. It was he who told me what he had to do to freshen herbs and plants. It would not work with older leaves, but I had gathered them recently and hoped they would hold enough of their essence to be revived. It seems they had."

Almin Bor sought out Jalor while food was being prepared and drew him away from the others.

"I'm worried," Almin Bor said without preamble. "If all of the guards have been ordered away from the citadel ... well, I'm worried about what might happen. Grall told me that the Faero had taken half of the Guard with him while he looked for a band of those ghazrak that had attacked some of the farms. He would have left about half of the Guard in the citadel, mostly to maintain law and order. But they're gone and it would seem several of these war-bands are heading that way."

Jalor nodded, waiting.

"We need to move faster," Almin Bor continued. "We're about half a day or so at a forced march, but closer to a full day at the pace we'll have to go with the full group. I'm thinking we need to take the guards and get there as fast as we can."

Jalor shook his head.

"If we did that then it's likely that the ghazrak will find and attack the children and those without military experience. And no matter how well any of them can fight, they'd lose. We can look to move faster, but we need to stay together."

Almin Bor grimaced. His war sense vied with concern for the largely unprotected citadel, and he sighed acceptance.

"Aye. You're right. But if we can move faster..."

"That's what we'll do. How big is this citadel? How many people are there? Does it have walls and gates that can be closed?"

"It's big, at least compared to most towns in the parts of Ennaris I've seen," Almin Bor replied. "There are many who can hold weapons, and quite a few who were in the militia or the Guard. And there's a single gate that can be closed and barred, so there's that to hold them out, maybe. The citadel has never been taken, even though enemies made it all the way to the walls in the past."

"But there were also armed men and women to hold those armies out at the time?"

"Aye," Almin Bor sighed, "and now there may not be. And you've seen those things. They're not fast but they're almost unstoppable with normal weapons and it will be the trained ones who have the best chance to kill them, not shop keepers and merchants."

"I've seen plenty of shop keepers and merchants who were willing to fight for their homes and families," Jalor said quietly. "Don't dismiss them completely. But I agree these ghazrak make it harder. So, early start and we push harder. The children will have to be carried and the injured helped."

"Aye. You have my thanks. I'll have a word with Flin and see what can be done to help the injured further."

"Flin? Why Flin?" Jalor asked, intrigued.

There were many questions about the supposed storyteller that Jalor would like to have answered. Maybe Almin Bor had some of them.

"That will be for Flin to tell," Almin Bor replied, hurrying away.

It was well after noon of the following day that the group reached a large open field and paused on the edge of the tree line. As planned, they had started with an early breakfast and called everyone together. Almin Bor had laid out the basic concerns and the plan to get to the citadel as fast as possible. Contingencies were put together in the event the group met more of the ghazrak troops. Almin Bor divided the trained fighters into two groups, taking the lead of one himself and, surprising many, directing the other to Jalor.

Amused, Blaine had moved close to Jalor, with Varna not far away.

"So, the plan to act like a group of minstrels and not military is going well so far, don't you think?" he asked with a grin.

Varna snorted while Jalor gave a long-suffering moan.

"It seemed like a reasonable plan when the Admiral suggested it," Jalor said.

"And I'm sure there may be one or two of this crowd who might even still believe it," Blaine said with a grin. "But they seem to be pretty smart and I'm betting none of them do."

"Yes, well, let's get across this field and up to that fortress town. Then we can work out what we can do to recover some of the mission. The Empire being here and involved with those things changed it anyway, and this seems to be the civil and military power of the area, so they're the ones we would have to deal with anyway. In fact, I think this is the large town we were heading towards. We've just come at it from a different direction."

The road they travelled crossed the field from where they stood, making a nearly direct line for the walled city. It was smaller than many that Blaine and Jalor had seen but it was large enough to hold a sizable population. A huge gate stood open as the entrance to the city. At a second look Jalor realised it was less a gate and more a wide and deep passage through the walls, which were very thick at that point. Low, squat towers stood to each side of the gate and the walls were crenelated at the top, allowing defenders to fire arrows or throw spears or other items at attackers. More towers could be seen along the front and side walls that stretched a long way back towards what looked like an escarpment. Blaine estimated the city walls could hold several thousand defenders at any one time, depending on how deep they were.

A stream meandered from the woods to the right and wandered across the field, under a stone bridge that carried the path, to pass into the city via what looked like an arch in the wall. A heavy grill filled the arch and protected the arched opening from incursions. Jalor could see that the city was built on top of some sort of ridge - later he would find that it was, in fact, a precipice and the same stream passed out a channel in the rear wall to cascade down that precipice. Down one side of the field and continuing along one side wall of the Citadel was a confusion of broken gullies and what could be old watercourses, which offered some protection for the city. The woods ended in open grassland on the other two sides of the city, with plenty of open space. Blaine looked on with approval - this place would be hard to take with the weaponry available to this planet.

Almin Bor led the way across the field. Magwyn led the group of children close behind him. They were ringed by most of the other adults and with Flin, Jalor and Varna next. The guards followed, along with Blaine, who had fallen into the squad leader role without any opposition. The group was making slow time, with Jalor and one guard being assisted, when they saw a second group emerge from a path on the other wooded side, running and looking behind themselves. Varna saw that this group comprised more families, several men and women with around twelve children of varying ages. Behind them came a small group of guards, no more than eight men.

Blaine took in the scene and, knowing what was likely to happen, gestured to the guards of his group while he growled a warning to the others. Blaine's makeshift squad stopped and waited, as did Almin Bor, Welkis and the other former militia. Jalor urged the rest of the group to greater speed, and women and children started to run towards the city. Jalor followed more slowly with Varna at his side. Just as the second group of refugees met and joined with them a large body of black-clad ghazrak emerged from the woods, with three Shadows in tow. Blaine snarled. Just how many of these creatures were roaming around out there? The presence of enemy agents he still did not understand, for they never worked with others who they considered to be beneath themselves, which was anyone not Empire.

The second set of soldiers met Blaine's group and without ceremony Blaine directed them into a defensive position. Blaine's team immediately responded and, with an uncertain glance towards their own team leader the others did likewise. Almin Bor merely fell in beside Blaine, which resolved any concerns that anyone had. The half-men responded with guttural growls and grunts but little real discipline, as Blaine now expected, and started a lumbering run towards the defenders. Blaine glanced towards the city to see the group of families was almost there. Jalor and Varna trailed them. He also noted with a frown that the internal gates had been closed, obviously when the creatures had appeared. He would have to hope that someone would get that gate open, and turned his thoughts back to the ghazrak approaching.

Varna and Jalor reached the group beneath the closed gate as Magwyn yelled an angry demand that the gate be opened. After a moment she hammered on the iron of the gate with her knife hilt, repeating her demand in no uncertain terms.

Clearly Varna heard a woman loudly cursing almost everyone and everything in sight before the gate resounded with a mighty crash.

"Open this gate, ye spume-faced son of a misbegotten arthrobok, before I ram this down yer scrawny throat," she yelled.

Magwyn relaxed slightly and smiled. She turned to regard the battle as a postern door that Varna had not seen was flung open. Out strode a tall woman, bareheaded, in a mismatched set of armour - a burnished bronze cuirass, a skirt of overlapping links of iron or steel, greaves and a single arm-guard of the same metal but differing in colour. She was pulling the other arm-guard on while adjusting a round shield, all the while muttering about the stupidity of all men and male gaolers in particular. She stalked past Varna without more than a brief appraising glance.

"Where's the fight?" she demanded.

Magwyn stepped in her way, forcing her headlong pace to be checked. "Helt, stop!" she said with authority, and Varna was surprised when she did exactly that. "Calm down or you'll be no use to anyone."

"Magwyn!" the woman said. "Where's Almin Bor? I should be in this fight. Those boys out there have no real idea."

Magwyn nodded. "Agreed, but we need to get the non-combatants inside and then get the rest of the militia out here. Where are they?"

"All out somewhere. I don't know where."

Magwyn nodded. "In the gatehouse again?"

Helt grimaced. "I'm what's left, so can we just get on with it?"

Magwyn nodded. She pointed to where the fight had just started and Helt nodded her thanks, starting to march to where the fighting was already taking place. The defenders were hard pressed and already two were down and not moving.

The postern gate remained open and the children were shepherded inside, Flin with them. Jalor stood outside the gate, leaning on his crutch, while Varna made sure all were inside before turning to him.

"Okay, you too Jalor. You'll be of no use standing there and they need to close this gate."

Jalor nodded and wearily made his way through the gate, only realising as the postern was closed that Varna had remained on the other side.

Varna, meanwhile, had unlimbered her staff. She dropped her pack at the gate and took off her cloak, placing it atop the pack. At a call from atop the city wall, she turned to see yet another band of attackers emerge from the woods, moving to reinforce those attacking the defensive line, which was now slowly moving back towards the gate. Helt had arrived to bolster the defenders and Varna watched open mouthed as Helt's strategy became obvious. Or non-strategy, perhaps.

The armoured woman merely walked straight through the defensive line, drawing a large broadsword from the scabbard across her back and immediately started to lay about her with barely controlled fury. The attacking line wilted in front of her as the half-men were cut down in a broad swathe. The huge sword sliced through their body armour with ease, surprisingly. Blaine merely smiled as he gestured to the remaining defenders to move up with Helt, which they did while ensuring they stayed out of reach of her sword, which continued to deliver death and destruction to the enemy.

The one time that Helt paused was when she swiped through a Shadow only to find the robes tangled in her sword and no body. The closest half-men immediately turned on her only to find Blaine intervening. The original invading force had been cut down significantly and Varna realised that three of the second, smaller force had bypassed that fight and were heading for her, or for the gates of the city with her in the way - two half-men and a Shadow. She frowned - one of the creatures she could handle, she thought, for they had little imagination that she had been able to discern, two maybe she could keep at bay but three would be a stretch, especially with the third a Shadow. Ah well!

Varna moved forward and positioned herself at the further end of the wooden bridge that crossed the stream and waited for them. A Shadow struggled to cross water and would have to use the bridge. She was not sure of the ghazrak but hoped they would have the same need or would follow the Shadow. Her staff was extended but she knew she was tired, and recent events had left her innate energy levels lower than she would like. Hopefully none of the three had ever seen a battle staff in use - most people dismissed the staff as a lesser weapon, but in the right hands it was lethal, even without the hidden blade. And this was a Warrior staff manufactured on *Starfire*.

As the three drew closer, Varna started to twirl the staff so that it presented a wheel, whistling as it whirled around. The half-men slowed and stopped outside sword range, uncertain at what this was and Varna's confidence grew. They didn't know! She continued to twirl the staff until, suddenly, she stepped forward and cracked the staff against the closest of them, directly across the point where the helmet and body armour almost met. She saw the half-man's eyes open wide and then cloud over as he collapsed, pushing the Shadow out of its place and causing it to stumble. Varna stepped back again, extended the blade and with a cry pushed it through the side of the Shadow's robes, retracting the blade immediately so the robes did not snag.

But in doing so she was exposed to the final half-man, who swung a mighty arc with his sword that just managed to clip Varna's upper arm as she sought to evade. A shaft of pain caused Varna to stumble. The creature did not hesitate and immediately lifted the sword again. As in a dream, Varna noted from close up that, as Blaine had described, the sword lacked any real workmanship. Still, it would kill her just as fast given it was at the top of the swing. She tried to lift her staff once again but her arm refused to provide strength. She did manage to hit the stud that retracted one arm, making it shorter and so easier to handle one-handed, and then threw herself backward onto the bridge, hitting the back of her head as she did so. Everything went into slow-motion as the pain in her head battled the pain in her arm. Both seemed to win, a sort of mist closing in as the creature roared in victory.

In the dream Varna saw the sword swing falter as the creature's head left its shoulders and bounced out of her vision. The sword clattered onto the bridge alongside Varna, who observed almost dispassionately as the mist closed further. The last thing Varna recalled seeing was the warrior woman kicking the half-man aside and reaching for her.

35. The Citadel

Inside the citadel, controlled chaos reigned. Recriminations were flying at the able-bodied men who had not rushed out to help defend the families as they were ushered across the large field - a well-defined field of fire, Blaine recognised - while many told of not being aware such a battle was being fought until it was too late. Looking around, Blaine could believe that was the case, especially with the fortress' troops of guards all out. In itself that move was being decried, and Creely's name - whoever that was - was being cursed by some, defended by others.

Blaine noted that those who were receiving the insults were all surly and had all the signs of being mercenaries. They were badly outnumbered by the citizens who were complaining, loudly, about their lack of action. Their leader, a shorter, vicious-looking individual, drew his men back from the confrontation and they clustered at the foot of a large building that occupied one whole side of the large town square. The defenders had made their way to the square on entering the citadel.

The brief battle was over. The half-men - the ghazrak - and the by now inevitable accompanying Shadows had been defeated but at cost - six of the Citadel guards were dead and almost all the rest carried wounds. Blaine knew that they had been lucky. His defending troop had found a small natural rise in the field and that, combined with the stream running across the field and thus defending that flank, had been enough to give them an edge. That and Helt wading into the attackers with her broadsword, which was something they obviously did not expect. Blaine smiled at the memory.

He was sitting in the main square of the citadel at a tavern. Tacitly acknowledging again that he knew the three were not what they claimed, Flin had tossed him a small bag of coins as the Teller had gone with Magwyn to settle the children from both parties - orphans most of them, Blaine thought grimly - in communal facilities that had already been prepared. In itself, that told Blaine that this was a caring society but that it also was one that found itself needing those facilities regularly enough for them to be available on demand. Varna and Jalor had been taken to a medical facility, where the attending physician had shooed Blaine away, telling him to come back tomorrow. In adjoining beds in the long room were several of the defenders, including Almin Bor and Sindelar, most with cuts and scratches, quite a few of which were deep. Flin had been concerned about infection, given what they had seen of the swords and spears being used by those creatures, and had promised to return with some of his herbs. Those swords and spears really were rubbish, Blaine thought. But they would kill as effectively as the best made weapon, and they probably carried infections that could kill just as effectively.

So, with nowhere else to go, Blaine had done what he would do in most societies where he tried to blend in, and headed for a drinking establishment. The one he found faced the main square, had an open front and tables with benches laid out across the back. A few individual chairs fronted the square. Blaine occupied one of the latter and ordered from the serving woman whatever the locals drank. He had not needed the coins for she had seen Blaine lead the defenders in the field and refused to take money, at least for the first, she had said with a smile. Thankfully, for even Blaine was weary after the last few days, it turned out to be quite a good ale. He looked around the square. It was close to what he had seen on most Union worlds - and there had been a surprisingly large number - where an attempt was made to return to simpler times, to leave advanced technology behind as far as possible and to use skills that were not even memories for many people of the Union. Inevitably, people thought medieval at those times, and agrarian.

The difference he could see here was that there were no little remnants of advanced technology as usually crept through for the Union worlds, or that had to be retained to maintain communication and supply routines. Everything here was done using what Blaine thought of as true medieval methods, or what he imagined they would be. In one corner of the square, a blacksmith was making a great din, rhythmically hammering some sort of metal into something. Blaine could not see him but could see a glow from what he assumed would be a forge. He made a mental note to make the smith's acquaintance and see if he could lend a hand. Blaine had enjoyed working with smiths on a number of missions and had become familiar with their working and layouts. In doing so, he had noted that the pattern rarely changed from forge to forge - it seemed there was a small number of logical and ruthlessly efficient layouts for smithies and almost all of those that he had seen had conformed to those layouts. He would be interested in seeing if this one, on a world that truly was at a medieval level, differed. A second, smaller tavern occupied another corner and between that and this tavern were a small number of stores - clothing, farm implements and wooden objects, from what Blaine could see.

On the opposite side of the square from the tavern where Blaine sat was what seemed to be a guards' barracks, taking up most of that side. The barracks seemed to be empty, Blaine noticed, with the exception of two elderly men sweeping and washing out the room, periodically sticking their heads out of the door to look at the board-walk above the gates, which could be seen across the square and a couple of blocks distant. Blaine glanced at the board-walk and could only see a couple of men, two of whom had fought with him and carried minor injuries. The fourth side of the square was the large building that looked like it might be official offices or similar. In addition to the mercenaries, Blaine had seen a number of people entering and leaving with the universal air of bureaucrats, files carried under one arm and that appearance of having important things to do somewhere.

In the centre of the square was a square stone-walled pool with a mound of rocks in the centre, the sort where usually there would be a fountain. There was no water spouting from any fountain, though, so maybe it was just a pool with a pile of rocks. There was water in the pool at least and it had to come from somewhere. Perhaps a spring fed the pool from below. Hitching posts told him that, at times, some sort of mounts were tied there, although there were none now. Efficient again - use the ornamental pool to water the animals, although that could become untidy. Blaine spent a moment wondering how the water was delivered to the pool and then gave that up as a useless thought vector.

So, Blaine thought after another look around the square, this was not exactly going to plan. Their first finding of what seemed to be the remains of a blitz mine usually indicated no survivors. Blaine was intrigued by the small patch of grass surviving in the centre of the blitz field. He had not said anything to Jalor but Blaine had a faint suspicion that the grass was important. He could not really imagine the Champion surviving a blitz blast. Still, Clay's exploits over a relatively short time had become legend to a particular group of Union Warriors, and Blaine was one of them.

Then they found Shadows in uncertain numbers already infesting Ennaris and those strange half men, half beasts - ghazrak he reminded himself again - with weapons of appalling quality and almost no real idea of fighting strategy beyond charging to attack and swinging hard. But they were being guided by Shadows, and probably controlled by them somehow. Added to those events was Varna being badly affected by something that seemed inherent to the planet and now both she and Jalor were in the infirmary after taking injuries during fights that they really were not supposed to take part in. Blaine snorted to himself. Another bureaucrat's rule. No Warrior of the Light could stand by and watch innocents get slaughtered, so that rule was broken almost everywhere. Blaine had done so on several occasions before this, and probably would again, assuming he came out of this one.

But something was going on. Flin was a storyteller like Blaine was a mountain goat herder, but exactly what Flin was Blaine could not tell. He probably knew what was happening but held it close to his chest, which Blaine could accept. For now. Then again, he thought that he would have little chance against Flin if he tried to make him tell something that he did not want to tell. And Flin had seen through their story with ease and was neither surprised nor concerned, which was another factor to consider. Blaine continued to turn over the events as he sat and slowly worked through his ale.

36. Balgor

Varna awoke - again, she thought bitterly - but this time she was in a bed, which was utilitarian but there was a white sheet covering her. The mattress was lumpy and may have been made with straw mixed with something softer, perhaps some sort of wool. She could feel that she had a bandage around her head, which fitted with the headache she could feel. Beneath the sheet she was wearing very little, a shift that extended to her knees. Looking around she saw that she was in a large room where there were five other beds, none of which were occupied. A small table placed beside the bed held a metal jug and mug, and on a second table she could see her clothes, folded neatly and with her staff laid on top.

She tried to sit up but a wave of dizziness told her that was not a great idea. The dizziness did not go away as she laid back down. She felt a surge of despair at the thought that she was returning to the state she had faced before Aldar did whatever she did. What was happening to her? She could be endangering the whole mission because she could not handle something that this planet was throwing at her. The frustration brought tears to her eyes, tears that she dashed away angrily. She had struggled to bring herself back together after her last mission shredded what had proven to be a somewhat fragile self-belief, and she could feel her partially rebuilt confidence ebbing away. It was only that spark of native stubbornness that had allowed her to get this far, she knew, but she was not sure that she had much more. A single tear escaped and ran down her cheek, and this time she did not brush it away. Reflecting on how useless she was in her current state, after a while Varna slipped back into an uneasy sleep.

Varna started awake again, or thought she did. The room was indistinct to her, not dark but overlaid with some sort of mist. A figure moved from one corner towards her. Varna struggled to reach her staff but could not make herself move. The figure moved to the bed and the mists parted to show a man with unruly hair that was the colour of wheat, wearing a long robe tied at the waist. He stood over her and looked down, smiling cheerfully.

"Well, so here you are, after all this time," the man said lightly. The smile reached his deep blue eyes easily and made them sparkle, although that may have been Varna's fantasy. He was very good looking and she thought this must be a dream.

"You have no need to fear," he continued, sitting on one edge of the bed such that he was partly side on to Varna, his head turned slightly to face her. "I'm Balgor and you're safe within my walls."

"You own this place?" Varna asked, more for something to say than because she was that interested.

He laughed. "Not really. It's more of an arrangement of convenience. The owner seems fairly happy with the arrangement and it is convenient for me, so ..." He left the remainder unsaid.

Varna found her responding to his open and friendly manner, despite her training, and relaxed.

"Better," Balgor said. "You'll need your rest, for you and your friends have trials ahead of you that will test you, individually and as a group. But you'll have support and assistance, from me and others. We're not supposed to intervene directly but will provide aid and assistance where we can."

Varna nodded, accepting this statement in her slightly dreamy state. Dream? Yes, that must be it.

"Is this a dream?" she asked warily.

"Kind of, but not really," Balgor replied. "You've not adjusted yet. There is that within you that holds you back, but your chains will be broken. You, Jalor and Blaine are important to Ennaris. To the galaxy, in fact. Likely to this universe. For now, you need to rebuild your strength.

But I need you to pass on a message for me. Tell Flin that it's time for the Nine. He'll know what that means."

"The Nine?"

"Yes, just that. It's time for the Nine." Balgor smiled. "Flin is about to get a bit of a shock so I suggest you don't tell him until he's sitting down." He reached out and placed one hand, one warm and gentle hand, on Varna's head. "For now, though, sleep. And when you feel that you cannot make sense of what is happening, seek out my Garden of Rest. It will bring peace."

With that Balgor appeared to fade back into the mist and Varna fell into a deep, restful sleep.

Flin found Blaine just starting on his second ale. Drawing a second chair up the storyteller signalled to the server for whatever Blaine was having and with a sigh settled into the chair. When the ale came Flin also ordered food for them both, then took a long pull of the drink, sighed and took a smaller drink.

"Better, much better," he said.

Blaine nodded as he drank.

"It's not bad at all," he said. "Everyone settled?"

"Yes," Flin said, his face gone bleak. "The children who lost their families will be looked after. The Faeronar have strong beliefs, and the Faero will want to know that the Blood seems to be re-establishing the gifts. Varna and Jalor have been patched up and both are sleeping. Jalor, I think, almost had to be tied down but he lost more blood than I thought so he couldn't really do anything about it. The nurse gave him a sleeping draught to make sure he stayed."

Flin now smiled.

"He knew he was losing blood, but we had to keep moving," Blaine said with a shrug.

"Yes, I guessed as much."

"So, you know this place," Blaine said. "Where are all of the guards? Those ones we had were returning, not coming from here. Without that Helt woman we would have been in trouble. And who is she?" he added.

Flin grimaced. "All of the guards were out, as is the Faero. My apprentice is with them. There was an alarm about the families being attacked and so the Faero decided to take half of them out. Creely sent the rest on what I think may have been a fool's errand. Creely," he explained, "is the Lord Chamberlain and rules in the Faero's absence. The lot we encountered and the second lot who joined in the fight were the first back. The citadel was left with no really trained defenders, which explains why the gates were closed so fast. The citadel has never fallen and I guess Intika felt he could afford to do that. Intika Ramesa," Flin explained to Blaine's enquiring look, "is the current Faero."

"And Helt?"

"One of the Faero's more interesting characters. She is from Escar, far to the north-east of where we are now, near what are now known as the border lands. Very few know that about her. Most think she is from Land's End, far enough away that no-one here knows anything about it. Except me and my friends. As you can see, she's trained in the martial arts, at least as they deal with sword play. The Faeronar are both in awe of her and a little unsure of her. You will have noticed that here there is no bar to women standing alongside their men but apparently where she's from that's considered to be very strange. So, even though she claims she could hold her own against most of the men of her land when it came to their form of sword fighting, she decided to leave. She doesn't talk about it but I gather she left under some sort of cloud." Flin smiled. "Beneath that tough exterior I think there's another Helt. I've always found her to be both respectful and polite." He considered. "Except when she drinks. Then she loses sense and sensibility and usually ends up in the cells which, it seems, is what caused her not to be out with the Faero, for she's part of his bodyguard."

The subject of their discussion exited the guards' barracks and strode across the square towards the other tavern, where she sat at a table by herself and leaned against one wall. Blaine watched as she leaned forward and ordered from the waitress, only to lean back once again, eyes closed. If she had seen Blaine and Flin she gave no sign.

"Well," Blaine said after a short while, once a platter of meats and fruits had been placed on a small table nearby, "she's worth having in a fight. But she needs to be a little less emotional about it all or she'll lose her head, probably literally. And that would be a pity."

He decided to ignore Flin's pointed comment implying that Blaine did not understand Ennaris' mores regarding women in battle. With one more appraising glance at Helt, Blaine fell to with a will, helping Flin to demolish the platter's contents.

Varna awakened to daylight, surprised to be feeling rested for the first time in what seemed like a long time, although their time on Ennaris had been a matter of days only. She still felt slightly out of phase somehow. Lying in the bed, with her headache mostly gone, she sought to recall each and every part of her most recent dream, and was surprised when she could do so. She recalled that Balgor had not said it was a dream, just "kind of" a dream. So, maybe not a dream. This planet had some strange things happening. Varna, who was less experienced than Blaine in on-world missions, still was aware that there were many things in the universe that were unexplained. And, she thought, Ennaris had not been known to anyone not that long ago.

She was still lying there when the physician, a young and robust man with a strange, straggly beard that seemed out of place with his strapping build, walked into the room, accompanied by the nurse and Flin. The doctor smiled to see her awake and alert, walked over and laid a hand on her forehead, held her wrist in the way every physician Varna had ever known did to take a pulse, no matter what modern aids they possessed, and nodded.

"Well," he said, "I think no real damage done. No headache?"

"I feel quite well," Varna replied, avoiding the direct answer.

"Excellent, then I can see no reason for you to stay here occupying a bed when you can be out doing whatever it is you do." He hesitated, his manner less brusque. "And I thank you, and your friends, for rescuing our children. One of them is my sister's boy, who will now be staying with us. The Faeronar value our children, and all know of the great service you did. It will not be forgotten."

He nodded to Varna and then to Flin before striding from the room. The nurse smiled also and left, heading in a different direction, leaving Varna alone with Flin.

"So, no ill effects remain? The cut was relatively shallow. It was the fact that you were unconscious and unable to be woken that concerned him most."

"Cut? Oh yes," she suddenly recalled her arm being clipped by one of the half-men's swords, "I can barely feel that now." She pulled back the sheet to see her right arm with an ugly welt already half healed. "That healed quickly."

"Some of my herbs," Flin replied blandly. "The healer was quite surprised at how effective they are."

"Yes, your herbs do seem to have properties all their own," she responded in a tone just as bland.

"Uh-huh. I'll leave you to get dressed and meet you outside in the square. Exit to your right and go down the stairs."

Having washed up and dressed, and again marvelling at the lack of pain or even discomfort in her arm, Varna made her way out of the infirmary. She thanked a different nurse as she did so and received an uncomfortable, awe-struck stare and awkward, bobbing curtsy. She walked down the wide stone stairway and through the main entry portico, standing on a wide porch to view the square. Flin was standing in front of what looked like a tavern, with Blaine, and was pointing out something across the square. Varna took a careful look around, making sure she memorised the square's layout - her experience was that knowing the layout of anywhere she happened to be was a good thing - before moving down the remaining steps to join them.

Blaine smiled to see her and gestured them both to the tavern, where the pretty serving woman gave him a warm smile before giving a table a swift wipe down with a rag. She headed into the tavern kitchen - the sounds and smells could be from nothing else - without being asked.

"I see you've been here before?" Varna asked dryly, eyes dancing as Blaine looked a little sheepish.

"Maybe once or twice," he replied, then grinned and shrugged. "Or four or five times. It's the closest to the infirmary, the service is good, food is reasonable and I seem to be acquiring a taste for the ale served here."

"Ah, food and ale. Of course, no other attractions at all," Varna teased as she watched the serving woman return with a laden platter of meats, fruits and cheeses, and then carefully place it in front of Blaine. It was only with great effort that Varna did not laugh out loud, and Flin was looking at something on the other side of the square with inordinate interest.

Blaine loftily ignored Varna for five seconds before saying, "I can see you're feeling better, then. Do you want something to eat or do you want to keep laughing at me?"

Varna did laugh then, a low, chuckling laugh that she stifled as the serving woman returned with three tankards, placing them carefully on the table, smiled at Blaine and returned to the counter at the back of the tavern.

For a few minutes the three availed themselves of the repast, Varna agreeing that the ale did, in fact, slide down rather easily. The food presented was similar to what she and Blaine were accustomed to in Union territories, and yet was different enough to seem exotic. It was tasty and very welcome. Varna realised that she had not eaten solid food for some time and was quite hungry.

"What of Jalor?" Varna asked after a few minutes had passed. "I know I was in the infirmary for two days, but nothing more than that."

"My herbs were of assistance to Jalor," Flin replied around a piece of some bright yellow fruit, "but it was not enough to heal him as you have healed. He lost a lot of blood and for that he needs to rest up for a couple more days. I'll repeat the treatment later today."

"Hmmm, herbs again. Sometime you need to let us know just how your herbs are so good." Blaine glanced sideways towards Flin, eyebrows raised.

"Sometime I will," Flin reassured him. "Not just yet, though."

"Well, that was delicious," Varna said as they all sat back, replete. "But I have a message for you, Flin. At least I think it is. While I was out, I had some sort of strange dream, a vision if you will, strange as that sounds. My visitor left with me a message for you."

"Nothing about you seems strange any more, my dear," Flin remarked, turning to look at her. "I believe you truly are experiencing some sort of adjustment to Ennaris, and I believe your visions may well be true. What message?"

"He said you would understand, but that I should make sure you're sitting," Varna said. "It's time for the Nine."

Flin's eyes shot wide open, which was the only external sign of the jolt of shock he felt. His skin felt clammy all of a sudden, and his breath caught. He saw nothing of the present for the moment, reliving a moment from the deep past when he had last heard of the Nine. Varna, watching carefully, saw Flin struggle to return to an even keel, and she reached over to put one hand over his. Blaine merely watched, aware of Flin's sudden internal struggle and interested that it should be so.

"Are you alright?" she asked quietly.

Flin nodded abstractedly. He waited a moment longer as his heart returned to its normal rhythm, moved his hand out from under Varna's and then patted Varna's hand.

"Do you know the name of the person who gave you the message?"

"Balgor, he said his name is."

Flin squeezed his eyes shut. He stayed very still for a long moment while both Varna and Blaine watched intently. The shock of a short time before was reflected ten-fold in Flin's hands, which were clenched and trembling. Varna could sense the turmoil that was churning beneath Flin's exterior. Flin was striving as always to appear in control.

Blaine stood and moved to the back of the tavern where he poured a beaker of water from a jug, bringing it back to place it in Flin's hands.

"Here, drink a little of this," he said quietly.

Flin raised the beaker to his lips without thinking and took a sip of the water, only to splutter and cough. Life returned to his face.

"What do you call this? Water! Who gives water to someone suffering from a shock?"

Flin's indignation pulled him out of the deep funk, and very deliberately he lifted his ale tankard and downed the remainder in a single go. Blaine caught the eye of serving woman and gestured for another round, while Flin turned to Varna.

"Can you describe Balgor to me, please?" His voice was steady. His hands no longer trembled but there remained a shadow over his features, a cast that spoke to the shock that still coursed through him.

"No, not really," Varna replied. "It was a dream, or enough like one, I suppose. Everything was sort of fogged, misty, and Balgor was just an indistinct figure, more a voice than anything physical. A masculine voice. So, just who is Balgor?"

Flin sighed. "I'm struggling with this. I lost faith in the Guardians, believed that if they had ever existed then they had all left us to our own devices well before the rebellion and civil war that led to the destruction of Ennaris. There was no sign of the Guardians during that whole period, no support, no help." His voice turned bitter. "Millions - billions - died across Ennaris as the very surface of the world changed under them. The Guides did everything we could to help for a long time, and most of those who survived the struggle with Goroth perished in doing so, while being blamed for what had happened."

His clenched fist struck the tabletop with enough force that the newly placed tankards jumped, each losing some of its contents as they did so.

"*We* were blamed after striving for such a long time, losing so much. *We* took the brunt of the people's anger. *We* were the ones who were stoned as a result of that anger, who were driven from the communities where we had been honoured such a short time before. *We* were the ones who saved and healed many and were left without help, without ... without any form of recovery for ourselves." A tear crept from the corner of one eye and made its way unheeded down Flin's cheek to lodge in his straggly beard.

"My friends, my *family* for so many cycles, were destroyed during the rebellion or while trying to recover this world after the rebellion. My Marjory, the greatest of the Battle Mages for so many generations, perhaps for all of Ennaris' history, gave her life for those same people who pilloried us. Our son ... our son died for these people."

His grief bowed his back and for a moment he covered his face with both great hands. Varna and Blaine sat mute as, with a super-human effort, Flin drew his grief and his memories back within himself, straightened and dashed the tears, the original one and several others that had joined it, from his cheeks.

"So," Blaine said neutrally, "not just a storyteller after all."

Flin smiled bitterly, apparently returning to his own internal balance. "As much as you are from 'over there'," he replied, gesturing broadly to various points of the compass, as Jalor had done when first meeting Flin.

Blaine and Varna both laughed, neither seeing any point in maintaining any charade with this man.

"And Balgor?" Varna asked.

"Balgor was - is - a Guardian. He was known as a trickster in the very early days, apparently playing tricks on the other Guardians as they did whatever it was they did. Legends are that the Guardians created Ennaris, that they made all of the land, the oceans and seas, the creatures great and small, and, of course, the Ennarisi. Our own history tells us that it is unlikely that was the case, though it is likely that someone, perhaps the Guardians after all, promoted the Ennarisi to higher intelligence and civilisation. The stories of Balgor are many and usually relate to silly things done during the creation of Ennaris. Like the story about Balgor waiting for Ana, the Guardian of the seas, to construct her sanctuary deep beneath the ocean depths and then turning it around so its door faced in the opposite direction. Or when Tanga had just finished his garden carved out of what had been a wasteland and Balgor somehow made all of the water turn into ice so that it just sat there, not melting in the heat."

Varna and Blaine laughed, as did Flin.

"Of course, all of that is myth, I thought. Or, maybe not," he mused. "Myth and legend often have a base in some form of fact. And it seems that Balgor has returned, at the same time as you have arrived. And called for the Nine."

He frowned, disturbed by something only he could see.

"So, I think we need you to tell us more of Ennaris' past. I think we probably need to get a better understanding. You were not surprised or even worried that we're not from, um, around here," Blaine kept his voice low, his expression neutral.

"Soon, when Jalor is able to join us," Flin replied, nodding. "I think it's time. Meanwhile, I think there is something I need to do. Varna, would you join me, please? I would value your perspective."

"Certainly, but about what?"

"There's something that has been disturbing me for a short while about the Citadel. Too many people are missing, no guards were remaining when we arrived and the ones who have stepped in are long past their prime. Most are retired, in fact. The Faero would not have left things like this, I'm sure. If we had not returned when we did, I believe the citadel may have fallen to those creatures, or at least been seriously damaged." Flin scratched his head. "This citadel has never been breached, though, even in the worst times, so maybe it's a case of over-confidence. I just want to test that out a little."

Blaine nodded, staying in his seat as both Flin and Varna stood again. He gave a sketchy wave as Flin led Varna back through the main doors of the administration building, taking a different corridor to that which led to the infirmary. At a reception area Flin politely asked to see the chamberlain, only to be told quite brusquely that Lord Creely was far too busy to be bothered, especially by itinerant storytellers. Flin merely nodded and turned as though to go, when a loud clatter echoed through the building, coming from the direction of another set of offices. With a groan of anticipated problems, the receptionist hurried off in search of whatever disaster had befallen.

Flin waited until he had gone then unhurriedly stepped past the reception point, moving unerringly through a maze of corridors to a room close to the centre of the building. He walked past a startled secretary into the Chamberlain's room.

"Ah, Creely, just the fellow," Flin said loudly, his voice full of good cheer. "When will Intika return, do you think? I've been waiting for him for a while and can't wait much longer."

Creely was a thin man, standing about mid-height to the Ennarisi that Varna had seen. His robes were dirty and dishevelled and his hair was awry, matching his unshaven face and bloodshot eyes. He stared at Flin incredulously before standing abruptly from behind an enormous desk, which caused a beaker of clear liquid to spill over the papers in front of him. Varna clearly smelt strong liquor.

"How did you get in here? I gave orders for no-one to be allowed in. Out! Get out! Guard, get these people out of here." Creely spluttered to a halt as he realised no-one was coming.

Flin smiled. "Well, there was no-one to stop me so I just came on in. And, as you know, all of the guards were sent on various missions. You also know that Intika gave me the run of the citadel, anyway, so those orders don't apply to me." Flin's tone dropped from light-hearted to glacial in a beat. "Do they? And I very much doubt your guards, the ones that are left, will bother me after that little run-in with strange visitors a couple of days ago. You do know about that, I'm sure. But you seem to have done nothing since."

Creely stepped away from Flin, close to the stone wall.

"Of course, you have free rein," he said in a wheedling tone, bobbing his head to Flin. "I never meant that to apply to you. And, of course, I know what happened and we are all very much in the debt of you and your friends but that is done and I don't see anything more to worry about there. This citadel has never been invaded, so I am sure we would have withstood whatever they tried to do anyway."

The Chamberlain's eyes were unable to meet Flin's, and one hand developed a sharp twitch, which he tried to hide by holding his hands tightly behind his back. Varna could see that he was under enormous stress. It took little of her reading skills to know he was trying to hide something.

"Hmmm," Flin said, non-committal. "And where is Intika at this time, and when will he return?"

"The Faero rode out with the main garrison troop to gather in the surrounding families of the Blood from the area towards the north-lands. I would expect him to return in the next few days." He gathered himself together. "Not that it is of any importance to you. Now, I have important work to do so please leave my rooms."

"Of course," Flin said, then gestured to the pool of liquid slowly being absorbed by the pile of papers on the desk. "You may want to clean that up, though. It will stain."

Flin swept from the Chamberlain's room with Varna in tow. They returned to the courtyard, with Flin deep in thought.

"Varna, I need to take care of something," he said glancing at her as they stood at the base of the huge stone steps. "I will be a couple of days, maybe a little more. I suggest that the three of you should stay here and rest up. Jalor will need that anyway, and I think you will also. If I'm not mistaken, you're starting to get those odd headaches again?"

Varna nodded. "Yes, I think they're starting again. I may try some other techniques," she said, thinking of Balgor's suggestion that she visit the Garden of Rest. "But if we're to stay here we'll need some spending money, or people will ask questions."

Flin nodded, fishing a small sack from the depths of his robes and handing it to her. It made a distinctive clinking sound, telling her it was full of coins.

"This will keep you out of harm's way for a bit," he said. "When I return, I'll bring you all up to date about what's happening on Ennaris and about the Nine. I think the three of you play roles in that, too. Two or three days," he repeated, turning to walk away. He stopped and looked at Varna closely for a moment. "And be careful. The Chamberlain is not the man he was, I think, and I'm not sure why. But he may not be a friend."

With that warning, Flin turned and strode off purposefully down one of the streets leading from the square. Varna stood and watched until he turned a corner, then walked back to the tavern, deep in thought. When she arrived, she found Jalor had joined Blaine. He was pale and his crutch was propped against the table. Both had tankards in front of them.

"Ah, here she is," Blaine said, looking around. "Where's Flin? I've been filling Jalor in on our discussion earlier. Flin obviously knows more about us than we do about him."

"He said he has something to do that will take two or three days, and suggested that we stay in the citadel. He said he would bring us up to speed on the situation with Ennaris when he returns, including our place in things." Varna paused, thinking back over the morning's events. She lowered her voice. "Well, we know he is a Guide, at least, whatever they are, and that he seems to have some of those 'gifts' the Blood referred to. Almin Bor and the others seemed to accept him as someone of importance. And the chamberlain is afraid of him, or something else that Flin seems to be involved in."

"Chamberlain?" Jalor asked.

"Yes. Flin and I visited the chamberlain, who is the authority here when the Faero is away. Apparently, Flin's on good terms with this Faero person, and I gather the chamberlain keeps things running day to day. Flin said the man has changed. The person I saw is scared, afraid of something to the point where he probably can't manage things very well. He's coming apart, I think. As we know the Faero took the citadel garrison with him to search out the Blood families in the north, but the chamberlain was the one who sent the citadel guards out also, leaving the place pretty much undefended. Before he left Flin told me to be careful also. He thinks Creely, the chamberlain, may try to do something to us, or perhaps me, as I was with Flin."

"And you have no idea what Flin is up to?"

"No. Whatever it is, it's the result of the message I gave him about the Nine, whatever or whoever they are, as well as his visit to Creely." She repeated for Jalor's benefit her 'dream' and the message imparted during it.

"Well," Jalor said. "I'm in no state to go chasing around anywhere at the moment, even though Flin turned his strange herbal remedy on me last night. I think I'll just laze around here, maybe seeing what I can see. How about the two of you make sure you know your way around the citadel. Keep your eyes open for things that seem to be out of place, not that we know what normal is like here."

37. Likki

Deep in the jungle, there was surprisingly little light. The tall trees with thick foliage blocked out most of the light so that the floor was in a permanent twilight, even in the middle of the day. Combined with the high humidity, the heat that did not fail to make its way through the foliage and the deep undergrowth, plus the tangle of roots as the trees and shrubs fought for their own patches of earth, the overall effect was of a land trying very hard not to allow anyone in.

Which was what Credar thought as she tried to hack her way through that deep undergrowth. She was trying to maintain as straight a path as possible through the jungle where there were no paths. Where the paths had been hacked, the jungle grew over again seemingly within moments. The jungle occupied that narrow neck of land between the north and south continents, running a little north of the neck and a little further south of it also. Legend had it that the neck was the remnant of a much broader piece of land that was all but destroyed during the rebellion, long in the past, but Credar knew enough of the world to know that legends were someone's way of explaining things they did not understood, so she treated all of that with healthy scepticism.

Still, she knew, just knew, that there was treasure somewhere in here. Rumours of a hidden city, long lost, persisted and after she put those rumours together with others that told of strange happenings and odd types of people attacking other people through various parts of the land, she was sure that something was there. And something usually meant valuable, especially when it was hidden away. That feeling had grown ever more certain when she was awakened by a roar and a blinding light flashing over her camp by the river, in a location that she knew was safe from the water-based predators. Of course, that still left the slithers and various stinging and biting insects, any of which could cause you real harm if you were not careful. But she and her friends were careful.

And so here she was, hacking through the jungle with her business partner, Emdur, and their two handlers, Ester and Maxnil. They were moving away from the river, heading in what she thought was a near enough to straight path from the camp to where she thought the strange light had come to ground. They were all feeling strangely driven to do so. In fact, they were driven to the point that they had rushed their morning meal, packed the camp and had been on the trail almost before first light. But now most of the morning had passed and progress was slow, even for this crew who had seen it and done it many times before. Frustration levels were rising, although they all knew that frustration never helped to carve a path through this jungle. Sometimes, though, frustration did add a little energy to the machete swings.

Credar had that thought just as her machete cut through what seemed like a particularly difficult tangle of branches, vines and vege-tation and came to an abrupt halt with a *clang*. Her machete vibrated violently and she felt the impact to her core. When she drew it back she could see the notches on the tough blade.

So, not just vegetation, then, she thought.

Emdur, following as close behind her as was sensible when someone was swinging a machete, moved up to examine the blade, followed by the other two men. As Credar rubbed her shoulder that had taken the brunt of the sudden end of her swing, Emdur attacked the vegetation with a small axe. It took a little while, but he managed to clear enough vegetation to display a stone column or, rather, part of a stone column.

Ester and Maxnil took their turns at wielding machete and axe and before long the whole stone column was exposed. It stood a little higher than Emdur, who topped Credar by a head. The column was weathered but in remarkable condition, which was the good news. The bad news was that the column, and the markings on it, unmistakably were the work of the Waslit. Credar considered. The Waslit, as they were known in these latter days, arose after the rebellion's destructive aftermath, according to the tales and limited documentation remaining, over-ran this region, practising cannibalism as a way to get past the food shortages experienced at the time. They had been all but wiped out after a couple of hundred cycles, but there had been periodic outbreaks for a long time thereafter, or so the stories told. Of course, as Credar and many who she grew up with knew, the Waslit had actually lived in an old city that had been destroyed in the rebellion. She could not recall any mention of recent events, though, and she and Emdur had been travelling in this region for quite a while now, so they probably had little to worry about.

The four stopped to take stock. Credar looked closely at the jungle around them, noting how there seemed to be an impenetrable wall of vegetation ahead of them. As a group, for none wished to separate at this time, they searched out to left and right, locating two more of the columns, each with the same figures etched into the stone.

The shapes included some that Credar had seen before, and she knew to read from bottom to top. At the bases were column supports, carved in waving lines but generally thought to have little meaning and to be ornamental. The stone above the foot-stone showed the stylised suns, shining on what seemed to be people making offerings of plants and vegetables. Above that was a scene showing the land swallowing the people, with a great rent into which the worshippers fell. Above that was a scene showing more worshippers, but this time with a person lying on the altar, and a being with a knife poised over the altar. Finally, above them all was a stone with an image of a wrathful being, wild eyes staring, a snarl or grimace carved into the features. This, Credar knew, was the face of Likki, the mythical Guardian of the jungle regions. Waslit tradition was that Likki had caused the destruction because she was unhappy with the offerings and demanded blood sacrifice, which they duly provided.

"What do we do?" Emdur asked quietly as the four regarded the three columns. "I've not heard of the Waslit still being around in great numbers, but these columns have not been left to rot, even though they were covered up."

"Hmmm," Credar agreed. "But we'll have to push through here to find where that thing came down. It can't be too far ahead now. I say we go on. I feel that we have to."

After a quick meal, they renewed their assault on the vegetation, moving around the first column, the centre one of the three. They could make some headway more easily now, leading Credar to consider Emdur's warning that the columns appeared to have been maintained not that long ago. Before too long they pushed through the wall of vegetation to find themselves above the steep bank of a small stream. A path in front of them paralleled the stream, while to the left was a narrow stone bridge, without any railings, spanning the stream.

Carefully, Credar bent over the bank to look into the water below, and immediately wished that she had not done so. Deep in the water, deeper than she would have thought possible for the width of the stream, she saw one of the water predators. Disturbingly, she was sure it was watching her in turn. The steep, near vertical, banks of the stream meant that it could not reach where they were but she nervously looked around to see if there were places where it could come out of the water.

"This is man-made," Emdur said. "The water course is not natural."

"And we have company in the bottom," Credar said, gesturing towards the water. "I'm sure it can't get to us, but it's a big one."

As though it understood what was being said, the huge predator pushed off from the bottom of the stream where it had been laying and, with a few swishes of its gigantic tail, launched from the stream, driving towards the bank where the four were standing. Its huge mouth, with its masses of razor sharp teeth, snapped shut as it fell just short of the top of the bank and then fell back into the water. It allowed itself to settle again to the bottom, but the group, who had jumped back from the edge as one, was sure it was watching them still.

Shaken, but still drawn to locate the strange object that had shone with such a bright light, the four moved to the stone bridge and, with bated breath, walked across. It was almost anti-climactic when they all reached the other side without incident. With a deep breath, Credar led the way again, this time following a defined path that led from the bridge. A short way along, the path passed between two more of the columns, with the same carvings. These were obviously cared for. Again the group stopped, concern etched on each face.

"Are we sure this is worth it?" Emdur asked Credar, nervously scanning the path behind them as well as the path stretching ahead of them in an arc.

Ester and Maxnil nodded their agreement to the question.

Credar opened her mouth to answer at the same time as a short, dark-skinned man stepped from the shrubbery, pointing what looked like a very sharp spear at her and smiling. Wearing a short breech cloth and a ring of beads around his head with a large red pendant stone centred on his forehead, he was well muscled and clearly confident. As she stared a further five of the short men appeared, each with a spear levelled at Credar and her companions.

Maybe not worth it, Credar thought, sharing a despairing look with her companions.

Guided and prodded by their six captors, Credar's small party moved along the path, which proceeded in an arc and ended in a clearing, or perhaps a meeting place. It now had a more sinister purpose. In the centre of the clearing a stone column of great height was surmounted by a round stone that glowed brightly. Beneath the column was what could only be an altar, with what could only be a priest standing behind it, garbed in a white robe and a feathery cape with a headdress made from the skull of a water predator, mouth gaping and teeth yellowed and showing many gaps. Credar cursed to herself, even while she noted that the skull headdress must be very old, for the realisation was dawning that maybe the Waslit were not as gone as people thought.

Credar nudged Emdur and shouted "Run!"

Both of them headed in different directions, while the two handlers leapt at the smaller man nearest to each of them. But escape was not to be had, as additional spear-waving people, men and women both, appeared from the bushes and formed a solid wall of spears around the clearing. A number raised the spears as though to throw them.

"Halt!" the first of the captors called out, and the spears were lowered again, but not put up. The four stopped also, Maxnil putting down the man he now carried above his head, having been preparing to throw him into his fellows as part of the escape attempt.

At a gesture, the party was swarmed and, within a very short time, they had been stripped of their clothes. Credar elicited some appraising looks from the men as she was lifted by four of the captors and carried to the altar. Despite her struggles and protestations, none of which were answered, she was strapped to the cold stone as the priest intoned a prayer for divine intervention.

"Oh great Likki, we beg you in your grace to look on us in joy and protect us from the demon that has taken root in the sacred stone."

He paused as the entire gathered congregation looked as one to the stone, which was pulsing now rather than maintaining a steady glow as it had been.

The priest's voice trembled as he continued, "We offer you this beating heart and the running blood, as our fathers did in the glorious past. Take our offering and save us from the ravening beast that threatens to tear us limb from limb, to rend our flesh and despoil our women." Spittle was running down his chin as he became more involved in detailing the deadly danger expected to arise from the light that inhabited the stone. His voice rose to a shriek as he brought the ceremony to a climax. "I cut this heart from the living breast for you, oh Likki, and beg you smite the demon. Aaiiiieeeeee!"

The last was a scream of pure fear as the stone gave an almighty flash, after which it no longer pulsed. But now, a strange woman, garbed in a robe of ancient style, floated before the altar, pure rage showing on her otherwise fine features.

"How dare you!" she said coldly into the complete silence that had fallen. "How dare you use my name for blood sacrifice! This abomination is ended," she continued glaring at the priest who now huddled in as small a ball as he could make of himself. "Begone, false priest, and never darken this place again, for if you do you will be destroyed. Go!" She pointed towards the jungle.

The priest and those who had acted as captors scrambled away along the path into the jungle, back the way Credar and her friends had come.

"Now," said the woman, "we need to set this right. I am Likki," she said, at which the assembled people moaned and fell forward on their faces, lying prostrate around the column. "Oh, get up, I'm no god for you to worship. I am Likki, Guardian of Ennaris. We have returned to assist the Children of Ennaris to defeat the evils that caused the destruction of Ennaris and that have once again awakened. It appears that some of that evil has taken root here, also. These four," and she gestured to Emdur and the two handlers, "I have chosen to assist me."

The people had scrambled to their feet, but now turned to face the three standing companions and bowed deeply.

"That's all very good, and we appreciate your help," Credar said from atop the altar. "And I think I speak for all of us when I say that we will assist you readily. But can you get me off this altar, please?"

38. Rest

Three days later Varna awoke with the now familiar feeling of lethargy. She had a heavy head coming on. As Flin had surmised, the feeling had been growing since she awakened in the infirmary and had grown worse across the last day, so she was not surprised. Knowing that it would not stop her completely - not yet, anyway - she decided to continue to explore the citadel. Hopefully, it would help her to clear her head, and she might find Balgor's Garden of Rest. She and Blaine had covered a part of the citadel during the previous two and a half days. It was surprisingly large, with a population that she put at somewhere around thirty or forty thousand, which probably made it more of a city in Ennarisi terms than merely a citadel. The latter implied a military fort to her mind. Of course, if it was built to protect the Faeronar, who all seemed to maintain a militaristic stance, then it may well have been a large fort, after all.

After a quick breakfast of fruit and bread at the same tavern where she had sat with Blaine and Jalor on previous days, she made her way to the main gate, and turned to follow a passage that ran against the wall. No buildings were against the wall, which she found odd when placed against most of the pseudo-medieval cities she knew of in the Union. Rather, there was a paved path that varied in width from a narrow passage to almost a broad road in places and ran around the citadel alongside the wall. She and Blaine had not come this way during their explorations of the previous days. The buildings facing the wall were all of a type in this part of the citadel, two or three storeys tall, made of a mix of stone and wood. They seemed to be slightly, or in some cases significantly, less well maintained than those she had seen with Blaine in the other quarters.

After a relatively short distance conditions changed from less well maintained to squalid. Refuse was piled against the Citadel wall, and scuffling sounds showed rodents of some sort were exploring. The light changed as the wall curved. The buildings now blocked the available sunlight, and Varna walked through a semi-twilight, still with sufficient light to see but with odd shadows making some detail hard to make out. The difference between the obvious wealth that she had seen in other quarters and the squalor and poverty of this part of the Citadel was marked. The alleys that ran between blocks of buildings were dark and increasingly noisome. Odours whose source she did not want to think about emanated from several alleys as she passed. Rodents - there are always rats, she thought, no matter which world it was - scurried through the gloom.

Varna could feel herself starting to drift, and thought she should turn back. This did not seem to be the sort of place to be when she did not have a clear head. But still she continued, now seeking one of the seats that she recalled seeing periodically along the wall on the other sides of the citadel. She was staggering slightly, one hand against the stone wall to support her balance as the symptoms of whatever was affecting her made themselves felt. The path started to swim in front of her. Distortions like rising heat waves caused her vision to ripple. Still, she forced herself to keep moving, not to let herself collapse, but it was now sheer willpower that kept her on her feet.

Finally, when she decided that she could go no further, she came upon a small, dusty park, with a small dry pool with an equally dry fountain backed against the wall. With a weary sigh, Varna made her stumbling way to the side of the fountain, dragging herself to the point where the stone fountain side met the Citadel wall and sat on the low wall around the pool, with her back to the Citadel wall. She leaned back and rested her head against the stone, feeling the cool against the back of her head. Almost against her will her eyes closed and she started on one of the waking meditations that she had learnt long ago as a remedy for headaches and extreme tiredness.

After only a short time she became aware of the sounds of stealthy movement nearby. Shuffled steps and scrapes of cloth on stone came from her right side, the direction from which she had come. Wearily, making an enormous effort, Varna opened her eyes and turned her head to find two ragged, dirty men trying to be stealthy as they crept towards her. In her normal state, Varna would have found it comical and been able to deal with the two would-be attackers without noticeable effort, but she was not in her normal state and she knew she faced trouble.

Seeing that she was awake, but also seeing that she was vulnerable, both men pulled knives from somewhere inside the rags they used for clothes. Their feet were bound with pieces of cloth tied on by scraps of rope, their hair was matted and filthy, and their faces had not seen any form of razor for a long while. One produced a gap-toothed leer, showing blackened teeth. Varna did not have her staff with her, and could see that there would be no-one to intervene - the surrounding area appeared to be deserted. So, with another supreme effort, she forced herself to her feet to face them, knowing full well that in her current state they had the advantage. Her movement caused them to halt, while they tried to decide if she would be as easy to take as they thought. Evidently, they thought she would be.

"Well, lookee here, Mac," the leering one said. "We got ourselves a nice little girlie, all clean and fresh looking. I've not had any sort of girlie for a long time." He licked his lips, eyes gleaming as he restarted his approach with his knife held inexpertly in front of him.

Mac was a man of few words. He said nothing but, like his companion, started a slow shuffle forward again. He ran his eye up and down Varna's form, and a small smile tugged at the corners of his mouth. Varna noted that he held his knife as though he was far more familiar with it, and decided that he would be the more dangerous of the two. They were only three or four spans away when both stopped and stared at something behind Varna, mouths agape, eyes wide and faces pale.

Varna felt a breath of air movement behind her and resigned herself to an attack from front and back.

"Not a good idea," said a gentle voice from a short distance behind her, a voice she thought she recognised.

The two men stepped backwards, holding their hands wide and, as one, turned and ran, turning down the first alley they came to. Varna carefully turned herself to face the newcomer, striving to hold herself upright. She could make out the shape of a man standing by the fountain where she knew there had been no-one a short while before. The man watched while the would-be attackers fled, and then turned to regard Varna.

"This place is not safe for you," he said in his gentle voice. "Not in your current state, at least. Those two were just the first. There will be others. I have a place where I think you will be able to feel both better and safer."

Again, in her now thoroughly confused state, Varna felt that she knew the voice and for some reason she could not understand she felt that she could trust that voice. In any event, she could now sense other movement in the alleys, and so agreed with a jerky nod of her head.

The man moved to her and grasped her arm, supporting her without in any way seeking to take advantage. As they walked further along the path, further along the inner wall, Varna sought distraction, more as a means of staying aware than anything else.

"You live here?" she asked her rescuer.

"Oh, I've been in the Citadel for a very long time," he replied with a smile in his voice. "It's not a bad place, although from time to time we do have a rough element take up lodgings. Usually, the Faero makes sure the people have enough to eat and a place to live, but there are always those who prefer to prey on others. I try to keep that down a bit also, even though it's not really my place."

"So, what do you do, apart from rescuing people from being attacked?"

"Well, not that much, I guess," he said, scratching his head. "It's not that I'm a wastrel, you need to understand. Just that I've got a job to do when it's necessary, but it hasn't been necessary for quite some time. So, I guess you can say that I just wait."

"That sounds boring," Varna said, her voice tailing off as she concentrated on walking upright.

"It can be. I think I may have some action coming up, though." He glanced to Varna. "Just a little further and you can rest."

Varna just nodded and they continued on their way. After a short time, Varna could see, through her wavering vision, that they were coming to another small park. This one, however, was green and lush. A similar fountain pool occupied a place against the wall, but this one had water splashing and tinkling from a centre fixture that resembled a great fish. Slender trees stood in a garden that framed the fountain, with bright-plumaged birds singing in the branches, diving into the water and back again as they trilled what Varna felt sure was a greeting. Grass, deep green and luxuriant, spread from the fountain and the garden to a defined edge, where it came to a stop. On the other side of that edge, the dry and dusty path continued.

"Here we are," he said, and they crossed what seemed to be a boundary separating this tiny lush place from the surrounding area. Even the light seemed to be brighter.

For Varna the change was dramatic and immediate. Her lethargy dropped away and the disorientation lifted - enough, at least. She stopped, amazed, as her full awareness returned. Her companion turned to see why she had stopped and smiled at her wide-open eyes, and the colour returning to her previously pale face.

"What is this place?" she breathed in wonder.

"This is my refuge, my small space where I can be who I am," the stranger said mysteriously. "It's also your place for so long as you need it. Occasionally others use it when they are sick in spirit, but their need is tiny compared to yours. Welcome to my Garden of Rest."

Varna stared for a moment at the fountain, garden, birds and trees. She recalled the words of her dream, urging her to find this place. Without a word she turned to step back past the boundary where the grass ended. Immediately she felt the heaviness crash back over her and she started to fall, only to be caught and helped back into the small glade. The effects left her once again, and she shook her head in amazement.

"You knew that would happen," she said accusingly.

"Yes, I did," he replied with a grin.

Varna stood and regarded him for a moment. Slightly taller than herself, sandy hair that dropped to his shoulders, clean shaven, dressed in utilitarian garb - pale linen shirt, dark trousers and sandals - he had the bluest eyes Varna could recall seeing and wore a slightly impish expression, a half-smile that told of a mischievous personality. Varna suddenly knew.

"Balgor!" she said in shock. "It was you in my dream!"

Balgor smiled again, genuine pleasure shining through. He bowed slightly.

"Guilty as charged," he said lightly. "It is my pleasure and privilege to welcome you to my garden, Varna. We have been looking for you and your companions for a very long time."

"Flin was, um, surprised when I gave him your message," Varna said, as much to continue the conversation as anything. She was intrigued to find Balgor, a Guardian and thus one of the most powerful beings on Ennaris, acting as though she was important. "He has some anger towards the Guardians for leaving him and his friends, and the people of this planet, to make their own way. And he seemed surprised that you returned."

"Flin has done a remarkable job," Balgor said kindly. "But he is mistaken. He and his friends were never abandoned. The people of Ennaris were never abandoned. Most of the Guardians were forced to leave Ennaris and undertake other work, but some of us stayed and have been here for the duration."

"You?"

"Me for one. I've been here for the whole time. Flin has had assistance, even though he may not have been aware. But you must understand that we were forbidden to intervene in certain things. The people of Ennaris had to make their own way after the rebellion's devastation. It was heart-breaking to see so many perish and we did what we could to reduce the impact but could not stop it. We're not all-powerful gods, after all. We have many gifts, and can perform what many people would see as miracles, but gods we are not." Balgor's gaze sharpened and his voice hardened. "But the time is coming when we can assist again. The destruction of Ennaris will not be repeated, and we will make sure of that. The Ennarisi must take the chance we will give them, however."

"How many of you?" Varna asked, curious at Balgor's change of mood.

"Oh, there were only a few who remained. But now the Guardians return, even as the evil rises once again. And you have returned also, as the Prophecy of Halfgar said you would. But you haven't had the chance to acclimatise and your gifts are running rampant. You need to have help to find your balance, to learn how to control your gifts or you will fail in your appointed task."

"You mean what I have been experiencing is because I have some sort of gift? Flin implied something of the type a little while ago but I haven't had the chance to talk with him any further."

"Yes, that's exactly what I mean. Those brought up on Ennaris are acclimatised from birth, of course, and as their gifts show they can be harnessed by people who know what to do. Or they could be. That was the origin of the Guides, by the way. They guided the gifted through that process of becoming aware and then developing their gifts. You're not from Ennaris, although you are of the Ennarisi line, but have not had the opportunity to come to your gifts gradually. Rather, you have had them thrust on you. They will have been there all along and you will have used them but only as a shadow of how they will develop here. Ennaris has certain qualities, and even we are not sure what they may be, that opens those gifts to their fullest extent."

"What do you mean that I am of the Ennarisi line?" Varna ignored the reference to her not being from Ennaris - it seemed that secret was done and dusted in certain circles. "I am from a planet called Earth, or my forebears were."

"Yes, but it was the Ennarisi who worked to lift the vestigial intelligence of your planet into the light, and who maintained contact up to a juncture only a short time ago, relatively speaking. Earth, as you call your home planet, was so similar to Ennaris that it received large doses of Ennarisi material, including the seed of the Ennarisi people that helped Earth people develop. You would have seen a steady development of ancient peoples around your world from very primitive to modern. That is the lift provided by the Ennarisi over time."

"But that process took a huge length of time," Varna gasped. "Hundreds of thousands of years, er, cycles."

"Yes, but you don't realise just how ancient Ennaris is. Ennaris reached a peak a little before the rebellion, and its influence stretched through much of the galaxy. Your planet was not the only one lifted, although it is most like Ennaris, almost a duplicate in many ways. But other planets have gone through the same process and some have yet to flower. My brethren have spent their time of exile in seeking to protect those nascent intelligences, as we did with the Ennarisi so long ago."

"The Guardians lifted Ennaris and the Ennarisi?" Varna asked. "Using the same techniques of injecting DNA into species?"

"Something like that. It was an extremely long time ago. We also did some early repairs to the planet but nothing like what the legends and tales tell of."

Varna picked up a thread and worked it through.

"So," she said thoughtfully, "that makes the Ennarisi descendants of your people, which also makes us descendants of your people?"

Balgor smiled. "Indeed it does. The gifted of Ennaris are those whose genetic combinations give them a shadow of our powers. Likewise, the gifted of your people, and others in the galaxy, will have particular combinations of genes that result in gifts being present."

"And some get more complete combinations, and so get more powerful gifts." Varna stared at Balgor.

"Many of them became the Guide Mages in days past," Balgor said, nodding at Varna's logic.

"So the Children of Ennaris, who we have been hearing about, are Jalor, Blaine and me." Varna made it a statement, her tone flat.

"Maybe so," Balgor said. "We think so, anyway. But remember that I said there are other intelligences raised by the Ennarisi. Another has landed on Ennaris also, and could also claim to be the Children."

"Shadows," Varna said with a scowl.

"Yes, the Shadows as you call them. The people of Andoreth." Balgor smiled. "They have been corrupted from a peaceful and gentle people. And you will have to deal with them and perhaps others also. But not right now. This Garden will give you a break from the stresses of adjusting and I will help you until such time as you can get to the Forest of the Guardians. Fernis, who the trees call Hollow Branch, is the best one to help you to make the change. For now, rest with me for a short while. I suggest you try to return every day."

"Will coming every day help me to build some sort of resistance?" Varna said as she settled herself on the wide fountain side, looking suspiciously at a cushion that seemed to have appeared without her noticing before using it to support her head.

"Maybe," Balgor said. "But mostly because I like your company."

Varna laughed tiredly. Here she was with one of the most powerful beings she could imagine and it was relaxing, comfortable and pleasant. She closed her eyes and allowed herself to drift into a half-sleep.

39. Tine

The hunt was going poorly. Xymin had been trying to locate the great narwa for hours now. He knew it was in this area but nothing he tried to do brought him closer. In fact, he had not even had a sighting. He had found signs of where the narwa had emerged from the water beneath the ice through one of the small number of holes carved by the Junda people. The holes' purpose was just that, to tempt the narwa onto the ice so they could be caught easily. But for Xymin today, nothing. He was cold, hungry and frustrated, which were all feelings and emotions that were constant partners these days.

The narwa was the chief source of the food, clothing and bone implements needed to survive the extreme conditions in this most northerly region of Ennaris. The meat and blubber of the narwa provided sustenance as well as lamp oil, and the latter had some medicinal uses also. The pelt would be used for warm clothing. Xymin knew his mother and sister were relying on him, thus the constant frustration when he was unable to return from a hunt with a prize. It had been many days now since he had been able to return with anything, and then it had been a few miserable fish, luckily snagged when they had been washed onto the ice by a passing leviathan that had seemed to be hurrying towards something.

The far north was a harsh environment, and not one he could say he loved, despite it being home. Ice, snow and bitter wind were the staples up here. The land, such as could be uncovered, was unable to grow any crops, so most of the food came from hunting the sea creatures, and then trading for other staple foods and implements that were needed for day to day living.

The Junda people, as a result, were as hard as the land. They had to be to survive. The bundles of narwa pelt and white vilta fur were layered, making the people who wore it look like they were short and rotund. Anyone who met an angry Junda knew that such was far from the case. Beneath the layers of clothing the Junda people, men and women, were shorter than some, but they also were lean and hard. Muscles, developed from repeatedly drawing the long sleds or dragging the heavy carcasses of the narwa, or the occasional leviathan that was unlucky enough to become beached, were long and wiry. The occasional rope-pulling contests between Junda teams often were long and exciting, being exercises in endurance and strength, of stubbornness and resilience. The poor food had an effect, of course, but the people found ways to compensate, in part. There even were some small valleys inland where coarse and hardy crops grew, and these were harvested to supplement the diet of meat and the all-important fat.

Life, however, had been made more difficult by the rise in recent years, starting before Xymin had been born seventeen cycles before, of a great evil in the lands between the ice and the mountain regions that framed the more habitable parts of Ennaris. There had been many strange happenings over the last ten cycles, one of which took Xymin's father. Xymin still did not know what had happened. His father left one day on a hunt and did not return, but his canoe had been found smashed into pieces, obviously by axes or swords, and strange tracks had been found in the vicinity.

And the hunt had become harder, so it was more common to return empty handed. Despite the slim harvests of rain crops, hunger became a close companion for the Junda people. Several groups had sought relief by migrating south but in at least one instance they had been wiped out completely. The other expeditions were not heard from again so no-one knew if they managed to get away or not.

Lately, however, the travelling story tellers were reminding people of the old tales, brought to life again by these strangers who seemed to know much of the times before the rebellion. Those old tales, legends and prophecies told of Ennaris as a great world, and reminded the people of the Guardians who helped its people and the Guides who worked with them. Xymin did not know whether he should believe any of it, but he did wish it could be true. Certainly, the idea of some all-powerful being, who could make the lives of his family and those that remained on the ice easier, was attractive. But his life experience did not lead him to think any such thing was real. Looking around for his landmarks in this ice-blasted landscape, Xymin reflected that belief in anything positive was hard to come by. He pulled up the hood of his anorak, which was becoming dangerously thin from long use, and decided to head back to the rocky outcrop that marked the boundary of land and sea, even though thick ice covered all of it.

He was moving closer when the wind dropped to nothing. There was a constant wind across the ice, so the absence was something to note. Xymin sighed with relief and tried to move faster. He was on the sea ice still, pushing his way through snow drifts towards the rocks when he noticed a high-pitched whistle, growing in intensity. Over the horizon came a ball of bright light, racing towards him, and then over his head, close enough that Xymin threw himself flat to the ice. Then he was up and running, as fast as his bulky clothes could go.

With growing horror Xymin saw the ball of light impact on the rocky headland that was his goal. The horror was followed by a sickening feeling in the pit of his stomach as he felt the ice shift from the shock. Loud cracks and groans were emitted as zig-zag fissures started to reach out across the ice towards him. The solid ice started to fracture into a crazed network of floes. Each floe jostled against its neighbours as the stresses and tensions of the ice were released. Sea water sloshed up and over the rim of several floes, some of which now piled up against others and broke apart from the forces unleashed.

Xymin stopped running and stared, aghast, as he found himself on one such floe with no way to progress. He struggled to hold his balance, even as he dropped to one knee for better stability. Leads started to open between the floe on which he knelt and its neighbours. Xymin knew he would not make it to shore now and his horror and fear were replaced by anger, not for himself but for his family. They would never know what happened to him but they would suffer anew and would have to rely on others for support. While the Junda did what they could, inevitably there would be privation and possibly worse. The floe rocked violently and Xymin struggled to remain upright.

Resignation settled in. The Junda philosophy, supposedly drawn from the teachings of those old and long-gone Guardians, was to do the best you can do and fight hard for life but when, inevitably, the time came, to be calm and accept your fate with dignity. Xymin settled himself on the floe in a sitting position, and prepared for his own death by reciting the prayer to Tine, who he now knew from the stories was not a god as he had thought but a Guardian of the people of ice and snow. Closing his eyes, Xymin delved for the calmness that the teachers taught.

After a short time, he realised the floe had stopped rocking. Opening his eyes and looking up, Xymin saw that a solid path of ice had formed between his floe and the rocky shore, where a shadowy figure waited, beckoning him to come. Not sure if he was dreaming or not, Xymin scrambled to his feet and moved as quickly as he could over the new ice, testing its stability as he went from habit as much as anything else. He reached the shore and stood, regarding the stranger with consternation. A woman. She wore little more than a simple robe, belted at the waist, with wooden sandals for shoes. It was so ludicrously inappropriate for this region that Xymin knew he was dreaming. Perhaps he had fallen through the ice already and this is what death was like.

"Xymin," the woman said, "come closer. I am Tine and I have need of your help."

Tine? The Guardian? Xymin stared.

"But you're a myth!" he said, immediately recognising that as one of his less intelligent statements.

"Not quite," Tine said with a smile. "But I have been away for a long time and there are things we need to do. I have chosen you to help me to do it."

"Why me? And how do I know you really are Tine?" Xymin remained sceptical, although the creation of an ice path from his sinking floe stayed well to the fore of his thinking.

"Because you are someone who stays true, who cares and who will be listened to. Also, because you have suffered a loss from those who we must oppose. As to how you can believe, you already do, but just have to accept."

Tine's body was enveloped in a glow, not bright but certainly shining out.

Xymin stared anew, considered, and accepted. Quite apart from the ice path, and the glowing figure in front of him, Tine represented an opportunity to help his family and people, and possible to oppose those who had taken his father, as he expected was the case from how Tine spoke.

"Why now? Why have you been away so long and allowed your people to be hurt so much? How can we believe the Guardians want to help us when you did that? Many have died during the hard times that the tales tell." Xymin's anger was stoking, and he was amazed to find himself speaking to a Guardian like this. "Why?" he ended on what was almost a plaintive tone.

Tine sighed, letting the glow fade and moving closer to place one hand on Xymin's shoulder.

"We had no choice," she said softly, sadly. "We have restrictions also. We are not gods, after all, and our guardianship did not allow us to stop what happened, although we tried to help the Guides as far as we could. But now the time has come when we can assist once more. For the Children of Ennaris have returned, and so do the Guardians. Will you join me?"

Xymin nodded. "Gladly. But you have to do better than last time," he replied, looking Tine firmly in the eyes.

She did not look away.

"Agreed. Let's get started. I have food and better clothing for your family and community to help them, and then we will begin our mission."

Xymin felt himself wrapped in a warm glow and was lifted into the air alongside Tine. *Well,* he thought wryly, *I've never brought a girl home to meet mother, but this might be hard to top.*

40. Lady of the Citadel

For the next tenday the three Warriors stayed at the Citadel, waiting for Flin to return. Jalor was concerned at their inactivity while awaiting the return of the Mage, but took the opportunity to recover his strength. They explored the Citadel's paths and buildings and made acquaintances of many of the people, most of whom knew of their feats in defending the fortress and not a few of whom had been watching from the walls. They were able to discern an undercurrent of anxiety among many of the inhabitants. Merchants discussed shipments that had not arrived, and some luxury items were in short supply, such as spices, finer materials and even the type of stylus used by the administrators for record-keeping.

Creely, it was noted by many, remained largely if not entirely out of view. However, stories were doing the rounds about his increasingly bizarre behaviour when he was sighted, and his descent into forms of depravity that the Citadel had not seen in the memories of even the oldest residents. The situation came to a head when he was accused of attacking a young woman one night in one of the seedier parts of town. When the watch commander attempted to interview him Creely's own band of guards, whose number included several who had been newly imported for the role and the mercenaries who had been confronted by the people of the citadel, had beaten the commander to a point near death, and threatened the same for anyone else who tried to arrest the chamberlain. Creely and his minions barricaded his office and the approaches to it.

Faced with a public outcry, and with too few guards available, many of whom still were recovering from their injuries or were far from being young, Crander, the watch second who was himself near to retirement, in desperation reached out for help to Jalor. In turn, because he was still convalescing, Jalor redirected the request to Blaine. Blaine listened politely, asked a few questions and agreed to do something, but said he needed time to formulate a plan. Crander was satisfied, posted a couple of guards at the administration building to try to keep Creely's protectors bottled up, and made it known that the strangers were going to help. He then went back to trying to maintain order in an increasingly restless citadel.

"So," Jalor said quietly after Crander had departed, his effusive thanks still ringing in their ears, "ideas?"

"Nope," Blaine said, taking a sip of his ale. Either it was getting better or he was becoming far too familiar with it, he thought wryly. "From what I can gather, they have that big office barricaded along with the two corridors leading to it from each direction. Varna said the office is in the middle of the building and not against any of the side walls, and the whole thing is solid stone anyway. This place was built to be defended, and it will take some effort. And the remaining guards are not really soldiers, even though most of them want to think they are."

"Helt?"

"Yeah, I think I'll try to get her in on it. She's in the lock-up again for fighting while drunk. I think she needs something to keep her occupied. And she can fight! That old longsword she has strapped to her back is enormous but is well made. What she lacks in any sort of real finesse she makes up for in power. And that misbegotten armour provides her with more protection than the guards with their leather breast-plates and old helmets." Blaine considered for a moment. "I need to figure this out a bit and then get her out."

Jalor nodded. "We should be able to come up with something. Creely's men are more thug than warrior and from what I can gather they dragged a whole lot of wine-skins in with them and have been going through them. Maybe when they run out, we may have an opening."

"It's a thought," Blaine said in agreement. "I'll take another day to come up with a plan. Crander has already passed the word that we're taking a role, and that will get to them soon. Let them stew on it for a bit." He smiled. "I wonder if we can get our own armour so we come across like some sort of space marine squad?"

"Helt will know where you could do that," Jalor said with an answering smile. "Maybe you need to get her out sooner rather than later."

Blaine nodded again, swallowed the remainder of his ale and stood. He sketched a salute to Jalor, who was seated with his leg resting on a bench, and ambled out of the tavern towards the watch-house.

Varna continued to visit Balgor's Garden of Rest, at least once daily. She found that she was able to keep at bay the disorientation and lethargy she had been feeling. She also found that she enjoyed Balgor's company, finding him a bright and witty companion. She relished the opportunity to relax and undertake deep meditation, something she had not been able to really do since landing on Ennaris. So far, her meditations and the effects of the Garden had been able to hold back the intrusive effects of her "gifts", whatever they were, but now she could practice the techniques taught over many long years. To her surprise she found that she was able to go much deeper than before, to establish links with the planet in some sort of way that she found both exciting and disturbing. She could almost sense Ennaris surrounding her, and with Balgor's guidance she started to separate distinct threads from the background noise that was what she had experienced almost as a psychic attack previously.

Her discussions with Balgor ranged far and wide, including aspects of the Citadel and the situation with Creely - Balgor was not prepared to play any part just yet, if ever, in that because it seemed not to impact on the safety of the Faeronar or Ennaris - and they discussed the role of the Guardians, some of the history of the planet from the earliest days of the Guardians' arrival, and the people of Ennaris across time.

Balgor described the heights of technology achieved by the Ennarisi - an advanced civilisation that grew and thrived over millions of Earth years before the calamitous fall. With deep regret, and no small anger, he told of many millions of Ennarisi dying during and after the rebellion, of the efforts of the Guides and Guardians to hold back the worst effects and the loss of almost all of the advances that had been made, with the result that Ennaris had reverted almost to savagery. There were parts of Ennaris, Balgor had told her, where barbarity was closer to being the norm than the fledgling civilisation that was so painstakingly being built anew.

Varna found that the Garden was the only place in the Citadel, and for some distance around, where she was able to escape the mental pressures brought to bear on her. The Citadel itself contributed a feeling of closeness that she had not experienced before on other planets.

At times, and at Balgor's urging, Varna sought out Aldar, daughter of Almin Bor and Magwyn, and took her to the garden with her. On the first occasion Aldar gave a squeak of shock, eyes very wide, when she saw Balgor.

"So bright," she said in awe when Varna asked her if she was alright. "He *shines*."

Balgor smiled broadly, welcoming Aldar warmly, and to Varna's mind not just to the Garden. The awe never really left Aldar when she spoke of Balgor, although she promised not to speak to anyone but Varna of his presence. Varna was pretty sure that Balgor had his first acolyte. Balgor had explained that the Guardians had usually attracted small bands of followers who were known as acolytes and who helped the Guardians to spread their word. That had died out as Ennaris became more sophisticated and the more direct contact between Guardian and Ennarisi, the people of Ennaris, had faded to myth and legend, although some had held onto small bands of acolytes to use as messengers until the Guardians had been forced to leave Ennaris.

Balgor encouraged Aldar to explain what she could see when she looked at people, and how she did it, helping Aldar as she explained that she was able to switch her other sight on and off, which allowed her to see people just as people when she wanted to do so. But Balgor's joy was obvious when he found that Aldar could see an aura surrounding plants and animals also. She could tell which trees were sickly based on a grey-brown aura, and which were healthy based on a green-brown aura. She could point to people walking past and tell Balgor which of the roughly dressed people were good-hearted and which were villainous.

"Fernis," Balgor said to Varna as they sat over an ale in the Garden one evening, "is going to love Aldar."

But then he would say no more of Fernis and, when Varna pressed, only said that she would meet him herself sometime soon.

Balgor encouraged Varna to open her sight to those auras also. At first, Varna was unable to see anything at all. Despite her efforts, or because of her effort expended, her sight remained stubbornly normal. And then, on a day when Varna was hurrying to the Garden with Aldar to stave off the disorientation, she was startled by a woman stepping out of an alley, holding her hand out and begging for a coin. Recoiling in surprise, Varna snapped a glance at the woman, noting that she had a faint glow of blue interspersed with a pale grey that Aldar had previously said was a sign of being malnourished, and allowing herself to relax rather than prepare to defend. In relief, and with a sense of compassion for the woman, Varna dug into a pocket and handed over enough coins for the woman to buy food for several days. Aldar touched Varna's shoulder and pointed to the alley where two small children's heads poked out, each of whom showed the same grey of privation. Varna glanced to Aldar, dug into her pocket again and extracted additional coins, pressing them on the woman who broke into tears when she saw the sum presented to her, clasping Varna's hand and thanking her repeatedly. Varna smiled and waited till the woman and her children had moved away before continuing to the Garden.

Balgor was waiting and Aldar excitedly told him how Varna had been able to see the aura of the woman they had encountered. Balgor nodded, his ever-ready smile on show once again, but did not press Varna for details. The latter was pensive, thinking back over various times in her life when she had felt that she knew whether to trust a person or not, but also other times when she had made the wrong call and given her trust to the wrong person or failed to trust someone worthy of it. Did the abilities that were starting to manifest on Ennaris have something to do with that? Were her innate psionic abilities that had been identified long before she joined the Academy part of it as well? Balgor referred to her gifts, plural, and Varna wondered just what this powerful being knew of her.

Still, during the course of the time she spent with Balgor and Aldar that day, and for the next couple of days, she was able to push those concerns to the back and relax, trying out her new-found ability as people passed. Inevitably, given the part of the Citadel where the Garden was located, those people were poor, many were malnourished and quite a few were inclined to regard the law as an obstacle. But Varna was amazed at what she was able to read of people, of their underlying personalities and motivations, of their state of mind and physical health.

She found herself weeping when she saw an old woman, kind of heart and gentle of spirit, struggle down the path, and could see that her life force was almost spent. She argued with Balgor that the Guardians should be able to do something about making people's lives better, but Balgor deflected that criticism, stating that life and death was not something the Guardians controlled. They did do what they could to help those who needed it, although perhaps not the way Varna may have deemed to be appropriate.

She also found herself glaring at a swaggering young man, his aura displaying shots of almost-black that Varna now associated with evil, or at least a complete lack of moral fibre. He stationed himself near the alley mouth, obviously awaiting someone, in clear view of Varna. It was only then that Varna realised that Balgor had shielded the Garden, for the young man should have been able to see Varna clearly. But when a middle-aged woman trudged along the path and was confronted by the youth, who demanded that she hand over all of the food she carried in a relatively small pack, Varna steeled herself for what she knew would be a return to her disorientation and stepped from the Garden to confront him.

"Stop," she called clearly as she stepped through what Balgor would later explain was a sort of veil hiding the Garden in plain sight.

The youth would later tell his friends that the beautiful woman appeared from the air without warning, carrying a long black staff and with eyes blazing in anger, demanding that he return the food and other goods to the woman. Not being the heroic type, the youth quickly handed everything back and without a backwards glance fled the scene. The woman, just as startled, stood and stared at Varna before getting down on one knee and bowing her head low.

Embarrassed, Varna bid her to rise. "Please, stand. There is no need for you to kneel to me."

The woman stood slowly, unsteadily. "I have seen you, my Lady," she said. "You were one who defended the Citadel, and I have seen you walking about the paths, keeping them safe for those of us unable to protect ourselves."

Varna was startled at that. "Yes, I helped to fight off those creatures and I have been walking around the Citadel from time to time. Why do you say that I have been protecting you?"

"Those who know of you have told others of your skills. Those who prey have no wish to be where you can deal with them, for it is said that you have protective spirits aiding you."

Varna thought back to the attackers who had been scared off by Balgor. Knowing him as she now did she wondered just what he had looked like when he appeared, for they had been terrified. She also realised that this episode would now add to whatever tales were being told of her.

"My protective spirits sometimes get ahead of themselves," Varna said, and was sure there was a snort from the Garden behind her. She thought she may as well make something useful come of this. "Let people know that evil will not be accepted and I will deal with miscreants where I find them."

The woman nodded eagerly. "Aye, my Lady, I will tell the people. And I thank you, my Lady," she said softly, reaching out to touch Varna's sleeve. "Thank you."

Varna nodded and stepped back, passing through the veil once again. The woman gasped as Varna disappeared from view, looked around once or twice and hurried on her way.

Balgor laughed delightedly, until Varna rounded on him.

"Just what did you show those two who tried to attack me?" she demanded, hands on hips.

"Um, well, nothing real," Balgor said with barely suppressed laughter. "But I had bulging eyes, two huge horns, some very impressive claws, really huge muscles and was red all over. And I was twice as tall as they were."

Varna stared at him, her eyes narrowed.

"And a long tail with an arrow-tip at the end," Balgor elaborated. "Really big teeth and ..."

"Enough," Varna said, her anger dissolving as Balgor refused to be cowed by her. "When were you going to tell me about that?"

"Oh, some time," he said blithely.

"So now you have me being the local police force? I have my own work to do, you know, apart from trying to keep my head from exploding."

"Yes, well it was either that or I would have to do something a little more drastic, and we try not to be too obvious about things." Balgor had turned serious. "There is trouble brewing. Creely, the Chamberlain, has been turned, I think. His behaviour is anything but normal. His guards are thugs and there has been an influx of the wrong people, the type Intika would never tolerate in the Citadel. It has yet to get to the point where the Citadel and the Faeronar are threatened, and I don't want that to happen."

"Why? What would happen then?" Varna could not read Balgor, either using her innate empathy or her new ability to read auras, but she could tell he was now very serious.

"My role is to protect the Citadel and the Faeronar living in it, as the last best hope for Ennaris. It is what I have done for more lifetimes than anyone except Flin and one or two others can understand. And when the situation requires me to do that, the limitations with which I have been bound for all that time come off, and I make decisions about outcomes."

"And you don't like that." Varna made it a statement.

"No Guardian likes to take a life, but we have had to do so at times of extremity, both on Ennaris and elsewhere. I have never had to do more than put a scare into people here, although I have assisted the Faeros to maintain order from time to time, and some people died as a result of that. So, I'm not completely innocent in that regard." Balgor sighed. "And I think it's time the big bad Varna made her way back to her companions. Flin has returned and will have need of you. I suggest you continue to keep your ability to read people to yourself for now. It may be useful."

41. Flin's Exposition

Varna steeled herself and made her way from the Garden to the tavern that had become their base, even to the extent of having semi-permanent rooms now. Jalor was standing, flexing his leg that seemed to be about normal again, while Blaine sat at a table mending a piece of harness from a stable in a side street. He had been meeting people and taking a greater interest in the goings-on of the Citadel, including helping out in the stable and one or two smithies. Also sitting at the table was Flin, a tankard of ale in hand and a large heavily bound book in front of him.

"Ah, Varna," he smiled as she arrived, "now we can begin."

"And hello to you, too," Varna said. "How was your trip? Have a nice walk? Was the weather good?"

"Um, yes, thank you. It was very good," Flin stammered, while Blaine smiled broadly at the ease with which Varna had brought Flin up short.

"Excellent!" Varna exclaimed. "Well, enough small talk. You were saying?"

She smiled a bright and winning smile, causing Flin to stare at her suspiciously.

"You," he said accusingly, "seem to be much better. I'm not sure it's an improvement," he grumbled, taking the time to have a long drink of his ale. "Well," he said, placing a hand on the book, "I have been checking on the Prophecy, which is what this is."

He opened the book and all three looked at it closely. It was heavily bound in some form of leather, with stitching that looked a little amateurish and was bearing a patina of age, but the pages revealed were not paper, nor any form of skin that many less advanced civilisations used in place of paper, or other traditional materials. Rather, all three recognised an advanced synthetic material, with no signs of age despite being thousands of years old going by Flin's previous statements.

Jalor reached out to touch the open page and just nodded.

"Ennaris was not always as you see it," Flin offered by way of explanation. "Anyway, as I said, I have been reviewing the Prophecy and mentions of the Nine that Varna was told of in her vision. To summarise, the Prophecy states that in the time of greatest need Ennaris will be saved and enabled to retake its place amongst the many peoples of the heavens, as Halfgar termed them. Those who will save Ennaris are the Nine."

Flin paused, considering. "You need to understand some of Ennaris' history."

"I think we also need to know what you know of us, and explain more about yourself," Varna said with a gentle smile. "Archmage Drewflin, last Archmage of the Council of Mages and accounted by some who know of those things as the greatest of those Mages."

Flin was startled, staring at Varna, as were both Jalor and Blaine, who then turned to stare at Flin. After a moment Flin started to chuckle, but all three saw tears form in Flin's eyes.

"Not the greatest, child. That honour belonged to another who is no longer with me." He brushed at his eyes. "And not the Archmage, although I am called that by my friends. Ironically, I might add. Well, you have been busy, I see."

Flin stood and bowed formally.

"On behalf of the Council of Mages and the Guides of Ennaris, such as we are these days, I bid welcome to the Children of Ennaris, after all these cycles. Varna, Jalor, Blaine, you are welcome, and badly needed." He sat again. "And it is, indeed, time I brought you up to speed."

He thought for a moment, planning how to proceed.

"To begin with, I know a great deal more than your names. I know where you are from - yes, more than 'not from around here'." All four smiled at that jest. "I know enough about your civilisation and your federation to be satisfied. I also know about your foes. And I know why you are here, although you may not know the whole story yet."

Jalor raised both eyebrows, which was as much surprise as Blaine had seen him display. But he stayed calm, outwardly at least.

"You're not convinced," Flin stated. "Well, I know that you are soldiers of a civilisation that started on a small planet near the further edge of the galaxy. The guiding principles of your civilisation are drawn from a form of pan-universalism, essentially worshipping or maybe honouring the physical universe via an energy which you call The Light. I know," he held up his hand as Varna opened her mouth to speak, "it is a very crude generalisation, but it will do for now. As I said, I know enough to be satisfied. I also know that you are in conflict with a civilisation that appears to be directly opposed to your philosophy and espouses militarism, rampant industrialisation and empire. Again, crude generalisations," he finished apologetically.

Jalor nodded. "Near enough. And why are we here?"

"To save our planet and, probably, the galaxy." Flin spoke calmly, so matter of fact that a moment passed before his outrageous statement sank in.

"That's a pretty tall order," said Jalor impassively, "just for the three of us."

"Oh, I expect you'll have some help," Flin replied, a steely glint in his eye.

"You seem to have a remarkable grasp of technology, considering our expectation of finding a somewhat static, unsophisticated rural culture. You personally, I mean. Our best analysis indicated this planet has progressed very slowly or not at all over the last few thousand cycles."

Flin nodded. "This planet, and its various peoples, are far older than you can imagine. It has struggled to overcome the cataclysm that occurred thousands of cycles ago. The brilliant civilisation of that time was erased and most of the knowledge lost in very short order. Our advanced science is a memory of only a very few now."

"Memories of thousands of cycles ago?" Varna considered Flin expectantly.

"Many thousands of cycles ago. I had hoped to take you to the Council's chamber, and I shall, but I have a feeling we may be short of time.

"Believe it or not, there is a Prophecy concerning your coming and the role you will play in the crisis that is building. The Prophecy comes complete with portents and dire warnings, the usual cryptic phrases to be deciphered. But one thing now clear, given that you are here, is that people from another world will be the salvation of our own. We have been able to work out some of the puzzles of the Prophecy. Others are still unknown. We will go through the Prophecy together some time soon. For now, just believe that it was the Prophecy that told us approximately when and where you would arrive. That, and my own knowledge of your earlier party. All I had to do was wait."

"Us?" Jalor interrupted quietly.

"My ... er ... colleagues, I suppose you would call them, and me, and my apprentice. We are all that is left of the last Council of Mages. In fact, only I was a member of the Council at the time. Our task over the centuries since the catastrophe that followed Goroth's rebellion has been to slowly guide the people back to a form of prosperity. Once we were an advanced civilisation. It's distressing still to see what we have become, and to know I had a part in it. The true dark ages immediately following Goroth's defeat are long gone, but now the threat has re-emerged.

"But to start at the beginning. Ennaris' civilisation was very advanced over a very long period of time. We had space travel before your ancestors entered the trees, let alone left them. No" - he held up one hand to forestall protest that was not coming - "please, I know exactly what I am saying, and I mean it quite literally. As you will understand soon. Ennaris' high civilisation lasted for millions of cycles.

"We were known and respected throughout the stars of our galaxy. Many of the legends known to the people are of this period, although now they are seen as fairy tales, and the facts have been blurred or obscured by verbal tradition, but it truly was a long golden age. At our peak, we had exploratory and colonising teams going to dozens of prospective worlds at once. Our colonies thrived throughout the galaxy and produced peoples that still thrive, although a number have ceased to exist. Yes," he said wistfully, "it was a time to remember."

"And you remember them?" Jalor watched Flin intently.

"Oh yes, quite well. It has been only around five thousand cycles since the rebellion that ended it. I remember it quite clearly."

"So you are five thousand cycles old?" Blaine asked flatly, part question and part incredulous statement.

"No," Flin replied gravely, a sparkle in the eyes belying his studied expression. "As a matter of fact, I am about twenty thousand cycles old. And I feel every one of those cycles right now, believe me."

"But," Varna interrupted, then paused as she collected her thoughts, "but what you said means that some of the civilisations in our federation were your colonies."

"We are quite sure of one, and reasonably sure of a number of others, based on genetic and racial characteristics. And not just of your federation, either. There are a similar number of characteristics in races that compose the opposing empire, with a similar range of probabilities that some are scions of our colonisation from long ago. As a matter of fact, one part of the controlling Prophecy mentions child against child determining the fate of Ennaris. Your coming and that of the Andorethi, who have been pressed into service by Goroth's minions, put a new complexion on that passage. We originally thought it meant a return to civil war, but while Goroth's supporters already have subjugated a small number of our provinces – kingdoms as they now deem themselves to be – the forces are not enough as yet to mount a challenge against the free provinces."

"But are the remainder unified?" asked Blaine thoughtfully.

"Ah, there you have our first problem. No, the remaining provinces have fallen apart from each other. Mutual distrust over the centuries has become entrenched antagonism in some areas. Again, it stems from the effects of Goroth's rebellion. He has much to answer for."

"This Goroth has Shadows in his service?" Jalor asked quietly.

"Indeed, but not yet Goroth directly. They seem to have arrived as explorers a short while ago and were captured by Goroth's lieutenant, Grensor. Or perhaps given to him." Flin mused on that for a short time. "Yes, that seems likely also."

"I cannot believe Shadows would willingly serve any master, especially on what seems to be a backward planet."

"Grensor would have given them no choice, and as I said they may not be serving him by their own choice. He has very unpleasant ways of overcoming objection, I have been informed. And Grensor was one of Goroth's key lieutenants. As was Likud."

"Likud?" Blaine's attention sharpened.

"You've mentioned Goroth and the rebellion several times. Who was, or is, Goroth? What did he do that constituted rebellion? And what about Likud?" Jalor watched Flin keenly, still unsure about trusting him or his story.

"Goroth was one of the strongest powers of the Council of Mages. In fact, when his ambitions led him to choose the dark path and he adopted the forbidden lore, he became nearly the strongest, for our self-imposed limits were abjured along with his oaths. Ironically, he was one of our best in the beginning. The aims of the Council were to protect Ennaris and the home worlds and to support the colonising efforts supposedly decreed by the Guardians. Goroth's counsel was for more direct involvement in the colonised worlds, but until near the end he always honoured our first principle that colonised worlds had to evolve in their own ways."

"So, who are the Guardians?" Varna asked, already knowing Balgor's answer but interested in Flin's.

Flin smiled, a private, self-mocking smile.

"The Guardians are remembered by many as our gods. Almost no-one remembers them today beyond stories and tales, preferring the more modern gods raised after the decline of the rightful leading clan of Ennaris - the Faeronar. The Guardians are mentioned in our most ancient myths, handing tablets of law to the early leaders, guiding them by signs and portents, miraculously intervening in the lives of the ancients as they helped to raise us from the stone age to civilisation. And always the myths exhort the Ennarisi to continue the work of the Guardians, to raise to sentience and civilisation other races throughout the galaxy.

"I have been alive longer than almost any other Ennarisi, and have never met a Guardian, nor seen signs of their work, beyond what legends seek to explain away by invoking magical actions. My calling was not attributed to the Guardians but I was drawn to helping Ennaris and its peoples, which I deemed to be an honourable task." He sighed, rubbing one hand over his face as though to dispel weariness. "From what Varna told me, I have been wrong all that time. I have had to reconsider many things over the last days. Perhaps there truly were Guardians, watching over us as we watched over the colonies we planted. Marjory always believed it was so. Whether that was true or not, the leading clan always maintained that it had a sacred duty to continue the Guardians' work. And it did so for many ages, from the time we could travel to other planets and stars.

"But for some reason Goroth seemed to become enamoured of power. He always advocated more intervention, pointing to the legends of the Guardians and their supposed interventionist policy with Ennaris as an example. However, he had not shown any sign of going against the Council's wishes. When he was selected to lead a team of colonists it seems he decided to test his own ideas. The party left for a distant planet that was first colonised when its most advanced species was very low on the evolutionary scale. It had been raised over the eons to the point where it had achieved true civilisation. Goroth's task was to guide the civilisations to organised government, on several models, so that the races had several examples from which to choose. Instead, he set himself up as a godhead, with the other colonists as lesser gods. They actively intervened in the affairs of the inhabitants over a period of about five hundred planetary cycles or more. Their actions completely changed the course of that civilisation, we have reasoned. Towards the end of the expedition the team's cohesion broke down, and the members fought amongst themselves, with numbers of the world's inhabitants becoming involved in the fighting. Many died, including numbers of the colonisation team. Eventually, the recall signal was acknowledged, and they returned to Ennaris.

"When the logs of the expedition were reviewed Goroth and the other Mages of the expedition were roundly criticised. They were ostracised, something that had not been done for as long as the Council's annals recorded. And so we had no idea what to expect. Most of us hoped he would display contrition and return to the Council. But, instead, Goroth established his own Council in opposition. He began to use the forbidden lore and he and his supporters used it to create monstrosities. It became evident that he had to be stopped.

"What we didn't know was that since his return and ostracism Goroth had attracted numbers of the Guide Mages and members of the major families of Ennaris to his line of thinking. When the Council announced its intention to stop Goroth and his minions from subverting the colonising work of Ennaris, we found members of the leading families and Council members defected to his cause. Rather than stop him, the Council did little more than provoke civil war.

"There were many more trained talents in those days. Unlike the way many think now, there was no shame attached to being a Mage of greater or lesser degree. But that also meant there were Mages on both sides. Effectively, the sides were matched almost evenly. And when the conflict spread beyond the Council and its adherents, the advanced technology that we had developed over countless centuries was used by those with no enhanced capabilities - the gifts I have mentioned to you before.

"During the rebellion and civil war, whole tracts of Ennaris were laid waste. Some of the most beautiful places on the planet were destroyed. But the real destruction came when Goroth and his subverted Mages began to lose the technology war and drew on their dark magic instead. They unleashed horrors beyond contemplation, dread illusions that drove whole cities mad, mutant creatures like the original ghazrak that destroyed other cities and fed on the inhabitants. Seemingly normal Ennarisi creatures were transformed into fell beasts. The rebel army was supplemented by mutated soldiers drawn from subjugated peoples. Armies were destroyed by forces called forth from nature by Goroth and especially by Grensor – winds, earthquakes, floods. Cities were destroyed to the last defender.

"Our efforts to counter the dark magic were always too late, for the damage was done. The population lost confidence in the Council and more terrible weapons were used. Much of our best work, our most beautiful cities, our basis for civilisation, was damaged near to total annihilation. So the Council decided that it had to be stopped. Our first thought was to remove the instruments of mass destruction from both sides. One of our number – his name was Halfgar – claimed to be able to render all advanced technology unusable, at least for a while. He claimed knowledge from the Guardians. He was very old, and we all thought him senile, but he convinced enough of the Council that he should try."

Flin gazed pensively into the distance, eyes unfocused as he recalled events that almost passed beyond legend, let alone the memories of his own people.

"And it worked, mostly." He smiled wryly. "We were astounded." His smile faded to a thin-lipped grimace. "But we lost Halfgar. The effort took him past his own threshold. He just faded away. He turned to us and smiled once, lifted a hand in farewell, and was gone. Many on the Council thought he was a crazy old man – he was the oldest of us by far – and that his powers were almost negligible. He proved to be the most powerful of us. And he was my friend."

Silence stretched moment by moment. None of the listeners were inclined to break it. Varna was weeping quietly, her empathetic abilities drawing her into Flin's grief. The old man reached over to hold her hand in comfort.

"Do not grieve, my child," he smiled sadly. "Halfgar knew the consequences of his actions, I am sure. He spoke often to me over the years, teaching me, I now realise, and one of the discussions concerned over-extending ourselves when we draw on our talents. He warned of the end result of profligate release of energy. It was his triumph, in a way, and his final lesson. And he allowed us to win. When most of the terrible weapons of destruction were rendered unusable, the Council could concentrate on the rebels. We were hardened to our task now, and we attacked rather than waiting to repair the damage. Many Council members and lesser talents on both sides died, but finally we brought the remnants to a final battle not far from where you landed.

"The Mage energy unleashed was incredible, so much so that it reverberates still in that place, as Varna found out so painfully. Local superstitions tell of voices, spirits of the dead, unusual happenings occurring there. It may be so. Many died. The last terrible weapon unleashed from space, that had not been nullified by Halfgar's interdiction, resulted in Ennaris convulsing mightily even as we destroyed it. Only Goroth was left and two lesser but still powerful talents on the rebel side - Grensor and Likud. There may have been a few minor gifted also, but we could not be sure. Fewer than twenty Council Mages were left on our side, of varying levels of talent. We pooled our talents, using a technique Halfgar had shown me long before. Goroth was imprisoned in a special stasis chamber built deep inside the northern mountains. Halfgar had prepared that, too. An array of nodes powered by the remaining Guide Mages was placed around the planet to maintain the stasis, and various safeguards were erected around the nodes. Somehow, they also survived the interdiction. And the rebellion was ended.

"But Ennaris was reduced to barbarism. Simple things had to be re-invented. Major starvation was averted for all of the survivors only by the remaining Guides and Council Mages using all of our knowledge and talents to provide crops. And, of course, there were far fewer people left and the land was changed beyond recognition. Our work was irretrievably damaged. We were not sure how to proceed. The debates we had over that!

"Oddly, it was Halfgar who decided that for us, too. We found what we thought was a diary, but it was a series of prophecies that had come to him in trances. From the Guardians, he had written in a note fixed to the top page. Much of it was old, having been written over thousands of cycles. The older writings detailed what would happen during the rebellion and how it would end. That established for us that the Prophecy, as we called it, may be valid. There was a lot more debate, but really, we all knew that we would rely on Halfgar's guidance, as we realised many of us had done for most of our lives."

He chuckled. "That old man had been the real leader of the Council for a long time." Flin shook his head to clear memories, and sighed gently. "Now he showed us the way forward. We were to maintain as many of Ennaris' traditions as we could, but let the people find their own way back. We were too few to do any of the works of old. Anyway, we could not use technology for whatever Halfgar did to disable it was still in force, and it still is today, in general. So, over the last five thousand cycles we have tried to guide the remaining Ennarisi out of the dark age and onto the path of civilised development. For some, the work was too much, or the memories of what we had been were too sharp. They just gave up and ... ended. The remainder decided to live in the midst of the different peoples for short times only, and to enter a stasis sleep between times. For some reason, our own Council complex was not affected by Halfgar's interdiction. And the planetary defences in space were intact still, as was Goroth's stasis chamber. We still don't know why, but we know that technology taken from the chamber ceases to work."

"How did our technology work then?" Blaine had been drawn into the telling, almost against his will, and now he gave Flin his entire attention.

Flin frowned. "That's right! Perhaps it was because it came from outside Ennaris. And the weapons of your earlier party and your enemies also worked." He rubbed his chin, musing. "Interesting!"

"So," Jalor tried to get Flin's tale restarted, "if Goroth's in stasis, why do you need us?"

"One of the power nodes was damaged by a micro-meteorite. It should not have got through to the nodes but it did. Our defensive systems estimated that the stasis field would fail over a period of about fifty cycles. We expected a further few cycles for Goroth to build a force of sufficient strength to attempt to restart the rebellion. We had no real idea but we also had no doubt that he would. I fear that Grensor has been doing that since Goroth's incarceration.

"Until now, we have merely held our own. We can't come out into the open and announce that the Council still exists. For one thing, the Council has faded into a mixture of myth and legend, and Goroth was a member of the Council. Most people don't believe Goroth could exist. His name is used to scare children, but few really understand what he did, and they are mostly scholars and tale-spinners who we have taught. And, there are only four of us left." As he said the last, his voice faded, and Varna sensed a surge of very personal grief, quickly suppressed.

"Haven't there been any Ennarisi born with, er, talents over all the thousands of cycles?" Jalor frowned.

"Of course," Flin replied, "but you must remember that the Council and its rebels were held to be behind the destruction of Ennaris' civilisation. In the earliest days of reconstruction, we did what we could to help, but we were blamed, and rightly so in a way. That blame turned to persecution very quickly. Those who exhibited talents were driven out, in many cases they were executed. Also, the rebellion destroyed a whole generation of those with talents. The families were not formed, the bloodlines not carried forward. The volume of talent was cut dramatically. Oh, there were and are those who have an echo of talent, but where they used it, they became oddities. At one stage the faintly talented became travelling conjurers, illusionists. Some were good enough to attain a measure of strength, and a school of sorcery was even formed."

He laughed bitterly. "The sorcerers are pale reflections of the Council, but were tolerated because they were so much weaker than we were. They are still in existence, seeking to maintain an existence among a gullible population using party tricks." He snorted his disdain. "And there are so many fakers. Still, it has left us with a useful means of getting around the lands. Those of us still alive travel as storytellers and conjurers. It means we can travel almost anywhere, and we meet most of the ruling class," he shrugged, "such as they are."

"So, how do you know we are here to help?" Jalor re-joined. "You seem to know so much about us, but do you know our reason for being here? We have no orders to save either the planet or the galaxy. And we have a ship waiting for us."

Flin was apologetic. "Actually, it's not waiting so much as trapped. Your fleet broke orbit to counter a threat from a rival fleet."

Jalor was unmoved at the news, but Varna gave a gasp of dismay.

"As for your own purposes for being here, why I assume it is to investigate what happened to your first party." He smiled as Varna stared and Blaine raised a questioning eyebrow. Jalor remained impassive. "It's not hard to deduce, given where you first appeared. And the readings you were taking." He frowned. "The readings," he muttered, "your instruments were working."

Jalor nodded. "The spell nullifying technology seems to be selective."

"Perhaps. It's something I need to consider. And it's not a *spell*," Flin said the last with distaste, causing Jalor to smile faintly. "But to finish answering your question, Halfgar's Prophecy mentioned that as Goroth's prison weakened – actually he said, 'as the Adversary's bands loosen' – our children would send us a Champion and three." He stopped as Varna and Blaine started. Jalor's eyes narrowed.

"I said something significant?"

Blaine looked to Jalor, who nodded.

"We were trying to find traces of an earlier party, as you surmised. One of those was the holder of our highest honour. He was the Champion of the Light." Blaine spoke quietly. "He had three companions."

Flin regarded Blaine steadily for a moment. "And this honour is not given lightly?"

Jalor took up the thread. "The Champion was reputed to have superhuman powers. The honour is not just the highest award of valour, but also recognises inherent abilities beyond the normal. Clay was said to be the strongest Champion ever, although there have only been a few."

"And you are looking for him?" Flin asked of all three.

"For them," Varna corrected him. "Yes, but it was long ago. And we found what Blaine explained is the result of a destructive charge used as a last resort." She focused on Flin. "You know something of this," she stated tightly.

Flin nodded. "One of our working sensors was very near the spot. It was destroyed in the final explosion, but we recorded what happened." He described the events leading up to Clay's use of the blitz mine in the clearing now marked by the dead circle. "You see," he concluded, "your party was destroyed completely. And, it seems, so was your Champion."

"Can we see that recording?"

"In time," Flin nodded absently. "I still think you are the others of the Prophecy, for Halfgar wrote that you would come after. I will have to re-examine the Prophecy."

"Where is the recording?"

"At the Council's chambers. It's quite a long journey, but I do think we need to go there. I'm afraid you have some travelling ahead of you."

"We can make a start pretty much immediately," Jalor said. "But I think tomorrow would be better. We can make it look like a planned journey if we just make leisurely preparations."

"What about Creely?" Blaine asked. "I don't think we want to leave that behind us if we can help it. And I expect we will want these people to think kindly of us in the relatively near future."

"Creely?" Flin asked no-one in particular. "What have I missed?"

While Jalor and Blaine brought Flin up to date with the Chamberlain's situation and fall from grace, Varna noticed and kept a wary eye on a group across the square. They had crept from a couple of streets that ran into the square, and now there were eight men converging on a small wagon that was parked in front of a store. A young woman and child sat atop the seat in front of the wagon and a man, dressed in nondescript clothes, had just emerged from the store to climb up to the wagon seat. The eight men, who Varna could see were unkempt, dirty and disreputable-looking, surrounded the wagon, blocking the way both forward and back.

Varna frowned and stood. To Jalor's questioning look she said, "I'll be right back. Something to take care of."

She reached into her pack and extracted the staff, attached it to her belt and left the tavern, walking unhurriedly towards what had become a confrontation. Varna pulled the hood of her cloak up so that it covered her hair as she walked. Blaine, following Jalor's gaze, took in the situation and started to rise, only to be held back by Jalor.

"No, wait. Varna is no fool. If she thought she needed us along she would have said so."

"But what is she doing, and why?" Blaine asked, neither expecting nor receiving a response beyond a shrug.

The young woman was holding the child close to her, while the man looked around the group. Several of the youths - for Varna could see they were just out of their teens, if that - leered at the young woman. The first of the youths, obviously the leader, pulled a knife from under his ragged garments, waving it around as he made demands of the man.

"Ye can give us what ye got in the wagon," he said with an evil grin. "Matter of fact, ye can give us the wagon, too." He looked around his gang, grinning, drawing strength and confidence from the numbers. "And I think we'll be takin' her as well."

"What we have on the wagon is all we have," the man said, looking around desperately for help. He saw Varna closing on the group and his eyes lit with hope.

The leader saw his expression change and turned to see Varna stop outside the circle formed by the youths. He frowned, then grinned again when he saw that it was a single person, and obviously another woman.

"I think you should leave them alone and get back into the sewers where you belong," Varna said clearly and loudly.

"Ye do, do ye?" The leader looked around his gang again, most of them turning to look at Varna. "And I think ye should mind yer own business or ye'll get what she's gonna get."

Varna unhooked the staff from her belt and held it ready in one hand. With the other hand she swept her hood back, revealing fine features, blonde hair and a calm demeanour.

One of the youths started. "Raf," he hissed. "Raf."

The leader, now identified as Raf, snarled at him. "Shut it, Sef. When I want ye to talk I'll tell ya."

"But Raf, that's her," Sef said, looking around worriedly. "The one with the demon."

"Well, I don't see no demon. And if she wants to butt in she can join in all the way," said Raf as he moved from the front of the wagon, knife extended. "Come on, pretty. You can go first."

Which was the last thing he was to say for a while. Varna thumbed the stud and the stub extended to a full-length staff, which she then swung in an underhand powerful strike right up between Raf's legs. With a squeak he stopped, eyes popping. Around the square every man grimaced while not a few women laughed. Varna swung the staff again, cracking it against the side of Raf's head, but without full force. He collapsed, unconscious.

Varna stood still, staff now held across her body in both hands, ready for any action. Then she backed out into the square as the gang, except Sef, started to move towards her. While the gang thought she was trying to get away, Blaine knew she was giving herself space, and allowing the couple and their child to make their escape, which they did once the gang was away from them. The man gave a grateful nod to Varna before starting the wagon moving. The gang let them go, pride and the wish for revenge taking precedence.

All of the gang, except Sef, now had knives in hand and ignored everything going on around the square. Had they taken notice they may have wondered why people who might have assisted were being held back by two men who had come from a tavern, and may have been cautious. Had they faced an experienced fighter before, rather than unsuspecting drunks, they may not have separated into three pairs. And they would not have been surprised when Varna stopped reversing, suddenly lunged forward with the staff flicking out to the closest pair, both of whom found themselves out of the fight, one clutching a badly damaged shoulder and the other staggered by a blow that split his cheek.

And then all of them stopped and stared at a point just beyond Varna's right shoulder, mouths agape. Hands dropped to their sides, knives dropping from suddenly nerveless hands.

"I tol' ya," Sef said in triumph. "I tol' ya she was the one."

Varna smiled, realising that Balgor had taken a hand. More of the legend, she thought wryly. But then, the reason she had decided to take a hand without Blaine or Jalor was to do the same, so she could not really fault him.

"Pick them up and go," she said, gesturing to the unconscious Raf and the two injured youths. "In fact, you may want to think about leaving the citadel. I don't think you will have a very successful time here."

The remaining gang members, this time with Sef, retrieved their comrades and beat a hasty retreat, looking over the shoulders all the time.

"Big red?" Varna asked of no-one in particular.

"Yes, but I added a big eye in the middle of my forehead," Balgor said from behind her. "I think it was effective."

Varna chuckled, retracting her staff and turning to see nothing behind her. "Did anyone else see you or was it just them?"

"Flin probably could make me out, judging by his expression, but no-one else. I think that will help the tale of Varna to develop nicely. I'll leave you to explain to Flin," he concluded and Varna was sure he was laughing as his voice faded away.

Varna was smiling still as she made her way back to the tavern, all eyes around the square on her. She sat back in her chair and nodded her thanks to the server who placed a cold tankard in front of her, shaking her head when Varna reached for payment. Varna took a long pull of the drink and then sat back.

Jalor cocked an eyebrow. "Happy?"

Varna nodded, smiling broadly. She caught Blaine's eye and winked when he grinned to her.

"Who was your friend?" Flin asked, eyes narrowed as he awaited her answer.

"Balgor," she said. "He made an illusion of some sort of monster, which is what scared them off in the end."

She said nothing of the stories spreading about her.

"Does that have anything to do with the stories I've been hearing about a woman patrolling and protecting the Citadel's poorer district?" Blaine asked. "A yellow-haired woman. Apparently, she is accompanied by a demon."

So much for not saying anything, Varna thought.

"Maybe," she answered. "And it may be that some of the stories are exaggerated."

"Some of them? Not all of them?"

"*Some* of them," Varna reiterated. "And it seems to be working. The number of assaults has dropped, according to the women who live there. And people feel safer."

"And Balgor has been helping you? Why?"

"He has been helping me get past the integration of my gifts with Ennaris. As Flin thought, that's the source of the disorientation, headaches, loss of control that I have been experiencing. And he thinks the rise in crime and lack of authority since Intika has been away, combined with an influx of people who are more predator than anything else, is a source of danger for the Faero and the Citadel. So we have been developing a legend of the Citadel's protector, in the hope that it will be able to prevail when we're not here."

"But why would Balgor do this, after being away for so long? I know he was the legendary trickster, but I would expect a returning Guardian would have other things to do." Flin shook his head, perplexed.

Varna felt sorry for him. "Flin, Balgor is Guardian of the Faero and this citadel. He never left but has been here all the time, protecting these people, keeping watch over them. Most of the Guardians left Ennaris, and not of their own choice, so Balgor said, but not all of them."

Flin's confusion fell back into despair. "He's been here all along? And we - I - never had any sign? Were we of such little note?" he said with an anguished tone.

Varna shook her head. "No, you have it wrong. The Guardians valued the work you were doing, even though many of you did not believe they existed. It was because you battled for the people of Ennaris that you were - are - held in high repute by them. You have a place of honour with them, believe me."

"But we were so alone," Flin groaned.

"Never alone, my friend," said a voice from behind Flin, as Balgor strode up to their table, wearing a tunic, trousers and sandals very similar to those of others around the Citadel. "You have always had one of us with you in one way or another."

Flin stared, and rose to his feet, shakily. "Balgor?"

"Indeed. I was not supposed to reveal myself to you just yet but events are overtaking plans, so I have changed the plan." His eyes twinkled. "No-one will be surprised that I couldn't stick to the plan, after all."

"Plans are like that," Jalor said, taking attention away from Flin, who was struggling with his composure. "I'm Jalor, and this is Blaine. I take it you've met Varna," he finished drily. "Or rather, your demon has."

"Well met, Jalor and Blaine." Balgor smiled. "On behalf of the Guardians of Ennaris, I welcome you to our little home. How do you like it so far?"

"It's nothing like the brochure," Jalor said, "but I think it can grow on you. Some of the natives are a bit unpleasant, but we've experienced similar elsewhere. And you do seem to have an infestation of Shadows."

Balgor nodded. "Yes, but then from what I can discover they're not too happy to find you here, either. So Archmage," Balgor said, looking at Flin once again, "what are your plans?"

"If you are Balgor you know well I am not the Archmage," Flin said, with his composure returned but still with some uncertainty in his tone, "I was planning on taking them to the Council chambers to show them the records of their previous party, such as we have them."

"Hmmm, and Varna must spend some time at the Forest," Balgor said. "But I don't think you all should go. Jalor and Blaine will be needed here, I fear."

"Oh? What makes you think that?" Jalor asked, curious.

"I can't see into the future, if that's what you mean. As I told Varna, we're not gods, no matter that some may want to see us that way. No, there are matters arising that will require a steadying hand for the Faeronar, and I believe Jalor and Blaine will provide that."

"Soon?"

"Very soon," replied Balgor seriously. "I must leave you to your discussion. Drewflin, they need to understand the reference to the Children of Ennaris, to make their knowledge more complete. And know that it may apply to the Andorethi equally."

He smiled to the group, turned and left the tavern. The four remained silent for some time before Flin gave himself a mental shake, that became a physical shrug.

"Well, I suppose we should finish the tale of Goroth and the reason we refer to the Children, as Balgor instructed," Flin said.

"I think I can guess part of it," Jalor replied. "So, what form did your colonisation take? And where did Goroth get it wrong?"

Flin nodded. "Yes, I think you have it right. Normally we undertook genetic engineering of species judged able to accommodate the process.

Depending on the species, that involved changing the genetic structure or introducing additional genetic material."

Jalor frowned. "But Goroth went further on his world. He set himself up as a god-like figure. That implies actual contact with the inhabitants of the world."

Flin nodded shortly.

"And that implies that Goroth and his people, the Ennarisi, resembled the inhabitants of that world."

Another nod.

"Almost exactly?"

A third nod.

"How could that be?"

"The world had been found long before, on our initial sweep through the galaxy. It was very like Ennaris, and the primitive species on its surface included a number with sufficient resemblance to our own genetic structure to enable colonisation. Over time, with multiple careful interventions, the genetic admixture produced two dominant species that almost exactly resembled us. One of them survived. At one time, there was very serious consideration given to establishing a true colony on the planet, but it was vetoed. That was around four hundred thousand cycles ago, or thereabouts. Instead, it was decided to leave it to the normal colonisation process. The question was raised again on occasion, but the Council always decided against the idea."

"But Goroth decided to finish the job." Jalor nodded to himself. "It fits. The colonist seeders spread over the planet, to the various seats of nascent civilisation?"

"Yes," said Flint, eyes glinting as Jalor worked through the situation logically.

"What are you driving at?" Varna asked, bewildered.

"Haven't you guessed? The planet was Earth. We are the result of that genetic tinkering. Goroth and his expedition became our ancient gods, and probably those of many peoples around our globe. Is that right?" he asked of Flin.

"Yes." Flin's glance took them in at one time. "In a very real sense you are our children. And we need your help."

"And from what Balgor was saying, the same probably happened with the Shadows. Which makes them Children of Ennaris, also." Jalor said. "So, which are the ones of the Prophecy? Us or them?"

42. Faero's Return

Their discussions were interrupted by a cry from the battlements. The watch guard, one of the older men available for service, called to his fellows at ground level.

"The Faero - he's under attack. They need help."

A horn rang out and the few guards left in the Citadel, those who had fought the ghazrak with the Warriors, spilled from the barracks across the square from the tavern, most tugging on armour or attaching weapons to belts. The citizens of the Citadel watched for a few moments and then several started to move towards the main gate. Blaine turned to watch as a number of guards exited the building that housed the infirmary, still sporting bandages from their earlier encounter with the half-men.

Jalor looked to Blaine and Varna, nodded once, and all three rose as one, each reaching for their packs. Jalor and Blaine attached to their belts the swords they had acquired. Flin smiled and rose also, tugging his own pack into place over one shoulder. The four moved towards the gate, the crowd giving way as they saw who it was.

"Never did get that armour," Blaine complained.

"Did you see Helt?" Jalor asked, glancing to Blaine.

"Helt!" Blaine stopped. "Did anyone see her heading towards the gate?" At shakes of heads all round, he turned back. "I'll bet the fools left her locked up. I'll get her out and meet you down in front of the gate."

Jalor merely nodded as Blaine broke away, returning to the square at a jog. Varna felt Balgor's presence as she walked beside Jalor.

Tell Flin that it is time for the Guide Mage to return, he said to her. This is likely to be one of the turning points for Ennaris. And I need you to stay at the Citadel with me, he continued.

Varna did not slow her pace as she replied. Why do I stay? They are likely to need every able-bodied fighter.

One more fighter will not matter that much, but your presence in the Citadel will. This I have been told by one I trust above all others. And tell Flin that it is Dharmoney's time also. Balgor's tone firmed. Varna, trust me on this.

The three had reached the front of the gate, where Jalor halted to see what was happening. The gate remained closed, with all of the remaining guards milling around in front. A couple of the more senior men were trying to establish order. Barring the way was a group of men wearing the red armband that Jalor had been informed was the symbol of the Chamberlain's private security force. *Or thugs*, Jalor thought as he considered them.

While they outnumbered Creely's men, without officers the Citadel guards were unsure of what to do. Jalor glanced to Flin, who merely looked back and shrugged. Varna frowned and took the initiative. She stopped in front of the line of men, with Creely standing behind.

"Creely, open the gates so we can relieve the Faero," she called loudly, so the whole square could hear. "Right now, Creely, while you have the chance."

The chamberlain snarled back, "Get away with you ya stupid little girl. My men will make minced meat of ya. The Faero can stay out there and dance with the ghazrak."

"And you take over, you think?" Varna said with a sneer in her voice. "You, who had to hide in your office from fear? You, who had to hire this line of bullies because no-one else trusted you? You think you can take over? I don't think so."

"Ha," Creely laughed scornfully. "Who's goin' ta do anythin' about it? You? You're not even armed and my men are the best I could buy."

"You must have been short of coin, then," Varna retorted. "You do realise that by endangering the Faero and thus the Faeronar people that you will draw the ire of the Guardian of the Citadel."

"Guardian, right!" Creely snorted and several of the men in the line sniggered. "Everyone knows the Guardians are figments of imagination, stories told to keep children in line. Get along with ye before I let my men loose."

Varna felt a now familiar presence drawing close. Two of the men in line let out gasps as they were hurled through the air to land in the middle of the square. Immediately they were set upon by the guards who were waiting to get through the gate. They were bound and unceremoniously rendered unconscious. Creely gaped and the other men stared around in sudden fear. One of the guards, after searching the two men, held up sacks.

"Hey, these two are carrying red gold," he called out. "Creely must be paying them with red gold."

The people of the Citadel stared, and outraged murmurs broke out. The guards angrily started forward, to be halted by Jalor's outstretched hand. Creely blanched and his men moved closer together, their confidence now battered.

"I did warn you," Varna said, not understanding the reference to red gold but determined to maintain pressure. "If you won't open the gates, then I will. I command you to open!" she shouted and made a grand gesture, flinging both arms wide.

Creely stared and, as nothing happened, started to laugh evilly, a laugh that came to a shuddering halt as, with a loud creak, the massive gates appeared to open of their own volition, swinging inward so that several of Creely's men had to jump or be crushed. Creely cringed and started to back through the gate, eyes darting back and forth, with his men forming an uncertain barrier. Once through, they turned and ran towards the forest. Balgor allowed them to go, although several sacks similar to those taken off the two men appeared in a neat pile in the centre of the gateway. Varna smiled, picked up the sacks and turned back to the square, where even more people had gathered to watch and now regarded her open-mouthed.

Flin glanced at her, one eyebrow raised mockingly. Varna coloured, but then smiled ruefully, and shrugged. She dropped the sacks near a hitching rail.

Across the field, Jalor could now see a group of soldiers in a defensive formation being harried by an attacking force of both ghazrak and men. The formation was protecting a large group of women and children, which probably meant parents formed some of the defensive force. As he watched two of the soldiers fell and the formation closed slightly. There were perhaps fifty defending soldiers, with about half that many attackers. But as he watched a second larger band of attackers emerged from the forest, hurrying to join to the first band.

Jalor turned to Varna.

"We need to get in there," he said. "As soon as Blaine gets here with Helt we go."

Varna shook her head.

"I have to stay in the Citadel. Balgor's direction. I don't know why but he was insistent." She turned to Flin. "Balgor said to tell you it is time for the Guide Mage to return, and that is it time for Dharmey also, or something like that."

Flin merely closed his eyes, as though to gather strength or to pray. "Was it Dharmoney?"

"Yes, that's it. Do you know what that means?"

"I fear so. Very well, so be it."

He squared his shoulder and reached into his bag, extracting a short length of what looked like wood. Varna saw Flin's personal aura flash and the object lengthened to form a staff, with a pale green stone embedded at the top. Seeing both Jalor and Varna staring at him he grinned. The crowd at the gates were very quiet, having seen Flin's staff appear.

"What? Did you think you were the only ones able to do things like that? Remember where you youngsters started!" He turned back to the field. "Jalor, if you would organise that rabble, please? If we're going to do this we need to get started."

"Yes," Jalor replied, turning to deal with the guards, just as Almin Bor hustled through the gates. The latter took one look at the waiting troops and started exercising his parade ground voice. Jalor stopped, realising there was no need for him to intervene.

"What in the name of the Guardians are you lot doing?" he bellowed. "Is this how you're trained these days? You, Fernly, get your troop lined up and ready to march. Pasfer, you too. Come on, get a move on."

In no time at all the Citadel guards were lined up, each with a spear in hand and short sword hanging from a belt. Almin Bor turned to Jalor and saluted, with a wink that no-one else could see.

"Citadel guards ready, sir," he shouted.

Jalor nodded.

"One moment," he said as he saw Blaine, followed by a scowling Helt, start through the passage from the inner court to the gate.

He gestured to them to move to the front.

"Now we're ready," Jalor said to Almin Bor. "They're defending something or someone, probably the Faero, so we will relieve them. The goal is to get everyone back to the citadel. Let's go."

Without looking at the guards, Jalor started across the field towards the beleaguered soldiers. Blaine fell into step on his right, Helt to the right of Blaine. Somewhere, Jalor realised, Blaine had acquired a broadsword along with the short sword attached to his belt. Behind them, Almin Bor gave the order to march.

"Forward," Almin Bor snarled, "and if any of you fall out of line before I say I will personally make you regret it."

Blaine smiled approvingly and said to Jalor, "Now that's how a sergeant-major does it."

Jalor returned the nod, turning back to find Flin marching to his left. There were no signs of age displayed as he strode along. His extended staff rested on one shoulder.

Varna turned back to the Citadel and spoke to the citizens who still crowded the gate.

"Move back into the Citadel," she ordered, as she extracted her own staff and thumbed the stud to extend it.

This staff was getting a lot of use, she thought. Not what was expected when they left the ship. Only a few of the people moved back so she decided to take a leaf from Almin Bor's book.

"Move!" she barked, startling many who reflexively moved back a few steps.

That started a more general movement and soon the gate mouth was cleared. In a few moments Varna stood alone in the centre of the gateway, ahead of the long passage leading into the citadel proper. She settled one end of the staff on the ground and stood at parade rest, looking out over the field as Jalor and his relief troop quick-timed across the field, over the bridge and towards the conflict. Experienced as she was, Varna retained a watch over the forest rim, remembering that the last time a group of half-men had come through the forest they exited in a spot closer to the citadel.

Jalor made his plans as they jogged across the field. As they left the bridge, he tapped Blaine on one shoulder and pointed to the centre of the defenders, then at Blaine and Helt. Blaine understood what he meant and in turn tapped Helt, pointing to himself and her and then to the centre of the battle once she turned to him. With a feral grin Helt nodded, reached to her back and removed her broadsword from its mount. Blaine gave Jalor a 'what the heck' shrug and the two of them moved off from the troop towards the defensive cordon. Flin followed.

Jalor slowed so Almin Bor could catch up, the latter breathing easily where Jalor could hear one or two of the troop starting to labour. He signalled to the troop to stop.

"Form into two equal lines abreast, tallest behind. When I give the order stop in place, front rank to kneel, rear rank to stand, all spears to the front."

"Aye, Sir," Almin Bor said, nodding approvingly, in turn slowing to repeat it to his troop.

After some short confusion, the small troop was in formation as two lines abreast. Although they lacked the tall shields, any historian of human warfare would recognise the basic formation of ancient armies. Jalor positioned himself to one side, took stock and mentally shrugged. It would have to do with the relatively poorly trained Citadel guards.

"Forward, slow march," he called, and the troop started to move towards the battle.

Meanwhile, Helt had arrived at the attackers' line with the force of an enraged bull, and as much finesse. With a roar to announce her arrival she swung her huge sword twice in massive overhand swipes left and then back to the right, inflicting enormous damage on four of the attacking men and opening a gap through which she and Blaine charged. Meeting the defensive line both turned and immediately started to deal severely with the attackers. Blaine moved slightly away from Helt, ensuring their two huge swords were not clustered in the one spot.

The captain of the guard, recognising Helt and watching Blaine for a moment, was content to allow them to fight their own battles, and concentrated on resetting his dwindling defences around the families and a stretcher that had been laid on the ground, with a man resting apparently unconscious on it. They now were outnumbered three to one still and had been in dire straits until the two arrived. With Helt's unusual armour and sword, even though her skill was not as advanced as she may have thought, and Blaine's obvious skill even though unarmoured, the sides were more even.

Flin swung his staff with vigour and surprising skill, knocking two of the attackers out of the way so he could access the inner circle. He made his way through the outer defensive ring towards the stretcher, glancing to one of the men attending the injured man - the Faero, Flin saw - who shook his head mutely. Bending, Flin laid a hand over the head of the Faero. Had Varna been there she would have seen the flare of energy released. Flin glanced to the one who had shaken his head and nodded, agreeing with the diagnosis. The damage was too far advanced even for him. The infusion of energy would help, but it would only delay the inevitable. The Faero settled slightly, before awakening and glancing around. Seeing Flin and the ring of defenders, he tried to rise but was held down by Flin and the attendant. He finally realised that he was badly injured and subsided. His eyes followed the course of the defence.

The defenders were struggling to contain the attack. One of the half-men rushed through a small gap, brushing aside two of the defensive guards. The ghazrak approached the stretcher with sword raised and a guttural cry when the stone atop Flin's staff spat a ball of flame that engulfed the attacker and devoured it completely. A second ball took another who had charged through the same gap, after which the gap was closed by the defensive cordon. Flin saw the Faero stare at him but turned to watch the battle progress. The defenders were hard pressed and needed some respite.

One of the attacking men turned and saw Jalor's troop approaching at a steady march and raised an alarm. A ghazrak - Blaine took note that there seemed to be no Shadows with this lot - roared something and about one-third of the attackers turned from the fight and started towards the approaching guards. *Part of the plan was working, any-way*, Blaine thought. The defenders would have a slightly better time now. And so they did. The greater skill of the Faero's defending force now started to take a toll on the attackers, although they were still outnumbered. Slowly casualties mounted and the captain could see a possible way through. Flin's staff continued to spit fire from time to time, although at longer intervals. He breathed deeply and obviously was tiring rapidly.

Jalor watched the approach of the detached attackers. As he thought from what he had seen in their other encounters, there was little discipline involved in the way they fought, relying on overwhelming numbers, inherent strength and all-out attack to rout their foes.

"Stop!" Jalor called out and the troop came to a halt. "Front rank kneel, rear rank crowd up," Jalor called, as the approaching mixed force of ghazrak and men started to shout and wave their swords around in a manner they probably thought was intimidating. "Front rank, spears grounded. Rear rank, spears forward!" Jalor called and every spear was either dug into the ground to provide support or thrust through the gaps between the front rank to produce a bristling defensive line.

The first of the attackers, men rather than ghazrak, threw themselves fanatically at the formation, only to die on the small forest of spears that met them, despite their very basic armour. The up-thrusting spears were calculated to get below the breast armour. The attacking numbers halved immediately. Now Jalor had a numeric advantage, although they faced ghazrak more than men now. The following attackers slowed and approached more carefully.

"Spears down! Swords! Go for the separation of the plates." Jalor called, watching as his troop, still intact, dropped their spears. Several who had not needed them in the first engagement thrust them point down into the ground so they could be retrieved quickly.

The two sides came together. Jalor's men were slightly less capable than the attackers, whose ferocity threatened to alter the balance once more. Jalor wished he had Blaine with him at this stage, for his own skill with these medieval weapons was not as great as his team partner. He found himself the target of two of the attackers, and was hard pressed. Luckily the first to reach him, an Ennarisi man rather than a ghazrak, showed no skill whatever, launching a huge swing of his poorly made sword that still would have decapitated Jalor had he not swayed back. Once the swing was past the intended target, Jalor's assailant was off-balance and open, and Jalor had no problem stabbing through the unprotected part of the poorly constructed leather armour under his arm, penetrating through vital organs. Jalor extracted his sword as the first assailant fell.

The second, a ghazrak, was a different matter. Still with less skill, it halted and snarled through its animal snout, circling Jalor while trying to establish a weakness. Jalor turned likewise, but continued to move back and sideways. Slowly the two moved away from the main fighting group, where the Citadel forces were winning.

At the main battle, the defenders had started to gain ground and the attackers were growing desperate. Helt had amassed an impressive pile of dead ghazrak and men, and moved to one side to continue, now taking the opportunity of gaps appearing in the attacking line to launch small counter-attacks, targeting individuals each time. The attacking force was being whittled down until there were only a handful, who were then dispatched by the defenders quickly. As they leaned on their swords and shields, the defenders started to check their wounded, and the captain immediately started to organise carriage of the stretcher once again.

Blaine looked over the field and saw Almin Bor deal with the last of the attackers at his point. Jalor, however, was being hard pressed by his opponent. They were now a significant distance from the others. His assailant, realising that he was alone now, redoubled its attack, fury bubbling through via grunts and growls, and Jalor could see red eyes almost glowing in anger. Jalor was growing tired. His previous injury meant that he was not fully fit still, and he knew that he had to end this. Both of them had cuts and nicks, but Jalor was only alive because of his greater agility, while the other was inherently armoured and many of Jalor's strikes were ineffective.

Finally, Blaine saw Jalor appear to fumble and drop his sword, and nodded in approval. This was a move he had taught Jalor some time ago, on another assignment. Jalor's assailant roared in triumph and stepped in, raising its sword high to deliver a blow that would cut Jalor from neck to navel if it landed, only to find Jalor recover his sword and thrust from ground level, through a gap in the armour where the upper body plating met the thicker muscle covering of the upper legs. Jalor's sword penetrated its full length, and he rolled as far as he could, not being sure of the result, but that proved to be the end. The ghazrak fell to its knees with Jalor's sword still embedded and fell to one side.

Jalor forced himself to his feet, bent to retrieve his sword and gave up after several hard tugs failed to dislodge it from the ghazrak. He forced himself upright and walked - staggered - towards his troop, where Almin Bor was arranging for his injured men to be treated while moving the dead attackers into a pile. Surprisingly, while two of the Citadel guards were seriously injured and several more carried superficial wounds, none had died.

As he reached the group Almin Bor grinned to him.

"You'll have to do some updates on your sword work, Jalor," he said, nodding towards the dead half-man. "That one nearly had you."

Jalor nodded his agreement, wearily, then turned to watch the group of the Faero's guards reform and start forward. They had lost several men during the fight but the stretcher had been defended and was now being carried carefully.

Suddenly, one of Jalor's troop cried out and pointed towards the Citadel. Jalor spun around and cursed. A similar cry rose from the other party and Jalor saw Blaine and Helt break from that group, starting a long run towards the Citadel, along with about half of the Faero's guards. Almin Bor was only a shade later to start back, accompanied by most of his men. Jalor knew they would be too late. He could only stare as he saw Varna stride forward from the gateway, alone and with her battle staff held in one hand. She turned to face the large group of ghazrak and men that had broken from the forest.

Varna watched the two groups as the battle surged back and forth. She watched as Helt and Blaine crashed through the attackers to reach the defenders and start to take a heavy toll. She also knew Jalor's strategy would be to divide the attacking force and was not surprised when part of the attacking force broke away to attend to this new threat. She recognised Jalor's tactic from her military history but was surprised at how effective it proved to be. But even as the two separate battles were ended, with Jalor's final victory over his opponent, she continued to scan the forest edge.

With some dismay, but without a lot of surprise, she saw a larger group of ghazrak and accompanying men emerge from the forest much closer to the Citadel. There were around fifty of them, and Varna could see three Shadows amongst them with robes swirling as they all advanced at a rapid trot. Stepping forward, she turned to face the newcomers, holding her staff firmly. She opened her sight to view their auras and recoiled. The men's auras were what she could only describe as filthy, roiling blacks and browns, shot through with deeper reds. She knew these were the dregs of the Ennarisi, without any form of morality or compassion. Perhaps they had been made to be that way and could be repatriated, but she doubted it for this lot.

The ghazrak had no aura that she could detect at first, then she noticed a very faint trace of different colours, all edged in a dirty crimson. There was no fluctuation of the aura, nothing to indicate anything other than what she sensed was a largely uncontrolled rage. That fitted with her experiences of these creatures, and what others had described. But she was troubled by the underlying colours, which were all too similar to what the common Ennarisi displayed.

Then she turned to the Shadows, expecting to find auras indicating aggression, savagery and hatred but instead she found herself sensing despair. Pulsing pale gold colours were tightly bound by the same almost-crimson colour. She was unable to fathom what that meant, and she could not spend the time considering, for they had covered a quarter of the distance to the gates already.

Varna set herself. She fell easily into one of the mental zones she had been taught, opening herself to nothing else but the upcoming fight and preparing to give her life at a severe cost. She noted a fireball sail from the lower meadow into the rapidly advancing group, destroying several, but it did not halt the advance.

Varna, fall back to the gateway, Balgor said, shaking her concentration so that she fell from the zone.

Varna, fall back to the gateway now, said Balgor more urgently.

Almost without volition, and trusting in Balgor implicitly, Varna stepped backwards towards the gateway. Behind her the huge gates swung closed with no visible assistance. The attackers saw her falling back and shouted, grunted or growled, believing that she was retreating. Following further instructions, Varna retreated up the passage until she was close to the gates, where she stopped.

Still far too far away to provide any help, Helt was nonplussed.

"What is she doing?" she shouted to Blaine, who could only shake his head, mystified. Flin, surprisingly, had caught up to them.

"Stop," he called urgently, his Mage sight seeing what none of the others could.

Both Blaine and Helt turned to him in surprise as he stopped running. Both stopped also. Helt turned back with a groan as the first of the half-men reached the Citadel wall, followed quickly by the rest. They entered the wide, deep passageway as a tight group with savage shouts, waving their swords in preparation for satisfying their thirst for bloodshed. Almin Bor and his troop joined them, to be halted by Flin's outstretched staff, and almost immediately by those from the Faero's party. Mystified at why Flin would stop them, all stood and stared.

Varna was clearly visible at the end of the long passageway. Her long blonde hair streamed behind her, although there was no breeze, let alone a strong wind. The attackers were boiling towards her in triumph when she dropped her staff and opened her arms wide. Only Flin saw the shadowy figure standing side by side with her. Only Flin saw the figure take the form of a man, sandy hair slightly awry, gripping Varna's outstretched hand. But everyone heard the awesome clap of thunder and saw the brilliant, eye-searing flash that swallowed the entire passageway, before slowly fading to show only Varna standing in place.

"By the Guardians!" Flin gasped, mouth falling open and eyes wide in shock.

Varna dropped her hands and seemed to speak to someone, then hung her head as though in exhaustion, staggered once and collapsed.

Flin made his way back to the Faero's party, past the bodies of the many slain in battle. The remaining defenders were standing in a group. The Faero still was lying on the litter, his attendant by his side, a young man dressed like Flin, but in cream robes.

"Very impressive," the attendant said to Flin.

"Not what I expected," Flin answered shortly. "What happened?"

"We were ambushed. Lost about a dozen. They were after Intika." He nodded toward the Faero. "He won't live."

"Comforting young cuss," the Faero muttered, opening his eyes and searching the faces surrounding him. "So Flin, we meet for one last time, it seems. I was not that far out of it that I missed seeing what you did. All this time, we thought you were nothing but a conjurer and storyteller."

Flin shrugged.

"Let me see you properly." The Faero was struggling to rise, but was gently restrained by the attendant.

Flin shook his head. "I'm sorry, Intika. It is not yet the time."

"And I'm not the one, am I?"

Again, Flin shook his head. "It seems not."

"A pity." The wounded Faero's eyes caught those of Flin and held him fast. "Mage, I charge you to help my son. He is Faero now. He must be the prophesied one."

"I accept your charge," Flin replied gravely.

Intika Ramesa relaxed into the stretcher.

"Now," he turned to his militia. "Get me inside. I want to die in my own bed."

He was lifted and carried off the field, surrounded by the men and women of the militia.

Flin followed with his head bowed and deep in thought.

Epilogue

Grand Admiral Serra stood from her chair on the bridge of *Starfire*. She surveyed the team she had around her. The bridge crew were all occupied in their several tasks, efficient and quiet. The most recent brief battle with a breakaway group of Empire ships had been dealt with easily and *Starfire* was back with the fleet facing the now reduced number of enemy ships.

"Did any of them try anything while we were away?" Serra asked of no-one in particular.

"No, Admiral," Kiri replied from her station to one side of the bridge. "The fleet held them in place while we took care of that cruiser and its escort."

"And we still have no idea what they were doing?"

"No, Admiral," Kiri replied. "It had to be something to do with the signal they received, but we still don't know what it was about."

"Put the planet on screen please, and the smaller moon also, please," Serra requested.

She stepped forward as the large view screen split, showing the planet dead centre with a small window showing the moon to one side. For a long time, she stood quietly, examining both closely. A small frown creased her forehead and she tilted her head to one side.

"Do we have any ultra-long-distance sensors available, Mr Rork?" Serra asked.

"Aye, Admiral," Rork replied. "Not our own, but there are sensors sewn into various systems around the sector, and into the next also, and the one after that, right up to the Empire's acknowledged boundary."

"Can you tap them?"

"I believe so, Admiral," Rork replied after a moment of thought. "It may take some time though."

"See what you can find, please? I'm thinking about that message the Empire ships received that caused the *Ygruk* to move suddenly. I'm sure it was an instruction of some sort." She thought further. "And can you do the same heading back towards the Union headquarters?"

Rork turned to look at her in surprise, as did Kiri.

"Fleet headquarters, Admiral?" Kiri asked.

"Well, we know that there has to be something odd going on at Fleet, because of all of the strange happenings with my old crew. Let's just be sure that we don't find ourselves being jumped from the other direction." Serra smiled as she saw Kiri frown in thought. "Always remember that we don't know everything, Kiri. And we need to make sure that we know what is going on around us at all times. Even where we should feel safe."

"Aye, Admiral," Colonel Kiri replied.

Bard, standing beside the Grand Admiral, smiled as he remembered a young ensign getting similar quiet lessons from Serra.

"Admiral, I've managed to contact the Epsilon Array and the Opus Array. Epsilon seems to be failing in sequence but one of the sensors sent an alarm just before it went silent." Rork pressed a few points on the control pad in front of him. "Admiral," he said quietly, "the Empire fleet has left its home base."

"How much of the fleet, Mr Rork?" Serra asked.

"The sensor showed seven large capital ships and over a hundred smaller vessels. It didn't get to finalise the count."

"Seven capital ships from the home fleet? That's likely to be all of them, then," Serra mused.

"And Admiral, the Copernicus Array shows a Union fleet heading our way also." Rork's fingers continued to dance across his control pad. "Shows as *Moonbeam*, Admiral Ghosten in command. It seems to be on routine patrol, but the route is not the normal one."

"Very well, Mr Rork, maintain a watch on *Moonbeam*, please. And the Empire home fleet."

"Aye, Admiral." Rork paused as an alert flashed to life. "And a new contact, Admiral. Much closer. It's an Empire battle group by configuration and it's definitely heading this way." A few more taps and Rork turned to face Serra, eyes wide. "Three hours at the most, Admiral."

Serra nodded, standing straight on the bridge and exuding calm.

"Thank you, Mr Rork. Colonel Kiri!" Serra turned slightly.

"Admiral?" Kiri replied, turning from where she was examining the telemetry from Rork's station.

Serra moved to her chair and sat, shifting her command pad to the front and tapped out a short sequence.

"Colonel, please send the message you have on your screen, encryption pattern Alpha-Nine."

"Alpha-Nine? We don't have an encryption pattern Alpha-Nine, Admiral," Kiri replied, confused.

"Try it, please, Colonel," Serra said, remaining relaxed.

"Aye, Admiral. Calling up encryption pattern Alpha-Nine." She stared in shock as the screen in front of her acknowledged her command and turned the strange message into a mess of odd characters and symbols. "Uh, Alpha-Nine loaded, Admiral," she said, obviously surprised. "Sending."

"Thank you, Colonel," Serra replied.

"Acknowledgement received." Kiri asked, "Admiral, what was the message, if I may ask?"

"Just checking on something I asked to happen a long time ago," Serra said calmly.

The message was received and acted upon immediately. There was no need for lights of course, for the facility was run by an artificial intellect that used sensors so advanced that light would have been superfluous. The work had been paused, as per its programming, after the major repairs had been completed. Now it commenced the upgrades. The design it understood, the nature of the upgrades was well known.

The materials were readily available. With smooth precision the range of mechanical devices that had stood idle for a long time reactivated. Stores were shifted from their long-term locations so they could be loaded up when the time was right.

The artificial intellect queried the subordinate AIs and came up with an estimate of completion. It sent the reply via the antiquated communication channel. It did not wait for a reply, but started on the next task.

"Reply received, Admiral," Kiri said, staring at her screen.

"Send it to my screen, please," Serra asked.

Kiri did as requested, and Serra glanced at the screen and nodded to herself. The relief she felt did not show on her face as she turned to deal with the current situation.

"Colonel, it looks like this part of space is becoming popular." She paused and smiled slightly, a smile that verged on feral to Kiri's way of thinking. "Sound general quarters!"

About The Author

James K. McVey is an author living on the New South Wales Central Coast, in Australia. The four novels that comprise *Children of Ennaris* are his first published works.

Visit www.jameskmcvey.com.au for further information and updates on these and other works.